The Hotel on the Riviera

rol Kirkwood is one of our most loved TV personalities. llions of viewers and listeners know her for her weather)orts on *BBC Breakfast*, Radio 2's *The Zoe Ball Breakfast)w*, Wimbledon fortnight and waltzing into our hearts *Strictly Come Dancing*. Carol's debut novel, *Under a Greek)n*, reached no.2 on the *Sunday Times* bestseller list and rol was inspired to write it through her passion for vel and her love of Hollywood glamour. Off-screen, rol can often be found buried in a book, singing, dancing d taking long walks in the countryside.

find out more about Carol Kirkwood:

@officialcarolkirkwood
CarolKirkwood

Also by Carol Kirkwood

Under a Greek Moon

Carol Kirkwood

The Hotel on the Riviera

HarperCollins*Publishers*

HarperCollins*Publishers* Ltd
1 London Bridge Street,
London SE1 9GF
www.harpercollins.co.uk

HarperCollins*Publishers*
Macken House, 39/40 Mayor Street Upper,
Dublin 1, D01 C9W8, Ireland

First published by HarperCollins*Publishers* 2022
This edition published by HarperCollins*Publishers* 2023
1

A catalogue record for this book is available from the British Library

ISBN: 978-0-00-839347-2

Typeset in Meridien by Palimpsest Book Production Limited,
Falkirk, Stirlingshire

Printed and bound in the UK using 100% Renewable Electricity by CPI
Group (UK) Ltd

I dedicate this book to you, my readers . . . never in my wildest dreams did I think this would ever be possible, but you made it so. Thank you for your support and encouragement. I truly hope you enjoy *The Hotel on the Riviera* xxx

Prologue

Tears slid down the woman's cheeks, unchecked. She couldn't stop them now; it was as if all the tears she had been trying to hide – from her husband, the children, and from herself – were now escaping from her in an unstoppable torrent.

She felt as if reality itself was slipping from her grasp. She'd been struggling to keep it together for so long, and now, like her tears, the lies and the secrets were coming out into the open.

'I know what you did!' the man bellowed at her from the top of the sweeping staircase. 'You betrayed me.'

'No! You were going to betray me. I had no choice but to—'

'Liar!' He staggered towards her as she rushed up the stairs to meet him, the handsome, debonair man she had married, unrecognizable in the dishevelled, alcohol-ravaged figure before her. Over the last few months as his situation worsened he'd become angry, suspicious and selfish, but he'd never looked at her with such hatred as she saw in his eyes now.

'You don't understand,' she sobbed, her voice echoing around the cavernous entrance hall. Despite the late hour, her blonde hair was still immaculately coiffed, her clothing elegant on her.

'You had everything you could have wanted, and this is how you repay me?' he snarled as he advanced towards her. 'Sleeping around behind my back – and I'll bet he wasn't the only one. You've probably screwed half the hotel guests too.'

'How dare you! Don't you speak to me like that.'

'I'll speak to you however I want. You're my wife – even if you don't act like it.'

He grabbed her arm and she gasped in shock.

'Let go of me,' she cried, trying to shake him off.

'You need to be taught a lesson,' he yelled, raising his hand to strike her.

As she recoiled, turning away to escape the blow, he tipped forward, arms flailing, groping blindly for something to break his fall. But there was nothing.

He let out an unearthly cry as he crashed over the banister. She could only watch horrified as his body plummeted to the black and white tiles below, striking the ground with a hideous sound that she would never forget as long as she lived.

And then, silence. Until a piercing scream sliced through the stillness, a scream that she barely realized came from her own lips . . .

Chapter 1

Ithos, April 2009

'Papa!' Ariana scrambled out of the chauffeur-driven Mercedes and threw herself into her father's arms.

It was almost midnight and he'd come out to meet her, the palatial villa behind him illuminated against the blackness, the moon bright and full overhead.

Ariana was exhausted. She knew she looked far from her usual groomed and glossy self after the long journey from Los Angeles but was shocked by the change in her father. He'd lost weight, his handsome features hollowed out, and there were dark circles under his eyes. His once-dark hair was thick with grey, and it looked as though he hadn't shaved for a week.

'Yaya,' Ariana blurted out. 'Is she . . .?' She trailed off, not daring to finish the question.

'Your grandmother is very weak, but she's still with us.'

'Oh, thank God.' Ariana collapsed against him with relief. 'I was terrified I'd be too late.'

'She's been asking for you. Come, I'll take you straight to her.'

A look passed between them, so many emotions and unspoken words, but now was not the time for questions. Those would come later. Instead, Demetrios Theodosis put his arm around his daughter and steered her into the house.

Shauna, Ariana's stepmother, was waiting inside. Like Demetrios, Shauna looked shattered. Her thick, red hair was pulled back in a low ponytail, and she was dressed casually in lounge pants and a fitted T-shirt.

'Ariana, it's lovely to see you. I'm so sorry it had to be under these circumstances.' Shauna enveloped her in a warm hug, then stood back. She knew this was a moment for Demetrios and his daughter.

Ariana followed her father through the house towards her grandmother's wing. Her stomach was in knots as the memories came flooding back: running along these same hallways as a child, bare feet slapping against the cool marble floor. Then later, as a rebellious teenager, slipping off her Jimmy Choo stilettos and sneaking back to her room in the early hours after breaking her curfew.

Her heart was pounding as they reached her grandmother's bedroom. Demetrios squeezed her hand and pushed open the door.

Inside, everything was calm and still and surprisingly peaceful. The curtains were closed and a low lamp burned in the corner, but there was no medical equipment as Ariana had feared; it still looked like her grandmother's sanctuary, not an impersonal hospital room. Elana's costume jewellery and perfume bottles were neatly arranged on the antique dressing table, while the familiar silver-framed portrait of Ariana's grandfather, Aristotle, remained on the bedside cabinet. Only the baroque mirror had been removed – presumably to prevent Elana from seeing how she'd deteriorated. Two nurses were present, checking Elana's vital signs and administering painkillers to make her more comfortable, but at a signal from Demetrios they left discreetly.

Ariana approached the bed, stifling a gasp as she glimpsed the tiny, shrunken figure beneath the sheets. She blinked away the tears, shocked by how frail her grandmother had become, the steely, venerable matriarch almost unrecognizable.

Tentatively, Ariana sat down on the chair at Elana's bedside. Her grandmother appeared to be asleep, her eyes closed, her breathing shallow. Her face looked grey against the crisp, white pillowcase. Gently, Ariana reached for her hand; the knuckles were gnarled, the liver-spotted skin paper-thin over the criss-cross of purple veins. But as Ariana slid her palm into her grandmother's, Elana's eyelids fluttered open. Her once bright eyes were dull and filmy, as though the light had gone out of them.

'Yaya,' Ariana burst out, overcome with emotion. She dropped her head, bringing Elana's hand to her lips, feeling the coolness of her grandmother's skin. Despite everything, Ariana had always thought that by some miracle Elana might recover – that Demetrios had got it wrong, and this wasn't the end. But now Ariana could see that her hope had been futile. She had to accept that her grandmother didn't have long left.

'I love you, Yaya,' Ariana sobbed. 'So much.'

Elana turned her head a fraction, just enough to see her beloved granddaughter. With what little strength she had left, she raised her other hand to caress Ariana's cheek.

'I love you too, Ariana. Always,' she whispered, before falling back against her pillow, exhausted by the effort of speaking.

Ariana lay in her childhood bed, staring blankly at the ceiling. She'd barely slept for the past couple of days, what with the jet lag and spending most of her time at her grandmother's bedside. Demetrios had employed a small army of nurses to care for Elana around the clock, and when they'd insisted Ariana should try and rest, she'd reluctantly agreed – although now the idea seemed impossible.

In the privacy of her room, Ariana had broken down and wept for the grandmother she adored, readying herself for the inevitable loss. She'd listened to the comings and goings outside – tyres on the gravel as friends came to say their final goodbyes; low voices in the garden as the nurses changed shift; the local priest making his daily visit to pray for Elana's soul.

Frustratedly, Ariana threw back the covers and moved over to the window seat, staring out at the night sky. The Greek moon was full and dazzling, a panorama of stars splayed across the inky blackness. Below was Ithos Bay, the dark water dotted with pinpricks of light from the boats that sailed by, and the harbour aglow in the distance. Ariana opened the window, the fresh air cooling her hot skin, and inhaled deeply, the familiar tang of the sea bringing welcome solace. No matter where she was in the world, she loved to be by the ocean.

Ithos, and the family villa, held so many memories for Ariana. She remembered Yaya teaching her to bake, the two of them sticky with honey and nibbling on pistachios as they made baklava together. She recalled how, as a child, she'd watched, mesmerized, as Elana made herself up so elegantly every day, with pressed powder from Elizabeth Arden and a classic red lipstick. With her parents frequently away – her father travelling for business, her mother for pleasure – Ariana's grandmother had been a constant in her life, the steady, loving influence she'd needed. Now the sands were shifting around her, and Ariana felt lost. She'd hoped to make Elana proud, but instead her life was one big mess.

Slamming the window shut, Ariana pulled a silk dressing gown over her La Perla slip and strode out of her room. The long corridors were silent and shadowy, the walls adorned with valuable works of art, but already the house felt different, as though her grandmother's influence was slipping away like the woman herself.

She'd intended to visit Elana, but as Ariana passed her father's study, she noticed light spilling out from beneath the closed door. Ariana hesitated. She knew that she and Demetrios needed to talk, but she was ashamed of the things she'd done and the way she'd behaved, scared of the confrontation that would inevitably follow. She also knew that her father was hurting right now, just as badly as she was, and that the two of them needed one another. She tapped gently on the door.

'Yes?' Demetrios's voice was filled with alarm, and Ariana rushed to reassure him as she opened the door.

'It's only me, Papa.'

'Oh, Ariana.' The relief on his face was palpable. 'I thought . . .' He trailed off. They both knew what he'd thought – that it was the nurse, coming to get him for the final time.

Ariana took in the scene: after Aristotle had died, Demetrios had taken over his father's study. He'd kept the same style – grand and imposing, all dark wood and leather-bound books – but tonight, rather than being in his usual spot behind the mahogany desk, Demetrios was sitting on the floor, surrounded by piles of paperwork and overflowing boxes. A photograph album was open in front of him, and he was holding a glass tumbler that was almost empty, just a splash of amber liquid in the bottom.

'Couldn't sleep?' Ariana asked softly.

Demetrios shook his head. 'No. I didn't want to disturb Shauna, tossing and turning all night, and I found myself here.'

Ariana sank down next to him, wordlessly picking up a photo. It was black and white, and showed her grandparents in the Luxembourg Gardens in Paris. They looked so young and in love; Elana in a stunning full-skirted dress that Ariana recognized as Dior and Aristotle handsome and distinguished in a three-piece suit and fedora. Ariana turned the photo over to see the date on the back: *September, 1948*.

'They look incredible. Like movie stars,' Ariana sighed, with a pang. She couldn't help but wonder whether she would ever find a relationship like that, with a guy who was crazy about her, the way Aristotle had worshipped Elana. Ariana had been unlucky in love over the years, with a penchant for bad boys that led to broken hearts, and worse . . .

Demetrios smiled sadly as he gazed at the picture. When he spoke, his voice was thick. 'Would you like a drink?'

He stood up and refilled his own glass with cognac from the bar in the corner.

Ariana watched him, struck by indecision. For the last few years she'd been living in LA, trying to make it as an actress. At twenty-six years old, she was still a long way from realizing her dream and, if she was being brutally honest with herself, she had little in the way of natural talent. What she *was* good at was having fun. Partying. She'd been drinking a lot – excessively, some might say. And it wasn't just the alcohol. There'd been drugs too. But across the villa her grandmother was dying, and right now wasn't the time for Ariana to address her issues.

She nodded at her father. 'Make it a large one.' She took a slug of the neat brandy, feeling the welcoming burn in her throat, and reached for another photograph.

The time slipped by, father and daughter sharing their memories of Elana, trying to pretend they weren't about to lose her. Although Ariana idolized her grandmother, she recognized that she could be domineering at times, formidable and controlling. She knew that Elana had played a key role in her parents' marriage – that it was merging dynasties, not hearts, which had made Elana push the union between Demetrios and Sofía Constantis. In doing so, Elana had separated Demetrios from his true love, Shauna O'Brien, and it had been almost twenty years and a world of heartache before the two of them had finally reunited. Yet, despite everything, Ariana knew that Demetrios adored his mother and would be devastated to lose her.

She picked up another album and a loose print fluttered to the ground. Aristotle and Elana were pictured with a glamorous couple – the woman petite and laughing, with expensive jewellery and thick blonde hair in Farrah Fawcett waves, the man sandy-haired and suave, bearing more than a passing resemblance to Robert Redford. They looked at least a decade younger than her grandparents, all four monied and carefree and clearly great friends. The bright, bold patterns of their clothing put the time-frame as the 1970s, the location likely the South of France, with its palm trees and golden light and distinctive archi-tecture. The building behind them looked vaguely familiar to Ariana, but she didn't recognize the couple.

'Who are they?' she wondered, turning the photo over to find the back was blank.

Demetrios frowned. 'I don't know. My parents knew many people, personally and professionally. Father had so many business interests it was sometimes difficult to keep track.'

'Perhaps—' Ariana began, but she never got to finish her sentence, interrupted by an urgent knocking. Her stomach lurched as Demetrios leapt up and opened the door to a sombre-looking nurse.

The woman's voice was calm as she delivered the words they'd both been dreading: 'You must come, quickly. It is time.'

Ariana scrambled to her feet, choking back a sob, and followed her distraught father out of the room, all thoughts of the photograph forgotten.

Chapter 2

Cannes, August 1987

The day was filled with sunshine, as though the weather had made a mistake and didn't realize the solemnity of the occasion. Alain was to be buried in the prestigious Grand Jas cemetery, situated high on a hill above Cannes, shaded by palm trees and full of grand stone tombs and impressive monuments. But Gabriel paid no attention to his surroundings.

His father's coffin was lowered into the ground, the oak smooth and polished, sunlight reflecting off the gold fittings. The graveside was surrounded by black-clothed mourners as the elderly priest recited words that Gabriel didn't hear. He remained silent and stoic, his head bowed, distantly registering that the sleeves of his suit jacket were an inch too short following his recent growth spurt.

How could it be possible that he'd never see his father's face again? That this man who'd been so full of life, a hero that Gabriel had idolized and worshipped, was now gone? He knew that Alain hadn't been himself recently, but that had done little to dent Gabriel's admiration for the handsome, charismatic, gregarious man he was proud to call his father.

How could it have happened? Perhaps if Gabriel hadn't been away he could have prevented it somehow. He glanced over at his mother, now a shell of her former self. She seemed to have aged a decade in a matter of days. It was as though she'd turned inwards, physically shrinking, her shoulders hunched as she stared at the ground, grief etched in every line of her face. Beside Madame du Lac, his sister Constance wept in great, heaving sobs that shook her whole body.

Gabriel was twelve years old and knew that his life would never be the same again. He was the man of the family now and he had to grow up, to support his mother and sister. He would do it to honour his father. He wanted to make his papa proud of him.

Portofino, April 2009

Gabriel du Lac admired his reflection in the mirror – tanned skin, gym-honed body, piercing blue eyes – before pulling on a freshly pressed white shirt and navy chino shorts. His hair was blond and wavy, curling over his collar, his stubble carefully maintained to ensure it remained at just the right length. Yes, Gabriel was pleased with what he saw. He was thirty-four now and almost unrecognizable from the awkward teenager he'd once been, the gangly adolescent whose clothes were unfashionable and ill-fitting, who stammered and blushed crimson when forced to speak to the opposite sex.

He made himself an espresso, relieved that the noise from the machine didn't wake the woman sleeping in his bed. Carla? Claudia? Camila? It was something classically Italian, he remembered that much. Her long, brown hair was splayed across her face so he couldn't see her features, although a sunkissed shoulder and the curve of a breast were visible above the Egyptian cotton sheets. She'd said she was a model, in town on a fashion shoot. Or was that the girl from the night before? Perhaps this one was a designer, travelling through the region for inspiration. Well, Gabriel smirked, he liked to think he'd given her a little of that . . .

With a soft click, the balcony doors opened and he stepped out, the warmth of the Italian sun hitting his face as he pulled down his aviator sunglasses. The view was incredible, looking out over lush green pine trees down to the sparkling turquoise waters of the Ligurian Sea. Below was a hidden cove with a private beach, barely a kilometre along the coast from the centre of Portofino.

He'd acted on gut instinct to purchase this property – the first in his rapidly growing empire. Back then, it had been a rundown private villa belonging to an industrialist from Genoa. Gabriel had offered him a good price and spent almost two years renovating the place, stripping it back to the bare bones and overseeing every aspect of the rebuild himself. But it had all been worth it. The Hotel del Mare was an exquisite gem, a luxury boutique hotel frequented by the rich and famous. Right now, Heidi Klum was ensconced in the Venetian Suite. Brad and Angelina had hunkered down here to escape the press. Tom Cruise and Katie Holmes had even spent part of their honeymoon at the hotel – one of the most successful in Gabriel's expanding portfolio.

He checked his Rolex: 7.30 a.m. Time to leave. Gabriel grabbed his Valextra bag and gave the room a cursory final inspection to ensure that all was in order. Everything looked stylish and refined, from the classic cream décor to the wingback leather armchairs to the vintage Murano chandeliers. He left the woman sleeping and closed the door silently.

'*Buongiorno*, Signor du Lac,' the receptionist greeted him warmly. She was young and attractive, with a great smile and a curvaceous figure concealed beneath her uniform. 'Can I get you anything?'

'Thank you, Giulia,' Gabriel smiled, reading her name tag. 'I have a guest in my room. If you could send up a breakfast tray in around thirty minutes, and make sure she's vacated the premises by ten.'

Giulia didn't bat an eyelid. 'Of course, Signor du Lac. Have a safe journey, and we hope to see you again very soon.'

In the private car park, Gabriel slid behind the wheel of his Ferrari Spider, retracting the roof and gunning the engine. Within minutes he'd reached the winding coastal road, high up on the cliffs, the sun beating down and the sublime Mediterranean views falling away to his left. Life was good; he wouldn't have it any other way. There was only one thing that blighted his otherwise perfect world, and today he was going to deal with that once and for all.

The sky was a cloudless blue, but Gabriel's mood was darkening as he neared Cannes, the familiar sights stirring mixed emotions. His relaxing start to the day was all but forgotten after spending more than three hours behind the wheel; construction around Nice had brought the roads to a standstill, and vehicles had been bumper-to-bumper on the autoroute.

But it was more than just traffic that had riled Gabriel, and as he approached Le Suquet, the picturesque old quarter of Cannes, he realized that his jaw was clenched, his body held rigid. The Ferrari made light work of the steep climb through the narrow, winding streets and then there it was: the Hotel du Soleil. Gabriel grimaced. It looked even more rundown than the last time he'd been here – half a dozen roof tiles were missing, and it badly needed a fresh coat of paint. The planters were overgrown, the flagstones cracked, and one of the lights above the entrance had stopped working. All so easy to fix – if anyone gave a damn about this place.

Irritated to find his parking spot occupied by his sister's shabby old Citroën, he pulled into a guest space. There was no doorman to welcome him at the entrance; instead, Marie, the ancient receptionist, scowled at him as he strolled across the lobby.

'Monsieur du Lac. We were not expecting you today.'

'Evidently,' he snapped, his practised eye taking in everything from the dirty floor tiles to the vase of flowers wilting on the desk. 'I'm going up. Is she—'

'Madame is in her room—'

'Where else?' Gabriel muttered under his breath.

'And is *not* to be disturbed,' Marie shouted after him, as Gabriel strode off towards the sweeping staircase that dominated the entrance, ascending the steps two at a time. It would be faster than taking the old creaking lift, and a great way to get a quick burst of cardio. He was barely out of breath when he reached the top floor and rapped smartly on the door at the far end of the corridor.

'Yes?' The voice was sharp, suspicious.

'It's me.'

Gabriel waited impatiently as he heard movement within, footsteps shuffling across the worn carpet, then the chain being slid off and the lock undone. The woman standing there was short and extremely thin, brittle and birdlike. She was white-haired, dressed entirely in black, and looked much older than her sixty-five years. The expression on her face made it clear that she was not pleased to see him.

'*Bonjour, maman*,' Gabriel said tightly, bending down to kiss his mother on both cheeks. '*Ça va?*'

'Gabriel.' She raised an unimpressed eyebrow. 'How lovely to see you. I didn't know you were coming.'

'Surprise.' His tone was thick with sarcasm. 'Aren't you going to invite me in?'

Madeleine du Lac stepped aside to let her son enter. The room was shabby but clean, Gabriel noted. At least his mother hadn't gone completely senile and stopped letting the housekeeping staff do their job.

The penthouse was the largest room in the hotel, with a separate bedroom, lounge and dining area, as well as a sweeping terrace that looked out over the port with its flotilla of yachts, and the sparkling azure sea. Unfortunately, his mother kept the curtains tightly shut, otherwise, Gabriel knew, the room also offered a magnificent view of the gardens – currently overgrown, he was willing to bet – within which lay a small, rectangular swimming pool, a secluded suntrap nestled amongst bougainvillea and oleander. It made Gabriel want to weep when he thought of the thousands of euros they were missing out on from not being able to rent the penthouse to paying guests. He'd repeatedly offered to move his mother to a modern apartment in town, comfortable and convenient, but she insisted on living at the hotel. She was as stubborn as a mule, he thought resentfully.

'I'll call down for coffee and Stefan's pastries,' said Madeleine, picking up the phone and speaking quickly into the receiver.

'Stefan's still here?' Gabriel raised his eyebrows. 'He's too good for this place.'

'Some people show loyalty,' Madeleine shot back, before settling herself in her favourite chair. She sat straight-backed and composed, looking Gabriel directly in the eye. 'So, to what do I owe the honour of this visit? Have you come to check on your dear old *maman*?'

Gabriel sighed, running his hands through his hair in frustration. He hated how his relationship with his mother had deteriorated over the years, the two of them always at loggerheads. They didn't seem able to be in the same room as one another without the conversation descending into an argument.

'Your welfare is always my primary concern, as you know, which is why I'm so worried that you're living like this.' Gabriel swept open the curtains, pretending not to notice the way his mother winced in the dazzling daylight, clouds of dust motes thrown into the air.

'It's my choice to stay here,' Madeleine replied defensively. 'I know what you want, and you're not getting it.'

Gabriel rolled his eyes. They'd had this discussion countless times already. '*Maman*, you make me sound like some crooked conman trying to swindle you out of your life savings. What I'm proposing is for everyone's benefit. Unless this hotel is properly managed, you'll go bankrupt within the year and be left with nothing. What would Father say?'

'Enough!' snapped Madame du Lac. '*Ça suffit*, Gabriel.'

Gabriel exhaled sharply, balling his fists in frustration. He'd grown up in the Hotel du Soleil and knew every nook and cranny. He and his sister, Constance, had spent hours playing hide and seek as children, riding up and down in the dumb waiter, and sliding down the laundry chute. They'd stolen petits fours from the kitchen and, as they grew older, bottles from behind the bar. Back then, the Hotel du Soleil had been one of the most celebrated and glamorous destinations on the French Riviera, a second home for the wealthy, the famous and the international jet set.

But those happy days of his childhood had ended abruptly. Gabriel still didn't know the exact reason behind the change in circumstances – his mother had done her best to shield him and Constance from the arguments and the accusations – but it was obvious that his father, Alain, had got into financial difficulty. Looking back, Gabriel suspected there'd been alcohol and gambling, perhaps even infidelity.

And then Gabriel's world fell apart. He'd been staying with a schoolfriend for the weekend when the accident happened. He still remembered the boy's poor mother having to break the news to him that his father, Alain, was dead, driving him back home while he sat numbly in the passenger seat. He hadn't cried – not even at the funeral. He'd still been in a state of disbelief, in denial. His sister had shed enough tears for the both of them; her sobs from the next bedroom had kept him awake night after night. Only a few weeks later, his mother had suffered a nervous breakdown. Since Alain's death, she'd been a virtual recluse, cutting herself off from the world and barely leaving the hotel.

A knock at the door pulled him back from his painful memories.

'Oh, Gabriel.' It was his sister, Constance, holding a tray with coffee and pastries. 'I didn't know you were here.'

Gabriel snorted in disbelief. He knew full well Marie would have run to find Constance the second he'd left the reception desk. 'I thought I'd pay a visit to see how much the place has declined in my absence. Maybe I'll stay the night – I'm sure you'll have a room available. What is the current occupancy rate? Twenty per cent? Ten?' His sister coloured, and Gabriel knew he'd hit a nerve. 'Do you have any guests staying here at all?'

Constance placed the tray on the coffee table and turned to him angrily. She was three years older than him and tall, like their father, slim, with a thick waist and flat chest. Her mousy blonde hair was scooped up in a bun, and she didn't wear a scrap of make-up. She'd never married, and remained devoted to Madeleine with an intensity Gabriel found hard to understand.

'Gabriel, what do you want?' she asked haughtily.

Gabriel ignored her, crouching on the floor beside his mother's chair and taking her hands in his. '*Maman*, I'm trying to do this for us. All of us. Give me twelve months and I could transform this place. You'd have so much money, you'd never need to worry again.'

'Some things are more important than money, though you don't seem to realize it. Security. Stability. *Family*.'

'Keeping this place the way it was when Papa died won't bring him back!' Gabriel regretted saying the words as soon as they were out of his mouth. His sister looked appalled and his mother's face hardened.

She spat out a single word: '*Non.*'

'*Maman, je t'en prie*. I'm sorry. I didn't mean—'

'I don't want your apologies.' Madeleine cut him off furiously. The room was silent, the tension palpable. Gabriel and Constance were both waiting to see what their mother would do next.

There was a long pause before Madeleine spoke. Her voice was calm and controlled, her words slow and deliberate. 'Besides, even if I wanted to give you the hotel, it is not in my power to do so.'

Gabriel frowned, trying to make sense of what his mother had just said. 'What do you mean?' he demanded. Had his sister somehow persuaded Madeleine to give the hotel to her? Had his mother sold it to a competitor for a price Gabriel would have more than matched?

Madame du Lac pursed her lips and sat back in her chair, closing her eyes. 'I'm tired. I don't wish to speak about it anymore.'

Gabriel fought the urge to shake her. 'You can't just . . . You have to tell me!'

His mother remained mute, mouth clamped, eyes shut.

'I think you should go,' said Constance, crossing her arms over her chest.

Gabriel stared at them – at these two implacable, infuriating women who made his life so difficult. It was impossible to fight them together.

'Fine,' he fumed, knowing he'd been temporarily defeated. 'But I'll be back.'

He stormed out of the room, sprinting down the stairs, pulling out his phone to speak to his lawyers. He didn't know what the hell was going on, but he was damn well going to find out.

Chapter 3

Ithos, April 2009

'I miss you, baby. When are you coming home?'

Ariana bit her lip. That was the million-dollar question. 'I don't know.'

At the other end of the line, several thousand miles away in Hollywood, her on-again off-again boyfriend, Jonny Farrell, sighed in frustration.

'I just need a little time, OK?' Ariana replied testily. Home. Where even was that anymore? She'd spent the past couple of years living in LA, but after everything that had happened, she wasn't sure whether she wanted to go back . . .

If she didn't return to the States, where would she go? Stay in Greece with her father? Head to England, where her mother, Sofía, lived with her third husband? No, she needed a new challenge, one that roused her passion and made her excited to get out of bed in the morning. If there was one thing Elana had taught her, it was that life was short; you had to make the most of every day and grab opportunities with both hands.

'Well, you know, Ariana, I'm not gonna wait around forever . . .'

Ariana was lying in the bathtub, the delicious scent of Acqua di Parma bath oil filling the air. She knew she should tell Jonny to go to hell but, somehow, the words never came.

'. . . Although, there are ways we can make the time apart go a little faster . . .' Jonny's voice had dropped an octave, his tone low and suggestive. He was bad news, Ariana knew that. Jonny Farrell: failed actor, failed model, successful junkie. Demetrios would string her up if he knew she was even speaking to him.

Oh, but there was something about him that she couldn't resist. He knew just the right buttons to push, knew exactly what she needed to hear, and he managed to worm his way back into her life every goddamn time. He was hot as hell, sexy and intense, with that shoulder-length black hair, those smouldering brown eyes and the ever-present black leather jacket. And they *always* had a good time together.

'I'm thinking about you now,' he growled. 'Are you thinking about me?'

'Jonny—'

'That's it, baby, talk to me. Tell me what you want, what you're gonna do to me when—'

Ariana hung up. She paused for a moment then opened her hand, listening to the soft splash as the phone fell into the water, watching it sink to the bottom of the tub. Then she stood up and reached for her towel, drying herself off as she padded through to her room.

She didn't know why she'd even picked up Jonny's call.

It was 2 a.m. in LA and he was probably high, probably with some other chick. Crazily, she'd thought that maybe he'd remembered. That he was ringing to show sympathy, offer a few words of comfort. Christ, she was an idiot.

Ariana reached for her body cream and began to moisturize her skin, scrutinizing her reflection in the mirror. She'd been blessed with good genes, but you could always improve on nature, and she made sure that she ate well and worked out. She was becoming increasingly aware that looks didn't last forever and that, at twenty-six, she should be establishing herself in the world, working her way up the career ladder, not working her way around the party circuit.

Ariana pulled on her underwear before reaching for the dress she'd already picked out. It was plain black and knee-length, sophisticated and demure – a far cry from the usual figure-hugging, attention-seeking numbers hanging in her walk-in wardrobe, row upon row of designer outfits by Gucci, Alexander McQueen and ROX.

But today was not a normal day. Today was the day they were burying her grandmother.

Rain hammered against the high, arched windows of the small chapel, the priest raising his voice to be heard over the almighty cracks of thunder. Right now, Ithos was far from the sun-soaked idyll the tourists adored. Powerful forked lightning illuminated the sky, the air humming with the intensity of the electrical storm. It seemed appropriate, somehow, as though it symbolized Elana's fiery nature, her momentous life.

Following tradition, the casket was open. Elana looked at peace, her eyes closed and her expression serene. Her grey hair was neatly styled in a low chignon, and she wore a classic Chanel shift dress, black with a white lace collar. *Elegant to the end*, Ariana thought, the tears running freely down her cheeks.

Averting her eyes, she glanced round at the congregation. Elana had wanted a small service, with family and close friends only, but this still meant over one hundred people had been invited to pay their respects, crammed into the local church. Beside Ariana was Demetrios. He was utterly broken, supported by Shauna, who had her arm wrapped around his waist as though she was the only thing holding him up.

Behind them was Níko – Demetrios's closest friend – and his wife Teresa. Christian, Níko's son, was also in attendance, with his wife Grace – Ariana's half-sister. Grace was seven months pregnant with their first child, and Ariana tried hard not to stare at the blossoming bump beneath the loose-fitting dress. As a headstrong eighteen-year-old, Ariana had nursed a crush on Christian – all the more embarrassing when she'd thrown herself at him to discover it wasn't reciprocated. Instead, he'd fallen for the level-headed, sweet-natured Grace, and the pair of them were still madly in love.

Christian was undoubtedly a good man – loyal, dependable, devoted to his wife – and Ariana couldn't help but wonder how different her life might have been if she'd settled down with someone like him. If she'd stayed on Ithos and married a local boy, accepted a quieter life instead of jetting all over the world in search of the next wild party. Perhaps she wouldn't be alone right now, with no one to hold her hand and reassure her that everything would be OK, no one to take her in their arms and kiss away her tears . . .

Ariana was openly weeping now, crying for Elana, for herself, for everything that had happened in Los Angeles. She was young, beautiful and rich. She should have had the world at her feet, but instead, she felt lonely and scared.

Outside, great cracks of thunder rolled through the heavens as Ariana's sobs reverberated around the small church. Now that she'd started, she didn't seem to be able to stop.

Three weeks later, Ariana was stretched out on a lounger in a secluded area of the garden, listening to Beyoncé on her iPod Touch. A Jackie Collins novel lay open in front of her, but her mind kept wandering and she was finding it impossible to concentrate. She jumped as a shadow fell across her face and looked up, startled.

'We need to talk.'

It was Demetrios. Ariana had been avoiding him. In fact, she'd been avoiding everyone. It hadn't been difficult – her father had been incredibly busy, constantly on the phone to his lawyers, travelling back and forth to Athens as Elena's will was executed. Months earlier, Shauna had accepted a theatre role in the West End, so had flown to London a few days after the funeral to start rehearsals, leaving Ariana with the villa mostly to herself. She'd been spending her days holed up in the garden, or on deserted spots of the beach where she knew no one would find her.

'Yes, Papa.' Ariana had been dreading this conversation. She pulled her kaftan over her bikini, feeling strangely vulnerable.

'Let's go for a walk.' Ariana caught a glimpse of the

newspaper under his arm, it was the *Los Angeles Times*. Her heart sank.

Ariana turned off her music and abandoned her book, slipping on her flip-flops as she accompanied her father through the extensive grounds.

'How are you?' he asked.

'Fine,' she replied carefully. The question was unexpected; her family weren't big on talking about their feelings.

'Shauna and I are worried about you. You're not yourself, and it's more than just losing Elana. What happened in Los Angeles, Ariana?' He took the paper from underneath his arm and tapped at the headline. Seeing the words in black and white made her feel sick.

Los Angeles Times
13 March 2009

STARLET'S TRAGIC DEATH

Up-and-coming actress Liberty Granger, 23, died tragically in mysterious circumstances in the early hours of Thursday morning.

According to reports, Ms Granger was found unresponsive in the swimming pool at a property in the Beverly Park neighbourhood. Witnesses confirm that a party had been taking place.

The actor, hailing from Sarasota, Florida, had made a name for herself in independent movies such as *House of Fire* and the critically acclaimed *Orla's Wish*. Her résumé also boasted minor roles in TV shows *Mad Men* and *Gossip Girl*, but it was her supporting performance in the soon-to-be-released *All Our*

Yesterdays which had generated considerable buzz in the industry.

The circumstances surrounding her death remain unclear, but sources say Ms Granger's on-off boyfriend Jonny Farrell, 31, has been interviewed by the LAPD.

Farrell, an aspiring actor, has also been linked with *Playboy* model Brandi Simpson, and heiress Ariana Theodosis, amongst others.

There was a long pause, and Ariana found she couldn't meet her father's eyes. This part of the estate was beautifully manicured, lush with greenery and brightly coloured flowers, with classical statues surrounded by ivy-wreathed stone columns. Yet despite the beauty of her surroundings, Ariana felt wretched inside.

'What about this incident in the newspapers, this . . . Liberty Granger . . .'

Ariana winced. She never wanted to think about her ever again.

'Did you know her? Was she a friend of yours?'

'It was . . . complicated,' Ariana said carefully.

Demetrios frowned, determined not to let her off the hook so easily.

Ariana had loved the party scene, but had also had times when she felt lonely and an outsider. Liberty was a small-town girl with big dreams, and the two of them had just clicked. Everything went wrong after she'd found out that they were both sleeping with the same guy – Jonny Farrell. It had come between their friendship, and it was impossible for Ariana to explain that to her father.

'But you were there, yes? At that party, the night she died?' he pressed.

Ariana looked away. Above them, the birds wheeled and called, lifted high on the warm winds. Buzzards. When she spoke, her voice was barely a whisper. 'Yes.'

Demetrios looked furious. 'What kind of life were you living out there, Ariana? How were you at a party where someone *died* – a young woman, with parents and friends who loved her, her whole life ahead of her – and somehow her name is being linked to yours?'

Ariana shook her head, wanting to run away and hide. 'Stop it,' she begged. '*Please.*'

'I deserve answers,' Demetrios roared. 'Do you know how much it cost to hire one of the best attorneys in the country when you gave your police statement? What strings I had to pull to keep your name out of the press? This could have wrecked your entire future. Not to mention the consequences for the family business.'

'I'm sorry, Papa. I'm so sorry. I never meant for this—'

'I'm sure you didn't, but it happened, and you owe me the truth. What happened that night?'

The two of them had stopped walking and were facing one another. They'd reached a small wooden gazebo that looked out over the olive groves. It had been her grandmother's favourite place to come and sit in later years, and Ariana found herself wishing she'd spent more time here with her.

'I don't know.'

'Ariana—'

'I'm telling you the truth. I can't remember. I . . . I'd taken something I shouldn't have.'

'Dear God, Ariana. After everything we went through before.'

'I know, I'm sorry. I was so stupid, I thought I was in

28

control. But that night . . . I can't stop thinking about it. I keep having flashbacks, but nothing's clear. There are shadows, voices, but . . . It's like trying to catch a dream. I don't know what happened, and I'm so scared. I'm sorry, Papa. I'm so sorry . . .'

She broke down in her father's arms and Demetrios held her, letting her find the release she needed. The possibilities were terrifying – had she been involved in some way? Was she somehow responsible? Liberty had been found floating in the pool, a cocktail of drink and drugs in her system. Ariana remembered there had been shouting. Had the two of them argued about Jonny? Had Ariana – God forbid – had she *pushed* Liberty? Had she watched her go under for the final time and stood back, doing nothing?

The not knowing was the hardest part, the fear that someone, somewhere, had witnessed what had happened. The memories could come flooding back at any second, and Ariana would discover she was guilty . . .

She cried until she was spent, straightening up and wiping her eyes. Then the two of them began to walk again, taking the path back towards the villa.

'If you give me your word, then I'll believe you,' Demetrios said gravely. 'But you must be completely honest with me. And you have to start making changes – you cannot continue to live your life like this. It's reckless, childish. A waste of your talents. You've come so close to ruining your entire future – and it's not over yet.'

'I know, Papa. I know.'

They continued in silence as the hot sun beat down on them. The craggy hills rose from the scorched landscape behind them, and a lone aeroplane left vapour trails across the clear blue sky. It was probably heading for Crete or Athens; there was no airport on Ithos, and the only way to access the island was by boat. Growing up, Ariana had hated being so remote from the rest of the world, but now she valued the isolation.

'I have some news for you.' Demetrios's tone was brighter, deliberately changing the subject.

Ariana looked at him, a spark of hope in those amber eyes.

'I'm sorry that I've been so absent these past few weeks. As you might expect, your grandmother's will is rather complicated. It's taking some time to work through. But she's left a number of things to you – personal items, and the majority of her jewellery collection.'

Ariana nodded. She remembered, as a child, Elana letting her play dress-up with her rings and necklaces, telling her that one day, it would all be hers. Ariana hadn't really understood what she meant by that, nor realized that the pretty beads and shiny baubles she was treating like toys were, in fact, worth hundreds of thousands of euros.

'There is one item that's causing something of a mystery.' Demetrios paused, reaching into his pocket and bringing out a ring so beautiful that Ariana gasped. Looking closer, she realized it was a rare pink diamond set on a narrow band of yellow gold. The stone was enormous, perhaps ten carats, cushion cut and flawless, its facets dazzling in the sunlight.

Demetrios handed it over and, almost as though she were in a dream, Ariana slipped it on; it fitted perfectly on the third finger of her right hand.

'Oh,' she breathed, twisting it back and forth, mesmerized by the colour and the sheer size. Ariana had seen some spectacular jewellery over the years, but this was exquisite and clearly very rare. 'It's stunning. Was it Yaya's?'

Demetrios frowned, looking puzzled. 'That's the thing. It was in her safety deposit box in the bank's vault, but there's no record of it. There are no documents, no provenance, and it wasn't on the inventory. I don't recall ever seeing it before, do you?'

Ariana shook her head. 'No, and I'd have certainly remembered it.'

Demetrios smiled indulgently. 'I'm sure you would. Well, it's yours now. Enjoy it. There's a considerable amount of money too – cash, but also shares and other investments,' he continued. 'We can go through the details later. Suffice to say that you're now a very wealthy young woman. I hope you'll reflect on everything carefully, given recent events – and I've taken the liberty of appointing an adviser to assist you.'

Once again, the news wasn't entirely unexpected. Of course, Ariana had always had money – the Theodosis family was one of the wealthiest in Greece – but this was hers directly. She was rich beyond most people's wildest dreams. But that didn't change who she was, or what she'd done. Much as she adored the private jets and the designer clothes and all the trappings of wealth, she realized that she'd never achieved anything on her own terms. Her grandfather had built a business empire, but she'd been handed everything on a silver platter.

They were almost back at the villa, but Demetrios was still speaking. 'There is one more thing. Did your grandmother ever speak to you about a hotel?'

Ariana frowned. 'No.'

'It appears that she owned a hotel. I was never aware of it, and nor were my lawyers.'

'Me neither. Where is it?'

'It's on the French Riviera. In Cannes, to be precise. It's called the Hotel du Soleil.'

Ariana wrinkled her nose thoughtfully. 'I haven't heard of it. Why do you ask?'

'Well, the reason I'm bringing it up is that your grand-mother has left it to you.'

Ariana's mouth fell open. 'To *me*? Why?'

Demetrios laughed, not unkindly. 'I have no idea. But it's yours now. Congratulations, Ariana.' They were back at the house, the familiar view of Ithos Bay spread out before them in all its glory, whitewashed buildings clinging to the hillside all the way down to the pretty harbour. 'You're the new owner of the Hotel du Soleil.'

Chapter 4

Cannes, May 2009

The helicopter sliced noisily through the shimmering sky, descending as it neared the helipad. The locals barely looked up; celebrities and VIPs regularly flew in by chopper on the final leg of their journey from Nice airport, and today they were as frequent as buses, with movie stars and moguls all arriving for the start of the world-famous Cannes Film Festival.

The helicopter touched down and a man and a woman emerged, ducking beneath the still-whirring blades. The woman's glossy blonde hair swirled around her face and the pair looked impossibly glamorous – him in sharply tailored trousers and a low-buttoned shirt, her in a white silk jumpsuit by Yves Saint Laurent that draped perfectly around her slender body.

Chivalrously, he reached for her hand and she took it, the two of them pausing for just a moment. To the casual onlooker, it was almost unnoticeable, but the pair knew exactly what they were doing: making sure the photographers got the pictures they needed.

They hurried across the red carpet to the waiting limousine, flashbulbs popping around them. But these photographers weren't unwanted paparazzi who'd inveigled their way into the heliport. They were 'friendly' snappers, specially invited to take staged pictures and make sure the couple looked like the megastars they were: sexy, flawless, unattainable.

They reached the limo and paused for one final time before sliding into the soft leather interior. Two black-clad security guards closed the doors behind them and the vehicle pulled away.

'Thank Christ that's over,' huffed Robert Chappell, in his broad, northern accent, as he stared moodily out of the window. The sea and the sky reflected one another in myriad shades of blue, the lush green hills between them dotted with lavish mansions and pastel-coloured villas.

'Oh, do stop complaining, darling,' groaned his wife, Elizabeth. 'Anyone would think you'd been sent to work down the mine, not to the South of France for a week to be wined and dined.'

'Quit whining, Rob. You guys did great.' Francesca Ballard, Robert's agent, was already waiting in the car, having flown in the day before to make sure everything was perfect. She was in her forties, small but fierce, with short, red hair and a penchant for dressing in head-to-toe black. Her no-nonsense style and take-no-prisoners attitude had earned her the nickname 'Balls' and she revelled in it. 'I'll get the photos sent across to you asap for final approval.'

Elizabeth looked mollified by the praise but scowled at her husband. 'All I'm saying,' she began, in her cut-glass

English accent, 'is that if he ruins our chances of winning the Palme d'Or because he has one of his tantrums . . .'

Behind his Ray-Bans, Robert rolled his eyes, reaching over to the minibar. 'Does this thing have any Scotch in it? 'Cos I need a drink.'

Both Elizabeth and Fran glared at him, and Robert slumped back like a naughty child who'd been caught with his hand in the biscuit tin. With his dark, curly hair and soulful brown eyes, Robert had classic movie-star good looks, his gruff, gravelly voice instantly recognizable.

'Can't you just keep a lid on it for one bloody day?' Elizabeth hissed.

'Maybe if you didn't drive me to drink I wouldn't need to,' Robert shot back.

Fran, busy on her phone, ignored them. She was used to their squabbles. Robert and Elizabeth Chappell were two of the biggest stars in Hollywood, their fights legendary and their passionate make-ups tabloid gold. While there was no doubt that they were both fine actors in their own right, there was something special – an alchemy almost – about the two of them together.

This time, however, the whole thing was threatening to implode. Before they'd left Los Angeles, Elizabeth had told Robert she wanted a divorce. She'd threatened it many times before, but now she'd gone as far as hiring a lawyer and drawing up papers. It seemed she was finally done with her husband's drinking and carousing, the wild nights and the strip clubs and the three-day benders.

Fran had done some frantic negotiating, and Elizabeth had agreed not to make the news public until they were done promoting their latest film, a First World War epic entitled *All Our Yesterdays*. But once publicity duties were completed, Elizabeth was moving out and officially filing. Robert was in denial, trying to bury his woes at the bottom of a bottle.

'I thought the point of taking the chopper was so we wouldn't have to sit in traffic,' he complained, as the limo ground to a halt amid a long line of cars. Outside, tourists and curious passers-by peered through the blacked-out windows, wondering excitedly who might be inside.

'Why don't you get out and walk then?' Elizabeth suggested sweetly.

'Maybe I will,' Robert shot back childishly, reaching for the minibar and defiantly pouring himself three fingers of whisky.

They were still bickering when they pulled up at the entrance of the legendary Hotel du Cap-Eden-Roc. Internationally renowned for its A-list guests and stunning location in Antibes, the Hotel du Cap was the quintessential hotel of the festival, the Grande Dame of the Riviera. Everyone who was anyone had stayed there, from Winston Churchill to John F. Kennedy, Cate Blanchett to Kate Moss. Liz Taylor and Richard Burton famously began their affair at the hotel, and later returned on honeymoon.

The reference was appropriate – Elizabeth and Robert had often been compared to a modern Liz and Dick, the two of them fiery, passionate and undeniably talented. Elizabeth was Robert's third wife. At fifty-four, he was fifteen years her senior; she'd been the one to finally tame him, according to the tabloids.

The two of them were polar opposites: Robert was a grumpy, northern hellraiser, a working-class boy made good. Elizabeth was elegant and sophisticated, well-spoken and privately educated, and part of the legendary Forbes acting dynasty. Her mother was Fenella Forbes, the acclaimed classical theatre actress, and her father was Charles Forbes, widely regarded as the 'heir to Olivier'. A steamy remake of *Lady Chatterley's Lover* had catapulted Elizabeth to fame and Hollywood had come calling, turning her into a bona fide movie star.

In contrast, Robert had been brought up by his factory worker mother and bricklayer father in Manchester. He'd left school at sixteen, moving to London and later LA, with no contacts, just raw talent. It had been a surprise to everyone – including Robert – when Elizabeth had jettisoned her famous surname to take his instead, but there was something old-fashioned and romantic in the gesture which greatly appealed to her. Despite their many differences, they'd been madly in love when they'd got married a decade ago, holding two lavish ceremonies on either side of the Atlantic.

'I'm going to freshen up,' Elizabeth announced, after they'd been shown to their room. It was an enormous 1,000-square-foot suite, with a wooden terrace that resembled the deck of a yacht. The balcony boasted plush loungers and even a jacuzzi, with mesmerizing views over the sparkling sapphire sea and the 'Bay of Billionaires'.

Robert leaned against the railing and lit a cigarette.

Fran watched him disapprovingly. 'You need to stay in control, Rob. Quit the drinking and the smoking.'

'What does it matter? She's going to divorce me anyway.' He was trying to brazen it out, but Fran could hear the sadness in his voice. She'd worked with Robert for almost two decades – longer than he'd known

Elizabeth – and she could be frank with him in a way most people couldn't.

'Well, if you want to get her back, you've got to try harder. The two of you are clearly still crazy about one another.'

'I think she means it this time. The love's still there but . . . it's not enough. I don't know if we can get past this one.'

He looked so sad, staring out to sea, lost in his own thoughts. Fran knew Elizabeth was good for him, and hated to think how he might go off the rails without her.

'Then you have to fight for her. But first of all you have to fight for this movie,' she said briskly, slipping back into professional mode. 'I've left your schedule on the table. You have a couple of hours free so make the most of them, but then we're straight into promo. We'll get some shots of the two of you down by the harbour, then you've got drinks with Penélope Cruz and Javier Bardem, who've just arrived in town. There's a charity dinner at the Majestic, followed by a yacht party hosted by the studio. But I'll be right with you the whole time, making sure you're where you're supposed to be. All you need to do is show up and behave yourself. Be charming, don't be an asshole. Don't drink too much. And don't smoke, it's bad for your health. See you in a couple of hours.'

Robert gave her an ironic salute as she marched out of the door, calling goodbye to Elizabeth as she went. He dropped his cigarette on the terrace, grinding it out beneath the heel of his boot, and went inside to fix himself a drink.

'Did Fran leave?' Elizabeth sashayed into the room.

'Yeah, she – wow.' Robert looked up from the bar to see Elizabeth had changed her outfit. She was wearing a sleek red trouser suit by Stella McCartney and she looked incredible. *Statuesque*, was how Robert would have described her, with her ice blonde hair tumbling down her back and shocking red lipstick emphasizing her inviting lips. The suit jacket was fastened with just a single button, and she clearly wasn't wearing anything underneath.

'Don't get yourself excited, Robbie, it's bad for your blood pressure,' Elizabeth teased.

Robert felt like an idiot; he was one of the most famous men in the world, and right now he was acting like a love-sick teenager, his tongue practically hanging out. 'You look good, OK? Is it all right for your husband to pay you a compliment? You *are* still my wife. For now.'

An awkwardness hung in the air between them. Robert could sense it and he hated it. Without stopping to think, he drained his whisky and poured himself another.

'Really, Robbie? Is that a good idea?'

Her tone irritated him, cutting across his attempt at conciliation. After Fran's lecture, it was more than he could take.

'I've got a lifetime of bad decisions behind me, love. One more won't make any difference.' He raised his glass in a toast. The gesture was designed to irritate Elizabeth, and it worked.

'I've only ever made one bad decision and it's standing right in front of me,' Elizabeth shot back. The words weren't true – they were designed to wound and she immediately regretted them, but she was too proud to take them back, and she couldn't stop them. All they seemed to do these days was hurt one another, and a decade of experience meant they knew exactly what buttons to push.

'Well, you'll be rid of me soon enough, Liz.'

'Why do you have to be such a child about everything? Take some responsibility for once. For your own actions, your failures.'

'Oh, has someone been talking to their therapist again?' His voice dripped with sarcasm.

'So what if I have? I've been working on myself. Maybe you should try it.'

'How very LA,' Robert drawled.

'And you're "keeping it real" are you, darling? Just the same down-to-earth lad from Lancashire?' Elizabeth scoffed. 'What would your mates from back home think if they knew you drank bottles of wine that cost more than their monthly pay packet?'

He glowered at her and she moved towards him purposefully, just hitting her stride.

'Oh that's right, you don't have any mates from back home, because you only hang out with celebrities and millionaires. Such a fraud.'

'At least I made it on my own. Didn't have Mummy and Daddy to get me a place at RADA then sign me up with their agent. Right, princess?'

It was his nickname for her. Elizabeth used to love it; he'd treated her as though she was royalty, worshipped her like a queen. Now all she heard was the dig – she was a prima donna, a spoilt brat.

Elizabeth laughed scornfully. '*I* made you relevant again. You'd have been some washed-up old loser with the best days of his career behind him if you hadn't met me.'

'Yeah, you tell yourself that, sweetheart. We both know the truth. You rode my coattails all the way to the top.'

'Go to hell.'

'That'd be better than being here with you.'

They were in one another's faces, their breathing coming fast, so close Robert could feel the heat of Elizabeth's body against his. Even after all these years together, she still took his breath away. He wanted to grab her and kiss her, to make love to her and forget the rest of the world existed. But his pride was wounded. If she wanted a divorce, he wasn't going to come crawling.

Elizabeth looked him straight in the eye, and he watched the expressions flicker across her face, from passion to anger and sadness. Finally, she shook her head and spoke: 'This isn't going to work.'

'Huh?'

'You, me, being here together. We'll be at one another's throats the whole time.'

Robert frowned, not understanding what she was saying. That was the whole basis of their relationship – the Chappells were famously tempestuous, forever fighting and reuniting.

'I can't be here with you.' Elizabeth was suddenly on the verge of tears. 'I'll check in somewhere else.'

'What are you talking about? It's the Cannes bloody Film Festival, everywhere's booked up. What are you going to do, pitch a tent on the beach?'

'I'll find somewhere. And don't worry about our commitments, I'll show up to everything that's scheduled. I just . . . I can't bear this any longer, it's tearing me apart, Robbie. I'm sorry.' She fumbled on the bed for her handbag, dashing tears away from her cheeks.

Robert Chappell stood, open-mouthed, watching helplessly

41

as his wife turned around and walked out of the door. What the hell had just happened? Sure, they'd argued before – every damn day, in fact – but he'd never felt the way he did now: lost, wretched, hopeless. He wanted to run out of the room and up the corridor after her, to grab her and tell her to come back. To make love and lie in each other's arms, like they used to. To be together again, like they were meant to be.

But he didn't, and his feet seemed rooted to the spot. Instead, he drained his Scotch, feeling the alcohol burn in his throat and surge through his bloodstream, the frustration building in search of a release. He paced the floor like an animal, finally letting out a roar and hurling the glass as hard as he could against the wall where Elizabeth had been standing moments earlier. It shattered like his heart, and he slumped to the floor amongst the shards, holding his head in his hands.

Chapter 5

Ariana adored the French Riviera.

She'd been coming here all her life with her parents, and never failed to be captivated by the golden light, the softly swaying palm trees, and the charming belle époque buildings along this magical stretch of coastline.

Cannes during the festival was like nowhere else on earth. Back when she was a teenager, Ariana had begged her father to take her and been blown away by the energy and atmosphere. Everywhere you turned there was another celebrity: Jude Law strolling along the Croisette; Uma Thurman sunbathing on a yacht; Jane Birkin lunching at Le Bistro Gourmand.

The Hotel du Soleil was apparently located in the old town, the cobbled streets and fishermen's cottages a world away from the glitz and glamour down by the marina. Ariana checked her satnav, but she was definitely heading in the right direction. She felt unexpectedly nervous, but excited too. She still had no idea why her grandmother had left the property to her – though Ariana had plenty of experience *staying* in luxury hotels, she knew nothing about running one – but the challenge was thrilling.

Demetrios had told her she didn't have to be involved; they could put a management company in place to deal with the day-to-day affairs, collect the profits and never have to worry about it again. In fact, Demetrios had advised her against visiting the hotel at all, but rather to leave everything to their lawyers, as Elana had clearly done. But Ariana was intrigued. She had no immediate plans to return to LA, and there was nothing going on in Ithos, so why not take a trip to the Côte d'Azur? She could check out the festival too, catch up with her European friends, and schmooze all the producers and directors in case she decided to revive her fledgling acting career.

The monotone voice of the satnav told her she was almost there. A discreet sign indicated the entrance and Ariana swung the steering wheel, looking round eagerly as she turned in.

At first sight, her heart sank.

The Hotel du Soleil was undoubtedly a beautiful building, designed in the classic Provençal style with honey-coloured walls and terracotta roof tiles. It was only four storeys high, and Ariana estimated it contained around eighty rooms, each with louvred windows and dark green shutters and a wrought-iron balcony. The property was nestled amid tiered gardens to allow for the steep slope, with cypress trees standing guard and brightly coloured bougainvillea running riot across the walls. Yet overall, despite the traditional architecture and impressive location – the view of Cannes from the hilltop was phenomenal – the hotel had clearly seen better days. Perhaps the inside would be better, Ariana thought optimistically.

She pulled into the car park and almost laughed out loud. An identical red Ferrari Spider to the one she was driving was already parked in the space marked *réservé à la direction* – reserved for the management. Perhaps this place was making more money than she'd realized.

Ariana parked beside it and walked up to the entrance, noticing the weeds growing between the flagstones, the rotten wood around the windows, the cracks in the plaster. She could see it had once been grand, and her mind was already racing as she thought of how to restore it to its former glory.

She strode up the curved stone steps and into the reception with its harlequin tiles and dramatic sweeping staircase. Off to the left was what looked to be a bar and restaurant area, decorated with classic cream walls and oak beams. The reception desk was on the right, and beyond lay double doors through which Ariana glimpsed overgrown gardens and the turquoise gleam of a swimming pool. It was crazy to think that all this belonged to her!

The hotel had an undeniable charm, a faded grandeur which appealed to the romantic in Ariana, and its boutique size gave it a different feel to the behemoths in town – the Martinez, the Majestic, the Intercontinental. The Hotel du Soleil was more welcoming, more personal. Well, it would be if there was anyone there to greet her . . .

'*Excusez-moi? Il y a quelqu'un?*' There was an old-fashioned bell on the counter and Ariana rang it impatiently.

A rather elderly woman with grey hair pulled up in a bun shuffled out from the back looking annoyed. '*Oui?*'

Ariana bristled at the rudeness. Was this why the place didn't appear to have many paying guests? 'Do you have any rooms available?' she asked, in English. 'I'll take a suite if you've got one.'

'Do you have a reservation? It's the festival, we're very busy . . .' Marie shrugged in a way that implied it wasn't her problem.

Ariana glanced round at the empty lobby. 'Really? It seems rather quiet to me.'

Marie sighed and began leafing through a large heavy calendar filled with looping handwriting.

Don't they even use a computer? Ariana wondered incredulously.

'Perhaps we can squeeze you in.' Marie's tone was grudging. 'What's your name?'

Ariana hesitated for a moment. 'Holly Wood,' she announced, feeling mischievous, trying to stifle a giggle.

Marie frowned, unsure of the joke. 'Very well, Madame Wood. Here is your key. Your room is on the fourth floor.'

'*Merci beaucoup*. Is there someone to help me with my bags?'

'No,' Marie replied sullenly.

'I see. Thank you for all your help.' Ariana smiled sweetly and set off in search of her room.

Later, Ariana was lounging by the pool in a tiny gold bikini that left little to the imagination. She felt like a spy, revelling in the thrill of going incognito as she watched everything going on around her from behind oversized Gucci sunglasses, listening in on conversations between the other guests and the staff. So far, she wasn't impressed.

The sunloungers were rusty and uncomfortable, the cushions grubby and the parasols broken. She'd ordered herself a kir royale cocktail which took forever to arrive. When it finally did, it tasted as though it had been made with cheap sparkling wine, and there was a lipstick mark on the rim of the glass.

Across the pool she watched a young woman, surgically enhanced and wearing a leopard print bikini, fawn over a portly businessman twice her age who was bellowing into a mobile phone. She was clearly only with him for his money, Ariana thought cynically. There was no tenderness or affection between them as the woman rubbed sun cream on his back, taking care not to break her long fake nails. And then Ariana had a moment of realization: the two of them weren't in a romantic relationship – this was a business transaction. The woman was clearly an escort, or a call girl. *Oh, fabulous*, thought Ariana. Had she inherited a seedy hotel that rented rooms by the hour?

What could she do about all of these problems? If she was the new owner, didn't that make her ultimately responsible? Her father was the head of a vast corporation, which he'd inherited from his father. Ariana had never been interested in taking over Hellenic Ventures, but maybe some of the family flair for business ran in her blood. If Demetrios could manage a multimillion-dollar empire, then she could handle a hotel, surely?

Ariana jumped up, deciding to do some more investigating. She wove through the gardens, not in the least self-conscious about walking around in little more than her underwear. Having grown up on one of the most beautiful islands on earth, she was never happier than under a warm sun feeling the soft sand beneath her bare feet, but her stacked wedges would do for now.

Ariana entered the hotel through a side door that had been left open. No one else seemed to be around, and she made her way into what appeared to be a former ballroom: high ceilings, parquet flooring, elaborate mouldings, and panelled walls. It was a huge space, empty save for a pile of chairs gathering dust in a corner. Ariana wondered if the room was ever used. The French windows offered a superb view over the bay, and it could be a valuable additional revenue stream. She made a mental note to ask someone.

Ariana exited through the rococo-style doors and found herself in a corridor beside the lift. On the walls were gold-framed black and white photographs of celebrities taken back in the hotel's heyday: Mick and Jerry, Simon and Yasmin, Rod Stewart and Rachel Hunter. The Hotel du Soleil had evidently once been *the* place to stay for the jet-set crowd.

As Ariana was perusing the pictures, the elevator pinged and a woman stepped out. There was something familiar about her; she looked chic and polished, in a blush pink Roland Mouret column dress that clung to her killer figure, her pale blonde hair straightened and pulled back in a sleek ponytail. As she drew closer, Ariana realized who she was – Elizabeth Chappell, the famous British film star.

'Elizabeth!' Ariana called out instinctively. The woman turned to her, and Ariana noticed that her eyes looked red, as though she'd been crying.

'Yes?'

'I'm so sorry, I recognized you and wanted to say hi. My name's Ariana Theodosis, and I believe you know my stepmother, Shauna Jackson?'

Elizabeth's face changed instantly, and she broke into that trademark megawatt smile, immediately professional. 'Yes! How wonderful to meet you, Ariana. And how is Shauna? Is she in town this week? I'd love to catch up, I haven't seen her in forever.'

Demetrios's second wife, Shauna, was an Oscar-winning actress who'd previously been married to director Dan Jackson. She'd had a summer romance with Demetrios many years earlier, and the two of them had reunited after Dan's death. Shauna had taken a step back from Hollywood since marrying Demetrios and now spent much of her time on Ithos with their adopted son, Alex, able to pick and choose the acting projects that fired her passion.

'She's in London right now, performing in a theatre show,' Ariana explained.

'Oh, of course, I remember reading the opening reviews, they were phenomenal. *Three Sisters* at the Donmar, isn't it? I really must try and get over to see it before it closes. God, I miss the theatre. Are you an actress too?'

'Aspiring. I was living in LA for a while, but . . .' Ariana trailed off, unsure how to explain herself. 'I'm a huge fan of yours. You were amazing in *The Moonstone*, and I can't wait to see *All Our Yesterdays*.'

'Thank you, you're too kind, my love. Fabulous bikini, by the way.'

'Oh . . .' Ariana faltered. She knew Elizabeth hadn't meant to embarrass her, but now she felt rather silly standing there half-naked. It was the kind of thing that cool, composed Elizabeth Chappell would never do.

'If you've got it, flaunt it. Isn't that what they say?' Elizabeth winked. 'Now I'm terribly sorry, my darling, but I must dash – I have a lunch to attend.' She rolled her eyes as though it was the dullest thing in the world.

'Of course – you're nominated, aren't you. Good luck.'

'Thank you, that's very sweet of you. Well, it was lovely to meet you, Ariana. Let's find five minutes to grab a drink sometime. I'd love to get to know you better, and hear all about Shauna.'

'Sure, that'd be amazing. Is Robert staying here with you too?'

Elizabeth's face darkened. 'No, he's . . . He's not. I'm sorry, I have to go.'

She walked off briskly, and Ariana stared after her, wondering if she'd said something she shouldn't. Perhaps Elizabeth really was running late, like she'd said. Elizabeth and Robert Chappell were on the cover of every magazine and tabloid around the world. Their fiery romance was the talk of LA and the rumour mill had it that their fire had run out of fuel. Her stepmother, Shauna, was an old friend of Elizabeth's and had mentioned the chaos that being married to Robert sometimes caused. 'They can't live with each other and can't live without either,' she'd said. Robert was a bit of an enigma to Ariana. She'd tried asking Jonny about him once or twice, after seeing him on the cover of *Empire*. 'The guy's a has-been, babe,' he'd told her.

Shrugging it off, Ariana realized she was hungry, a wave of mouth-watering aromas drifting out from the kitchen, so she decided to go dress for lunch and check out the restaurant.

She was heading towards the lift when she heard a man's raised voice coming from an office further along the corridor. Ariana stopped curiously, wondering what was going on. She guessed he was on the phone as she could only hear one side of the conversation.

'It's not good enough, I need answers,' he snapped. 'Well find out. Yes . . . Ariana Theodosis, that's right . . .'

Ariana froze, her heart pounding.

'I've looked her up,' the guy was saying. He was speaking in French, but Ariana's well-travelled upbringing meant she was almost fluent. 'She's some spoilt little rich kid. Her father owns a shipping company and she's had everything handed to her on a silver platter, no doubt.'

Ariana's pulse was racing, the adrenaline flowing. She flattened herself against the wall, knowing that no good ever came from eavesdropping, but unable to help herself.

'Look, just make her an offer. We can buy her off. No, I don't know how the hell she got hold of it either. My mother has clammed up and won't tell me a thing. But as far as I'm concerned, this hotel belongs to my family and it's going to stay that way. The idea that I would give it up for some Z-list actress with more money than brains is simply impossible—'

Ariana had heard enough and before she knew what she was doing, she'd stepped into the room. Just who was this man who thought he knew something about her? With her hands on her hips, she approached his desk. She hadn't expected him to be so good-looking, with that athletic body and intense blue eyes, but she wouldn't let that distract her.

The man's jaw dropped as he looked her up and down, taking her in from her perfectly painted toenails to her immaculately manicured eyebrows and everything in between. Ariana enjoyed the little surge of power as he lingered on her taut, tanned torso before recovering himself.

His eyes narrowed. 'I've got to go,' he said quietly, hanging up the phone.

They eyed each other for a long moment, Ariana biding her time before speaking.

Recovering himself, the man spoke first. His accent was French, but he spoke in a clipped, precise way which spoke of long periods spent in England, and which lent a touch of arrogance as he regarded her steadily.

'My name is Gabriel du Lac, and this is my office. To what do I owe this pleasure?' His eyes flickered across her body once again.

Throwing her dark hair back over her shoulders, she looked him straight in the eye and flashed him a feline smile, savouring the moment. 'My name is Ariana Elana Aphrodite Theodosis, and your hotel now belongs to me.'

Chapter 6

Estée dressed quickly, pulling on her leggings and flip-flops, with a bodycon top that showed off her long, lithe dancer's figure.

'I can't believe how busy it was tonight,' she commented, as she hung up her costume – a ruffled corset and can-can skirt in red, white and blue, the colours of the French flag.

'It's all the tourists in town for the festival,' explained her friend Nicolette, rolling her wide blue eyes. 'They think they're getting the authentic French experience.'

'Well at least the tips should be good,' Estée said optimistically, glancing into the mirror as she wiped off the heavy stage make-up, revealing her tanned skin and deep brown eyes. She tied her dark, curly hair back in a ponytail and was about to leave when the owner, Victor, entered the dressing room without knocking. There were half a dozen women in various states of undress, and his gaze flickered proprietorially around the room.

'Good show tonight, girls. The crowd loved you,' Victor praised them, his French heavily accented with Russian.

Physically, he was short with a wiry build. He had closely shaved dark hair and small eyes that missed nothing.

Estée smiled and tried to slip past him, but Victor shot out a hand, grasping her arm firmly. 'Going so soon? Perhaps you should stay later, Estée. I'm sure it'd be worth your while.'

'Not tonight I'm afraid, Boss,' she brazened it out, shaking off his grip. 'See you tomorrow.'

Estée walked out of the cramped dressing room and headed for the exit at the back of the building – Victor didn't like them using the main door in the bar when customers were there. It spoiled the magic, he said.

She knew that some of the girls stayed in the club after the show. There were always men willing to buy them drinks, and sometimes other services could be purchased for the right price. It was a way for the women to supplement their meagre income, but Estée shuddered at the thought. Victor was always pushing them to keep the punters happy, whatever that might involve, but it wasn't a road Estée wanted to go down. She had bigger dreams.

Outside, the night air held a faint chill, but Estée found it refreshing after the past few hours working in a hot, sweaty club. She always walked back to the old town to save money, and tonight it felt exciting, soaking up the atmosphere of the festival.

It was after midnight and, as Estée cut through the narrow streets to the Boulevard de la Croisette, she found it was busy even at this late hour. The noise from the yacht parties grew louder as she neared the port, drowning out the ever-present sound of the sea as it kissed the shore and raced back again. Some teenagers had lit a bonfire on the beach and half a dozen police officers had shown up, trying to extinguish the fire and move the youngsters on. For a moment she stopped to take in the glamour, the hubbub of laughter and the lights dancing beautifully off the water in the harbour. How lucky these people were, so carefree and well-heeled.

As Estée began the steep climb up the hill to the Hotel du Soleil, she realized how exhausted she was. Not physically, as though she merely needed a good night's sleep, but bone-weary. It was so draining, always trying to stay positive, to keep hold of her dreams. She'd been working at La Châtelaine, a cabaret and burlesque club on the rue Hoche, for six months now and told herself it was merely a stepping stone on the way to fulfilling her real ambition: being a successful dancer.

Estée was classically trained. Despite her poor background growing up in the Paris suburb of Saint-Denis, she'd won a scholarship to the world-famous Paris Opéra Ballet School, but somehow her big break had never quite happened. She'd fallen prey to the usual teenage distractions – boys, alcohol, partying – and now here she was, performing six nights a week to rowdy tourists who were living out their Moulin Rouge fantasies. It was fair to say, life had not turned out the way she had planned.

'*Bonsoir*, Estée.'

Tonight, Constance was manning the hotel reception. Estée didn't particularly like her, and sensed the feeling was mutual, but tried to keep on her good side.

'*Salut*, Constance.'

'Another late night tonight. Make sure you're on time for work tomorrow or you're fired.'

'Of course,' Estée replied meekly. She hated the way Constance spoke to her, but kept her mouth shut as she desperately needed the job.

Estée had first arrived in Cannes almost a year ago, after being offered a job as a chorus girl at La Châtelaine; it hadn't turned out the way she'd hoped. The pay was less than they'd offered, and to make more she would have to work front of house 'entertaining' the customers. Instead, she'd found extra work as a chambermaid at the Hotel du Soleil. The hotel was quieter than some of the other bigger hotels, and Estée didn't have anywhere to live, so Constance had let her rent a tiny cramped room in the hotel – next to the kitchen – at a reduced rate. The money Estée earned was barely enough to live on, even with two jobs, but she told herself that at least she was dancing. She sent money home to her mother whenever she could, but there was rarely any to spare. She told her mother that she was dancing in big shows that were building her career. She could never tell her mother the truth, the mother who had held down three jobs to afford to keep her in ballet school, it would break her heart to know Estée was just a chorus girl, after all the sacrifices she made, and was still making for her. The lifestyle was exhausting, and Constance was always watching her, looking for an excuse to sack her or throw her out.

Estée headed towards the stairs – she preferred that to being stuck in the confined space of the lift, often as not with overweight businessmen who did nothing to hide their leers – when out of nowhere came the sound of a man yelling in fury, a crashing and commotion by the entrance as he shouted and swore.

Estée jumped and turned to see what was happening, shocked by the noise.

'Monsieur, please!' Constance ran out from behind the reception desk as the dark-haired man crossed the lobby. He was clearly drunk, dressed in jeans and a burgundy shirt that was open to the navel, displaying a tanned torso and plenty of chest hair.

'Where is she?' he slurred. 'Where's my wife?'

'*Mon Dieu!*' Constance stopped in her tracks as she realized the man's identity. 'It's Robert Chappell.'

Estée watched curiously. She often saw celebrities in town, especially during the festival, but Robert Chappell was strictly A-list. And he appeared to be roaring drunk.

'Can I help you, Monsieur Chappell?' Constance asked, in soothing tones.

'I want to speak to my wife. I know she's staying here.'

'I'm afraid we can't disclose the names of our guests,' Constance explained, taking his arm and trying to steer him out of the door. 'But perhaps in the morning, once you have had some rest—'

Robert shook off her hands and staggered clumsily towards the grand staircase with a battle cry.

'Monsieur, you are intoxicated. Please leave the premises, or I will have to call the police!'

'It's OK, Constance,' Estée heard herself say. She approached Robert carefully as though he were a frightened animal. 'Can I help?'

Robert looked at Estée and his face unexpectedly crumpled, all the fight going out of him. 'I love her,' he wailed. 'I just want to talk to her. Will you help me?'

'Go back to reception,' Estée told Constance. 'I'll take care of him.' She looked around for somewhere they could go.

'Not the bar!' Constance shrieked. 'Don't give him any more to drink.'

'We'll go to the kitchen. Stefan should still be there. We'll try and get him sobered up.'

'Now *you* are a nice lady.' Robert squinted at her unsteadily, as Estée steered him towards the stairway. 'Not like that battleaxe over there . . .'

'Shh,' Estée warned him. He reeked of alcohol, his velvety brown eyes unfocused and his clothing dishevelled, yet there was something endearing about him. He was incredibly good-looking, Estée thought objectively, with that coal-black hair and chiselled jawline half-hidden beneath sexy day-old stubble, yet he was clearly a troubled soul.

She guided him through the heavy metal door into the kitchen, sitting him on a stool and pouring him a glass of water. 'Here. Drink this.'

Robert downed the entire thing as though it were a pint of beer, then pulled a face. 'Water? Bloody disgusting. I haven't drunk that stuff since 1998.'

Estée laughed, as Stefan headed over. He was head chef at the Hotel du Soleil, with sandy red hair and freckled skin, his heart-shaped face honest and open. He was solidly built, with broad shoulders and a powerful chest. Undeniably talented in the kitchen, he was dedicated and focused when it came to his work but, contrary to the chef stereotype, was easy-going and respectful.

'Hey, Estée. What's going on?' Stefan eyed Robert curiously. He'd worked in the hotel trade for over a decade and very little fazed him – certainly not inebriated movie stars turning up in his kitchen late at night.

'This gentleman was getting rather overexcited in the

reception area. Could you make him a bite to eat, something to soak up the alcohol?'

Stefan looked at her, a question in his eyes, but he didn't ask it. 'Sure. Would you like something too?'

'I'm fine,' Estée replied automatically. A lifetime of dance training was hard to break. She had a birdlike appetite, often forgetting to eat entirely.

'On the house,' Stefan encouraged. 'I won't tell Constance.'

'All right. Thank you.' She smiled gratefully, sitting down beside Robert.

'You're lovely,' he rambled. 'D'you know where my wife is?'

'Hang on,' Stefan said. 'I recognize you, aren't you that actor, Robert . . .'

'Chappell! Chap by name, idiot by nature.' Robert sighed dramatically. 'Have you seen my missus? She's absolutely gorgeous.' He made the universal hand signal for an hourglass figure. Stefan shook his head, his green eyes twinkling good-naturedly.

'I'm sure she must be missing you. Have you tried calling her?' Estée suggested.

Robert shook his head. 'She won't answer her phone when she sees it's me.'

'Have you had an argument?'

'About a million. What's your name?'

'Estéc.'

'Nice. Means "star", right? Your friend here is right, I'm Robert.' The three of them took turns to shake hands. 'Are you married, Estée?'

She shook her head, avoiding Stefan's eyes. He was now at the large stove, delicious cooking smells drifting across the kitchen.

'You should be. You're very nice. Would *you* pick up my calls if you were married to me?'

'That would depend on what you'd done,' Estée laughed.

Robert frowned. 'Nah, on second thoughts, don't get married. It's more trouble than it's worth.' He slumped onto the counter, his head falling into his hands, and let out a groan. 'What's wrong with me? Why do I do this to myself? I bet you wouldn't know what it's like to completely mess up your life.'

'Try me,' Estée replied, with feeling.

Robert stared at her, as though trying to decide whether she was serious. 'My wife wants a divorce. I've not been the best husband in the world. She says I'm selfish, that I need to grow up. She's probably right. For most of my adult life, I've had people around me who just say yes to whatever I want. No one ever says no. But Liz is different. She *gets* me. I love her so much. I miss her. I just want her back.'

'Have you told her?' Estée asked gently.

'You don't know my wife. She's stubborn as hell. Once she's set on something, she won't back down. We used to be so good together, but lately . . . She wants a baby, y'know. I'd love that too, but she won't. Not while I'm like this, that's what she says. A "man-child".'

Robert made quote marks in the air. Estée tried not to laugh – she could see what his wife meant – but she stayed quiet and let him talk.

'This is my third marriage, y'know? I feel like such a failure. I've got a kid from my first marriage that I barely see. I wasn't there for him growing up – his mum did everything while I ran around like I had no bloody responsibilities. Now he's growing up just like me, going off the rails. I've already paid for rehab twice, some detox place out in Palm Springs. Bloody useless . . .' Robert trailed off, feeling sorry for himself. His eyes had glazed over, and he seemed to have forgotten he was talking to someone. Then he blinked, noticing Estée beside him. 'Do you have children?'

Estée paused. 'Yes. A daughter. She's almost ten.'

Estée watched Robert's face as he did the maths and realized that Estée must have been little more than a child herself when she'd given birth. It was true – she'd been seventeen, with her first proper boyfriend. She'd been so naive, by the time she realized the consequences, it was too late.

But Robert didn't comment on her age. He simply said, 'Lucky you. It must be nice to have a daughter. Your face lights up when you talk about her. What's she like?'

Stefan returned carrying a club sandwich with fries for Robert, and a small plate of Dijon chicken with baby potatoes for Estée.

'She's like a little ray of sunshine, she never stops talking, loves watching *Dancing with the Stars* and can run faster than me.' Estée felt her heart lurch, wishing she was at home watching TV with her daughter right now.

'Your favourite, right?' he smiled.

Robert was devouring his food with gusto. 'Mate, this is fan-bloody-tastic,' he groaned, speaking with his mouth full.

'Your accent's funny,' Estée giggled. 'Where are you from?'

'I'm from Manchester, love.'

'Like the football club? Manchester United?'

Robert put down his sandwich and gave her a look of disgust. 'Please – Manchester City.'

'What's the difference?' Estée shrugged, as Robert shook his head in despair.

'Where's your little girl tonight?' he asked.

'She lives with my mother, back in Paris. I moved here to create a better life for her. I hope one day we'll all be together again, but . . . not yet.'

Her mother had insisted that Estée wouldn't need to give up her dream – their dream – and would help raise the baby. After she was born, the most perfectly beautiful baby girl, her mother looked after Emilie while Estée worked and auditioned; sometimes she was away from Paris for months on end if she landed a touring role. Then, when Estée was offered the job in Cannes, she and her mother agreed that it would be best for Emilie to keep her routine the same, and not to uproot her from her school or her friends. It broke Estée's heart to say goodbye to her daughter, and each trip was getting harder and harder while she seemed to be getting further away from the dream.

Robert was staring at her, momentarily sober. 'That's some sacrifice. Now I feel like an idiot, going on about me when you—'

'It's fine,' Estée assured him. 'Everyone's dealing with something.'

Estée stopped speaking as Robert's phone began to ring, Liz's name illuminated on the screen.

'It's her! I gotta go. Cheers, Estée, you're a star,' he winked, as he crammed the last of the food into his mouth and ran out through the metal door.

Stefan had been keeping a safe distance, wiping down counters and prepping for tomorrow's service. Now that Robert had gone, he came over. 'What was that all about?'

'I don't really know. I was just trying to take care of him. He seemed . . . lost.'

Stefan looked sceptical. 'I'm sure Robert Chappell can take care of himself. You should worry about yourself more.'

'Thanks, Stefan. You're always so sweet to me.'

'I'm serious. Who's going to look after you?' His eyes were full of concern.

For a moment, Estée didn't have an answer. She'd been running after her dreams for so long that she didn't dare to think what would happen if she stopped. She'd missed out on her daughter's formative years; if she didn't have anything to show for it, then the sacrifice was for nothing. All she could do was keep believing, keep battling, and focus on her future. That was the way it had to be.

Chapter 7

'Montana! Over here!' Ariana cried, waving her champagne coupe in the air.

Montana Morgan raced up the gangplank towards her, screaming with excitement, causing heads to turn even in a town used to flamboyance. Ariana watched as her friend strode onto the superyacht and climbed up to the top deck, the crowds parting for the tall, leggy blonde dressed in six-inch heels and a sequinned catsuit.

'This is awesome!' Montana squealed, as the two of them finally found one another and hugged tightly.

'I can't believe you're here. You know how to make an entrance.'

'I try, girl, I try. And you – you look, like, unbelievable!'

Ariana blew her a kiss, bobbing a playful curtsey in her fuchsia-pink Marc Jacobs dress. Short and strapless, teamed with a pair of sky-high Manolos, the look was fashionable, fun, and outrageously sexy. 'Come on, let's get you a drink.'

They were on one of the largest yachts in the harbour, at a party sponsored by Bulgari. David Guetta was DJing, and everywhere you looked people were dancing, drinking, making out, having the time of their lives. It was an international crowd full of beautiful people. Ariana had spotted a few famous faces – Sienna Miller, Jake Gyllenhaal – but everyone was too cool to bother them.

'I'll take a mojito,' Montana winked at the attractive barman.

'Do you want to dance first, or catch up?' Ariana asked.

'Let's catch up. I wanna hear everything that's been going on with you,' Montana grinned, as the barman did his best Tom Cruise impression with the cocktail shaker. She grabbed her drink and followed Ariana down to the lower deck where it was less raucous, and revellers were chilling out on oversized chairs and comfy white sofas.

Montana was one of Ariana's best friends from her time in LA. Montana had grown up around the movie business – her mom was a screenwriter, her dad a camera operator – and Montana was desperate to make it right to the very top. She had all-American good looks, regularly being cast as 'the dumb blonde' or 'the cheerleader' and, while she could be a little shallow at times, Ariana adored her energy, her zest for life. Together they'd had a ball trying to take Hollywood by storm.

'So, tell me *all* the gossip,' Montana insisted, as the two of them squeezed onto a day bed together, lying back against the enormous cushions.

'Where do I start?' Ariana sighed. There was something incongruous about seeing Montana here in Europe, as though two worlds were colliding. Montana was loud and brash and superficial – traits that worked perfectly well in Los Angeles but seemed out of place on the French Riviera. Ariana had grown up fast in recent months; after university, she'd spent a hedonistic few years doing what she pleased, but Liberty's death and the passing of Elana had made her realize she was in danger of heading down a self-destructive path. Ariana found herself wondering how much she and Montana still had in common.

'I was so sorry to hear about your grandma,' Montana said, as though she'd read Ariana's thoughts. 'I know you really loved her. She sounded awesome.'

'Thank you. She was.' Tears sprang unexpectedly into Ariana's eyes and she blinked them away. 'It's hard. I miss her every day. I still don't think I've got my head around the fact that she's gone. But so much has happened, and of course the hotel has been a big distraction, so that's—'

'Hotel?' Montana frowned.

Ariana clapped a hand over her mouth. 'I can't believe I didn't tell you. My grandmother left me a hotel in her will. It's right here in Cannes, in the old town.'

'Shut. The. Front. Door!' Montana exclaimed, over-emphasizing every word. 'Wait, so you're telling me that your grandma, like, *gave* you a hotel? Do you get to live there and be, like, the boss of everyone?'

'Not exactly. Although I *am* staying there. You'll have to come and visit, I'll show you around.'

'OMG! Is it like the Beverly Hills Hotel? Or – even better – the Chateau Marmont?'

'Not exactly . . . It's smaller. More boutique. To be honest, it's pretty shabby and run-down right now. There's a hell of a lot of work to get it anywhere near a luxury, five-star experience. Would you believe I've been staying up until the early hours making lists and creating plans, researching architects and tradesmen and suppliers . . .

Last night I didn't even go out, I sat in my room and went through the books. Literally. Everything's recorded in these enormous black ledgers, they barely have anything on computer, it's insane.'

Montana gave her a serious look. 'You've changed, girl. Like, what have you done with fun Ariana, and can I get her back?'

Ariana smiled ruefully. 'Tell me about it.'

'Can't you just ask your dad for help? Isn't he some billionaire mogul or something?'

'Sure, I will, I just want to get my head around everything first. He thinks I should forget all about it and either sell the place or get a management company to run it and take a share of the profits. That would be the easiest solution, but . . . I don't know. I feel like I've been drifting for a few years, and maybe this is the project I need. My grandmother obviously left it to me for a reason.'

'You think that's your destiny? To run a hotel?'

'Well, when you put it like that . . .' Ariana laughed. 'But I need a challenge, something that'll give me a chance to use my brain for once. I know I can't do it all on my own, but I want to learn. I've been doing some reading, trying to find out about the history of the hotel. It's fascinating. Back in the seventies *everyone* stayed there – Jack Nicholson and Anjelica Huston, Warren Beatty, Sophia Loren. Now it seems to be businessmen and call girls.'

Montana shrieked with excitement. 'A-may-zing! It's like a real-life movie. Like *Pretty Woman*!'

'If only. At least Richard Gere would be hanging around. I reckon a hot older man is exactly what I need right now.'

'There's gotta be some gorgeous guys staying there,

right? I mean, it's the French Riviera, everyone's a ten out of ten.'

Ariana pulled a face. 'The only guy I've met was the previous owner's son, who was ridiculously entitled and seemed to think the hotel still belonged to him.' Ariana shuddered at the memory of how rude Gabriel had been, and the huge argument that had ensued between them . . .

She'd seen the look on Gabriel's face as she announced her name. He was clearly shocked by the revelation, but there was something else there too . . . His piercing blue eyes flickered over her body, and she sensed that he was intrigued by her, that she wasn't what he'd expected. But his expression quickly turned neutral, putting on his poker face.

'Mademoiselle Theodosis. *Enchanté de faire votre conaissance.*' He stood up and offered his hand but remained where he was – a power play which meant Ariana had to approach him. He was taller than she'd realized when he was sitting down, and his grip was strong and confident.

'*Le plaisir est à moi,*' she said coolly, as she returned his appraising look.

'You speak French?' he asked, switching to English, and sounding surprised.

'Of course. Although my name sounds the same in any language,' she added pointedly, and was gratified to see his look of discomfort as he realized that she must have overheard him discussing her earlier.

Ariana glanced around, taking in the bijou office. In stark contrast to the rest of the hotel, it was fresh and modern, with contemporary furniture and stylish accessories. On the sleek desk was a framed black and white photograph of a silver-haired man, with the same chiselled jawline and strong nose as Gabriel. The man looked familiar, but Ariana couldn't place where she'd seen him before.

Gabriel caught her staring. 'May I assist you with anything?'

'Yes, actually. I wondered when you'd be vacating this office, given that the hotel no longer belongs to your family. If you need any help packing, I'll send one of my staff to assist you.'

To Ariana's surprise, Gabriel roared with laughter. 'You think it's that easy? You kick me out, the staff are yours and – *voilà* – you're running a hotel!'

Ariana bristled. She'd expected him to be deferential – technically he was trespassing, and she could order him off the premises – but he was arrogant beyond belief.

'Well, I hardly think I could do a worse job,' she shot back, then remembered what she had seen on the company website. 'This place is an embarrassment, I thought that your hotels were "the essence of luxury and class".'

Gabriel's steely eyes bored angrily into hers, his cheeks flushing, and Ariana felt a thrill of victory that her barb had hit its target.

'Perhaps you can ask your father for help,' he retorted.

'You think I can't achieve anything without him? You underestimate me, Monsieur du Lac. You wouldn't be the first. But I like proving people wrong.'

'We'll see about that,' he replied arrogantly.

'Is it because I'm a woman?' Ariana wondered, stepping closer and placing her hands on his desk, dominating the space and ensuring he couldn't look anywhere but at her.

'Because you strike me as a conceited man with a misplaced sense of superiority.'

'On the contrary.' Gabriel smiled, his gaze never leaving her face. 'I adore women. Everything about them.'

The air was thick with tension. Ariana could feel the heat rising through her body, her heart beating faster, but she was determined to teach this arrogant bastard a lesson.

Gabriel leaned in closer. 'If you think I'm giving this place up without a fight, you're mistaken.'

'There is no fight – you've already lost.'

'Oh please, stop behaving like you're in some little soap opera. Your acting wasn't convincing in Hollywood, and it's not convincing now. You clearly have no idea what the hell you're doing here.'

'You're taking this far too personally,' Ariana remarked, keeping her cool. 'It's a business transaction, that's all. No need to get so emotional about it.'

'I don't think you understand, Mademoiselle Theodosis. This is far from over. I don't know how you've come to own this hotel, but rest assured I have my lawyers looking into every single detail.'

'No, *you* don't understand.' Ariana pulled herself up to her full height, her amber eyes blazing. 'It *is* over. You've lost. I'll give you time to arrange your affairs – which is very fair of me – then you must leave.'

On the surface she seemed bold and fearless, but inside Ariana was shaking with anger. How *dare* he speak to her like that. One thing was for sure – the sooner Gabriel du Lac was out of the Hotel du Soleil, the better.

* * *

'Urgh, what a douchebag,' Montana sympathized. 'He sounds like a total snake. At least there's always Jonny Farrell . . .'

At the mention of Jonny's name, Ariana felt her stomach flip. 'Have you seen him recently?' she asked, trying to sound casual.

Montana shrugged. 'I've seen him around. We've hung out a couple of times. He *always* asks about you.'

'Does he?' That stomach flip again. 'I've stopped answering his calls.'

'Well, it's clearly a case of treat 'em mean, keep 'em keen, 'cos the last thing I heard he's planning on flying over here.'

'Really?' Ariana hated herself for caring.

'Uh huh. Girl's got it bad, hmm?'

Ariana was saved from replying as a waiter passed by with a tray of tequila shots. They both took one, clinking glasses and knocking them back with salt and lime proffered by the waiter, grimacing at the sharp, distinctive taste. Ariana blinked, the world blurring and refocusing. She realized that she was doing exactly what she'd promised her father she wouldn't and was in danger of slipping back into the old ways: drinking too much, partying too hard. The lifestyle had been a blast, as long as you were in control, but she'd seen what happened to some of her friends and it wasn't pretty – addiction, rehab, worse. Ariana wasn't that girl anymore. She didn't want to be one of the idle rich, living off her parents' money. The Hotel du Soleil was the perfect opportunity to make something of herself.

'So what's happening with you?' she said to Montana, deliberately changing the subject. 'Any exciting projects?'

'I had an audition for the new Sofia Coppola movie. I didn't get it, but I'm on the casting director's radar, right? And I shot a commercial for In-N-Out Burger. My line got cut, but I'm still featured.'

'That's amazing, congratulations.'

'Thanks.' Montana glanced around to see whether anyone interesting had arrived – any hot guys or cool directors. She lit a cigarette, offering one to Ariana, who declined. 'The police are still hanging around, asking questions,' she said casually.

Ariana's stomach clenched as though she'd been punched. 'What?'

'Yeah,' Montana replied, with studied casualness. 'Brandon said they questioned him again last week. He's given them all the surveillance tapes, but the camera by the pool wasn't working properly.'

'So they . . . they still don't know what happened to Liberty?' Ariana hardly dared to speak her name, keeping her voice low even though no one was paying attention to them and the sound of Lady Gaga pumping out over the speakers made it almost impossible to eavesdrop.

'Nuh-uh.' Montana exhaled languidly, watching the smoke disappear into the night air. 'What can you remember?'

'Me?' Ariana's heart was pounding but she tried to keep her face neutral. Even the mention of Liberty's name unsettled her. 'Very little, if I'm being honest. That's what I told the police. I'd drunk a lot – it's all just a blur.'

'You were out of it,' Montana nodded. 'I don't know • what Jonny had given you, but you ate it right up like it was candy.'

Ariana felt ashamed of the way she'd behaved back

then. In truth, she'd been longing to talk to Montana about the night Liberty Granger had died. To finally share her fears with someone, to try to piece together her memories and figure out what happened. 'How about you?' she asked. 'What do you remember?'

'I left early,' Montana said, grinding out her cigarette in the ashtray. 'I had a casting the next morning and had to be up early,' she said airily. 'I was long gone before anything happened, thank God. Don't you remember me saying goodbye?'

'Oh,' Ariana faltered. 'I . . . I don't know.' Her mind was a jumble of misremembered memories and snatches of conversation. She had no recollection of Montana leaving and was no closer to working out what had actually happened that night.

'I mean, Liberty's death was, like, totally shocking and really sad, but nothing to do with me or you. Right?'

'I guess so . . .' Ariana trailed off as her BlackBerry started flashing. She opened the message, raising her eyebrows in surprise.

'What?' Montana asked eagerly.

'It's Gabriel.'

'Who?'

'The guy I just told you about. The arrogant ex-owner of my hotel!' Ariana turned her phone around to show Montana the message:

We need to talk. Dinner tomorrow?

'A man of few words,' Montana giggled.

'That's . . . weird. I wonder what he wants to talk about?'

'Honey, he probably wants to do a hell of a lot more than just talk.' Montana wiggled her eyebrows suggestively.

'Oh, stop! So what do I say?'

'You say yes, of course. Or do you want to give me your cell and I'll do it for you?'

'No! I hope he's going to apologize. He was horrible to me.' Ariana scowled as she remembered how unpleasant Gabriel had been. He'd been so rude, so entitled, seemingly expecting her to give up her inheritance because it suited him.

'Well, message him back and accept,' Montana grinned. 'Otherwise, you'll never know.'

Chapter 8

Elizabeth Chappell was undergoing her transformation from ordinary mortal to breathtaking superstar.

Right now, final touches were being made to her hair, make-up and outfit – toning down a smoky eye, adding a pair of diamond ear studs, making sure the finished look was immaculate. Elizabeth stood regally in the centre of the melee, completely unflustered as one assistant dabbed her lips with a sheen of gloss, and another slipped her feet into a skyscraper pair of Louboutins.

'You look stunning,' breathed Shannon, the make-up artist she'd met on a *Vogue* shoot three years ago and worked with ever since.

'If they gave out Palmes d'Or for the best-dressed, you'd win every time,' grinned her stylist, Kris.

'Thank you, my darlings,' Elizabeth smiled, indulging herself briefly in the flattery. Looking in the mirror, she had to agree they'd done an incredible job. Today was the press conference for *All Our Yesterdays*, held at the famous Palais des Festivals, where they were currently getting ready in a small anteroom that served as a makeshift dressing room. Sitting behind a desk answering questions from the world's journalists didn't require a ballgown, so they'd opted for a style Kris was calling 'Cannes cool': Elizabeth's long legs were encased in black leather trousers, teamed with a classic white vest and sleek blazer, her blonde hair backcombed and artfully dishevelled. The entire look was by ROX; it was part rock chick, part Barbarella.

That kind of style would never have worked in the States, but one of the things Elizabeth loved about the Cannes Film Festival was its alternative mindset. Compared to ceremonies like the Academy Awards or the Golden Globes, which were all about extreme glamour and razzamatazz, the European festivals were inevitably more arthouse, more experimental. Being included on the programme at Cannes or Deauville or Venice gave a film a certain cachet, a depth that went beyond the shallowness of Hollywood. Elizabeth felt incredibly lucky that her career spanned the two worlds.

There was a knock on the door, and Shannon opened it to see Francesca, who walked in without acknowledging her. She'd made no concessions to the Riviera heat and was dressed in her usual head-to-toe black, her red pixie cut swept up and off her face.

She shot Elizabeth an approving glance. 'Looking good, Liz. Are you ready? We're due out there in five, but . . .' She hesitated for a moment.

Elizabeth rolled her eyes, 'Don't tell me.'

Fran shrugged, 'Don't shoot the messenger, Liz. Robert would like a word first.'

'Where is he?'

'Just outside.'

Elizabeth sighed, then said coolly. 'I think we're done here. Thanks, everyone.' The team recognized the dismissal and turned to leave. Fran shooed them out, then melted away as Robert sloped in sheepishly. He was dressed in a simple black T-shirt and jeans, a paisley cravat draped loosely at his neck, and he was wearing his sunglasses, which Elizabeth knew meant he was hungover. He was *always* hungover – the only time he wasn't was when he was drinking.

'Everything all right?' he asked nervously.

'Good, thanks. And you?' The stiff and formal conversation sat awkwardly between them, and for a moment Elizabeth couldn't bear it. 'You look like something the cat dragged in,' she said with a small smile.

'Something the cat spat out, more like,' he grinned back, and there it was again – that characteristic swagger in his voice, the handsome smile that made Elizabeth want to melt. But she knew she had to be strong and stick to her guns, as hard as it was.

'What do you want, Robbie?'

He shrugged. 'Just to say hi. And . . . I miss you . . . And, I'll be honest, I can't remember exactly what happened last night.'

Elizabeth raised an eyebrow. 'Darling, you'd drunk enough to sink a ship. You were rambling incoherently when you turned up unannounced at my hotel. The management weren't very pleased with me – I had a very disgruntled receptionist inform me that a "gentleman" had come looking for me. When I asked for a description they said he was extremely intoxicated and it was impossible to understand a word he was saying.'

'How did you know it was me?'

Elizabeth raised a perfectly sculpted eyebrow.

'Joke! Did you tell them I'm from Manchester and that's just how I sound?'

'I'm being serious! You can't go around behaving like that. Have you apologized to the staff?'

Robert looked confused, as though the idea had never occurred to him. 'I could ask Fran to send flowers.'

Elizabeth wanted to scream. 'Getting Fran – or me – to clean up your mess every time is not good enough. You can't keep crashing your way through life like a bull in a china shop, getting someone else to pick up the pieces for you afterwards. We've all had enough. Start taking some responsibility.'

For Robert, it felt like Groundhog Day. He decided to change the subject. 'Why are you staying in that dump anyway? Is that place *really* better than a suite at my gaff, the Hotel du Cap, even if you do have to share it with me?'

'It brings back happy memories,' Elizabeth said defensively. 'I stayed there with my parents when I was a child.'

'Think they've still got the same old dear working on reception by the look of it.'

'I'm surprised you could see straight to even notice. I like it. Some of the staff remembered me – how sweet is that?'

'I think they'll remember me too after last night.'

'Robbie!' Elizabeth sounded exasperated. 'These aren't the sixties, you're not Oliver Reed or Richard Harris. You could lose your career. You're definitely going to lose your marriage.'

'Christ, Liz, will you stop going on about it.' Robert pulled off his sunglasses to reveal bloodshot eyes, heavy with bags, as he rubbed his hand tetchily across his face.

Even when he was rough as hell, he still looked great, Elizabeth thought irritably. He seemed to get better with age, personifying all those descriptions that only worked for men: craggy, seasoned, mature. Whereas she was fighting like hell in an industry that prized youth, her life an incessant treadmill of diets, workouts, injections, procedures, as though ageing wasn't natural and inevitable. Robert would probably move onto his fourth wife within weeks of their divorce, while she'd be over forty and cast on the scrap heap.

'You don't care, do you?' Elizabeth said, her voice trembling. 'You just—'

The door opened and Fran walked in without knocking. 'Ready??' She sensed the tension immediately, saw the strained looks on their faces. 'Look, I know you two are having a hard time, but we had an agreement. You're both professionals, at the top of your game.'

Robert raised his bloodshot eyes heavenward.

'Even you, Rob. The world wants the fairy tale, the glamour of the Chappells, and that's what we're going to give them. For the good of the movie. OK?'

Elizabeth and Robert nodded, glances passing between them, telepathically calling a truce.

'Great. Now get out there and make the magic happen. It's showtime.'

'. . . So we absolutely wanted to make this on an epic scale but, at the heart of it all, you're focusing in on these two lives with these big, universal themes that everyone can recognize – love, heartache, regret, grief. The pressure of expectation. I'm sure we've all experienced those emotions – even a bunch of hard-hearted hacks.'

The journalists smiled politely, scribbling in their notebooks as Ross Anderson, the grizzled Canadian director, expounded his vision for the film.

All Our Yesterdays was a First World War saga. Elizabeth played Lady Courtenay, an aristocrat trapped in an unhappy marriage, whose country house is turned into a convalescent home for wounded soldiers. She falls in love with Tom Brown, played by Robert, a northern, working-class serviceman who'd lost his right arm at Ypres. The two of them go on to have a passionate, yet unconsummated, affair. But Tom is married, his wife waiting back home in St Helens, and following his recovery he and Lady Courtenay go their separate ways and lose touch. Liberty Granger played Edith, a small but pivotal role as a nurse who works in the home and witnesses their growing relationship. Years later, when Lady Courtenay is dying, Edith cares for her and reunites her with Tom, giving the two of them an opportunity to enjoy fleeting happiness before Lady Courtenay's death. It was a real weepie, and the two leads in particular gave powerhouse performances.

Currently, there were over two hundred reporters, from all corners of the globe, packed into an auditorium in the building which had been specially designed to host the film festival. For the rest of the year, the Palais des Festivals et des Congrès housed exhibitions and conferences, so right now was about as glamorous as it got.

'Jon Feldman, *Entertainment Tonight*. There's been a lot of awards buzz around this movie. What would you rather win – the Palme d'Or or an Academy Award?'

'Why not both?' Robert suggested, making everyone laugh. His comment could easily have sounded arrogant, but he had enough charm to pull it off. 'Come on, Jon. Where's your ambition?'

'Right now, I'd say a Palme d'Or, but ask me again in February,' Elizabeth joked. 'In all seriousness, we're thrilled that everyone who's seen it has taken this movie to their hearts, and we hope the public does the same when it's released. You never know how a creative work is going to be received, but I think I speak for everyone when I say we knew we had something special on our hands.'

The rest of the panel – including Colin Firth, who played the husband of Elizabeth's character, and Chen Li, the producer – nodded in agreement.

'Chloé Laurent, *Madame Figaro*. This film is full of strong female characters, which is wonderful to see. However, I'm sure we're all aware that there's one person who should be on the panel today who isn't here – Liberty Granger, who died tragically earlier this year. The details of her death are still unknown. Do you think it's right to release the film under these circumstances?'

Chen Li leaned forward and spoke into the microphone. 'We were all terribly, terribly upset to hear of Liberty's death. She was a remarkable young woman, a fantastic actor with a promising future ahead of her. But I think we all felt – and we had the blessing of her family on this – that the best way to honour her memory was to go ahead and release the film.'

'We were all devastated.' Elizabeth took over the tributes from her producer. 'As Chen has said, Liberty was an incredible young woman, and the two of us grew particularly close during filming. What happened was a tragedy, and our hearts go out to her family and friends.'

'I'd like to echo what everyone has said,' Ross chimed in, rubbing his beard thoughtfully. 'I've spoken to her parents, who agreed that she absolutely would have wanted the movie to go ahead. Liberty was passionate about her work, passionate about her career. She was excited to be playing the role of Edith and I'm sure she would have gone on to much greater things had she been given the opportunity. It's a stellar performance and deserves to be seen by a wider audience. We miss you, Liberty. This is for you.'

'Ash Kumar, BBC. I have a question for Robert and Elizabeth. Is there any truth to the rumours that the two of you are getting a divorce?'

Like the consummate professionals they were, neither of them so much as flinched.

Elizabeth smiled brightly. 'I think the more pertinent question would be, when are there ever *not* rumours we're getting a divorce.'

A wave of laughter greeted her quip, and Elizabeth hoped they might move on. But Robert wasn't finished.

'Of course we're not getting divorced, we're bloody crazy about each other. You want proof?' He threw his arms around Elizabeth, pulling her to him and kissing her passionately. She had no choice but to go along with it, and the journalists went wild, cheering and whooping as shutters clicked and flashbulbs popped.

When he pulled away, Elizabeth kept the same fixed grin on her face, while Robert looked around smugly. Under the table, away from the prying eyes of the reporters, Elizabeth stretched out her leg, running the tip of her shoe tantalizingly all the way down Robert's calf to his ankle. Then, very slowly and deliberately, Elizabeth pushed the heel of her Louboutin down into his foot as hard as she possibly could.

Chapter 9

La Palme d'Or restaurant was the most celebrated in Cannes. It was located in the Hôtel Martinez and boasted two Michelin stars. Getting a table during the festival was hard. Getting a table in a prime location on the terrace was almost impossible. Ariana was impressed; Gabriel clearly had clout.

She followed the maître d' as he led her through the dining room. People were looking over at her as she passed by, the men checking her out, the women wondering who she was. It was a good feeling.

Ariana was wearing a white plunging bodycon dress that clung to every curve, accentuating her deep tan, and contrasting dramatically with her long, dark hair that tumbled in soft waves almost to her waist. Pulling out all the stops, she had accessorized with the pink diamond ring that had belonged to her grandmother, enjoying the heaviness of the stone and the way it sparkled in the overhead lights, spilling out a thousand shards of crystal. Ariana wasn't trying to impress Gabriel – at least, that's what she was telling herself. Rather the designer clothing and immaculate make-up were like armour, giving her the confidence to deal with whatever he might throw at her.

Gabriel stood as he saw her approach – a sweetly old-fashioned gesture, Ariana noted – and kissed her on both cheeks. He smelled delicious, freshly showered and spritzed with expensive cologne, and he looked even better than she remembered. He was dressed all in black, his shirt open at the collar to reveal a glimpse of smooth, tanned chest, his body lightly muscled and his slim waist emphasized by a narrow leather belt.

'I took the liberty of ordering champagne,' Gabriel said smoothly, as a waiter appeared and poured her a glass of Dom Pérignon.

'Are we celebrating?'

'That depends if you accept my offer.'

They clinked flutes, Ariana wishing Gabriel *'Yamas'* and him responding with *'Salut'*, and Ariana settled back in her chair. The view over the bay was magnificent, the sea darkening from turquoise to indigo, a riot of red and orange streaking the sky as the sun began its descent. A warm breeze drifted through the restaurant, the flames on the candles flickering softly. Ariana felt a thrill of excitement rush through her. She had something this man wanted, and it made her feel powerful. For the first time, she understood why her grandfather and her father had been so addicted to making deals and taking risks. She could only hope she'd inherited their killer instinct.

'It's no surprise that you haven't bought me dinner in the Hotel du Soleil,' Ariana teased.

'What do you mean? Stefan is a world-class chef, diners come from all over France to sample his menu.'

'Well they don't seem to have been in the restaurant since I arrived. Face it, your little hotel is past its best. You should be glad to let me take over.'

Gabriel visibly bristled, and Ariana enjoyed seeing him on the defensive. 'Oh, quite the expert, aren't you?' he said calmly. 'I've been reading about you – from what I can tell you've hardly been at your best recently either, judging by what the tabloids have to say about you. Aren't you rather out of your depth?'

Ariana narrowed her amber eyes, giving her a cat-like appearance. 'What do they say? Oh, don't be afraid, I've heard it all before, but I think you'll find there's more to mc than meets the eye.'

Gabriel appeared to be mulling this over. 'Perhaps others should be the judge of that.'

Ariana took another sip of her champagne, savouring its sharp, dry acidity, then she leaned in, so close that Gabriel caught the scent of Chanel No. 5 and saw the flecks of gold in her eyes. 'Monsieur du Lac, *qu'est-ce que vous proposez, exactement*?'

Gabriel stared straight at her. His jaw was set firm, his blue eyes intense. 'Twenty million euros.'

Ariana laughed out loud. 'The real estate the hotel is on is worth twice that alone.' She grabbed her Chanel clutch and stood up. 'I think the negotiation is over for the evening, don't you?' She turned to leave.

'Ariana, wait!' Gabriel reached out to grab her hand. His fingers clasped around her wrist and she felt a jolt, a shot of electricity travelling through her body. Their fellow diners were turning to look at the commotion, but at that moment they held each other's gaze, and Ariana felt a heady moment of connection. For a second, there was no one else in the room and it was as if Gabriel could see right inside of her. She'd never felt anything like this with Jonny, and it startled her for a moment, rendering her speechless.

'Please,' Gabriel broke first. 'I have been clumsy. I'm sorry. Can we start again?'

Slowly, Ariana pulled her hand from his before sitting back down. 'No, *I'm* sorry,' she heard herself say. 'I have somehow given you the mistaken impression that my hotel is for sale. It isn't.'

The moment was broken, and a flash of annoyance crossed Gabriel's face, which he quickly suppressed. The two of them stared at one another, the tension crackling between them, each silently daring the other to make the next move.

At that moment, a waiter appeared beside them, a quizzical look on his face. 'Are you ready to order?'

'I'd like the asparagus, followed by the lobster,' said Ariana, without even glancing at the menu.

'Very good, madame.'

'Would you care to join me for dinner?' she asked Gabriel, trying to hide her smile.

He broke into a grin, feeling outplayed. 'I'll have the ravioli to start, then the tenderloin.' The waiter nodded and departed. 'In England they would say we have "got off on the wrong foot". Perhaps we shouldn't discuss business.'

'In Greece we say, "a drop of wisdom is like a sea of gold". That sounds like a good idea.'

'So tell me about yourself. I imagine that's a far more interesting subject.'

Ariana laughed. He was clearly going overboard with

the flattery, but she didn't have any complaints. 'Where do I start?'

'At the beginning. We have all night.'

'Well, I was born in Greece,' Ariana began. 'On the beautiful island of Ithos. Have you ever been?'

'Greece? Yes. Ithos, no.'

'I imagine you've been to Santorini?'

'Of course, we have hotels all over the world.'

'Ithos is very different. Much smaller, much quieter. No airport, no mass development. A handful of tourists come by ferry for the day and then . . . they leave.'

'Sounds like a great place for a luxury hotel, I'll call my scout.' Gabriel couldn't resist provoking her.

'Don't you dare! There's a small guesthouse, and a handful of rooms to rent, but a development would ruin the island completely. It's so peaceful, so tranquil.'

'I can't imagine you being content with that kind of life. I thought this was more your scene.' Gabriel gestured round at their glamorous surroundings. A few tables away sat Keira Knightley, stunning in a vintage slip dress. Over by the door, Daniel Craig was arriving with his entourage, causing a huge buzz even amongst the celeb-weary Cannes crowd.

Ariana considered Gabriel's observation. 'Ithos was a wonderful place to grow up, very safe and free. My heart is in Ithos, but for the moment, my head is here in Cannes. Anyway, you don't know me at all.'

'Maybe not, but that's easy to change.'

Ariana stared at him, feeling the heat rise in her cheeks. She couldn't work out whether Gabriel was being serious. Was he genuinely interested in her – or in her hotel?

A month ago, Ariana hadn't even heard of the Hotel du Soleil, so why was she so reluctant to sell it to him?

Twenty million euros would mean she could do anything she wanted. And yet . . . Ariana couldn't explain why, but she didn't want to give up the hotel. Elana must have given it to her for a reason – selling it would be like rejecting her grandmother's legacy. And she still didn't know how Elana had come to own it in the first place. Her lawyers were unable to give her any further information, and despite Ariana trawling through online archives, she'd found no connection between her grandmother and the Hotel du Soleil. Ariana wanted to uncover the secret, to solve the mysteries that the hotel had so far managed to keep hidden.

'That's quite a rock, by the way,' Gabriel commented, indicating Ariana's ring as she lifted her glass to take a sip of champagne. 'It reminds me of something . . . what sort of stone is it?'

'A pink diamond,' Ariana replied proudly. 'It's incredibly rare.'

'You must have a generous admirer.'

Ariana smiled, wondering if he was goading her. 'My grandmother left it to me.'

Gabriel raised his eyebrows. 'A diamond *and* a hotel. How fortunate.'

Ariana's face changed instantly. 'Perhaps. But I'd trade both in a heartbeat if I could have her back,' she retorted, her voice catching in her throat.

'Of course. I'm sorry. It was a thoughtless remark. I know what it is to lose someone you love.'

'Thank you for the apology.' Ariana placed her champagne flute back down on the table. 'Now it's your turn. Tell me about yourself. Where did you grow up?'

'Here. In Cannes.' Seeing Ariana's look of surprise, Gabriel explained, 'My parents owned the Hotel du Soleil, and I spent most of my childhood there. I know every inch of it.'

'Oh,' Ariana faltered. 'Is that why you want it so badly? It must have a lot of happy memories for you.'

Gabriel flinched almost imperceptibly. 'Not necessarily, no . . .'

Their entrées arrived before she could question him further, and the waiter refilled their glasses.

'You called the hotel past its best, is that what you really think?' Gabriel asked.

Ariana smiled. 'It has a kind of charm, I guess. It must have been stunning twenty years ago, but it needs a little TLC.'

'My thoughts exactly,' Gabriel concurred, pleased that they were on the same page.

'So why haven't you updated it? Your other hotels are immaculate.'

'Thank you,' Gabriel inclined his head, accepting the unintended compliment. 'But the Hotel du Soleil never belonged to me. As far as I understood, it belonged to my father, and ownership passed to my mother when he died. I had – and still have – no idea how your family came to be involved.'

'Neither do I. Have you asked your mother what she knows?'

Gabriel hesitated, running his hand through his wavy blond hair. 'My mother . . . has not been the same since my father's death. She rarely leaves her room, let alone the hotel. I've asked her, many times, to hand responsibility over to me so that I can restore it to its former glory, but she will not. She is incredibly stubborn. I think, perhaps, the two of you have something in common, *non*?'

Despite herself, Ariana smiled. 'Do you have any other family you can ask?'

Gabriel shook his head. 'There is only my sister. It's true that she is closer to my mother than I am – I'm regularly away travelling – but Constance lives and works at the hotel. You may have seen her on reception – she's tall, slim . . .'

'Constance is your sister . . .?' Ariana looked stunned. 'I would never . . . The two of you are very different,' she finished diplomatically.

'I guess it's fair to say we wanted different things out of life.'

'And you wanted money? A hotel empire? A profile in *Forbes* magazine?'

'You've done your research. I should be flattered.'

'It's more flattering than the research you did on me. What did you say again? *"Spoilt little rich kid"*? *"Z-list actress with more money than brains"*?'

Gabriel had the good grace to look embarrassed. 'I'm sorry. I shouldn't have said those things.'

'Apology accepted. You hadn't met me then. Do you still think that now?'

Gabriel seemed to be weighing up his words for a moment but then smiled and said, 'You are certainly a surprise – and a very pleasant one.'

'You're teasing me.' She raised an eyebrow and felt an undeniable spark of chemistry swirling in the air between them again.

Gabriel leaned back in his chair. 'Why do you want the hotel? What difference would it make to you?'

'Does it matter? I don't have to justify—' But before Ariana could continue, her eye was caught by a flurry of flashbulbs and a hubbub at the entrance to the restaurant. 'Oh God, no . . .'

'What is it?' Gabriel asked, following her eyeline to where a tall, snake-hipped guy was swaggering through the restaurant towards them. He was wearing sunglasses indoors, his dark facial hair making him look like an extra from *Pirates of the Caribbean*, and he was heading straight for their table, a lazy grin on his face.

Gabriel looked at Ariana, who was stock-still in her seat, her face hard to read.

'Hey babe,' the guy said as he reached them, bending down to kiss Ariana full on the lips. 'You look hot. Did you miss me?'

Before she could answer, Jonny took off his sunglasses and stared directly at Gabriel. 'Hey, who the hell's this guy?'

Gabriel felt surprised by a jolt of jealousy at this gesture but kept his voice steady. 'Ariana, I think perhaps some introductions might be needed?'

She closed her eyes, hoping it was all a bad dream. When she opened them again, Gabriel was looking from her to Jonny with questioning eyes.

The contrast between the two men was stark – Jonny looked like a rockstar who'd just rolled out of bed, dripping with confidence and easy charm. Gabriel, on the other hand, was more reserved but clearly hugely successful, rich, and undeniably attractive. Intelligent and enigmatic, there was something intriguing about him that made Ariana want to know more.

'Jonny, this is Gabriel du Lac. Gabriel . . .' Ariana gestured between them, suddenly wishing she was back home on Ithos. 'This is Jonny Farrell.'

Chapter 10

Gabriel stormed through reception and into his office. It was almost midnight and the hotel was quiet, the moonlight streaming in through the unshuttered windows. He flicked on the notary lamp on his desk and poured himself a double measure of Armagnac. Gabriel wasn't a big drinker, but tonight he needed something to centre him.

He felt unexpectedly furious at the way the evening had played out, with that *boy*, Jonny, showing up out of the blue and interrupting his dinner with Ariana. It wasn't just anger, it was . . . What exactly? Disappointment, perhaps? A blow to his ego?

Ariana was undoubtedly stunning, but it was more than that. There'd been a real spark between them, and he'd enjoyed their jousting and her quick wit. Gabriel had dated many women over the years – he wasn't vain, but he knew he was attractive, worked hard at being charming, and was a multimillionaire, so it was no surprise that he was never on his own – but there'd never been anyone special, no one who could hold his interest for more than a few months. He'd been told by past girlfriends that he cared about his business more than any woman, and he suspected it might be true; there was nothing quite so thrilling as striking a hard-won deal and making a new acquisition, the latest addition to his empire. After his family, it was the thing he loved most in the world.

Gabriel knew he was lucky to live the lifestyle that he did, but recently he'd been thinking that he wanted something more meaningful. A connection that went deeper than a one-night stand. What was the point of experiencing the finer things in life if you had no one to share them with?

He shook his head to clear it, swirling the rich, dark liquid in his glass and taking a slug. What was he thinking? There was no way in hell that Ariana Theodosis could be that person. The woman had waltzed into his life out of nowhere, expecting to steal his hotel right from under his nose. The Hotel du Soleil was his birthright, his father's legacy. He didn't understand how Ariana had come to own it, but there was no way he was giving it up without a fight. His father would never forgive him.

Gabriel placed the glass down on the desk, beside the framed photograph of Alain du Lac, and walked over to the cabinet. Crouching down, he opened the door and pulled out a pile of folders, revealing the safe hidden behind. He entered the code and the door clicked open. Gabriel paused for a moment, preparing himself. He wasn't sure why he was doing this tonight, reopening old wounds. His meeting with Ariana, and the prospect of losing the hotel, had given him a sense of urgency.

Reaching into the safe, he took out a newspaper. It was a copy of *Nice-Matin*, yellowed and crisp with age. He stared at the article:

24 August 1987

FRENCH HOTEL LEGEND KILLED

Alain du Lac, 53, the renowned proprietor of the Hotel du Soleil in Cannes, died at his hotel in the early hours of Sunday morning.

Details are still emerging, but early reports indicate a tragic accident.

Du Lac leaves behind his wife, Madeleine, and two children, Constance, 15, and Gabriel, 12.

He was a popular figure and successful hotelier, turning the Hotel du Soleil into the favoured haunt of the beau monde in the 1970s, although its popularity has declined in recent years . . .

Gabriel lowered the newspaper, not wanting to read any further. He'd looked at it so many times over the years he could have recited the words by heart.

The face of his father stared out from the front page, the same strong nose as Gabriel, the same thick, wavy hair that curled over his collar.

There were so many unanswered questions, and Ariana's arrival had prompted even more.

What should I do, Papa? Gabriel raised his eyes to the heavens, wishing he was able to ask his father. *What didn't you tell me?*

He strode back over to the safe, replacing the newspaper

and removing a letter. It was addressed to Gabriel in his father's distinctive handwriting – elegant, but written in haste, as Alain was always so busy. Gabriel held it for a moment, closing his eyes, the paper feeling suddenly heavy as lead in his hands. He'd read it countless times since his father died, and there was one paragraph that had never made sense to him.

The day will come when you will be the man of our family. Perhaps you will do a better job than I have. All I ever wanted was to be a good husband, a good father, but I failed, and I drove your mother away. She trusted another man because she couldn't trust me, and now it will blight your future . . .

Gabriel turned the lines over in his head, not needing to open the envelope. He had found the letter when he had been sorting through his father's papers years after his death. It was something his father had started but had not finished, it was full of regret and recrimination, but also of love, and Gabriel had treasured it anyhow, even if it didn't show his father at his best. Those few words had always nagged away at him, however. *Now it will blight your future . . .* is that what was happening now, what did it mean?

After a few minutes, he placed it back on top of the newspaper, locking the safe and closing the cabinet, just another piece of the puzzle he could never solve.

Uncertainty was swirling in his mind, but he knew one thing without a shadow of a doubt – the hotel was his. His father had founded it, and it had been his life's work. He was legendary, just like the newspaper article had said. The du Lacs were the rightful owners of the Hotel du Soleil, and it would never belong to Ariana Theodosis – not while Gabriel had breath in his body.

Despite the late hour, he snatched up the phone on his desk and dialled a number. A voice at the other end answered almost immediately, which was no more than he expected. He paid them enough.

'Get me everything you can find on Ariana Theodosis,' he demanded. 'The whole family, in fact. Scandal, secrets, anything that's out there. There must be something – and I want to know *everything* . . .'

Estée ran off stage, cheers and applause ringing in her ears. It was hardly the Opéra Garnier, but it would sustain her for now, and it was good to feel that her performance was appreciated.

Her forehead was streaked with perspiration from the exertion and the hot stage lights, and she quickly wiped off her make-up before changing out of her skimpy costume into denim shorts and a loose vest. Some of the other women were repairing their make-up and redoing their hair, slipping into short and sexy outfits or glamorous cocktail dresses. Soon, they would head back out to the bar and mingle with the clientele; Victor would give them a bonus if they could talk the customers into buying the most expensive bottles of champagne.

Estée needed to be up at 6 a.m. to start cleaning rooms at the hotel, and she was already exhausted. She called goodnight to the others, grabbed her bag and walked out of the dressing room. The corridor outside was dark – the bulb had blown, and Victor was too tight-fisted to give anyone petty cash to go and buy a new one. Estée headed for the exit at the back of the building and almost collided with Victor.

Estée immediately felt uncomfortable. She and the other girls had an unspoken agreement never to leave one another alone with him.

'Someone's in a rush.' He smiled suggestively.

'Afraid so. I'm all done here so time for me to head off. I'll collect any tips tomorrow,' Estée said breezily, trying to get past him.

'Hmm, I'm not sure there'll be any,' Victor said. Estée knew he was lying, but didn't want to confront him. 'You know, Estée, there are a lot of girls out there who would be grateful for a job like this.'

'Oh, I'm sure,' Estée agreed, trying to sound genuine – who would want to be sleazed on by Victor night after night? 'And I *am* grateful, I really am. I have to be up early, so I can't stay.'

'That's a shame. There are men out there who are willing to pay handsomely for a little one-on-one time with a pretty girl. A sexy thing like you could make a lot of money.'

'I just want to be a dancer, Victor, nothing else. I've told you that before.'

'Look, sweetheart, I know you have that pathetic job in that pathetic hotel. Why don't you give it up and come and work for me full time? You'll earn ten times as much – and you might enjoy it too,' he winked. 'Don't you have a daughter? Imagine being able to spend the extra money on her. Sending her a new dolly for her birthday. Or a pretty dress for her to wear, just like mama . . .'

Estée fought to stay calm. How did Victor know about her daughter? One of the other women must have told him, though Estée rarely talked about her. She didn't want Victor to even know of Emilie's existence, let alone be talking about her, thinking about her . . . But Emilie was Estée's weak spot, and what Victor was saying made financial sense. Perhaps it wouldn't be so bad. She didn't have to *do* anything – just chat with the customers, be fun and flirty and ensure they were kept liberally supplied with expensive alcohol.

'I'll think about it,' she promised, desperate to bolt for the door and hoping that would be enough for him to leave her alone for now.

'Make sure you do. Because I could find another girl – one who's more . . . amenable, shall we say.' Victor snapped his fingers in Estée's face and she jumped. He laughed, and stalked off towards the dressing room.

Estée exhaled shakily, fighting back tears. She couldn't afford to lose this job. It wasn't much, but if it was taken away from her, what else did she have? She couldn't call herself a dancer. She'd simply be a badly paid chambermaid in a hotel that was past its prime.

At that moment, Nicolette emerged from the dressing room and noticed Estée's shadowy figure in the darkness of the corridor. She looked gorgeous in the light that spilled out from the room, her long, blonde hair tumbling over her shoulders, her curvaceous figure poured into a sequinned dress that emphasized every curve.

'Hey, what's the matter?' she asked as she drew closer, realizing that Estée looked shaken up.

'Nothing. Just the usual from Victor. He wants me to stay on, to go out to the bar and mingle . . .' Estée chose her words carefully. 'Entertaining' the male clientele wasn't her scene, but she didn't want her friend to think she was criticizing her or judging the choices she'd made.

Nicolette pulled a sympathetic face, looking at her supportively from beneath enormous fake eyelashes. 'You've been lucky to get away with it for so long. Victor always puts the pressure on. Once he's singled you out, he'll make it hard for you to refuse.'

Estée swore under her breath.

'Maybe time to start looking for something else?' Nicolette suggested gently.

'Perhaps.' Estée looked torn. 'I know it sounds ridiculous, but as long as I'm performing, I feel like I'm still following my dream. Sure, I could go and get a job in a shop, or an office, but what then? I've officially given up, I've let my mum and my daughter down. I promised I'd change things for us.'

Nicolette hesitated, as though trying to decide whether to tell Estée what she was thinking. She pursed her red glossy lips and began to speak. 'You know, I heard they're holding open auditions at the Palais for a new production of *Notre-Dame de Paris*. It's touring, and they're looking for dancers for the chorus. I was thinking of trying out. Do you want to come with me?'

'That sounds incredible,' Estée exclaimed, her spirits lifting immediately. Although she knew that the odds of being successful were minuscule, it was worth a shot. The possibility, at least, would buoy her up a little longer.

The other girls spilled out of the dressing room, chatting and giggling and dressed in their finery, as they headed for the bar. Estée knew they'd have had a few fortifying shots of cheap vodka before they went out there.

'Look, I've got to go,' Nicolette said. 'I don't want them to get all the best guys. And remember – we've all got our dreams and ambitions. This was never mine. None of us grew up longing to be a minimum-wage dancer in a crummy nightclub, but here we are, and we've got to make the best of it. I'll see you tomorrow, OK?'

'Thanks, Nicolette.' The two women hugged before Nicolette sashayed through to the club and Estée turned to leave, wanting to be gone before Victor returned. She would go to the audition with Nicolette, and she would give it her all. But if it didn't work out, she might have to accept Victor's proposal, or it would be time to go home . . .

Chapter 11

Cannes, May 2009

The room came blearily into focus: the old-fashioned bedside lamp and chintzy floral wallpaper. Ariana was in her bed at the Hotel du Soleil, naked beneath the covers. Startlingly, there was someone lying next to her, and it took a moment for the memories to come flooding back before she realized who it was: Jonny Farrell.

He was still sleeping, and Ariana was glad. She pushed her hair out of her eyes, rolled over and squinted at her phone. How the hell was it one o'clock in the afternoon?

She sat up slowly and tried to gather her thoughts, taking long gulps from the bottle of water on the bedside table. Her mouth felt dry and tasted like an ashtray; urgh, she had hazy memories of smoking cigarettes last night.

Ariana crept out of bed and stole over to the bathroom, examining her reflection in the poorly lit mirror. Despite the fact she'd just rolled out of bed, she still didn't look too bad, even though her hair was messed up, black kohl smudged around her eyes.

She needed time to think. Ariana had promised herself that she wouldn't do this again – Jonny was old news. *Bad* news. But oh, there was something about him she couldn't resist. It was like a weakness, a fatal flaw.

With a start, she remembered how Jonny had crashed her dinner with Gabriel. Ariana had been caught off guard, too stunned to protest when Gabriel remembered a prior engagement, paid the bill and made his excuses. Unexpectedly, she'd been enjoying his company. He was clearly sophisticated and well-travelled, intelligent and quick-witted, the tension between them undercut with a simmering chemistry. He was undoubtedly attractive, and she'd felt blindsided when he left. Worse, with Gabriel gone, Ariana had once again been sucked into Jonny's orbit, unable to resist, all her resolve dissipating with the smoke rings he blew with his Gitanes cigarettes. She always did find it impossible to say no to him . . .

Jonny had taken her to an incredible rooftop bar full of beautiful rich people. The views had been insane: 360 degrees from the mountains to the city, the lights from the waterfront buildings spilling out onto the dark mass of the Mediterranean. Montana had joined them, along with some other friends from LA who were in the South of France for the festival, but Ariana and Jonny only had eyes for one another. It was just like old times – dancing, drinking, flirting . . .

'I flew out here for you, babe,' Jonny had murmured, kissing her neck in the way she adored. 'I thought I was losing my mind – I had to see you again. You're even better than I remembered,' he told her, his arms pulling her against him.

Ariana knew it was sweet talk, but it was so good to hear. She'd forgotten how he could sometimes make her feel like she was the only person in the room, that when they were together the rest of the world didn't exist.

'You're the only one who can tame me. You make me a better person. I *need* you, Ariana.'

Jonny had been so attentive that she could almost forget all the bad things that had happened, thinking only of the feel of his body against hers, the familiar scent of cigarettes and alcohol and musky aftershave.

After freshening up, Ariana padded back through to the bedroom, sliding noiselessly between the sheets. Jonny stirred sleepily, nuzzling her ear.

She watched him sleeping, taking in his long eyelashes, his LA tan, the hint of a broken nose that gave him a wounded vulnerability though in reality he'd received it after sleeping with the wife of a director on one of the pictures he'd been working on. What was it about him and women?

His eyelids fluttered, opening slowly to reveal two brown soulful eyes that already seemed to have only one thing in mind. 'I'm so hot for you, baby,' he murmured, his voice gravelly with sleep, his stubble tickling her neck. 'I missed you so much. You drive me crazy, Ariana.'

She turned to him, the brief thought that she hated how he could do this to her – overcome her doubts, her resolve, her self-control – lost in the heat of his presence. He kissed her deeply and she melted into him, resigning herself to the fact that she wasn't going to be getting out of bed anytime soon.

It was late afternoon by the time Ariana and Jonny finally surfaced. They'd ordered room service and fallen back into bed, but Ariana was starting to emerge from Jonny's spell and felt anxious to get away. Jonny didn't seem to have any plans and was content to just hang around. 'I just wanna be with you, babe. We need to make up for lost time,' he winked.

When Ariana confessed that she owned the hotel they were staying in, Jonny insisted that she give him a guided tour.

'This is wild. It's insane,' he kept repeating, as she showed him the pool and the gardens, the view stretching for miles past the old port to the Pointe Croisette and the cerulean waters beyond. 'And your grandma just left all this to you?'

Ariana nodded. She'd pulled on a brightly coloured sundress, and a pair of oversized sunglasses that hid her tired eyes.

'Of course, there's a lot of work to do,' she said, looking around with a critical eye. 'This place has been kind of neglected. It's a shame, as it could be spectacular . . .'

For a brief moment, she considered asking Jonny for his input but knew he was little better than useless. He tended not to think much beyond the next drink or next party, no grand ambitions except scoring a megabucks modelling shoot or a lead-role acting gig. It wasn't his fault; Jonny had been raised in a Hollywood bubble, with people waiting on him his whole life. Ariana might be an heiress, but she knew the value of money – Demetrios had insisted on it. He'd taught her how to strike a bargain, how to push for a good deal, even with the local traders on Ithos market. A childhood spent on the small island, mixing with the locals, meant she'd been sheltered from some of the excess and extravagance that had been Jonny's world.

'It's hardly the Sunset Tower, is it?' he smirked, looking around.

She bristled at his comment, feeling unexpectedly defensive. Sure, the hotel needed some work, but it was *hers*. What had Jonny achieved in his life? It was infuriating, being constantly underestimated – by Jonny, by Gabriel, by her father. While it was true that she had no experience of hotels, Ariana knew she was more intelligent than people gave her credit for. *Let's see if Jonny's laughing in a year's time*, Ariana thought, letting the anger spur her on.

'Hey, let's go check out the bar. You get free drinks, right?' Jonny grinned, oblivious to her annoyance, as they headed inside. 'Large Jack and Coke,' he said to the surly-looking barman. 'And . . .?'

'A bottle of still water.'

'Come on, babe. Don't be boring.'

'I need to rehydrate. Maybe you should try it sometime.'

'What? This is the best form of hydration,' Jonny winked, picking up his glass and taking a satisfying slug. 'They're on the house – she owns this place,' he informed the confused-looking barman.

'Charge it to room 412,' Ariana told him, as Jonny strode off to find a spot on the terrace.

'I'm so glad we're back together, babe,' he said, pulling her in for a kiss, as they sat down at a table. 'I can't live without you. I know I've been an asshole, but I'm a changed man, I swear.'

Ariana tried hard not to roll her eyes. She'd heard it all before. Jonny was fun, great in bed, and there was a sizzling chemistry between them. But he wasn't boyfriend material and she knew it.

'And you know, we gotta stick together. Especially about this whole Liberty thing.'

Ariana's stomach churned nauseatingly, and she instinctively looked around, afraid someone might overhear. 'What do you mean?'

'Don't play dumb, Ariana. I got hauled in by the cops for that crap. It's still floating around, not going away. I'm not taking the rap for what someone else did.'

'Me too, Jonny. They questioned me too. But they're still investigating, right? No one knows what happened.'

'I'm innocent, man, I told them. Don't know a thing. What did you tell them?'

'The same,' Ariana said defensively, wondering where this conversation had suddenly come from. It felt strange discussing Liberty with Jonny. Before she died, she'd been a running sore between them; Ariana had known that Jonny was dating her too, that they were sleeping together even when he'd told Ariana *they* were exclusive. Sure, she'd been angry and jealous at the time, but she had mostly been hurt. The truth was she hadn't known where to direct her anger; she had become hooked on Jonny but Liberty was the only real friend she had made in LA. Should she have been more angry at him for destroying their friendship? Or had she confronted Liberty that night instead?

'I don't really remember what happened,' Ariana continued, trying again to remember, but it was like a big mist. All she could remember was Liberty's soulful eyes looking at her sadly. 'I asked Montana, and she said I'd taken something – that *you'd* given me something, and—'

'Montana needs to keep her big mouth shut,' Jonny snapped. He'd been tapping his lighter furiously on the table and now he pulled out a cigarette, sparking up and inhaling deeply, staring into the distance. Already the shadows were lengthening in the late afternoon, a handful of white clouds rolling in over the bay as shafts of sunlight sparkled on the water. His eyes narrowed and he eyed her for a moment before speaking. 'So you really don't remember anything?'

Ariana shook her head, a chill settling over her despite the warm day.

Jonny rolled the ice around in his glass then leaned into her, stroking her hair. 'You don't remember the two of you fighting, babe?'

'We had an argument?' Ariana closed her eyes, desperately trying to remember more. Now there were hazy memories too, of screaming, yelling. She felt nauseous.

'What, you blacked out or something?'

'I guess so. It's all a blur. What were we fighting about?'

He cocked his head, a smile playing on his lips. 'About me, I think. Kinda cute, right?'

Ariana wanted to slap him. 'Jonny, she's dead.'

His smirk disappeared into a petulant pout. 'I know. And it's nothing to do with me.' He downed the rest of his drink.

'Or me – right?'

'Sure, babe. Whatever you say. Don't worry, I didn't tell the cops anything. I mean, they knew you were there, obviously. But I never told them about your little catfight.'

Ariana felt a shiver wash over her. 'Jonny, I would never have hurt her.'

'No, of course not – not intentionally . . . I don't know, I wasn't there the whole time. I'm sure you're as pure as the driven snow, Ariana.' He finished his cigarette and ground it into the ashtray. 'Look, I gotta go back to my hotel and take a shower. Change my clothes.' He stood and eyed his reflection in one of the hotel windows, dragging his hand through his hair, carefully curating his tousled just-out-of-bed appearance. 'You in town tonight?'

Ariana didn't answer him, and for a moment she wished she had never set eyes on him again.

As if sensing this, Jonny leaned across, forcing her to look at him. 'Hey, this whole Liberty situation is under control, there's nothing to worry about.' He took her head in his hands and kissed her. Against her better judgement, Ariana kissed him back, wanting to believe what he was saying. 'Look, let's just look after each other, sweetheart, I won't say anything, I've got you.'

She nodded, pushing the negative feelings down. Jonny was right, there was no reason to believe she had done anything wrong, or that her argument with Liberty was anything more than a little clash, the usual Hollywood bitch-fest. Whatever happened to Liberty couldn't have had anything to do with her.

'I'll see you later,' Jonny murmured, nibbling on her earlobe. 'Wear something hot.' He picked up his phone and his cigarettes and strode away.

Ariana sat back in her chair, her cheeks flushed, her body still humming from Jonny's kisses. She glanced around, wondering if anyone had witnessed the passionate display, and locked eyes with Gabriel, who'd clearly stepped out onto the terrace at just the wrong moment.

Ariana swore under her breath. He turned to walk away, but she called his name, getting up to follow him. 'Gabriel! Please forgive me, I'm terribly sorry about last night.'

'I'm the one who should apologize,' he said tightly, as she reached him. He looked good, tanned and healthy, in contrast with Jonny's grungy, pale-faced appearance. 'I had other pressing business to attend to and I fear my departure was somewhat hasty.'

'Yes, but we were rather rudely interrupted. Please, let me buy you dinner in return. Maybe we could pick up where we left off?' She was hopeful he'd say yes. There were still so many unanswered questions surrounding the hotel and its history, and Ariana felt confident that over another dinner, with the wine flowing and Gabriel's guard lowered, she could tease the information out of him.

'Really, what more is there to discuss? You made it quite clear my offer wasn't acceptable to you.'

'Think of it as an apology.' Ariana smiled seductively, tilting her head to one side and letting her long, dark hair flow over one shoulder. It wasn't a hardship to flirt with him; he was an attractive man, and flirtation was second nature to her.

'Thank you for your offer, but I'm leaving this evening.'

'Leaving?'

'Yes. I have business to attend to in Capri.'

'Oh.' Ariana felt foolish, the rejection stinging. His coolness towards her had returned and she didn't like the way that made her feel. She wasn't used to men turning her down; usually her powers of persuasion were excellent. Ariana was about to say something else but then the phone in her hand beeped and she automatically looked down to read the message:

I KNOW WHAT YOU DID THAT NIGHT

Ariana gasped, the colour draining from her face. She didn't recognize the number and instantly closed the message, but the damage had been done, the words imprinted on her brain. What did it mean? And who'd sent it? She quickly looked around, as though expecting to see someone watching her, waiting for a reaction, but no one appeared to be paying attention.

'Is something wrong?' Gabriel asked, evidently concerned.

'No, it's . . . it's fine,' Ariana whispered, her mind racing. Was the message referring to that night back in LA? Had someone witnessed what had happened, and knew that she was responsible? But then why not contact the police? Why send Ariana a cryptic message? It didn't make sense.

'Was it that guy?' Gabriel demanded. 'Jonny?'

Ariana shook her head.

'If there's a problem, I can try and help. Whatever I can do – just tell me how.'

Ariana raised her eyes from her phone to meet his, and saw genuine concern there. She held his gaze for a moment and felt that connection again, almost as if he knew how she was feeling; it unnerved her, so she looked away again quickly. 'No, no, it's fine,' she repeated. Despite what her heart was telling her, her head didn't want Gabriel to know that she was rattled. *Never show your weakness to your enemy* – that's what Demetrios had always taught her. 'Enjoy Capri,' she smiled brightly, as she turned away. She longed to be alone in her room, to read the message again and process her thoughts.

'Ariana—' Gabriel stopped her, looking at her thoughtfully. 'Not dinner, but . . . perhaps something else?'

Ariana frowned. 'Something else?'

'Yes, something better than dinner. I'll be in touch.'

He smiled at her and walked off. Ariana watched him go, wrestling with a mixture of emotions. She was confused about the message, frustrated with Jonny – and she wasn't sure how she felt about Gabriel. She stared after him, watching his athletic body, his confident gait, clearly a man at ease with himself. She found herself wondering what his touch on her body would feel like instead of Jonny's and quickly pushed the thought away, wondering where the hell it had come from. She bit her lip, feeling a blush spread across her cheeks. When she looked back again, Gabriel was gone.

Chapter 12

Robert ambled up the steps of the Hotel du Soleil, crossing the now-familiar reception to be faced with the now-familiar scowl of the receptionist. As far as he could remember, it wasn't the same woman who'd been on duty when he'd made his late-night appearance; this lady was older, shorter, but still with the same dour expression that implied he'd ruined her day just by existing.

'*Bonjour*,' he called, in a broad, Mancunian accent, wondering whether she might be won over by his charm. She wasn't.

She eyed the bunch of dusky pink peonies he was carrying with displeasure, pursing her lips as though she'd recently sucked on a lemon. '*Oui*?'

'I'm here to see Estée, but I don't know her room number. I don't know her surname either. I was hoping you could help me.' Robert gave her his movie-star smile once again, but Marie remained unmoved. Instead, she looked rather scandalized.

'Monsieur, I'm afraid we cannot send male visitors to the room of a female staff member.'

'Oh, she works here? Anyway, come on,' Robert scoffed. 'I'm hardly going to—'

'But I will telephone her for you, to see if she is in residence, and if she will come down. May I take your name?'

'My name?' Robert wondered if she was joking. 'My name is Robert Chappell.'

The woman didn't display any flicker of recognition, and Robert realized that the last time she went to the cinema was probably to see Charlie Chaplin's latest flick. Marie picked up the receiver on the old-fashioned phone, speaking in French too rapid for Robert to follow.

'Mademoiselle Estée will be down momentarily. Please take a seat.'

Robert did as he was told for once, settling himself in a faded velvet armchair and looking round the lobby. He could see what Elizabeth meant about the hotel having an old-school charm. It could be spectacular if they smartened it up – although it appeared they'd got the memo and were making a start, as there was a handyman up a ladder replacing the blown bulbs in the dusty but enormous chandelier.

Moments later, he saw Estée making her way down the dramatic central staircase. She looked young and pretty, wearing no make-up, and dressed casually in drawstring linen trousers with a loose vest top.

'Monsieur Chappell,' she greeted him. 'I didn't expect to see you again.'

'I'm a little more sober than the last time you saw me,' he said, shamefaced. 'That's why I'm here. I wanted to apologize. In fact, my wife insisted I apologize, and I always do what my wife tells me.'

'Do you?'

'No, but now's a good time to start trying. Better late than never. Oh, and these are for you.' Robert thrust the flowers at a bemused-looking Estée. 'I'm sorry if I caused you any embarrassment or did anything to upset you. My memory of the other night is . . . somewhat incomplete. My agent's very grateful that this stayed out of the press. One less fire to fight.'

'You're more than welcome. I did what anyone would have done.'

'Well, maybe not. Most people would have called the tabloids and taken a fat wodge of cash for photos of me in that state. So the flowers are to say thanks, and it's the premiere tonight of my new film. Should be a good do – posh frocks and free booze, that kind of thing. Do you want to come? I can put you and a friend on the guest list – a small token of my appreciation.'

'Tonight?' Estée was momentarily flummoxed. A movie premiere? She felt a jolt of excitement at the prospect of mingling up close with celebrities and sweeping down the red carpet. Perhaps for one night, she could feel part of that world, as though she'd finally made it . . . The only problem was her usual shift at La Châtelaine this evening. Victor would go crazy if she cancelled, but a small part of her was feeling rebellious.

Why not me?

Opportunities like this rarely came along. Estée never called in sick, no matter how bad she was feeling, so what if just this once . . .?

'Thank you,' she said, before she had a chance to change her mind. Beaming at Robert over the bouquet of peonies, it was almost as if another part of her was speaking as Estée heard herself say, 'I'd be delighted.'

Gabriel strolled into his office and locked the door behind him. He hadn't vacated it yet; it would take more than a fit of hysteria from Ariana Theodosis to make him leave the Hotel du Soleil. One thing he'd learned in life – give them an inch, they'd take a mile. Ariana was surely joking if she thought she could order him to get out and he'd scuttle off meekly with his tail between his legs. She might have other men dangling for scraps, but he wasn't one of them.

Gabriel settled himself at his desk, switching on his MacBook and waiting for it to boot up. His business in Capri had been concluded swiftly, and now he had a short window in his diary for a little . . . research . . . He'd asked Constance to call him if she saw Ariana in the building; the last thing he wanted was her trying to gain access to his office right now. He'd asked around, but no one had seen her today. Perhaps she was with Jonny, Gabriel thought darkly.

It had seemed as though he and Ariana were making some headway at dinner the other night. He hadn't expected her to accept the twenty million euros he'd offered, but it served as a useful yardstick, to gauge her reaction and determine if she had any idea of the hotel's real value.

Gabriel had to confess that she intrigued him. He'd meant it when he said she was out of her depth, but she was clearly going to put up a good fight. She was more intelligent than he'd given her credit for, naturally astute and far from the vacuous airhead he'd expected He could tell she wouldn't be a pushover, but with a little of the famous du Lac charm he was confident he'd be able to persuade her to see things from his point of view . . .

Then her boyfriend, or whatever he was, had turned up and ruined everything. Jonny Farrell, that was his name. Gabriel typed it into the search engine and waited for the results. The Wi-Fi was awful here. So slow. Perhaps Ariana could make that her first task, he thought wryly.

The sun streamed in through the window, falling on the framed photograph of his father that had pride of place on his desk. Alain would approve of what he was doing, he felt sure. The hotel had meant everything to his father, and he wouldn't want Gabriel to give it up without a fight.

The investigator he'd tasked with looking into Ariana had come up with something unexpected that had given Gabriel pause for thought. It was a photograph from a magazine – his father and Aristotle Theodosis – Ariana's grandfather – leaving the famous Casino de Monte-Carlo together. At first, Gabriel had been shocked to discover that the two men had met; in hindsight, perhaps it wasn't quite so unexpected. They were contemporaries, although Aristotle was a decade older than his father, and both were movers and shakers on the international circuit. But was their meeting merely a one-off, or did the two men know one another better than anyone realized?

The web page Gabriel had been waiting for loaded and the results about Jonny Farrell flashed up on the screen. There were mentions of bit parts in films, the occasional modelling job, minor scandals on gossip sites. So far, so Hollywood brat.

Gabriel remembered how upset Ariana had been when he'd last seen her, and wondered what the reason was. Partly because, despite himself, he discovered he was genuinely concerned about her and partly . . . While he didn't consider himself to be ruthless, he did like to keep himself well informed. If there was information out there which might encourage her to sell the hotel to him, something that could be used as gentle persuasion, then he'd make it his business to find out. And if he got one over on that idiot, Jonny Farrell, at the same time, then that was simply a bonus.

Gabriel clicked through the pages of stories, many relating to Jonny's drink and drug issues. He'd been to rehab a couple of times, and he'd spent twenty-four hours in prison for a DUI before being released to do community service. Some entrepreneur – possibly Jonny himself – had printed his mugshot on a range of merchandise, from T-shirts to lighters. Jonny was clearly a troubled guy. He saw an article about Jonny and his father: *Like Father Like Son – troubled star and his hellraiser dad*. He wondered what Ariana was doing with him, and what the extent of their relationship was.

Gabriel hesitated for a moment, then typed: *Jonny Farrell, Ariana Theodosis*.

A stream of paparazzi pictures popped up, showing the two of them out and about in LA. Ariana looked stunning in every photo, whether leaving a nightclub in a Swarovski-studded minidress, or wearing a tiny vest and running shorts to pick up a Starbucks.

A third name seemed to keep cropping up in the search: Liberty Granger. It looked like she'd also dated Jonny and, if the dates were correct, there'd been a degree of crossover between the two women. Like Ariana, Liberty was brunette but, despite being American, her looks were classic English rose; a contrast with Ariana's olive skin and fiery Mediterranean temperament.

Gabriel remembered reading about Liberty's death a few months ago. It had been shocking, because she'd been so young, and the circumstances were mysterious. She'd been found in the swimming pool of a mansion in the Hollywood hills, where she'd been attending a party. Jonny had been there too – as had Ariana, it seemed from the reports, although her name featured far less frequently.

Interesting, thought Gabriel.

Not long afterwards, Ariana had returned to Europe. He knew that her grandmother had died, which was why she'd inherited the hotel – though neither of them understood how Elana had come to own it. And he knew, of course, that her father was Demetrios Theodosis – wealthy, powerful, successful. He imagined that Ariana would struggle to live up to his name and carve out her own niche. Perhaps that's why she wanted the hotel so badly, Gabriel mused.

He jumped to his feet, pacing the room as he mulled over the information, trying to make connections. Could it simply be a coincidence that Alain and Aristotle appeared to have known one another, and now Aristotle's granddaughter owned the hotel that had once been Alain's? Gabriel wondered if Ariana knew that the two men had met, and resolved to ask her. He wondered how much his mother knew. Madeleine had never mentioned the connection, not even when she discovered that Ariana had inherited the hotel. But was that because it was irrelevant, or because Madeleine was trying to hide something?

There were too many missing pieces, too many uncertainties, Gabriel thought, sitting back down and resuming his search on Ariana. It appeared that she'd got caught up in a bad crowd in LA. That could be useful. Jonny seemed to be at the centre of it – there was certainly enough evidence of his destructive behaviour out there. And now he was back on the scene, back in Ariana's life. Gabriel hated to admit it, but his ego was wounded, his sense of competition ignited. What did this guy have that he didn't?

Gabriel remembered a contact, Felipe, who used to run his property in Palma – the Hotel de la Catedral – and was now the general manager of the Sunset Tower in West Hollywood. Gabriel checked his Rolex – just gone 3 p.m., which meant shortly after 6 a.m. in the States. Felipe was an early riser; he'd be up by now. Gabriel dialled his number.

'Felipe! It's Gabriel du Lac. How are you?'

'Gabriel! Good to hear from you. I'm in the gym, getting in 10k before work.' Felipe sounded short of breath.

'You've changed – you've gone Hollywood,' Gabriel joked.

'I'm embracing the lifestyle,' Felipe laughed. 'No more *frito mallorquín* or *churros* for me. Anyway, how can I help?'

'I'll cut to the chase. I wondered if you'd heard of a guy called Jonny Farrell.'

Gabriel could hear the scowl in Felipe's voice. 'Sure, I've heard of him. I've had the displeasure of dealing with him too – I've had to throw him out of here on more than one occasion. Thinks he's God's gift and he can do what he likes.'

'Sounds like him,' Gabriel muttered.

'Yeah, he's bad news. He has quite a reputation. Why, what are you asking about him for?'

Gabriel smiled, thrilled to have made a breakthrough. 'Felipe, my old friend. Tell me everything you know . . .'

Chapter 13

Alone in her room, Elizabeth was trying to relax. Tonight was the official festival screening of *All Our Yesterdays*, which meant pressure, judgement, being on stage in front of the world and having to look polished and immaculate while she was scrutinized for any perceived flaws – in her appearance or her marriage. Before the premiere, the cast had endured a back-to-back afternoon of press, speaking to interviewers from all over the world, each with their allocated ten-minute slot.

It was why they were here, part of the deal, and she'd known it would be exhausting, which was why she'd insisted on having a couple of hours to herself this morning. Her plan was to take a leisurely bath, eat something light but nutritious, maybe run through a few yoga poses to leave her energized and positive. Instead, Elizabeth had made the mistake of asking reception to send up a selection of newspapers and magazines to peruse while she got ready, but one look at the front covers and she was already regretting it.

Elizabeth Enceinte? screamed the headlines. *Is Elizabeth Pregnant?*

Voici magazine had run a series of photos from the last few days in Cannes: Elizabeth looking a little round-tummied following dinner at the Carlton Restaurant. Another, wearing a beautiful billowing dress that she'd chosen for its exquisite colour and masterful draping, was apparently 'concealing a precious secret'. Then there were staged shots of her and Robert on the Plage du Midi, his hand around her waist, speculating that he was 'tenderly caressing the much-longed-for baby bump'.

A whole host of emotions surged through Elizabeth – humiliation, anger, sadness. Why didn't people understand how hurtful these kinds of spurious stories were? Not about her size, or her bloated stomach – she didn't give a damn about those. No, the most upsetting part was that she would have given anything to actually *be* pregnant. To have a new life growing inside her and know that she would be blessed with a little boy or girl. But she wasn't.

Elizabeth had seen the top gynaecologists in Los Angeles, who'd all made the right noises and told her what she wanted to hear – she was paying them enough after all. They talked about follicle count and ovarian reserves, scanned for polyps and cysts, did intrusive, invasive examinations and discussed her reproductive system as though it were entirely separate from the rest of her.

There was no obvious problem, nothing to stop her from conceiving naturally, in their professional opinion. She knew there were no issues with Robert; he already had a child, and anyway, couldn't men go on forever? Look at Mick Jagger, Michael Douglas, Eric Clapton.

And therein lay the rub, as Hamlet almost said, Elizabeth thought. Did she even *want* to have a child with Robert? He certainly wouldn't win any Father of the Year awards for parenting his son from his first marriage. Robert had barely seen the boy when he was growing up, sending the occasional belated birthday card then making up for his failings by splurging on something expensive and inappropriate – like the year he'd bought him a pony when the kid had never expressed any interest in horse riding. About the only useful thing Robert had done was to pay for rehab when his son inevitably went down the cliched Hollywood offspring route and spiralled out of control with a drink and drugs addiction. She'd tried to intervene over the years, but there was too much water under the bridge between father and son, it seemed, and she now avoided reading the gossip columns, which never seemed to have anything good to say about Robert's offspring.

Robert himself was unreliable – drinking heavily, staying out all night, rumours of infidelity. Elizabeth had lost count of the nights she'd fallen asleep on the sofa, waiting up for him, only to see pictures in the press the following day of him stumbling out of a strip club in the early hours. Of course, the tabloids adored his wild image – an old-school hellraiser in the mould of Richard Burton or Peter O'Toole – but it was hardly the right environment in which to raise a child. Elizabeth had long ago lost hope that he might grow up and become a mature adult. If it hadn't happened by the age of fifty-four, it probably never would.

The worst part was that Elizabeth had had to endure endless column inches over the years about how she was putting her career before a family, the underlying implication being that she wasn't fulfilled as a woman because she didn't have a troop of children like Angelina Jolie. She'd considered adopting, like her idol Elizabeth Taylor; few people realized that, as well as giving birth to three children, Liz had adopted a German orphan called Maria. Surrogacy was another possibility; she'd heard all kinds of outrageous rumours – celebrities who wore prosthetic bumps but paid another woman to secretly carry their child. The star was then lauded for popping back to their pre-pregnancy size mere days after the birth, when in actual fact they'd never really been pregnant at all.

It was all getting too much, Liz thought, throwing the magazines onto the table and sinking down onto the bed. She was constantly fighting for her career, fighting the ageing process, fighting for her marriage, fighting to have a baby. She was sick of fighting; she simply wanted to give in. What did they do in the old days? Retire to the country to breed horses, or drop out of the spotlight and let age come to meet them naturally like those iconic beauties of yesteryear, Brigitte Bardot, and Jean Shrimpton?

Perhaps, if *All Our Yesterdays* won the Palme d'Or or an Oscar, she'd jack it all in. Go out on top, move on from Robert and start again. She could move back to London, or perhaps the English countryside, and live a simpler life: go to the theatre, take long walks in nature, cook a roast dinner on Sundays and invite all her friends over – her *real* friends, not the fake LA ones. And yet she'd always envisaged children as part of that idyllic life. Could she ever give up her acting? She knew deep down she loved it, it was part of who she was and she didn't know how to be anything else. Maybe she was part of the problem too?

Could she ever give up on Robert?

A knock on the door startled Elizabeth. Was it time for hair and make-up already? She jumped up, snapping out of her melancholy mood, not wanting anyone to see her like this.

'Hi Liz.'

She pulled open the door to see Robert standing there.

'Robbie . . . I wasn't expecting you.' He looked more handsome than ever, evidently sober for once, and she felt her heart flip.

'Just thought I'd pop by,' he said casually, but his hopping from one foot to another told a different story.

'Of course. Come in.'

'Actually, I'm here because I took your advice,' Robert said, as he strolled into the room. 'I apologized to Estée – the woman who looked after me the other night. Gave her a bunch of flowers and a couple of tickets for the premiere.'

Elizabeth raised her eyebrows. She was surprised that he'd listened to her. She wondered if he'd taken the initiative himself, or whether Balls was behind it. 'That was sweet of you. I was about to start getting ready, so—'

'I hear congratulations are in order.'

Elizabeth frowned in confusion, then realized he was looking at the magazines she'd left strewn across the table. Feeling foolish, she gathered them up and dropped them in the bin.

'Is it mine?' Robert teased, misjudging the mood.

'Isn't it ridiculous? Am I not allowed to have a fat day?' Elizabeth tried to joke, turning away from him. She didn't want Robert to see her upset. But he knew her too well.

'Hey, love, what is it? Come here.'

He took her in his arms and she sank into him,

closing her eyes, savouring the feel of his strong body pressed against her, the deliciously masculine scent of him. Everything felt right when they were together like this, all her problems shared and halved, as though the two of them could handle anything together. She could have stayed there forever, but reluctantly pulled away, knowing she had to stand by the decision she'd made.

'You know what the problem is,' she said quietly.

Robert rubbed his hands over his stubble, reflecting on her words. 'Is there any chance you might be? There was that one night . . .'

Elizabeth reddened. After she'd told him she wanted a divorce, he'd moved out of the home they shared in Beverly Hills to their beach house in Malibu. A couple of weeks later, he'd come over to collect some of his belongings ready for Cannes and one thing had led to another . . .

That had been the last time, Liz had insisted to herself. It was their final goodbye.

'I took a test,' she admitted. 'Just in case. Three in fact. All negative.'

'Right.'

The two of them stood in silence, the atmosphere shifting completely from the closeness they'd shared only moments ago. It was Robert who spoke first.

'Liz, I've said it a million times before, but I'll say it again. I love you, I'm crazy about you, I want to be with you. Whatever you want, I'll give it to you. I can be the man you want me to be, just give me a chance to prove it. I've stopped drinking—'

Elizabeth shot him a look.

'Stop-*ping* drinking. I'm trying, OK? I can stay home every night if that's what you want. We can spend our time doing jigsaws and rescuing kittens if that'll make you happy?'

She didn't laugh. 'It's too late, Robbie. And yes you have said you love me a million times, but it's actions that count and you've had chance after chance to change. I've given you so many opportunities and every time you've let me down. I can't live like this anymore, it's not healthy. It'll be better for us to be apart.'

'No, it won't! Elizabeth and Robert, Robbie and Liz. That's how it's always been. Everyone knows we work better together. We bring out the best in each other.'

'Not anymore.' Elizabeth shook her head sadly. 'We've stopped working. Look, I'll see you for the press conference later, but Kris and Shannon will be here any minute and I've—'

'I don't care about the fucking press conference!' Robert sounded desperate. 'I only care about you. Liz, I—'

'Please, Robbie . . . don't make this harder than it is already.' She kissed him softly on the cheek, and it felt horribly like a goodbye as her heart broke into a thousand tiny pieces. 'Just go.'

10 December 1987

My dearest friend Madeleine, I can't even begin to think about what you must be going through now that Alain has gone. It seemed like only yesterday when we were all together, laughing and enjoying ourselves, drinking cognac on the terrace of your hotel as the sun set over the bay. Our husbands setting the world to rights, while you and I gossiped about all the guests at dinner. I have tried to

see you my darling, but the doctors said you were not well
enough yet. I pray for you and the children . . . One day
I hope we will laugh again, until then, I shall keep writing
. . . I will look after your precious gift . . . I will always
be your dear friend . . .

Madame du Lac was standing at the window, looking out
through a crack in the curtains. Her room was dark, and
from her vantage point at the top of the building she had
a sweeping view out over the city. During the daytime,
she would watch the waves cresting on the iridescent
sea, sleek white boats slicing through the sparkling water,
vapour trails criss-crossing the sky as planes droned overhead, the cars and the people making their way up and
down the Croisette.

Now it was night-time and the sky was dark, the sea
invisible. The curve of the bay was illuminated, spotlights
beneath the exotic palm trees, light spilling out from the
busy restaurants and bars. Madame du Lac could hear
the music from the boats in the marina below, the babble
of voices drifting up from the yacht parties, the roar of
traffic on the boulevard. Yet she was numb to it all.

Oh, she'd been like that once – carefree, sociable, happy.
But now she knew how life could change in an instant.
How your world could be turned upside down in
moments, all your hopes and dreams and plans destroyed.
She envied the naivety of the partygoers; those fools had
no idea what could possibly happen to them.

There was a knock at the door and Madeleine froze,
then folded up the faded and yellowed letter and put it
into the pocket of her cardigan.

'*Maman*?' It was Constance.

Madeleine waited silently, unmoving. She could hear the sound of her own breathing and tried to control it, inhaling slowly, exhaling noiselessly. The seconds ticked by and she counted them inside her head. She'd almost reached sixty when she heard Constance retreat, probably assuming that her mother had already gone to bed.

Good.

Tonight, Madeleine wanted to be alone. She needed time to think, to formulate a plan.

Panic had consumed her since she'd first heard the news, anxiety clutching at her stomach and making it impossible to sleep, leaving her exhausted and restless. For the past twenty years, Madame du Lac had been content to simply exist – to keep to her room and not trouble the world; in return the world didn't trouble her. But now everything was going to change, she could sense it – could almost smell it, the sensation was so visceral.

Her lawyers had contacted her to say that Elana Theodosis had passed away. With one phone call, her life had gone into freefall. The hotel had been left to Elana's granddaughter, the lawyers explained, although they couldn't say yet what that would mean. For now, the instructions they'd received from the beneficiary were that everything was to remain the same, and so Madeleine had done just that.

She closed the curtains, blocking out the bright lights and the revelry, and found her way to her chair in total darkness. She sat down, her knuckles gripping the arms, her eyes adjusting to the blackness.

The Hotel du Soleil had been part of her life for almost forty years now. She'd seen its rise and fall, seen the great and good pass through its doors, witnessed their most intimate moments, their triumphs, their shame. She had kept their secrets. But Madame du Lac had secrets of her own.

It's so unfair, she thought furiously. Why couldn't Alain have kept his word? He'd promised her that everything would be all right, that it was all taken care of, and she'd never have to leave the hotel. That's why she'd agreed, when he'd suggested that they . . . that she . . . What was it that Alain said? Why was the letter in her pocket so important? Madeleine squinted into the shadows, trying to remember. If only everything wasn't so hazy and unclear, the past opaque and her memory composed of elusive fragments that she could never quite piece together.

The only thing she recalled with clarity was that dreadful night, the terrible scream and then Alain's body, cold and unmoving . . .

Feeling old and alone in the darkness, a tear rolled silently down Madeleine's cheek.

Chapter 14

'I'd forgotten how exciting these things are,' breathed Ariana, as they stepped out of the limo onto the red carpet, a crush of excitable fans pressed up against the crash barriers.

Gabriel smiled, delighted by her enthusiasm. They were at the premiere of *All Our Yesterdays* and the buzz was incredible, with flashbulbs popping like fireworks and reporters calling out for interviews. Colin Firth had just arrived, looking chiselled and handsome in a Tom Ford suit, and was generously signing autographs for the crowd, posing for pictures with giddy admirers.

'How did you get tickets for tonight?' Ariana asked Gabriel. She looked stunning in a backless Versace gown, which showed acres of tanned skin, a jewel-encrusted waistband drawing attention to her toned figure. The dress was demure yet provocative all at the same time.

'The hotel may be a little, how do you put it, *chic minable*?' Gabriel said with a Gallic shrug. 'But the Hotel du Soleil and the du Lac name still mean something in Cannes.'

'I don't doubt that for a moment.'

Gabriel's eyes twinkled at her appealingly. 'When I was offered tickets, I thought of you. Shall we?'

He placed his hand on the bare skin of her back to guide her to the entrance, an intimate gesture that made Ariana's skin tingle. Gabriel had an innate confidence, an air of self-assurance that was extremely attractive – and he looked hot as hell in a tuxedo. Ariana didn't know if tonight was a date, or a peace offering intended to show there were no hard feelings after their aborted dinner and awkward conversation at the hotel. Either way, she intended to enjoy herself.

Being in the limelight and performing for the cameras was Ariana's natural arena. She revelled in being the centre of attention, and adored the whole process of dressing up and getting glam for occasions like this. She felt completely at home as she strutted along the red carpet on Gabriel's arm, soaking up the atmosphere.

Just before the entrance was the 'step and repeat', a standard fixture at high-profile events, where the stars posed in front of a backdrop covered in the logos of the sponsors. Right now, Catherine Deneuve was having her photograph taken. Ariana was used to rubbing shoulders with the rich and the famous, but even she had to stifle a gasp.

'I love her – she's a legend. Such an amazing actress,' Ariana marvelled. She had come to Cannes before with her parents, but tonight was different; being on Gabriel's arm made her feel somehow more polished and sophisticated than when she was in LA. 'She's so chic and elegant. And look at her skin. I read that her secret is drinking lemon juice every morning . . .'

Madame Deneuve walked into the building ahead of them and Ariana turned to Gabriel. 'Our turn.'

Gabriel laughed. 'I don't think anyone's interested in what I'm wearing.'

Ariana deliberately looked him up and down, her gaze running over his lean, muscular body. 'You'd be surprised,' she said flirtatiously, her amber eyes shining.

'What can I say? I don't like being upstaged,' he grinned.

'Now you're teasing me.'

'I'm being serious. You look incredible tonight.'

Ariana knew she looked good, but wasn't sure if Gabriel was just spinning her a line. She'd been reading up on him – some of the more gossipy articles that didn't make the business pages – and there were countless photos of him attending parties and charity galas and gallery openings. He was always accompanied by stunning women, and rarely the same one twice. Well, two could play at that game. 'You know, you're probably right. Best leave it to the professionals,' she winked, stepping forwards into an explosion of camera flashes.

Ariana's name was better known in Europe than the States. The feisty, glamorous heiress had provided the European press with some excellent headlines during her party years and the photographers called her name now, clamouring for pictures.

Ariana turned around to show off her backless dress, peering over one shoulder and blowing a kiss to the camera, posing up a storm. She'd undoubtedly grown up in recent weeks, the sensible and mature side of herself coming to the fore, but crazy and wild Ariana was still in there somewhere and tonight she was coming out to play.

She was laughing as she stepped away from the melee, her eyes shining, her face radiant. She turned to Gabriel and saw the beaming smile on his face as he watched her, but there was something else too – a wolfish gleam in his eye, which suggested that beneath the staid suit and professional veneer there was a whole other side to him.

He offered his hand to lead her inside and Ariana took it, her palm slotting neatly into his, a bolt of excitement shooting through her. It was just the adrenaline, she insisted to herself, pushing away the butterflies as she followed Gabriel into the Palais des Festivals.

Outside, Estée and Stefan were approaching the security cordon that led to the red carpet, although theirs was a far more low-key arrival than Ariana and Gabriel's had been. The venue was less than a kilometre from the Hotel du Soleil so they'd decided to walk, strolling along the Croisette together in the early evening sunshine. Their conversation was a little awkward at first – they weren't used to spending time together one-on-one, outside of the hotel – but they soon relaxed, enjoying one another's company.

Stefan had clearly made an effort now that he was out of his chef's whites, wearing a smart blue suit with a pale blue shirt that fitted snugly across his muscular chest and broad shoulders. Estée was hoping to catch a casting director's attention in a sweeping red dress that looked sensational with her shimmering skin and slender dancer's frame.

'Everything OK?' Stefan asked, noticing Estée glancing around wide-eyed.

She nodded, grinning. 'Just taking it all in.'

Estée had been thrown into turmoil after Robert had given her two tickets. He'd clearly expected that she would have someone to bring, but Estée was embarrassed to admit she had no one. Ordinarily, she could have asked one of the girls from La Châtelaine, but tonight that was impossible as she was supposed to be off sick. She'd left a voicemail earlier for Victor claiming to have a bout of food poisoning, and was feeling quite proud of her acting skills.

When Estée had bumped into Stefan that afternoon in reception, she'd blurted it out, asking if he'd like to accompany her to the premiere. The two of them had chatted a few times – he was often finishing his shift in the kitchen in the early hours, just as she was returning from work, and they'd stand outside on the front steps while he smoked a cigarette before driving home. It seemed appropriate to ask him, it was his one night off, and as he'd also helped out that night with Robert.

'It's quite something, isn't it,' Stefan marvelled, letting out a low whistle as he stared round at the lights and the cameras, hearing the shouts of the photographers and the cheers from the crowd. He offered Estée his arm and she took it gratefully, brimming with excitement as they entered the Palais. She felt like Cinderella going to the ball, promising herself that tonight she would enjoy every single minute.

'So tell me about your acting career and Hollywood?' Gabriel asked innocently. 'Before you became a seasoned hotelier, I mean.'

Ariana narrowed her eyes. 'It's never wise to underestimate one's competitors, Monsieur du Lac.'

'I wouldn't dare,' he winked. 'Did you always want to act?'

'I guess you could say I've always had a flair for the dramatic,' Ariana grinned. 'I enjoyed performing – I did a few plays and short films at university. It was fun. I think I wanted to make my mark somehow. My family are high achievers – I'm a Theodosis and must live up to that. We're used to success, but we all have to work for it.'

'I understand. Sometimes we're hardest on ourselves,' Gabriel said thoughtfully. 'Are you planning on going back to Los Angeles?'

Ariana wondered why he was asking – because he wanted to know about her plans for the hotel? Or for some other reason? 'I don't know,' she replied. 'I haven't decided anything yet.'

Gabriel nodded, unfazed. 'And is everything OK now? You seemed upset when I saw you the other day.'

Ariana hesitated, remembering the unsettling text she'd received. She'd been trying to put it out of her mind – probably it was just some crank playing a practical joke, or perhaps the message had been sent to the wrong number – but she hadn't quite been able to dismiss it. 'Everything's fine,' she insisted brightly.

'Look,' Gabriel said, 'I know we don't know each other well, but if you are in some kind of trouble, you can trust me.'

Ariana regarded him; his handsome face was open and seemed honest. Maybe it would be good to tell someone about her fears, someone who wasn't an air-head like Montana. Or worse, Jonny, who only seemed to intensify her anxiety.

She hesitated. 'It's just . . .'

Robert and Elizabeth Chappell were making their way up the walkway and the crowds were going wild, screaming and calling their names.

Ariana shook her head, the moment gone. 'Never mind, I can handle it. Look, there's Elizabeth and Robert.'

Elizabeth was wearing a gold foil sheath dress with a thigh-high slit, and a matching cape that trailed along behind her like a wedding veil. She looked statuesque, the outfit bold, avant-garde, and certain to make the front page of every paper the following morning. Beside her, Robert was playing up to his image, wearing a black velvet tuxedo with the bow tie undone and slung around his neck, his shirt open and his Ray-Bans on. He looked rakish and cool and like he could show you one hell of a good time.

'They're fabulous together, aren't they?' Ariana sighed wistfully. 'Did you know that Elizabeth's staying at the hotel?'

Gabriel nodded. 'But her husband isn't. Strange, *non*?'

'One thing you learn in Hollywood,' Ariana began, as Robert and Elizabeth approached the building and everyone was ushered to their places, 'is that nothing is ever what it seems.'

Estée and Stefan were sitting on plush red velvet seats on the balcony of the Grand Théâtre Lumière, *All Our Yesterdays* playing out on the enormous cinema screen in front of them. It felt oddly like a date, and Estée wondered if Stefan thought so too. She hoped he didn't get the wrong idea. He was a nice guy, but she had no time for anything like that right now.

The film was wonderful, utterly absorbing and exquisitely shot, showcasing the English countryside and set in a gorgeous Oxfordshire manor house. Elizabeth was perfectly cast as the aloof, composed aristocrat whose passion simmered below the surface, waiting for an opportunity to be unleashed. Robert was more than a match for her as the troubled soldier trying to remain loyal to his wife while overcome by his feelings for Lady Courtenay.

Estée was having a ball, her head twisting this way and that as she tried to take in every glamorous detail. She'd been within touching distance of Colin Firth – although she'd restrained herself and hadn't actually tried to touch him. She recognized the actress Montana Morgan looking excited on the red carpet in a revealing sequinned dress as she chatted to the press. She was starting to realize that there was a whole world out there and it was passing her by while she worked all the hours God sent.

You could be spending time with your daughter, a nagging voice popped into her brain. Emilie was almost ten. How much longer could Estée be absent from her life, chasing this dream that might never come true? The odds of success lessened with every passing year; no one wanted an ageing dancer. Perhaps it was time to get real, to start thinking about what was truly important.

Estée had thought by leaving Emilie with her mother in Paris, she was taking the best course of action to secure all of their futures, but suddenly she wasn't so sure anymore.

On the screen, Lady Courtenay was falling in love with Tom Brown, even though she knew that she shouldn't, and despite the two of them being from completely different worlds. It was lovely – romantic and idyllic – but it was a fantasy, Hollywood's version of what real life could be. For Estée, it offered a diverting, temporary escape, but tomorrow it would be back to reality. And she had some big decisions to make.

Ariana and Gabriel were sitting side by side in the darkness of the auditorium, so close that Ariana could feel the heat from Gabriel's body. She stole a glance at his profile; he was undoubtedly handsome, with that well-defined jawline, his blond hair curling over his collar, and those sea-blue eyes focused on the screen.

The film was every bit as poignant as the press had said it would be. The two leads were phenomenal, the chemistry between them so powerful it almost oozed off the screen and into the theatre. Right now, Tom and Lady Courtenay were having a heartfelt conversation in the grounds of the manor house, but were interrupted by a young, brunette nurse. Her heart-shaped face slowly came into view, radiant and compelling, with alabaster skin, rosebud lips, and unforgettable green eyes that seemed to look straight out of the screen and find Ariana—

She gasped, her heart rate tripling, her stomach going into freefall. Gabriel turned to her, a question reflected in his eyes, but she shook her head in answer, unable to speak.

How could she have been so stupid? When Gabriel had called her to say he had tickets to the premiere of *All Our Yesterdays* and asked if she'd like to accompany him, Ariana said yes without thinking, her head filled with thoughts of what she would wear and the best place to get a last-minute mani-pedi. How could she have forgotten . . .?

On the screen in front of her, twenty feet high and sixty feet wide, was the image of Liberty Granger, so close that Ariana could see every detail of her face – beautiful, luminous, vital. Ariana closed her eyes, but she could still hear that voice; she longed to clamp her hands over her ears and make it all go away. Liberty's features were so familiar, her voice the same as Ariana recalled from that fateful night.

And then she remembered: those deep green eyes, staring at her in accusation, in anger – and then fear. Snatches of memory, as though in a dream. There was shouting, although Ariana couldn't make out the words, and then she was back there, standing by the eerily lit swimming pool, Liberty and her screaming at one another like banshees. Ariana tried to look more closely, to see the next piece of the puzzle, but it was like trying to catch water, and the flashback faded away.

Ariana opened her eyes and saw that she was still in the cinema, her heart racing, her mouth dry. The girl on the screen was dead, and Ariana was terrified it might be because of her. She felt the panic rising in her chest, blackness threatening to overwhelm her. She needed to get out.

'I'm sorry,' she blurted out to Gabriel, standing up and pushing past rows of disgruntled VIPs. There were annoyed mutterings, an outraged cry as she stood on the hem of someone's designer gown, but Ariana didn't care, she just wanted to escape.

She headed for the lobby but stopped abruptly as another thought occurred to her – the photographers! Ariana had posed outside on the red carpet like she didn't have a care in the world. Suppose someone put two and two together – that the girl who'd attended the party where Liberty Granger died was now swanning around the South of France trying to steal the limelight at the premiere of Liberty's film. It was too horrible to think about.

Ariana turned abruptly, searching for another exit. She ran towards the back of the building, her gown billowing out behind her, her skyscraper heels sinking into the carpet. She heard Gabriel calling her name but she didn't care, focused on the freedom that lay beyond the doors.

Then finally Ariana was outside, gulping in the fresh air, standing in the golden light as the sunset streaked the sky and a warm breeze drifted in from the sea, the palm trees rustling and the birds calling.

Ariana stood alone, trying to calm her racing heart and slow her breathing as Gabriel came running towards her. She felt her bag vibrate and instinctively pulled out her phone, her amber eyes skimming over the words before she had time to realize what was happening:

HOW DARE YOU AFTER WHAT YOU DID

Gabriel caught up with her. 'Ariana, what's happened?'

Ariana couldn't speak, unable to utter a single syllable. She stared at him, searching his face, suddenly suspicious. Why had he asked her to come with him? All those questions about her movie career, and her time in Hollywood. Did he know more than she realized?

'Why did you invite me here?' she demanded.

Gabriel's forehead creased in confusion, bewildered by what was happening.

'I thought you might enjoy it. I thought this was your kind of scene. And it was an apology for leaving our dinner so abruptly.'

'Oh really?'

'Yes, really.'

Ariana stared at Gabriel. She felt as though she was going mad. 'Liberty – the girl on screen playing the nurse. She died, earlier this year.' Ariana watched his face carefully, scrutinizing his reaction. 'I was at the party where it happened. And now . . .' She gestured around at the venue, as though that would explain what she was thinking.

'So why did you come?' Gabriel replied, his face neutral. 'Why did you accept my invitation?'

'Because I . . . I didn't realize. I mean—' Ariana covered her face with her hands, wishing everything around her would simply disappear and she could start over. She felt guilty, confused, overwhelmed. It had seemed like she was turning a corner with Gabriel, but now this had happened. She couldn't help but wonder if it was all part of some elaborate ploy to get the hotel, or if she was going crazy with paranoia. 'I don't know,' she repeated, more quietly this time. 'I've been getting these messages and—'

'Messages? What messages?'

'Forget I said anything.' Ariana regretted her words as soon as they were out of her mouth. She had no idea who she could trust right now.

'Is it Jonny?'

Ariana frowned. 'Jonny? What would Jonny have to do with this?'

'I don't know . . .' Gabriel said carefully, and Ariana sensed he knew more than he was letting on. 'Look, like I said before, if you're in some kind of trouble, I'll try and help.'

'Why?' she shot back. She realized how she must look

right now – poised and groomed and completely put together on the outside, while inside she was falling apart.

For once, Gabriel was almost lost for words. 'Ariana . . . I don't know if I understand the reasons myself, but you have my word, if I can help you, I will.' Almost unconsciously, he took a step towards her, compelled to take her in his arms. At that moment she seemed so fragile and vulnerable.

But Ariana moved back and held up her hand. 'Look, if you really want to help me, just get me back to the hotel,' she pleaded. She was exhausted. All she wanted to do was collapse into her bed and pull the covers over her head, to forget about everything.

'Of course,' Gabriel said smoothly. 'Whatever you wish.' He held out his hand. Ariana stared at him for a moment, then took it, letting him guide her towards the waiting car.

Chapter 15

Nice, May 2009

Sweat dripped from Gabriel's forehead, his muscles burning as the lactic acid began to build. He ignored his discomfort and pushed on, pounding the trails that wove uphill through the park where the old citadel had once stood, high above the spectacular Baie des Anges.

It felt good to be doing something physical, to focus on his pace and breathing and try to push all other thoughts from his mind. It was the reason he'd shunned the hotel gym in favour of running in the great outdoors, the morning air deliciously warm on his skin before the temperature soared later in the day.

He'd been called away from Cannes on urgent business; the general manager of the Hotel du Château, along the coast in Nice, had quit, effective immediately, for personal reasons, and the situation was chaotic. Gabriel had spent yesterday speaking to contacts and finding a solution, but he was eager to get back to Cannes. He told himself it was because the situation there was so uncertain, that it wasn't fair to leave his mother and sister when the Hotel du Soleil was in a state of flux. But he knew the real reason he was so desperate to return – Ariana.

'*Bonjour*,' Gabriel called to an elderly couple out for a morning stroll, who acknowledged him as they passed on the path. He increased his pace, lungs pumping, muscles straining, taking care not to trip on any loose rocks or hidden tree roots. The next section was particularly punishing: a steep uphill comprised of stone steps beneath the shade of sprawling pine trees, before emerging unexpectedly at a stunning waterfall. The spray soaked the rocks below, wonderfully refreshing in the Riviera heat, as a handful of tourists milled around taking photographs of the picturesque scene. Here, Gabriel stopped, taking in great gulps of air as he placed his hands on the back of his head to open up his chest, stretching out his limbs on the stone balustrade as he took in the view.

It was breathtaking. The full panorama of Nice was spread out before him, the glorious sweep of the Promenade des Anglais stretching west into the distance, flanked by the incomparable blue of the Mediterranean on one side and the distinctive pastel-coloured buildings with their orange roofs on the other, the mountains rising like waves behind. To the east, beyond the port with its glossy, white, millionaires' yachts, was Antibes, the famed rocky peninsula jutting out into the sparkling azure waters. Ariana would adore it here, Gabriel thought, before realizing that she'd pushed her way into his thoughts once again, just like she'd pushed her way into his life – an unstoppable, irresistible force of nature.

Even here, he couldn't stop thinking about how Ariana

had been so upset when she'd run out of the premiere. Gabriel wondered what the problem was, certain he could fix it if only she would confide in him. He'd become increasingly mesmerized by her; she was intelligent, vivacious, witty – and one of the most dazzlingly beautiful women he'd ever laid eyes on.

Gabriel started back down the path, wanting to keep moving before muscle fatigue kicked in. He could feel the pressure in his calves, his thighs, at the change of angle, his body taut and glistening with a light sheen of sweat, as he raced down the path, picking up speed.

Felipe had told him how he'd had to ban Jonny Farrell from his hotel for openly taking drugs, inhaling a line while sitting on the sunloungers or snorting coke off the bar top. He'd caught him dealing a few times too, pestering celebrities and VIPs to try and sell to them.

The worst story Felipe had shared was when Jonny had turned up in the early hours with a girl who was so wasted she could barely stand. She was feebly pushing Jonny away, slurring that he should get off her, but he'd laughed, before asking to book a room for the two of them. Felipe hadn't been working that shift, but the night manager had refused Jonny's request and told him they were full.

It was sickening. Jonny was clearly sleazy as hell, and Gabriel would have staked his empire that there were worse stories out there. He'd got in touch with a few more contacts – he'd stopped short of hiring a private investigator – and was waiting to see what they came back with. He told himself he was doing this for leverage over Ariana, that he was merely discovering a rival's weakness to give himself a business advantage. But Ariana was already under his skin, and he knew it. Gabriel had been involved with plenty of women, some of them were more than casual, though none of them had ever found a place in his heart. He knew it was something lacking in him, a way to shield himself from pain. He'd done what all successful entrepreneurs should do, had therapy and looked inside himself, and what he'd learned had been noted, compartmentalized, and packed away for another distant day. Was Ariana the one to change all that? He stopped dead in his tracks, and shook his head. What was he thinking? Ariana Theodosis was right, he shouldn't underestimate her. Somehow she had got him daydreaming like a schoolboy. He smiled wryly to himself; another point chalked up to the Greek heiress.

However, something wasn't right, and he was sure that in some way Jonny Farrell was entangled in it.

Gabriel was almost back at the Hotel du Château, the elegant, honey-coloured building with its suntrap pool and bougainvillea-covered walls emerging dramatically out of the cliff face below. He had a full day of work ahead of him, but the second that was wrapped up he was gunning the Ferrari and driving straight back to Cannes. He needed to see Ariana, there was no way she was going to bewitch his hotel out from under his own nose. It was time that they sorted it out once and for all, but it was purely business, he told himself firmly, and nothing to do with the way she had started to inhabit his dreams.

'Thank you.' Ariana smiled at the young man who'd assisted her with carrying two heavy boxes out onto the terrace. She had work to do, but it was far too nice a day to be inside, so she'd decided to set up out here at the little round table with a picture-perfect view of the bay, shaded by a striped parasol overhead. She knew that Gabriel was away on business, so there was no risk of him catching her with what she was about to do. 'And could you bring me a pot of coffee and a basket of pastries, *s'il vous plaît.*'

'*Bien sûr,*' the young man said shyly, and scurried away. He was a trainee concierge and only looked to be around eighteen, but he was polite and efficient, and Ariana was impressed.

She took the lid off one of the boxes and peered inside. In the archives, stored in the messy basement, Ariana had found all kinds of interesting documents. The du Lac family clearly didn't like to throw anything away; there were receipts dating right back to the 1970s, for all manner of inconsequential items such as an order of cheese for the kitchen, or hardware from the local *quincaillerie*. This box, however, looked as though it might prove particularly enlightening.

Ariana pulled out the folders, brushing the dust from the top. The papers were faded and yellow, some torn or water damaged, but most were readable – even if the looping French handwriting on some was hard to make out. Most of the documents were addressed to Alain du Lac. Ariana felt momentarily guilty, snooping through Gabriel's father's private papers, but technically everything in the hotel belonged to her. If the family didn't want her to see them, they should have removed them before she assumed ownership.

On the top were legal documents from various *avocats*. They seemed to increase in number and get more serious in tone as the dates on them neared the mid-1980s. Ariana's cat-like eyes skimmed over the words and she frowned. Her French comprehension wasn't strong enough for her to completely untangle the legalese, but she understood enough, and it was clear that legal action was being threatened; that Alain had considerable debts. There were words like 'repossession' and 'foreclosure'.

A waiter arrived with her order, and Ariana thanked him distractedly, before moving on to the next folder. This contained letters from what appeared to be Alain du Lac's accountant, expressing concern about the finances of the hotel, and the large amounts of borrowing that had taken place. There were bank statements, showing the accounts were in the red, that considerable sums of money were being withdrawn. But everything only went up to 1986 and then stopped. There were no more legal letters, and one statement from the same year showed that a large amount of money had been deposited, putting them back into the black.

Ariana could find nothing to show where the money had come from. There was no name associated with the transfer, but amongst the jumble of numbers that made up the account reference were the letters ATH.GR. Ariana frowned, making a note on her pad. She would ask her lawyers to try and trace where the money had come from, in the hope that would solve another piece of the puzzle.

In the next folder were a bunch of casino receipts. Ariana gasped as she saw the amounts and the dates, all with Alain du Lac's name. He'd clearly been a prodigious gambler, betting tens of thousands of francs over a few months, the amounts and the frequency increasing.

Well, that explained why the hotel had suffered such

a serious decline, she realized. Alain was clearly spending the profits faster than they could make money. But it still didn't explain the link with her grandmother. Had Alain sold the hotel to pay his debts? But then why were the du Lacs still in residence? And if Elana had been the buyer, why had she never told anyone?

Every time Ariana found an answer, it only threw up more questions.

She decided to take a break, pouring herself a cup of coffee and reaching for a mini *chausson aux pommes*. It was delicious – buttery and flaky, with a tangy apple filling. Gabriel wasn't wrong when he'd praised Stefan's skills. Perhaps Ariana should go and speak to the chef. She wondered how long he'd worked at the hotel – he might be able to give her an insight into its history . . .

'Hello, darling. How lovely to see you.'

Ariana heard a cut-glass English accent and looked up to see Elizabeth Chappell sashaying towards her. She looked wonderfully chic in a halterneck jumpsuit, and Ariana felt rather underdressed in a simple broderie anglaise sundress that highlighted her tanned, olive skin.

She smiled warmly at Elizabeth. 'You too. By the way, I was at the screening last night, and the movie was amazing. *You* were amazing.'

Elizabeth smiled graciously. 'Thank you, that's so sweet of you. The critics seem to have been kind, so we celebrated rather too hard last night. The party went on until the early hours, which is why I'm feeling a little delicate this morning.' She pointed at her sunglasses.

'You look incredible, as always.' Ariana didn't want to mention that she'd only seen half the film. She was still kicking herself for going in the first place. How on earth could she have forgotten that Liberty had a supporting role in *All Our Yesterdays*? She'd got caught up in the excitement of the day, and being in Europe had left her feeling so far removed from everything that had happened back in Los Angeles that she hadn't made the connection.

'Oh, you are a sweetheart,' Elizabeth smiled. 'But what are you doing?' She gestured at the boxes and the piles of paper surrounding Ariana. 'It looks terribly complicated.'

'Research, I guess you'd call it. No rest for the wicked.'

'Gosh, what on earth for? An acting role?'

'Oh no,' Ariana laughed at the assumption. 'I never put this much work into my acting – which probably explains a lot. I'm learning about the history of the hotel – these are some old documents I found.'

'I see,' Elizabeth frowned, though she clearly didn't.

Ariana decided to be honest. 'I know it seems hard to believe, but in fact this hotel belongs to me. I inherited it.'

'Good heavens, I didn't realize. How marvellous!'

'I'm still getting used to the idea myself. My grand-mother died earlier this year—'

'Oh, I'm terribly sorry.'

'Thank you. She left this place to me. I'm aware that a lot needs doing, but I'm looking forward to the challenge.'

'Well, it's a fantastic inheritance, I feel quite jealous.' Elizabeth seemed genuinely thrilled. 'Don't change it too much, will you? It would completely lose its charm if it became some huge, soulless beast where all the rooms are painted magnolia and everything's terribly inoffensive. Its dilapidation is part of its appeal. It needs smartening up, that's all. Oh, what a fun project!'

Ariana realized Elizabeth was still standing, beginning to turn pink in the hot sunshine. 'Would you like to join me?' she offered, gesturing to the chair across from her.

Elizabeth quickly checked the time on her Cartier watch. 'I'd love to. Though I have a press call at two, and it's going to take forever to make me look human, so I can't stay long.'

'Would you like a coffee?' Ariana asked, looking around to summon a waiter as Elizabeth sat down opposite her, placing her 1950s style sunglasses on the red-and-white checked tablecloth. 'Or something for breakfast?'

'I'll have the scrambled egg with black truffle shavings, and a freshly squeezed grapefruit juice. That's exactly what I need after last night,' she grinned at Ariana, as the waiter made a note and hurried away.

'Help yourself to a pastry while you're waiting.'

Elizabeth hesitated, then took a miniature *pain au chocolat*. 'They look yummy. To hell with the waistline,' she joked.

There was something Ariana was curious about. 'Elizabeth, if you don't mind me asking, why did you choose to stay here? Why not the Martinez, or the Hotel du Cap?'

Elizabeth relaxed into her chair and smiled. The warm air enveloped the two women, bringing with it the famous *garrigue*, the distinctive, intoxicating scent of the region made up of crisp pine and sweet flowers and aromatic herbs. 'I used to come here as a child,' Elizabeth explained. 'Apparently it was a riot in the seventies, and my parents adored it, so in the eighties they brought me and my brother here too. We came most summers when I was growing up. I have very fond memories of this place, but it's years since I was last here.'

'What can you remember?' Ariana asked casually, feeling a tingle of excitement. Elizabeth could be the perfect person to shed some light on the hotel's mysteries.

'It was owned by a family by the name of du Lac back then. They had two children – a girl who was around my age, and a boy a little younger, the same as my brother. It was always lots of fun playing with them, but I don't recall their names.'

Ariana realized she must mean Gabriel and Constance. It seemed strange to think that she was now the owner of their childhood home. It almost felt as though Gabriel had more right to it than Ariana, even though legally it belonged to her, and she felt her conscience prick. What if Gabriel arrived on Ithos and tried to take their family villa?

Elizabeth's words made Ariana remember there was a second box. It was full of old newspapers and press clippings; she'd commandeered Demetrios's office team to compile everything they could find and send them through. She pulled out a pile and laid them on the table. There was a black-and-white article from *Nice-Matin* featuring the hotel's opening in 1972; a feature from *Vanity Fair* dated 1981; Alain and Madeleine du Lac looking glamorous and untouchable on the cover of *Paris Match*.

'That's them!' Elizabeth exclaimed. 'Madeleine was very sweet to me as a child. I remember she always looked immaculate, in fantastically chic outfits from the boutiques on the rue d'Antibes, and she had the most incredible jewellery. Look at the size of that ring,' Elizabeth marvelled, poring over the photos. 'It's divine.'

Ariana looked at where Elizabeth was pointing and almost gasped in shock. The picture was grainy, taken from a distance at a party, but on Madeleine du Lac's finger was a gold ring with an enormous pink stone.

Ariana frowned, pulling the photo across the table towards her to see it in more detail, her heart beating fast.

'Is everything all right?' Elizabeth asked, surprised by Ariana's reaction.

'Yes, of course . . .' Ariana replied distantly. At that moment, the waiter arrived with Elizabeth's breakfast, and Ariana changed the subject quickly. 'What else do you remember? There must have been some good gossip,' she grinned conspiratorially, pushing down thoughts of the ring for the moment.

'Oh, the parties were outrageous. My parents would put my brother and me to bed then we would sneak back down – you could do that in those days. They thought we were asleep, but we'd stay up, watching out of the window at everyone dancing by the pool. I remember being so excited to see George Michael – I had such a crush on him back then,' Elizabeth giggled, spearing a forkful of fluffy yellow egg with decadent truffle. 'And Bono, and Simon and Yasmin Le Bon were friends of my parents, and we all had the most tremendous fun.

'I suppose the last time we stayed here must have been the mid-eighties. It was different then. It had started to decline, and didn't have quite the same carefree, luxurious feel. They were cutting corners – silly little things like cheap juice from a carton at breakfast, nothing fresh. Usually they closed for four weeks in the off-season to spruce the place up, but that year they hadn't – they needed the extra money, I suppose – but everything began to look rather shabby.

'Madeleine and Alain had always seemed like such a dazzling couple, but they were clearly having marriage problems. One evening they had the most explosive row, right on the terrace, in front of all the guests. I didn't really understand it all – they were speaking very fast in French – but he seemed to be accusing her of having an affair. She replied that he was the one "*avec toutes les jeunes femmes*". They were arguing about money too. It was all terribly embarrassing for us stiff-upper-lipped English types.'

Ariana smiled, she knew all about that after spending five years at an English boarding school.

'Of course, he died not long afterwards – I remember my parents talking about it at the breakfast table, it was a shocking story which made all the headlines, as you can see.' Elizabeth gestured to the old newspapers on the table in front of them that Ariana had requested. 'We never came here again. That's why I thought it might be nice to revisit it – though, it's far from the place I remember, but I'm sure you'll change all that.' Elizabeth smiled encouragingly at Ariana.

'Do you know how Alain died?'

Elizabeth wrinkled up her face in thought, and Ariana was gratified to see her face crinkle appealingly, she clearly hadn't had Botox. 'There was an accident. Here, at the hotel. I don't recall the details, though I'm sure it will all be there for you to find out.'

Ariana was about to ask another question, but Elizabeth noticed the time and pushed aside her plate, jumping to her feet.

'Darling, you've been the most delightful company, but I'm afraid duty calls. My team have the impossible job of making it look like I *didn't* stay up until three a.m. last night,' she laughed. 'Do give my love to Shauna, by the way, and best of luck with the hotel. I'm in room 420, if you ever want to chat.'

The two women kissed one another goodbye, and Elizabeth glided off across the gardens.

Ariana snatched up the photo of Madeleine du Lac, eager to see it once again. She held it close, scanning it thoroughly, but it was impossible to tell whether the picture showed the same ring that was in Ariana's room right now. Which reminded her, she really ought to put it in the hotel safe. She hadn't had it valued yet, but she felt sure it was worth a considerable sum.

Ariana sipped her coffee thoughtfully, staring at the photograph. Could it be the same piece of jewellery? If so, how had Elana come to own Madeleine's ring, and why? The coincidences kept piling up, along with the questions. Elizabeth had unexpectedly proved an invaluable source of information, but there was still so much that Ariana didn't know.

She began leafing through the rest of the clippings, hoping they might provide some answers, when she came across an article:

RIVIERA HOTELIER FOUND DEAD IN CANNES

Alain du Lac, the well-known French hotelier and darling of the jet-set has been found dead at his hotel in Cannes. Reports from the scene suggest that he died after a fall at the Hotel du Soleil, but others say it may have been the result of a heart attack. Previously able to count Michael and Shakira Caine as friends, the hotel has been host to the rich and famous, including stars such as Brooke Shields and Elton John.

There had been rumours of money problems, as well as his recent hellraising lifestyle making the headlines.

His wife, Madeleine, has not been seen since his death and a lawyer for the family has asked for privacy at this time.

Her reading was interrupted by the sound of her phone beeping loudly on the table beside her. A sick feeling clawed at her stomach, a jolt of horror shuddering through her body. She'd managed to temporarily forget what had happened last night, but hardly dared to read the message:

Back soon. I want to get to know you better. Let's get away somewhere . . . just the two of us. G

Ariana exhaled shakily, relieved it wasn't yet another sinister message and intrigued by Gabriel's text. Of course, it would be the perfect opportunity to find out more about the hotel – that was the only reason she was agreeing to spend time with him, she told herself.

But as she sat back in her seat and re-read Gabriel's message, Ariana found that she couldn't stop smiling.

Chapter 16

Cannes, May 2009

Estée was waiting outside the Palais des Festivals when Stefan pulled up in his scruffy old Peugeot. She'd changed out of the leggings and crop top she'd worn for her audition into a brightly patterned playsuit. She'd added a slick of lip gloss and mascara, and her curly hair was tied up in a brightly coloured scarf.

'How did it go?' Stefan asked, as she slid into the seat beside him and they kissed on both cheeks. It was rare that he had a day off and, after their evening at the premiere, he'd asked Estée if she'd like to spend the day with him. She'd instinctively said yes and was trying not to overthink her decision.

'I think I did well, but it's hard to say. You can never tell what they're looking for.'

'I'm sure you were amazing. They'd be fools not to choose you,' Stefan assured her, as he pulled out onto the Croisette. He was dressed in shorts and well-worn canvas loafers, and he was more tanned than Estée would have expected, given how much time he spent working indoors. His T-shirt was loose but couldn't disguise his broad shoulders and muscular chest.

'You've never seen me perform. I could have the grace of an elephant,' Estée teased.

'Maybe I should,' Stefan called her bluff. 'Next time I have a night off, I'll come and see your show.'

'No way!' Estée exclaimed with feeling. 'It's tacky and trashy – strictly for tourists and lonely locals only. I'd hate for anyone I know to see me in it.' Estée shuddered at the thought. 'Although I did see that actor, Jonny Farrell, in the club the other night. You know, he was in that terrible movie, *Wolf Heart*.'

'I haven't heard of him,' Stefan frowned.

'I'm not surprised – he's no Robert Chappell. Some of the girls think he's hot, but I think he looks like trouble. I wonder what he was doing there?'

'Didn't you say the costumes are quite revealing? I expect that's the reason,' Stefan joked, as Estée laughed.

She couldn't quite put her finger on why, but there was something odd about Jonny Farrell showing up at La Châtelaine. He hadn't stayed for long, speaking briefly to Victor and heading into the back with him. He'd seemed furtive and guarded; Estée assumed he must have been embarrassed about potentially being recognized at a back-street cabaret club.

'Where are we going?' Estée asked, glancing out of the window as they headed north on the Boulevard Carnot. She'd expected them to take the coast road.

'It's a surprise.'

'I don't like surprises,' Estée said, only half-joking.

'You'll like this one,' Stefan replied confidently. 'We're driving into the countryside, and it'll take about half an hour, but that's as much as I'm telling you. OK?'

'OK,' Estée agreed, turning her head to watch the scenery flash past. They were leaving the city sprawl behind and approaching Mougins, driving through a lush landscape dominated by the Alpes-Maritimes mountains. They passed pretty little hillside towns, ruined buildings and quaint rural churches, with a picturesque backdrop of craggy cliffs and dense forests of pine and olive trees. All the while Stefan chatted to her, telling her about funny things that had happened in the kitchen and recipes he was trying out. She felt herself relax as the beautiful French landscape opened up in front of them.

'Have you been out here before?' Stefan wondered, noticing how Estée was drinking in the view.

'I don't think I've left the city since I arrived. Isn't that terrible?'

Stefan shrugged. 'Life gets in the way. Work, commitments . . . But it's important to take time out now and again. It's good for the soul.'

'It doesn't seem as though you have a lot of time off.'

'True. I enjoy my work and take pride in what I do. I'm lucky to have a lot of independence, to create the menus I want and be bold with my choices. Madame du Lac has been very good to me, giving me a chance when others wouldn't.'

'I hardly ever see her. She scares me a little,' Estée admitted.

'She keeps herself to herself. I guess we all have our secrets.'

Estée looked across at him, wondering what he meant.

While not movie-star handsome, Stefan was undoubtedly attractive, with a quiet confidence and self-assurance that was incredibly appealing. He glanced at her and she looked away, not wanting to be caught staring.

'Not far now,' he told her.

In the distance, Estée could see a large town on a hill, a jumble of terracotta rooftops and higgledy-piggledy stone houses that were characteristic of the area. Off to one side was an ancient cathedral with a square-shaped bell tower, and Estée imagined that the view looking over the surrounding fields must be spectacular.

'Wind your window down,' Stefan instructed. 'Go on,' he laughed as Estée looked at him uncertainly.

'Oh, it smells wonderful,' she exclaimed, as the car was filled with a powerful floral scent. 'What is it?'

'Just about every type of flower you can imagine. Jasmine, mimosa, lavender and probably a hundred different species of rose.'

'It's incredible. But why are there so many?'

'The town up ahead is Grasse,' Stefan explained, nodding at the patchwork of buildings that Estée had been admiring. 'It's the perfume capital of the world. They produce flowers here for all of the big names – Dior, Hermès, Maison Guerlain. Even Chanel No. 5 was born here.'

'Wow. It's incredible,' Estée said sincerely, taking in row after row of delicate roses and vibrant broom and orange trees heavy with blossom. It looked wonderful and smelled even better.

Stefan turned down a series of country lanes, each one narrower than the last, before pulling to a stop by the side of an orchard bursting with peach trees. 'Here we are,' he announced. 'Time for lunch.'

Confused, Estée stepped out of the car. She couldn't see anything nearby – no restaurant, no bistro. It was only when Stefan pulled a chequered rug and a wicker basket from the boot that she understood what was happening.

'Follow me,' he smiled, as they made their way through the meadow, the long grass tickling Estée's ankles as she walked through in flip-flops.

'Many of the fields round here are protected,' Stefan explained. 'You're not allowed to enter, as the flowers are so delicate and they're grown especially for the big perfume houses. But I know the guy who owns this farm. He also happens to produce some of the best brandy outside of the Cognac region. Here?' he asked, as he stopped walking and indicated a pretty spot beneath the fruit trees with outstanding views over the valley.

'Perfect.'

Stefan spread the blanket on the ground and began unpacking what he'd brought: a freshly baked baguette, roast chicken, duck pâté, ripe tomatoes, a wedge of soft, buttery Brie, green grapes and the first strawberries of the season.

'It looks too good to eat,' Estée joked, suddenly feeling shy. She found herself wondering why Stefan had gone to so much trouble, and what he might expect in return.

'Think of it as a thank you for taking me to the premiere. I had a wonderful time and wanted to do something nice in return. Would you like a glass?' he asked, proffering a bottle of white wine.

'My favourite,' Estée smiled, as Stefan poured them each a drink and they toasted with a '*Santé*'.

Estée clinked her glass to his, then took a bite of olive fougasse, a bread that was a speciality of the region. 'This is delicious. You're such a good cook. How did you decide you wanted to become a chef?'

Stefan munched thoughtfully on a chunk of bread slathered with rich, creamy Brie. 'I grew up in Marseille, and my father walked out on us when I was very young. My mother was always working, so I was left to look after my younger brother. We didn't have a lot of money, so I had to cook everything from scratch, and I tried to make it tasty and wholesome.

'I wasn't interested in school and left without passing my exams. I was looking for a job – anything, I didn't care – and got taken on as a potwasher at the Hotel Dieu. It's the lowest rung on the ladder, but one profession where you can really work your way up is in the kitchen. So that's what I did. Talent is the most important thing, not your background.'

'You're so lucky that you get to do what you love for a living.'

'Well, I'm not quite there yet. I don't want to stay at the hotel forever. I dream of one day owning my own restaurant – and being awarded a Michelin star, of course.' Stefan grinned, reaching for a perfectly ripe apricot. 'How about you? What does your future hold?

'Hopefully I won't be at La Châtelaine for much longer, but the older you get, the harder it becomes as a dancer. I need a plan B, and I'm not sure what that is yet.'

'You have to go with your gut and do what feels right. If you hate working at the club, then leave,' Stefan said simply.

'I guess you're right . . . I hate it there. The girls are

nice, but the boss is a creep. He keeps pressuring me to—'
Estée broke off, realizing that she'd said more than she
meant to.

'To do what?' Stefan narrowed his eyes, instantly alert.

'He . . . The girls can earn bonuses if they stay after
the show, socialize with the clients, encourage them to
drink more . . .'

Stefan scowled, and Estée realized he understood
exactly what she was talking about. 'You're better than
that,' he said quietly.

'I know, but . . . I've told you about my daughter,
haven't I?' Estée knew she talked about Emilie in their
late-night chats, and Stefan nodded. 'Having a child
makes everything more complicated. I need to earn
money to support her. I *have* to be successful so she
doesn't see me as a failure, and I can't behave as though
I have no responsibilities. I have to consider her first
when I make decisions.'

'I understand, but think about how you'd feel in ten,
fifteen years' time if your daughter was in this situation.
What advice would you give her?'

'I'd be furious. I'd tell her to quit immediately,' Estée
admitted, shaking her head and biting her lip. 'You're
right, I need to leave. I'll hand my notice in tonight.'
Now that she'd said it out loud, it felt like there was no
going back. 'Let's hope I get this audition – cross your
fingers for me.'

'You said it's a touring show, so you'd be leaving Cannes
if you got the job? I'll cross my fingers because it's what
you want, but there's part of me hoping you'll stay . . .'

They smiled at one another, but Stefan seemed to sense
not to push things too far, and Estée appreciated how

considerate he was being. It would have been all too easy for him to lean across and kiss her, to take advantage of her in this secluded location, with no one else around. Would she want him to?

The sun was rising higher in the sky, the heat all-encompassing. They'd finished eating, and Stefan began to pack away the leftovers before the wasps and insects took an interest. Estée couldn't help but feel disappointed that their trip was coming to an end.

'What are your plans for the rest of the day?' asked Stefan, as he stood up and shook out the rug.

'No plans. Although, I have to go to the club this evening. I need to speak to Victor, and I'll have to work my notice period . . . But I'm not going to think about that now.' Estée shook her head, not wanting those thoughts to intrude and spoil the day.

'I'll get you home in time,' Stefan promised. 'But would you like to visit Grasse? It's a charming little town. We can explore, go for a coffee . . . And I need to pick up some supplies if you want to come with me – they have an incredible *confiserie* and the best *fromagerie*.'

'Yes,' Estée nodded eagerly, realizing she didn't want their time together to end. She looked up at Stefan and smiled. 'I'd like that very much.'

Chapter 17

'What's your lucky number, babe?' Jonny was looking expectantly at Ariana.

'My birthday,' she grinned, laughing as she saw his face drop.

'Um . . . That's the . . .'

'Twelve, you idiot,' she shot back, her eyes flashing playfully.

'Sure, sure, I knew that,' he protested.

'And you know the month, of course?'

'Yes, of course! It's Decem— I mean, March. July? Hey!' Jonny yelled, as she pinched his arm. 'OK, twelve. Be lucky for me.'

Jonny leaned over the roulette table, placing a stack of chips in the centre of number twelve. There were ten chips – one thousand euros in total.

'No more bets,' said the besuited croupier, as the ball began to bounce and stutter in the wheel.

Around the table, everyone was breathless with excitement. It was a mixed crowd of high rollers and those who were there for a flutter, some clearly monied and others there just to soak up the atmosphere and gamble vicariously.

Jonny had seemingly made an effort for the occasion and was wearing a shirt – albeit untucked and unbuttoned halfway down his chest. Ariana had stepped up the glamour, in a metallic silver Roberto Cavalli dress that clung to every curve of her body. Low cut and shimmering, with a fringed hemline that swung tantalizingly around her tanned, toned legs, Ariana looked like a Bond girl, her dark hair styled in voluminous waves, her cat-like eyes lined with kohl and teamed with a nude lip gloss.

Jonny had one arm slung around Ariana's waist, the other hand gripping a Jack and Coke, as the ball jumped one final time and came to rest.

'Black, thirteen,' the dealer announced, sweeping the unlucky chips – including Jonny's – off the table.

Jonny swore and unceremoniously let go of Ariana. He took a gulp of his drink, his face black as thunder.

'Thirteen, unlucky for some,' Ariana quipped, but Jonny didn't seem to find it funny. He turned to walk away, but Ariana stopped him.

'Running scared?' she goaded him, but he shook his head.

'Nah. Let's try blackjack.'

'Then let me try,' Ariana said confidently, leaning over to place her chips on the table. She put a stack on twelve, as Jonny had done, and covered surrounding numbers too – the 'split', 'street' and 'corner' bets. The dealer waved his hand to close the betting and everyone watched in anticipation as the ball spun in the wheel, tripping over the numbers like a tap-dancer before landing for the final time.

'Red, twelve,' said the straight-faced dealer, as Ariana let out a screech of joy.

'I can't believe it!' she cried, hugging Jonny as the non-winning chips were swept away and an enormous pile was pushed across to her. She'd won almost a hundred thousand euros from a thousand-euro stake. She flipped a chip at the grateful croupier and scooped the rest into her purse, her expression ecstatic as she walked away.

'What are you doing?' Jonny demanded. 'The luck's clearly on your side. Keep playing.'

Ariana shook her head. 'You've got to know when to walk away, Jonny.' She was enjoying the thrill of anticipation of the night ahead and a little of her old hedonism had crept back in. 'What shall we play next?'

Jonny looked annoyed, his usual buoyancy deflated. 'I'm not interested. Let's go get another drink.'

'What's wrong with you tonight, Jonny? You're so uptight.'

'Nothing's wrong, Princess Ariana. We're not all around to please your highness, you know.'

Ariana frowned, thinking over the last few days, to all of Hollywood descending on Cannes – the cameras and the flashlights on the red carpet and the press intrusion – to Jonny's petty jealousies and resentments. 'Is this because your dad is in town?'

'Don't mention that prick, you hear me?'

'Jesus, forget I said anything, OK? You want some chips? Here, take some of these.' Ariana handed him a stash, keen not to let the night descend into one of Jonny's petulant episodes; however this only seemed to infuriate him more.

'I don't need *pocket money*,' he spat angrily, but still thrust the chips into his pocket. 'I'm going to the bathroom. I'll meet you at the bar.'

'OK . . .' Ariana watched him thoughtfully as he walked away, surprised by his attitude. He may have had his faults, but you were usually guaranteed a good night out with Jonny Farrell. That was part of his charm – he could always get the party started, determined that everyone would enjoy themselves. When his attention was focused on you, you felt like the most special thing in the world – although Ariana wasn't naive enough to think she was the only one to receive this treatment. His relationship with his entire family could at best be described as strained, and to Jonny it was as if his own father didn't even exist. She'd learned to pretend that was the case too.

Ariana sashayed across to the bar, pleased to note that she was causing something of a stir, eyes following her as she strutted by in the silver lamé dress. She ordered two Old Fashioned cocktails and nervously pulled out her phone. She'd tried to put the texts to the back of her mind, but it was impossible to forget about them. Who'd sent them, and why? She'd tried calling the number but it always went straight to voicemail. Did they have information about the night Liberty died, or were they just bluffing, trying to cause trouble? It nagged away at her, even tonight when she was supposed to be having fun. There was no more fun for Liberty, and she could never forget that. Perhaps she'd speak to Jonny about it when he came back – to finally get the subject off her chest and see what he thought of the whole situation.

There was a notification on her phone, and Ariana held her breath as she opened it. It was a text from Montana, and she exhaled slowly, her shoulders dropping in relief.

Where ru? X

Ariana quickly typed back:

Casino with Jonny. Come? X

The reply was almost instantaneous:

Be there in 10. VIP Room is soooo lame X

Ariana sat down on a bar stool, crossing her legs, her dress riding up to display acres of toned, tanned thigh. She wondered where Jonny was, he was taking forever. For the first time, she was tempted to walk out and find another party somewhere else – Gabriel flitted across her mind, and she wondered what he was doing right now. Probably poring over some acquisition spreadsheet, she guessed.

She glanced around, scoping out the room to see if anyone she knew was there, and then, almost as if she had conjured him up, her cat-like eyes settled on Gabriel, and he was staring right at her, as though he'd been waiting for her to look across. What on earth was he doing here? She'd thought he was still in Nice.

Her gaze slid to the girl on his arm. She was stunning, with legs that never seemed to end and her honey-blonde hair cut in a sophisticated long bob. Ariana felt sure she was a catwalk model she had seen last season in Paris. They were at the baccarat table and as Ariana watched the woman placed her bet and stood back, slipping her arm through Gabriel's. She said something to him, and Gabriel's eyes slid away from Ariana and back to his female companion.

Ariana exhaled slowly, surprised to find how unsettled she felt, a spark of competition igniting and firing through her veins. Gabriel looked gorgeous in a tuxedo, and Ariana wondered if it was the same one he'd worn to the premiere of *All Our Yesterdays*. *The same suit, a different woman*, she thought cynically. Still, at least she knew where she stood. She wondered if this woman was a casual date, or if she and Gabriel were serious. She wondered why she cared.

After his text, Ariana and Gabriel had made plans to meet at the old port on Tuesday. She'd asked herself whether there might be any romantic intention behind the invitation, but that notion seemed faintly ridiculous now. It was probably just another attempt to wine and dine her in order to convince her to sell the hotel to him.

She looked back to the baccarat table, but it seemed Gabriel had moved on. Instead, she spotted Jonny making his way back through the casino, weaving through the bank of slot machines that jangled and whirred invitingly, flashing in garish neon colours. Jonny's mood appeared to have been transformed – he'd rediscovered his trademark swagger, his eyes were glittering, and he was full of energy, practically bouncing off the walls.

'Thanks, babe,' he said, grabbing the drink. 'Let's play blackjack, I'm feeling lucky.'

'Jonny, what—' Ariana began, and then she realized: the dilated pupils, the manic energy, the way he was grinding his jaw – he'd clearly just indulged.

'C'mon, babe.' He grabbed her hand and pulled her along, oblivious to her frustration. There was no way that she could talk to him about anything serious now. Plus, she'd moved on from the drug and partying she'd slipped into in LA and made a deliberate decision to avoid that kind of lifestyle. She was conscious that Gabriel might be watching them, and didn't want Jonny to embarrass her. Then it dawned on her that it mattered what Gabriel thought of her and she wished fervently that she was with somebody other than Jonny.

She followed him hesitantly to the blackjack table, where he sat down on one of the stools. Ariana remained standing, leaning on his shoulder, revelling in the anticipation, as he began to play with the chips she had given him. Jonny might have complained about being given pocket money, but he'd still taken it from her and was more than happy to gamble with someone else's cash.

She sipped her cocktail as she watched Jonny play, her foot tapping the floor tensely as he lost hand after hand, growing more and more exasperated with every bad call he made.

'Maybe call it a day, Jonny?' Ariana suggested, after watching him bust five hands in a row. 'It's not your night. We could get another drink, get something to eat?' She placed a hand on his arm and he shrugged it off angrily.

'Shut up, Ariana, we're not all prissy little rich girls like you. I need to concentrate.' He glanced up and saw her shocked face. 'I know what I'm doing.'

Ariana's cheeks were flaming, torn between causing a scene and drawing even more attention to herself, which was the last thing she wanted, but still furious that he'd spoken to her like that. This was the Jonny that she hated, the arrogant, selfish and volatile man-child who was never very far from the surface.

She glanced up, wondering if anyone had seen her, and stared straight into Gabriel's eyes. He looked concerned.

'Are you OK?' he mouthed silently across the casino.

Ariana nodded. There it was, that connection again, inexplicably, even though they had barely got to know each other, in that moment she felt that if Jonny did anything to hurt or upset her, she could rely on Gabriel to step in. She reminded herself that wouldn't be necessary and pasted on a smile; she could look after herself, but instead of bolstering her confidence, she found herself both grateful for his concern and humiliated that he'd witnessed Jonny speak to her like this. The blonde woman took Gabriel's hand, and his attention, and led him away. They melted into the crowd and Ariana turned back to Jonny, watching in silence as he continued to play – and continued to lose – his entire focus on the cards as though she wasn't even there. Sweat was beading on his forehead, his eyes darting from side to side. The occasional win was greeted with a triumphant roar, but the pile of chips in front of him was slowly but surely depleting.

Ten minutes later, when he lost the final chip, Jonny slammed his fist on the table, swearing loudly. The croupier glanced over in concern, and Ariana gave her a reassuring look, hoping he wouldn't cause a scene. The last thing she wanted was for them to get thrown out, or for the police to be called – especially with Gabriel there to observe it all. *You can always judge someone by the company they keep, Ari,* Demetrios had told her. She wondered what that said about her right now.

'Come on, Jonny,' she said, tugging his arm. 'Let's go get a drink or something. Montana will be here any minute, and I'm done here even if you're not. We're supposed to be having fun, remember?'

'Fun?' Jonny shot back, refusing to snap out of his dark mood. 'I'm sure you think it's "fun" to lose ten thousand dollars in one hit. Jesus, Ariana. Try living in the real world. Oh, right, you don't have to because Daddy bails you out every time your bank balance drops below one million dollars.'

Ariana was floored by the vitriol coming from him, furious at being spoken to like that. Besides, the money he'd lost was *hers* to start with. She opened her mouth to tell him to go to hell, but at that moment they heard a screech from across the casino. It was Montana, wearing the shortest, tightest dress that Ariana had ever seen, her breasts pushed up to eye-popping levels. Her blonde hair was ironed poker straight, her enhanced lips covered in fuchsia-pink gloss, and she was waving excitedly. She was with a group of mutual friends, and they were all heading over.

Jonny's face changed instantly and he turned to Ariana, wrapping his arms around her, leaning close to whisper in her ear. 'I'm so sorry, babe. I didn't mean what I said.'

Ariana stepped back, pushing him away. She knew he was embarrassed by his behaviour and didn't want the others to see him like that, but he was a fool if he thought he could take his frustrations out on her then act sweetness and light around everyone else. She was a Theodosis, and she wouldn't be spoken to like that by anyone.

'Please, Ariana.' His dark eyes searched hers, his face now as contrite as it had been venomous a moment before. 'I'm an asshole, I know I am. I just . . . I really needed to win some money tonight, OK, got a few expenses I need to take care of. You know how it is. I'm sorry, baby, come here. Ariana, I'm begging you.'

She relented a little, allowing him to wrap his arms around her.

'Look, can you do me a favour,' Jonny continued. 'Can you lend me some money?'

She pulled away. 'Is that all you're interested in?'

'Please,' Jonny hissed, his eyes darting over to where Montana and her crew were fast approaching. Ariana wondered why he cared so much what Montana thought. Montana flirted outrageously with everyone, but could there be more to it with Jonny? 'I'll give it back to you tomorrow, I swear,' he continued. 'I just . . . got a little cashflow problem, it's these stupid French ATMs. I just want us all to have a good night, y'know?'

His arms were around her waist, his body pressed against hers as he nuzzled her ear.

Ariana sighed. 'How much?'

'A few grand.'

Ariana knew she had the money, and it would barely make a dent in her bank balance. Jonny had borrowed money from her before, more than once, and she knew her chances of ever seeing it again were slim.

'Please, I swear I'll give it back to you tomorrow as soon as my card gets sorted. That's chicken feed to you, babe. You won, like, fifty times that on the roulette table.'

Ariana said nothing, feeling torn. She'd always been wary of people using her for money – her father had drummed it into her that she'd be a target for fortune hunters and those whose intentions weren't the best. Yet she was also aware that she was very privileged and able to live a life others could only dream of, but Jonny wasn't one of those, he was a spoilt actor from Hollywood who thought the world owed him a living. Her brain knew that but why didn't her body? He was kissing her neck, and Ariana felt muddled by the familiar scent of him, the feel of his body against hers. She'd had a few drinks and didn't want to argue.

'C'mon, babe, don't embarrass me in front of everyone. Just enough to have a little flutter. If I win, I'll give it straight back.'

'Fine, but don't make me regret it.' she agreed, dipping into her stash of chips and handing some over to Jonny.

'Get a room, you guys!' Montana pulled a face and pushed them apart. Ariana noticed a flash of annoyance cross Montana's face as she quickly greeted Ariana, then practically threw herself at Jonny, letting out an ear-piercing squeal as she jumped up into his arms, so that he was forced to catch her. Montana was with a dozen equally loud and outrageous people – friends from LA, as well as a few hangers-on she appeared to have just met – and everyone said hi, hugging and air-kissing.

Before she was able to decipher the vibe between Jonny and Montana more thoroughly, Ariana felt a touch at her shoulder and turned, expecting it to be another of Montana's followers. Instead, Gabriel was standing behind her. She was momentarily disconcerted to see him, as she inhaled the expensive cologne she remembered from their dinner, so close that she could pick out flecks of deepest blue in his eyes.

'I'm leaving now,' he told her, in his gravelly French accent. 'But I wanted to make sure you were all right.' His gaze slid to Jonny, who was speaking to Montana, regarding him coldly, as though he were something he'd scraped off the bottom of his shoe.

'Thank you,' she nodded. 'I'm fine.'

The blonde on his arm was staring at her aloofly.

'I'll see you on Tuesday?' he said quietly.

Ariana nodded once again, and as he departed, she followed them with her eyes, before turning back to the group, expecting Jonny to be jealously watching the conversation. Instead, he was paying no attention. Montana had her arms around him, hanging off his neck. They were both giggling hysterically, their faces pushed close together. As Ariana watched, Jonny pulled a small packet of white powder from his trouser pocket, a handful of poker chips coming with it. Montana reached over and discreetly palmed the packet, raising an eyebrow as she noticed all the chips. 'Ooh, someone got lucky tonight!' she squealed.

Jonny shrugged, like it wasn't a big deal. 'Here,' he said, tossing her half a dozen. 'Try your luck.'

Ariana's eyes narrowed. 'Jonny—' she began, but he threw his arm around her and steered her across the floor to follow Montana.

'It's all good, babe,' he said casually. 'Now, let's go have some fun.'

Outside the casino, Gabriel kissed Elodie on both cheeks and helped her into a taxi. The street was lively, and Elodie was going on to a bar to meet her friends, but Gabriel planned to call it a night. He felt bad; Elodie was a beautiful young woman, and was good company, but tonight he had been distracted. They had been involved in an on/off liaison for a few months, though it wasn't serious. She was in Cannes for the festival and Gabriel had asked her out for the evening. Now he wished he hadn't, his mind was elsewhere, and it wasn't fair of him, or gentlemanly.

Seeing Ariana had thrown him. Seeing Ariana *with* Jonny. Gabriel was worried about her – he couldn't see what she saw in the guy. Jonny was clearly bad news. The way he'd spoken to her . . . Gabriel had seen the shock and hurt on Ariana's face. It had taken all his restraint not to storm across the casino and spark him out.

Since speaking to Felipe, Gabriel had made a few more enquiries, putting the word out amongst his contacts. He didn't like the reports that were coming back. It seemed like Jonny was in serious trouble. He was involved with some dangerous guys, ones who didn't mess around. The kind of guys who'd come after anyone you were close to, just to teach you a lesson.

Yeah, he was definitely concerned about Ariana, and what she might inadvertently be mixed up in.

Gabriel hated the thought of anything bad happening to her, and knew he needed to warn her as soon as possible. He didn't want to consider what his motives were.

Chapter 18

Juan-les-Pins, May 2009

Estée slung her bag over her shoulder, and made her way through the jostling girls in their stage costumes, in various stages of dress and undress. After she'd talked to Stefan, he had given her courage. She had been doing the matinee today, on her day off, and after her set, she had made the firm decision that it would be her last show.

She made her way towards his office; the door was ajar, he was sitting at his desk, and was on the phone. She hovered uncertainly in the doorway as she heard him growl into the receiver.

'Just make sure you are there for the pick-up,' he said. 'Don't screw it up like last time, or you know what will happen.' He looked up and saw Estée, beckoned her over, pointing at the chair in front of him.

Estée sat down, avoiding his eyes by looking at the framed pictures on the wall of Victor with various famous footballers and sportsmen, who looked like they had been visitors to the club. Judging by their clothes, and by the fact that Victor had much more hair than he did now, it must have been over a decade ago. Estée hadn't noticed a single famous face coming into the club since she had been there.

'Just do what I tell you.' Victor abruptly ended the call, never taking his eyes off her. He leaned back in his chair, 'I don't very often see you in my office, Estée, to what do I owe this pleasure?'

'I wanted to talk to you,' Estée said, trying to keep her voice calm.

He stood up and walked past her, closing the door. 'That's better, a bit more privacy,' he said, and came and sat opposite her, resting himself on his desk, getting so close that Estée could smell his stale cheap aftershave. She suddenly felt trapped, with no escape behind her and Victor so close in front. 'I hope you have seen sense and taken me up on my offer. There's no future in your dancing, Estée, no matter how good you think you are. There are one hundred girls in front of you, all better, prettier . . . smarter.'

Earlier that day, Estée had learned that she hadn't passed the audition that she was desperate to. It was time for her to realize that she needed to make some tough decisions, so she didn't rise to the bait; she just had one thing to say, she would do it quickly and never have anything to do with Victor ever again.

'Getting friendly with the customers,' he continued, 'making them happy, that's where the money is.'

'Well, actually . . . no, that isn't why I'm here.' She braced herself. 'I've decided to leave the club. I'm resigning.'

Victor's face immediately changed, anger flashing across it. He set his mouth in a hard line.

'Leave? Where to, some other nightclub where no one is interested in what happens on stage?'

'That's not really your concern, but I don't want to do this anymore.'

Victor eyed her, almost like a cat deciding when to pounce on a mouse. 'If you are sure about this, there is nothing I can do to stop you.' Then he stood and walked around to his desk and took out a ledger. 'If you just settle up what you owe the club, then I can return your passport and you can be on your way.'

Estée felt the ground shift beneath her. 'What are you talking about? I don't owe you or the club anything.'

A cruel and sly smile spread across his face, 'Oh, but my dear, yes you do. There are the costumes that we provide that must be paid for, the drinks and the free food we give you, all of it costs me something and that's why we make sure it is in your contract that all those cost must be reimbursed in full when we part ways.'

He reached for a calculator on his desk and made a show of adding up some numbers, 'It looks like you owe me sixteen hundred euros.'

Estée laughed nervously, 'You're joking?'

The smile disappeared from his face. 'This is no joke; if you don't want to be part of our happy family any longer, then we must let you go . . . but you'll have to pay for your freedom.' He unlocked another drawer in his desk and took out a piece of paper and what she recognized as her passport.

She gasped, she had completely forgotten that he had her passport; he had taken it for 'verification' when she had signed the contract, and had never given it back to her.

'This can't be legal?'

Victor didn't even try to hide his enjoyment now and took pleasure in pointing out the clause.

Estée felt hot tears sting at her eyes as she looked at it, barely even taking in the words. She grabbed her bag and stood up. 'You're just a con artist,' she said, her voice unsteady.

'Now now, better be nice to me,' he said, '. . . and I'll be nice to you. Now don't be late for your shift tomorrow, or call in sick – if you do, I'll dock your pay and it will take you even longer to pay me back.' He laughed, but she didn't give him a chance to gloat, turning on her heels and running from the room, not stopping until she was outside the club and gulping in big mouthfuls of air, tears falling down her cheeks.

What on earth was she going to do now?

She dabbed at her eyes and shook herself. She needed to think. She crossed the road and headed towards one of the late-night bars that she knew some of the other girls went to, where she would be safe.

She asked the garçon for a Diet Coke and tried to compose herself, thinking about everything that had happened. She felt as though she'd well and truly messed up her life, that every time she'd been at a crossroads, she'd taken the wrong path. She was a twenty-seven-year-old failed dancer with a beautiful daughter who she barely saw due to her terrible decision to move to the opposite end of the country. Where had it all gone so wrong?

Moments later, a well-dressed woman walked by holding hands with a girl of around five or six. Estée remembered when Emilie had been that age – so adorable, so innocent. The girl was skipping along without a care in the world, her brightly patterned sundress dancing around her skinny legs, a straw sunhat perched on her head. She looked up at Estée and smiled; Estée smiled back, suddenly feeling close to tears once again.

Estée finished her drink and got to her feet, trying to quell the rising sense of panic that threatened to engulf her. With no idea of what to do next, or where she was going, she set off walking.

Robert's feet were pounding the pavement as he kept his head down and moved fast, hoping that no one would recognize him. In sports shorts and an old T-shirt, teamed with a baseball cap and dark glasses, it was a far cry from his usual image, and so far he was managing to go incognito.

He wasn't sure where this crazy idea to go for a run had come from, but he was starting to regret it. Did people really do this for enjoyment? At least the view made up for the exertion and it was keeping him out of the hotel bar, he thought, as the sweat began to bead on his forehead. He'd followed the winding coastal path, heading north as he left his hotel. This was the part of town he usually sped through in a limo, shuttling between the Hotel du Cap and Cannes, but moving at a slower pace revealed its true beauty: the rocky inlets and secluded sandy beaches were a delight, the clear waters deliciously inviting. He'd certainly come a long way over the years, Robert reflected.

A short way out to sea was a fisherman in a rowing boat, his line set as he allowed himself to drift with the tide. Robert envied him the solitude, the simplicity of his life. That was downright patronizing, he realized; he felt sure this bloke had his problems like everyone else. But out on the ocean without a care in the world seemed like a good place to be.

From the outside looking in, it seemed as though Robert had everything. So why did he feel so disillusioned with his life, terrified that he'd messed it all up and he was about to lose everything? He felt that if he could explain his feelings to Liz – if it was just the two of them without all the crap that intruded on their everyday life – then it would all be OK. Why hadn't he tried harder before?

He knew Liz desperately wanted a baby, and he'd move heaven and earth if it would make her happy. This would be his chance to make up for his failings as a father; he could be present for this kid the way he hadn't been for his son. Imagine if they had a little girl – she'd be the image of Elizabeth, the apple of her daddy's eye. Christ, when did he get so sentimental?

He decided to cut through a small park to see if there was a bar in the parade of shops on the other side. It was getting late, but there were still plenty of people around; a few families were using the playground, their children sliding and swinging. The walkways were beautifully laid out, bordered by rose bushes and ranunculi, with pine and palm trees providing shady areas during the hottest parts of the day.

Robert rounded a corner and almost did a double take as he noticed the woman sitting alone on a bench.

'Estée?'

She jumped as he said her name, clearly lost in her own thoughts.

'Hey, it's me.' Robert removed his sunglasses and it took a moment before she placed him.

'Robert . . .' Estée seemed dazed. 'I'm so sorry, I was . . .'

'Are you all right?'

'Just feeling sorry for myself,' she smiled ruefully.

'Sorry to hear that. Anything I can help with?'

'No, I just . . . A quarter-life crisis, I guess you'd call it – if I'm not too old for that. I'm feeling a bit lost right now.'

'You and me both,' Robert said with feeling. 'Listen, do you want to go grab a drink or something? I was thinking about getting one myself.'

'No thanks. But you go ahead. I'll be fine.' Estée wrapped her slender arms around herself as though she was cold, despite the balmy evening air.

Robert hesitated, then sat down on the bench beside her. 'I can't leave you here like this, can I?' he grinned jovially. 'Come on, tell Uncle Robert what's wrong. I'm a good listener – when I manage to stop talking.'

In spite of herself, Estée laughed. 'It's nothing really.'

'If it's making you feel bad, then it's important. Lord knows I'm the last person to judge what someone else is going through.'

'Thank you,' Estée said quietly. 'You're a good man.'

'I wish my wife thought the same,' Robert said wistfully.

She stared at him for a moment, her brown eyes searching his face, wondering whether to unburden herself. He was a famous movie star, so why did he care about her life? Equally, he'd probably gone through his fair share of trials and tribulations on his way to the top, so perhaps he would have some good advice.

'All right,' Estée began to talk, telling Robert all about Emilie, about how she'd lied to her mother and pretended she was far more successful than she really was, but how she really worked as a chambermaid in the Hotel du Soleil where Elizabeth was staying. Estée told him about the club, about Victor and his shady business dealings, his blackmail and his threats. Robert listened without interruption, offering reassurance and comfort, letting her speak until she had nothing left to say.

Neither of them noticed the photographer hiding in the bushes, crouching behind the oleander to get the snaps that would make him a small fortune, his camera clicking rapidly. The light was fading, but it was still possible to identify the shadowy figures on the bench, bodies turned towards one another, his arm around her and their conversation intimate and intense.

The paparazzo stole away silently, then pulled out his mobile phone.

Chapter 19

Cannes, May 2009

Ariana burst out laughing. 'You've got to be kidding me.'

'Good morning,' Gabriel grinned as he saw her approach. 'Aren't you impressed?'

Ariana had walked past dozens of superyachts – sleek, white, some as large as two hundred feet, the largest the marina could accommodate – to reach the end of the jetty where Gabriel was standing aboard a small wooden boat.

It *was* beautiful, Ariana realized, looking closer. It was a Riva Aquarama, the famous Italian speedboat, in immaculate condition – dark, glossy mahogany, with the interior upholstered in pristine white and turquoise. It looked like something from a classic movie – *To Catch a Thief*, or a vintage James Bond.

'My father would love it,' she told him honestly.

'Great. Should I take him instead?' Gabriel asked, straight-faced, and Ariana laughed once again.

He held out his hand to help her aboard and Ariana took it, a frisson of excitement rippling through her. He was perfectly dressed for the occasion in stone-coloured chino shorts and a white polo shirt that highlighted his toned, athletic body.

Ariana felt almost underdressed for once. She'd deliberately chosen a low-key outfit of a red halter-necked sundress teamed with strappy gold sandals, and a bikini underneath in case they went swimming. Her dark hair was clipped up in a casual style, and she carried a designer beach bag with all her essentials thrown in. Today, Ariana wanted to look like a beautiful country girl from Ithos, not the glamorous starlet she'd been in LA.

'So, where are we going?' she asked, taking the opportunity to stare at Gabriel from behind her Jackie O-style sunglasses, his biceps flexing as he untied the lines from the dock piling.

'You'll see,' he grinned infuriatingly.

'You really know how to drive this thing?'

'Of course. I grew up next to this marina. I could pilot a boat before I could walk.'

Ariana felt her competitive streak surface. 'As the daughter of a shipping magnate, I know a thing or two about boats myself.'

'A woman of many talents,' Gabriel teased. 'You can drive a boat, run a hotel . . .'

'I wondered how long it would be before that came up,' Ariana said, her eyes flashing a warning. 'We've not even left the harbour.'

'I'm sorry,' Gabriel was conciliatory. 'Shall we make a rule? No hotel talk today, OK?'

'It's a deal,' Ariana agreed and felt her shoulders relax.

Gabriel turned the ignition key and pushed the throttle, and they steered out of the harbour, increasing the speed as they headed out into the open water. They bounced over the white-tipped waves, the wind whipping tendrils of dark hair around Ariana's face, the sun beating down on her bare shoulders. It felt wonderful to be back on the ocean. Like Gabriel, she'd grown up around boats and her father adored them. Demetrios had even built his own, a schooner called *Beauty*.

Ariana glanced across at Gabriel, who was standing by the wheel, his posture upright, his shoulders set. He looked powerful, attractive, like a man in control with the world at his feet.

'My turn,' Ariana grinned, striding over and nudging him aside. Gabriel laughed and gave way, the boat slicing across the Bay of Cannes as Ariana daringly pushed the throttle faster.

Gabriel was still standing by her shoulder, close enough to make himself heard over the noise of the engine and the wind, and for Ariana to smell his Acqua di Parma cologne.

'You don't know where you're going,' he smiled. He reached out in front of her and placed one hand on the wheel next to Ariana's, turning it gently, their bodies only inches apart. Ariana didn't move, her back almost against his chest, as she stared straight ahead at the flat, tree-covered islands that hove into view, but she was intensely aware of his presence and she could feel a tingle on her skin at his nearness.

The Lérins Islands lay just off the coast of Cannes. There were four in total, the largest of which was the Île Sainte-Marguerite, famous for being the location where the 'Man in the Iron Mask' was held prisoner.

Gabriel steered the boat around the rocky coastline and Ariana caught glimpses of a soft, white, sandy beach in front of a dramatic walled fortress, beautifully clear turquoise waters pooling close to shore that fell away to a deeper blue the colour of lapis lazuli. She expected them to head for one of the moorings, but Gabriel continued, circling the smaller Île Saint-Honorat and heading east towards a tiny strip of land.

'Îlot Saint-Ferréol,' Gabriel announced. 'Have you ever been?'

Ariana shook her head.

'It's uninhabited,' Gabriel told her. 'Hardly anyone knows about it. There are very few visitors.'

He killed the engine and they drifted nearer, pushed by the gentle waves. Ariana realized why they'd taken the smaller boat – it would have been impossible to get anywhere near the little island in a larger vessel. The water here was dazzling and crystal clear, myriad shades of green and blue like the Caribbean. It lapped softly against powdery golden sand, the beach deserted and impossible to access except by boat.

Gabriel dropped the anchor a few metres from the island and, with him carrying a cool box and basket, they waded ashore through the deliciously cool shallows.

'What do you think?' Gabriel asked expectantly, as they set foot on the velvety sand.

'Pretty good,' Ariana teased. 'Not quite as good as Ithos.'

'I'm sure,' Gabriel agreed. 'Although I think you'll find there's one thing the French do better,' he grinned, spreading out a large beach blanket before reaching into the cool box and bringing out a bottle of perfectly chilled Taittinger champagne.

'I don't agree at all,' Ariana teased, accepting a glass and sipping it appreciatively, wondering why Gabriel had gone to so much trouble. She glanced over at him to see him pulling off his shirt and stretching out languidly, almost as if he knew she was watching. Ariana couldn't help but check out his body. He clearly took care of himself, with well-defined muscles and the outline of a six-pack, his chest bronzed with a smattering of blond hair. It was a real contrast with Jonny and his pale, rangy physique, slim but untoned and covered in tattoos.

'It's so beautiful here,' Ariana said quickly, as Gabriel caught her looking at him. The eucalyptus trees waved lazily overhead in the balmy breeze, surrounded by lush greenery that provided the utmost privacy, making Ariana feel as though the two of them had been marooned on an idyllic tropical island. 'So peaceful. It's hard to believe we're so close to Cannes.'

'I thought we could both do with a change of scenery. Something slower paced. Or are you missing the buzz of the city?'

'I'm an island girl at heart, never happier than with the sand between my toes.'

'Of course. The sea is so calming, don't you think? Around here, the whole coastline is full of hidden inlets and little spots to escape, if you know where to look.'

'You grew up around boats?'

'Yes. My father owned a few – not as many as your father,' Gabriel added wryly, 'We were always out on the water when I was a child.'

'Sounds idyllic.'

'Sometimes. I have good memories of my childhood. Not so much as I grew older . . .'

'I have to admit, I've read a little of your family history. If you don't mind me asking, what happened to your father? How did he . . .'

Gabriel said nothing, and Ariana couldn't read his expression behind his aviator sunglasses. She hoped he wasn't angry with her. Then he laughed hollowly. 'The crazy thing is, I don't entirely know. No one ever really told me. I was staying with a friend the weekend he died, and my friend's mother was the one to break the news. She didn't explain the details. And then my mother was so distraught, I didn't feel I could ask. I found out a little more afterwards, reading accounts in the papers, and digging around a bit, though I've tried to respect her wishes – some said it was an accident, others said a heart attack; whatever it was he could never have survived the fall.'

'Haven't you ever asked your mother how the fall happened?'

Gabriel sighed. 'I've tried. She won't talk about it. She's barely left that room since the funeral.'

'I wondered why I'd never seen her around the hotel. I'm sorry. That must be hard.'

Gabriel waved his hand, batting away her words. 'I don't want to bring the mood down. Come on, let's change the subject.'

The sun rose high in the cloudless sky as they got to know each other, lazing on the sand and chatting easily. They'd both spent time at boarding school in England; Ariana had chosen to go to Marlborough, while Gabriel had been sent to Abingdon after his father died. It hadn't been a good experience for him – he'd struggled to make friends, grappling with the language and weighed down by grief – and the two of them spoke about how it had felt to be separated from their families during their adolescent years.

They talked about their travels, the places they'd been and the places they wanted to go. Ariana adored Indonesia while Gabriel preferred Japan, and neither had been to Central America but both dreamed of exploring Costa Rica. They compared their favourite foods, favourite music, favourite movies, discussing their plans and ambitions.

'And this guy, Jonny Farrell, that I had the pleasure of meeting the other night,' Gabriel began, his tone sarcastic. 'What's the story with him?'

'Oh, Jonny is just . . . Jonny,' Ariana shrugged, not meeting his gaze. 'He's not always as you've seen him, he has his good side, and we do have history . . .'

'History can be bloody and brutal.'

'Not as bad as that,' Ariana said ruefully.

Gabriel raised an eyebrow. 'How did you two meet?'

'On the party circuit. Once Jonny gets you in his sights, you get caught up in his orbit.'

'Is that how you feel? Caught? I'm intrigued by your interest in him. To the outsider, he seems . . .' Gabriel hesitated.

'. . . Like an entitled asshole?' Ariana finished for him, and they both laughed.

'You said it.'

Ariana felt a stab of loyalty. 'Jonny's just messed up. A mother in and out of rehab, his dad a famous actor who never showed up when he was a kid. He's a little boy lost really.'

'Can I ask you something?' Gabriel said, looking at her intently.

'Sure.'

'What happened, the night of the premiere? Why did you react like that?'

Ariana tensed instantly, avoiding his gaze.

'I know something's wrong. I want to help you if I can.'

'Why?'

'Because I can't stop thinking about you. And I know you're not as strong as you pretend to be.' Gabriel reached across and took her hand, forcing Ariana to look at him.

She gazed into his eyes, searching for answers. She wanted so badly to confide in someone, to unburden herself and feel less alone. But she was afraid that if things went badly between them, he might use the information against her.

'It's a long story,' she said, stalling for time. 'Long and complicated. I'm sure that isn't why you brought me here.'

Gabriel shrugged easily. 'I'm not going anywhere.'

Ariana stared at him, at the sunlight dancing across his features, at the solid bulk of his body that made her feel protected. She took a deep breath and decided to trust him. After she had told him everything, about Liberty and the party, Gabriel looked at her thoughtfully, his blue eyes holding hers. 'Somebody must know something.'

'But who? I keep expecting to get a call from the police. I wish I knew what really happened to Liberty. Things got . . . complicated between us, but she was a good person, and a good actress too, one who was going somewhere. Better than me.'

'You're a good person, Ariana,' Gabriel said gently.

'She had her whole life in front of her.'

Gabriel took her hand. 'So do you. Everyone has to

grow up sometime. And perhaps you need a man, and not a boy?'

'A man like you?' Ariana held his gaze, which he returned.

'Perhaps. Jonny is more than just a Hollywood bad boy, he's also a stupid brat who's caught up in some serious stuff and he's way out of his depth. You need to be careful.'

'How do you know that, have you been snooping?' She narrowed her eyes, warily.

'I don't need to snoop, his reputation precedes him, and the stories about his nasty habits. It's hardly a secret, but he's worse than you think he is.'

Ariana sighed and stood up, pulling her dress over her head to reveal a red halterneck bikini that made her look like a classic pin-up girl, with her hourglass figure. She could feel Gabriel's eyes on her body, and something had shifted in the air between them. 'Maybe you're right, but I don't want to talk about Jonny today.' She felt lighter after unburdening herself to Gabriel, but could she really trust him? She narrowed her eyes, appraising him for a moment, then said playfully. 'Right now, I'm feeling hot! Come on, enough talk.'

Laughing, Ariana ran into the sea, the cool Mediterranean water wonderfully refreshing on her sizzling skin. She plunged beneath the waves, swimming underwater like a dolphin before coming up for air, droplets settling on her flawless skin like diamonds, the swell lapping at her slender shoulders. Gabriel surfaced beside her, his blond waves slicked back, rivulets racing down his powerful torso. They stared at one another, and it was impossible to ignore the electricity crackling between them.

'Why did you invite me here?' Ariana asked, their faces inches away in the water.

'Like I said, I thought it would be nice to get away from the city for a day. And I wanted to get to know you better.' Gabriel's voice was husky, desire in his eyes.

'How much better?' Ariana's pulse was racing in excitement and anticipation. Yes, she was attracted to him, she could no longer deny it.

A burst of longing surged through her, making her feel reckless. She tilted her head and Gabriel responded, his lips finding hers, their bodies melding together like it was the most natural thing in the world. Her fingertips slid over the taut muscles of his back as his strong hands grasped her waist and Ariana surrendered to his touch, lost in the moment and unable to think of anything except how good it felt to finally kiss him, and—

Suddenly she pulled away, full of uncertainty. What if Gabriel had deliberately planned to seduce her, and she'd fallen straight into his trap? She knew how badly he wanted the hotel, and it seemed suspiciously convenient that he would pursue the woman who now owned it.

Gabriel burned with intensity, as though he'd read her thoughts. 'I've never met anyone like you, Ariana. You're beautiful, and an enigma. I can't stop thinking about you.'

Ariana didn't respond, her heart beating fast. She wanted him to kiss her again, but her mind was whirling and she couldn't seem to think straight, afraid of making any impulsive decisions she might come to regret. No, this could wait. 'Don't they say never mix business with pleasure?' she said, slipping out of his arms and swimming back towards the shore.

Gabriel took the bait and gave chase, ploughing through the shallow waters after her as Ariana shrieked and giggled, the two of them falling, exhausted, onto the powdery sand.

'I won,' Ariana laughed, as Gabriel collapsed beside her.

'No, *I* won,' he grinned, leaning over to kiss her once again. 'I always win.'

Ariana could taste the salt on his lips, running her fingers through his damp hair, her breathing coming fast. She could feel the heat rising in her body as Gabriel pulled her closer. It would have been so easy to get carried away with the warm Mediterranean sun on their bodies, the azure sea lapping at their toes. It was idyllic and it would be simple to give in to her longing and let him do all the things her body was crying out for.

'Not this time,' she whispered, sitting up and pulling away. 'Not like this.'

Seeming to understand, Gabriel sat up and wrapped his arms around her, 'We can't ignore this,' he said, and kissed her gently.

'We have to, for now,' she answered. Her body and her mind were fighting against each other. She was used to getting what she wanted and right now she knew exactly what that was. But inside she could hear her grandmother's voice: *If it is real, it is worth waiting for, Ari.*

As they finished the champagne and ate lunch from the cool box Gabriel had brought, Ariana felt the time slip by, and knew that the voice was right.

La Provence
20 May 2009

HUGE BLAZE AT LE MARTINEZ

A huge fire broke out at the historic Cannes hotel, Le Martinez, late on Tuesday night.

Plumes of smoke could be seen rising from the art deco building, which has played host to film stars, VIPs, and royalty since opening in 1929.

The hotel had been preparing to host the Palme Gala, a prestigious event for Palme d'Or nominees and jury members, this Saturday, ahead of the main prize-giving on Sunday.

While the cause of the fire has not yet been confirmed, early reports suggest that the blaze, which began in the Palmier ballroom where the gala was to be held, may have been started by a construction worker overloading an electrical circuit.

Due to the festival, the hotel was at capacity, but all guests were evacuated safely with no casualties, and the fire was quickly extinguished.

Le Martinez is expected to remain closed for a number of weeks while renovations take place.

Chapter 20

It was early morning, and Ariana was slicing through the cool water in the swimming pool of the Hotel du Soleil. She had the place to herself and was enjoying the workout, refreshing her body and focusing her mind. She needed it after last night. She'd barely slept.

She and Gabriel had returned to the hotel after their date, unsure where the evening would take them – perhaps a drink in the bar and a chance to deepen the connection they'd formed on the island. They'd only just sat down, in a cosy corner with two glasses of cognac, when they became aware of a hubbub outside and were alerted to the fire at Le Martinez by shouts of alarm from guests who'd spotted the billows of grey smoke from their rooms. Everyone immediately dashed out onto the terrace, which had an unrivalled view over the famous Croisette where the Martinez was situated, watching in shock as fire engines came wailing down the street.

It was growing dark, but the lights on the shoreline illuminated the scene as guests streamed out of the hotel, evacuating onto the beach. The road was temporarily closed, and passers-by stopped to stare as police tried to move them back.

Not long after that, the reception phone started ringing off the hook with guests displaced from the Martinez who were trying to find a bed for the night. They hadn't been allowed back into their rooms, and many had nothing but the clothes they were standing up in. Ariana and Gabriel, aided by Constance, had swung into action, checking people in, allocating rooms, offering food and drink, sourcing spare clothes and whatever was needed. They'd waived the bill; Ariana had insisted on it. Not only was it the right thing to do, but she had a less altruistic motive too – it was the perfect opportunity to re-establish the reputation of the hotel, to show that they could offer great service and step up in a crisis. Ariana found that she loved the adrenaline high of having to swing into action; perhaps, after years of watching her father and grandparents direct operations, it came naturally to her.

It had been almost three in the morning when Ariana had finally fallen into bed, but the buzz had kept her awake, her mind racing, her body humming. She'd finally given in and got back up at six for her swim as the sun rose in a stunning wash of soft pink and pale yellow. The sky was hazy, the smell of smoke still lingering in the air. Thank God no one had been hurt.

Ariana could only imagine how she would have felt if that had been the Hotel du Soleil. The thought caused her heart to race and made her stomach clench with fear. She felt proprietorial towards this place already, she realized. It was under her skin, just like it was under Gabriel's, she thought, a smile playing around her lips at the thought of him.

She'd been hoping to see him that morning – he'd been on her mind as she slipped into her white high-cut bikini and sauntered down to the pool – but there'd been no sign of him. It was still early, she told herself, pushing down the feelings of disappointment.

In truth, Ariana wasn't sure how things stood between them. She'd opened up to him about Liberty and her wild time in LA, confessing shame-facedly that she'd been drunk and high and didn't remember what happened. It had felt cathartic, being able to talk openly and honestly about the situation, as Gabriel listened intently without interrupting.

He'd urged her to go to the police about the messages, but what could she say? There was no law against sending messages. They weren't even threatening; there was no blackmail or extortion. Their sole purpose seemed to be to try and frighten her. Besides, Ariana had heard nothing from the police since she'd left LA and she wanted to keep it that way. She had no intention of drawing more attention to herself, to dredge up the past and flag her name alongside Liberty's.

Now a prick of anxiety began to steal over Ariana. She wondered if now he'd had time to think about everything, he viewed her differently. Or maybe it had been what she'd feared all along – nothing more than a ruse to discover her secrets and exploit her weakness. She *did* like him, Ariana admitted to herself, and she wanted him to like her too.

And yet, she'd come no closer to finding out *his* secrets. She didn't know how his father had died, or why his mother hadn't left her room since. She didn't know how

Elana had come to own the hotel, or why it seemed to be so important to the du Lac family. Instead, Ariana had been carried away with Gabriel's kisses, distracted by the way his touch had made her feel, overcome by the heat flooding through her body . . .

She swam to the edge of the pool and climbed out, rivulets of water streaming down her body, as she wrapped herself in a branded hotel towel that had seen better days.

Ariana pulled on her sunglasses and looked up at the hotel. *Her* hotel. If she wanted answers, she mused, perhaps she should go straight to the woman who could provide them: Madeleine du Lac.

Right at the very top of the building, in the largest suite with the best view, was where Madame resided. It seemed bizarre that the two women hadn't met yet, and that Gabriel's mother still seemed to be calling the shots despite the fact she no longer owned the hotel and hadn't for some time.

Ariana narrowed her eyes as she stared up at the top floor. Gabriel had said his mother rarely came downstairs, and Ariana imagined her like Miss Havisham, or Mr Rochester's wife – the madwoman in the attic. Why shouldn't she go and introduce herself? Ariana thought determinedly. It was her hotel, after all, and it was the perfectly polite thing to do.

She squeezed the water from her hair, patting herself down until she was completely dry, before slipping on her wedge heels and heading inside. It was time to meet the mysterious Madame du Lac at last.

* * *

Ariana emerged from her room, locking the door with the old-fashioned key and set off along the corridor. She was intrigued and somewhat nervous to meet Gabriel's mother. She wondered whether they looked alike, or if Madame du Lac more closely resembled Constance. She wondered if Madeleine would like *her*; inexplicably, Ariana wanted Gabriel's mother to approve of her. And more importantly, would *she* like Madeleine? After all, Madame du Lac's continued residency at the hotel depended on Ariana's goodwill.

After her conversation on the island with Gabriel, Ariana was feeling uncharacteristically sympathetic. She understood both his and his mother's position – they'd spent years at the hotel, and it was their home. She didn't want to cast them out into the street, but she had to think like a businesswoman too.

She'd dressed smartly, in a powder-blue Ralph Lauren suit and white silk blouse, as she wanted Madame du Lac to know that she meant business. Madeleine had lived at the hotel for almost forty years, longer than anyone else; she was best placed to advise Ariana on how to move on from the mistakes of the past, and what she could do to restore the property to its former glory.

In return for letting Madame du Lac stay, Ariana wanted honesty: what was the connection between Madeleine and Elana? Why had it remained a secret that Elana was the real owner? Out of sheer curiosity, Ariana wanted to ask what had happened to Alain, and why Madeleine had barely left her room since his death.

She reached the end of the corridor and knocked smartly on the door, her heart thumping.

Silence.

For a moment, Ariana wondered whether Madeleine was even in residence, but Gabriel had said that she never went out. Perhaps she was still sleeping?

She raised her hand to knock again, but stopped as she heard a movement inside, and footsteps slowly coming closer. Then a voice – gravelly, suspicious – demanded, 'Who is it?'

Ariana cleared her throat. 'Ariana Theodosis.'

There was a long pause. Ariana wondered if Madame du Lac might refuse to open the door, but then she heard the sound of a chain being unlatched and the next moment the two women were face to face with one another at last.

Madame du Lac was petite and poised, dressed immaculately in a tweed Chanel suit, her grey hair swept back in an elegant chignon. There was something in her elegance, her bearing, that reminded Ariana of her grandmother.

Madeleine's sharp, blue eyes stared at Ariana, who spoke first.

'*Bonjour*, madame, my name is Ariana Theo—'

'I know who you are. I wondered when you'd come to see me.'

She stood aside and Ariana entered, looking around curiously. The suite was enormous, and it was like stepping into a time warp. The furniture clearly hadn't been updated since the 1980s, and the walls were covered in floral paper, the pastel pink carpet worn and threadbare, and there was a strange sense of stillness, as though even the air itself was stale, though it was clean. Ariana longed to pull aside the curtains and throw open the French doors, to let sunlight and the scent of the sea brine flood the room and cleanse it, but she remained standing where she was.

Madame du Lac sat down in her armchair and indicated that Ariana should take a seat opposite. She smoothed her skirt and crossed her ankles, feeling as though she were back at Marlborough College and had been summoned to the headmistress for being caught smoking.

For a moment, Madeleine didn't speak, simply scrutinized Ariana, taking in everything from head to toe. The elderly woman's eyes were quick and keen, though Ariana noticed that she held an old-fashioned lace handkerchief tightly in her hand, worrying it beneath her fingers. Ariana tried not to feel intimidated, reminding herself that she owned the hotel, but her grandmother had drummed into her to defer to those that were older and wiser, so she kept respectfully quiet until she was spoken to.

Finally, Madame du Lac began to speak. Her voice was strong, with only a hint of a tremor that suggested her frailty.

'Ordinarily I'd offer you some coffee and pastries, but my daughter watches me like a hawk and will be up here to see what's going on before I put the receiver down. We might prefer that this meeting stays between us, for now,' Madame du Lac said carefully. Ariana noticed that she spoke in the clipped style of the well-heeled French person.

'As you wish,' Ariana replied. 'I have a lot of questions. I'm hoping that you can answer them.'

Madeleine laughed scornfully. 'Just like Gabriel. Always asking questions, always thinking I can provide the answers. I understand you're well acquainted with my son.'

Ariana's mind flashed back to yesterday on the island, kissing him passionately in the sea, their bodies pressed together on the soft, golden sand. She felt her cheeks flush and replied primly, 'Yes, he's been very helpful.'

'Indeed,' Madame said, through pursed lips.

Ariana reasserted herself, putting Gabriel to the back of her mind for now. 'Madame du Lac, as you're aware, the Hotel du Soleil was left to me in the Will of Elana Theodosis, my grandmother. I had no idea that she owned the hotel, and nor did my father. Did you know?'

'I am not an idiot,' Madeleine snapped. 'Of course I knew Elana owned the hotel.'

'So you knew my grandmother?'

Madeleine hesitated, as if she realized that she'd revealed more than she'd intended. For a moment she looked contrite. 'Yes, I was very sorry to hear from Gabriel of her passing. Please accept my condolences.'

'Thank you. Were the two of you friends?'

Madeleine looked uncomfortable, and Ariana reminded herself to go slowly, but it was so hard to restrain herself when she finally seemed to be getting somewhere.

'At one time, yes, I would say we were great friends. You remind me of her, you know,' Madeleine observed through watchful eyes. 'You have the same spirit, the same strength . . . The same beauty.'

'Thank you,' Ariana murmured. She felt a poignant mixture of pride and sadness as she thought of Yaya, momentarily lost in her memories, before remembering that her grandmother would have admonished her to stop daydreaming. 'Did she buy the hotel from you, when you were struggling financially? Is that what happened?'

Madeleine shot her a sharp look, and Ariana wondered whether she'd gone too far. She didn't want to embarrass Madeleine by talking about money troubles.

'Alain, my husband, dealt with all the finances,' she explained, waving her hand dismissively. 'It was all very . . . distressing. He promised me that everything would be all right, and I trusted him. I made my sacrifice, and he said I would never have to leave the Hotel du Soleil. He *promised*,' she said forcefully.

While she had no intention of asking Madame du Lac to leave, it was impossible to promise her that she could stay forever.

'I'm trying to understand how I came to be the owner,' Ariana explained gently. 'What my grandmother's connection was. The news was a surprise to the whole family – we don't understand why she never told us.'

'How would I know?' Madeleine retorted, her eyes flashing stubbornly.

Ariana thought for a moment, deciding to try a different approach. 'When was the last time you saw Elana?'

Madeleine stared into space as she murmured, 'Alain's funeral.'

Ariana was shocked, but tried to hide her surprise. The two women must have been close friends if Elana had flown from Greece to attend Alain's funeral. She wondered if Gabriel knew Elana had been there, if he remembered her, if he knew how close the two families had been at one time. Madeleine was still talking.

'It was sweet of them both to come. Aristotle was always so busy, but he was a true friend to us when we had very few left.'

'Why?' Ariana pressed, sitting forward in her eagerness. 'What did he do?'

Madeleine's voice was shakier now. 'He promised, don't you see? And now it seems we are to be thrown out.' The woman started to tug at a set of pearls at her neck. 'I feel hot, please get me a glass of cool water.' She indicated the dresser against the wall. 'Over there.'

'Why don't you let me open the windows for you to get some air?'

'No, don't touch them, just the water.'

Ariana did as she was told, and poured Madeleine a glass of water from the carafe. As she watched Madame du Lac gulping from the glass, she noticed the frayed cuff on her Chanel jacket, the yellowing collar of her shirt and felt a stab of compassion. How had this lonely and frightened woman come to be trapped in her room this way – what on earth had happened to the du Lac family?

Madeleine handed Ariana the drained glass and then dabbed at her brow with her handkerchief. 'Thank you for coming to see me, but I'm afraid I must rest now. Your visit has been rather upsetting, and I'm very tired. I'm sure you understand.'

'Madame du Lac—'

'Goodbye, Mademoiselle Theodosis.'

With that, Ariana was dismissed. The shutters had come back down and Madeleine had retreated.

As she made her way back to her room, a sense of frustration settled over Ariana. She was on the cusp of making a connection, of unlocking the secret, but she couldn't help feeling that her meeting with Madame du Lac had raised more questions than it had answered.

Chapter 21

September 1986

Madeleine and Elana were sitting at a table on the terrace at the Hotel du Soleil. Madeleine looked chic in an Emanuel Ungaro dress with shoulder pads and a nipped-in waist that showed off her petite figure, still tiny even after two children. Elana was a decade older than her, but still looked striking in an electric blue, one-shoulder gown, her mane of dark hair perfectly coiffed.

It was almost midnight, and the two women were drinking dry Martinis, garnished with Greek olives. It was nearing the end of the season, and the hotel was quiet – although that wasn't the only reason for the lack of guests. There was a peculiar feeling in the autumn air, as though everything was coming to an end.

Madeleine sipped her drink and checked the watch on her slim wrist.

'What time will the boys be back, do you think?'

'Who knows, with Aristotle, once he gets the bit between his teeth. The last time he went to Monte Carlo he came back having

lost a yacht in a game of poker, but he won a Rolls-Royce so wasn't too disheartened.'

'I hope Alain doesn't do anything silly . . .'

Madeleine looked worried. Elana watched her as she played nervously with her engagement ring, twisting it round her finger, the enormous stone glinting in the candlelight.

'Is everything all right?'

Madeleine hesitated. She was desperate to share her fears but hated the thought of betraying her husband. The situation felt like Pandora's Box – once you'd let the bad things out, it was impossible to put them back in again. But she needed to talk to someone.

'I'm worried about Alain,' Madeleine admitted. 'Not just him – our future, our marriage.' Now that she'd begun speaking, it seemed impossible to stop. 'I asked him not to go tonight, but he refused, and we had the most terrible argument. Oh, nothing to do with Aristotle,' she explained quickly. 'We simply don't have the money for him to keep spending like this, but night after night he goes out to gamble. I'm terrified. It's like he doesn't understand the consequences. We've emptied our savings, sold the car, fired staff, cut back everywhere we possibly can . . .' Madeleine was close to tears with the relief of letting it all out.

Elana looked mortified. 'I'm so sorry. I never realized things were this bad. I sensed there was some tension between you, but Alain loves you deeply, I know he does. We've been friends for years, and I know how much he adores you.'

'Not anymore.' Madeleine shook her head. 'He's like a different person. All we do is argue. I don't know what to do. I'm so scared for us, scared for Constance and Gabriel. What future can we offer them? If we have to sell this place, we'll be left with nothing . . .' She broke down, sobbing.

Elana took her friend in her arms, letting her cry. By the time Madeleine had calmed down, Elana had devised a tentative plan. 'You won't lose the hotel, I promise you. I won't let that happen. I'm sorry – I would never have let Aristotle take Alain out tonight if I'd known. I'll speak to him. But don't worry, my dear. Everything will be all right, I promise you . . .'

Gabriel strolled smartly past reception and through the Hotel du Soleil, greeting the staff on his way, most of whom were still dealing with a flurry of requests and complaints from the sudden influx of well-heeled and demanding clientele. He'd woken early, after the drama of the previous night and the arrival of the guests from the Martinez. He suppressed a grin now, unable to avoid a shot of enjoyment that the lethargic staff were finding themselves having to run a proper bustling hotel for once. As usual these days, his thoughts turned to Ariana. The hotel was completely full, with every room booked, and if she needed his help he'd be there. Maybe she would be good for this place, perhaps if they could come to some arrangement . . .

He'd gone for an early breakfast, hoping to bump into her, but there'd been no sign of her. Perhaps she was still sleeping – they hadn't got to bed until the early hours. Gabriel wondered whether he should go and knock on her door, or whether that might look too eager. He'd never previously had a problem working out how to behave around women – certainly not since he'd left his teenage years behind – but, then again, he'd never felt like this about anyone before. Ariana Theodosis made him feel like a nervous schoolboy, unsure how to act, what to do, what to say.

He remembered the feel of her from their time together yesterday; the way her skin had shimmered in the water, the rivulets of water running down her flawless body, the feel of her lips on his, the heat of her . . . He shook off the memory, knowing he needed to focus on other issues today.

Aside from that, their conversation yesterday had set him thinking, reflecting on painful issues he'd pushed to the back of his mind. He'd always avoided speaking to his mother about his father's death and her subsequent behaviour, accepted being fobbed off and placated with half-truths. But no more. As he strode through the hotel he'd grown up in, the place he knew arguably better than anyone, but which had never truly been his, he was determined to get some answers.

'Gabriel,' his mother sighed, weary but resigned, when he knocked on the door.

They exchanged pleasantries, but Gabriel could see in her eyes that she knew why he was there. The sands were shifting, and Madame du Lac couldn't hide her secrets for much longer.

'*Maman*, I met with Ariana Theodosis yesterday.'

'Yes, I heard the two of you have been spending a lot of time together.' Madeleine remained straight-backed and upright despite her diminutive stature. She was clearly not going to make this easy.

A flicker of irritation crossed Gabriel's face. 'You have Constance well trained. She's wasted here, she should have been a spy.'

'Perhaps you're not as discreet as you think you are.'

Madame du Lac looked infuriatingly smug, and Gabriel bit back a smart retort. They'd barely said two words to each other, and already they were fighting. They'd achieve nothing if they carried on this way. Yet, despite his mother's triumphant expression, Gabriel knew that the power balance had tilted. Previously, Madeleine had held all the cards – or so he'd thought. Now, despite still living in the hotel, her situation was precarious; she didn't own the hotel and hadn't for some time.

But before Gabriel could speak, his mother announced, 'I have met with her too. Perhaps I am one step ahead of you?'

'What? When?'

'This morning. She came to see me. She's very beautiful. I can see why she has you wrapped around her little finger.'

Gabriel exhaled slowly, not wanting to start another argument. He was still reeling from the revelation that Ariana had spoken to his mother. He wondered why – had he said something yesterday to encourage her? Was she deliberately going behind his back, plotting to get Madeleine onside?

He kept his voice even and asked, 'What did she want?'

'Questions, questions and more questions – just like you. Did you put her up to it?'

'*Maman*, why must you always think the worst of me? She's curious – as am I. She wants to understand the history, to know what happened. And she's starting to put the pieces together.'

'She should mind her own business.'

'She's smart,' Gabriel continued, warming to his theme and instinctively defending Ariana. 'Ambitious. And she has plans for this place – plans that don't involve you.'

'You always were a pushover for a pretty face – just like your father.'

'I'm trying to help you, *Maman*!' Gabriel burst out. 'But I can't do that unless you tell me what you know.'

He saw his mother weaken, confusion and uncertainty crossing her features. For a brief moment she looked vulnerable and defeated, but then it passed and she grew defiant once again, her expression resolute.

'I don't know anything. She can never make me leave this place. Your father promised me.' She jammed her lips shut in a stubborn line.

'Of course she can, don't you see? The truth will come out one way or another. Ariana hasn't had to look very hard to find out about our past – she knows all about father's debts, about his gambling. I'm sure there's more to come. Don't you think it's about time you were honest with me? How am I supposed to help you if you see me as the enemy? I am your son.'

To his surprise, Madeleine's eyes filled with tears. Gabriel was stunned. He didn't think he'd ever seen her cry, not even at his father's funeral. He moved towards her, embracing her, and was shocked to feel his mother's bones through her dress. When was the last time he had held her like this?

He helped her to her armchair and sat her down, taking a handkerchief from the drawer and pouring her a glass of water.

'*Maman, je t'en prie,*' Gabriel began softly. 'Tell me everything.'

He looked into her eyes imploringly. Madeleine du Lac stared back, and Gabriel could see the doubt and fear. He gently took her hand, crouching down beside her, and waited.

* * *

'It's so frustrating, Papa. I'm trying to discover the link to Yaya, and how she came to own the hotel, but everyone's keeping secrets and I don't understand why. Madame du Lac seems to be living in the past, and no one seems to accept that *I'm* the owner now. I feel like I'm being blocked at every turn.'

'Now I'm the one who doesn't understand. Why is this so important to you, Ari?'

'I don't know,' Ariana burst out, although she had her suspicions. She hadn't mentioned Gabriel's name to her father; Demetrios knew her better than anyone in the world, and Ariana was certain he'd hear something in her voice that would betray her.

'Look, my darling, last week you wanted to live in Los Angeles and be an actress. This week you want to live in the South of France and run a hotel. You're finding your way, I understand that, but don't get so overemotional about everything.'

Ariana was incensed by her father's patronizing tone. 'You don't understand,' she snapped back, realizing too late that she sounded exactly like a petulant teenager.

'Look, when the festival's over, come home and we'll talk. I'm sure you're having a lot of fun out there – I remember how you adored Cannes when we went together many years ago. I know it's glamorous and exciting, but don't get carried away. Regarding the hotel, I haven't changed my opinion that the best way forward would be to bring in a management company and leave well alone.'

'But I want to try and—' Ariana broke off, thinking how best to explain herself. 'It's giving me a purpose,' she said eventually.

'Ari, you weren't born to run a hotel on the Riviera. When you're ready to talk seriously, give me a call. I love you, but I'm very busy right now.'

To Ariana's fury, Demetrios hung up. For a moment, she stood completely still with shock, staring in disbelief at her phone. The television was on silently in the background, the news channel, France 24, playing footage of the fire at the Martinez. Without thinking, Ariana turned up the volume, listening to interviews with the hotel manager and the firefighters, along with some eyewitnesses. Then the reporter spoke about the illustrious history of the Martinez, the great and the good who'd stayed there, and how the hotel had been due to hold the celebrated Palme Gala that weekend . . .

Sparks were firing in Ariana's brain. Not simply anger at her father's dismissal, but the beginnings of a plan . . .

She remembered her first day at the hotel. It was barely a week ago, but it felt like a lifetime. So much had happened since then. She remembered exploring the grounds and strolling into the ballroom, an impressive, cavernous, empty space, with an incomparable view over the Bay of Cannes and the palm-fringed peninsula of the Pointe Croisette. What if . . .?

Ariana knew it was madness, that events like this took weeks – months – of planning. She had mere days. But if Gabriel could help – he'd said himself that the du Lac name still meant something in Cannes – and Shauna, her stepmother, a famous actress with connections right across the industry. If Ariana could pull it off – and it might just be possible – it would put the hotel on the map and show her critics exactly what she was capable of.

Her mobile was still in her hand and she called Gabriel's number. It rang then cut off, going through to voicemail.

'It's Ariana,' she said, hearing the excitement in her own voice. 'Call me as soon as you can.'

She walked out of the room, heading down the grand staircase to go check out the ballroom. As she descended, she couldn't help but think about Gabriel's father, and the night that he died. How many other events had this staircase seen, what other secrets did it hold? Ariana paused for a moment, her hand resting on the beautifully curved wooden banister as her foot stepped onto the Italian marble stair. The hotel really was beautiful, she thought, she would never want to change it too much.

When she reached reception, she noticed Constance standing guard like a wolf.

'Do you know where Gabriel is?' Ariana asked, smiling politely.

'He's speaking with our mother, *Madame Wood*,' Constance replied sarcastically.

It took Ariana a moment to realize what she was referring to and then she remembered – the false name she'd given when she'd originally checked in. She'd only meant it as a joke; she was certain now that everyone knew exactly who she was.

'Thank you. That's very helpful,' Ariana smiled brightly, amused by Constance's look of confusion. As she was about to turn away, she remembered something, 'Oh, while you're here, can you put this in the hotel safe?' She put her hands out and pulled the ring off her finger, the diamonds catching the lights overhead. She handed it to Constance, who took it, and looked at it, seemingly flummoxed for a moment.

'Well, you do have a safe, don't you?' she said.

Constance seemed to be struggling for words, and looked flushed around the cheeks, but said, 'Yes, of course we do. I'll put it there now.' She placed the ring in her pocket.

Ariana turned around and walked back the way she'd come. The ballroom could wait until later – now was the perfect time to run her idea past Gabriel *and* Madame du Lac.

As Ariana approached Madeleine's suite, she raised her hand to knock and heard Gabriel's voice. What perfect timing, she thought, unable to deny the flutter of butter-flies at the thought of seeing him again.

She took a moment to compose herself, sweeping tendrils of hair away from her face and smoothing down her clothes, before realizing that an argument was taking place inside. Gabriel's voice was raised, and Madeleine was crying.

In spite of herself, Ariana's curiosity was piqued. It felt horribly reminiscent of when she'd overheard Gabriel talking in his office, the very first time they'd met. She'd thought then that no good ever came of eavesdropping, and she'd been proved right, yet there was an old Greek saying, *Know how to listen and you will profit*, and here she was again . . .

'She's a sweet girl – trusting, naive. She should be careful that no one takes advantage of that.'

It was Gabriel's voice, and he was speaking in French. Ariana wondered whether she'd fully understood. Were they talking about *her*?

His mother mumbled something that Ariana couldn't hear, then Gabriel replied, 'Listen, *Maman*, don't get upset.

Ariana Theodosis has no idea what she's doing. She has no experience of running a hotel – no experience of much in life apart from wearing designer clothes and going to parties. This place belongs to us – always has, always will. But don't worry. I have a plan . . .'

Ariana was in shock, unable to believe what she'd just heard. This was part of a plan? What she'd suspected all along, and convinced herself was paranoia, was actually true? Gabriel's convincing lines, his apparent concern for her, even his kisses – all a lie. All a trick.

The voices became muffled, as though they were speaking more quietly, or had moved to a different part of the room, but Ariana had heard enough. Cheeks flaming, she turned on her heels and marched away.

Ariana felt sick. She felt like an idiot. But most of all, she felt furious. Gabriel, and Madame du Lac, were going to feel the full force of her wrath.

Chapter 22

Robert was nervous. He was standing on the main deck of a superyacht, surrounded by the dazzling waters of the Bay of Cannes. The boat was too large to be moored in the harbour so it was anchored out at sea, its white paintwork glistening in the golden hour light.

It was another beautiful evening on the French Riviera, the air fragrant and balmy, the sun beginning to sink as the shadows lengthened over the rugged hills. Robert could see why artists and creatives had been drawn to the region over the years – Picasso, Monet, Matisse, Hemingway, Fitzgerald. Even the Hotel du Cap where he was staying had originally started life as an artist's retreat. That kind of lifestyle had its appeal. Sometimes Robert thought about giving it all up, saying 'sod you' to Hollywood and buying a rambling pile in the countryside to spend his days writing and painting. If Elizabeth wanted him to do that, then he would. He'd do anything for her – and that's what he intended to tell her tonight.

Behind his sunglasses, Robert squinted, scanning the port and watching the boats zipping in and out. He was conscious of his appearance, but knew he looked good in light grey trousers and a loose white shirt, the sleeves pushed up casually past his elbows, the buttons undone to mid-torso revealing the dark hair on his chest. A few hundred metres away was a flotilla of smaller boats; Robert knew that on board were photographers, organized by Fran, with the aim of capturing every intimate moment during the romantic evening ahead. Robert guessed he owed Fran a favour; he doubted Liz would agree to dinner with him right now, but if it was presented as a work gig then she could hardly refuse.

In the distance, Robert made out a small speedboat, skimming across the water and heading straight for the yacht, white waves cresting behind like a plume of feathers. That was her, he felt sure. God, he wanted a cigarette. Or a drink. Though neither would go down well with Elizabeth, he reckoned.

Robert stood up a little straighter, smoothing down his dark hair, surreptitiously checking his reflection in the gleaming metal railings. Glancing round, he made sure that everything was immaculate. The table arrangement was flawless, white porcelain on white linen, and every-where he looked there were bunches of Liz's favourite white avalanche roses, along with a bottle of Dom Pérignon Rosé 1996 – the year that they'd met – on ice.

The vessel drew closer and then he could see her, her blonde hair tucked neatly beneath a colourful Hermès scarf, oversized sunglasses hiding her face. She looked spectacular, elegant in a white lace dress that clung to her perfect hour-glass figure, diamonds glittering at her wrists and throat.

Robert's heart ached with longing. She was so perfect, he couldn't believe she was married to him. And then he remembered that she didn't want to be married to him anymore. Well, he was hoping to change her mind tonight . . .

Robert bounded down to the lower deck to greet his wife. One of the crew members helped her on board and then she was right there in front of him in a cloud of Joy by Jean Patou, her blonde hair spilling out around her shoulders as she pulled off her scarf. Robert felt like a tongue-tied teenager. She leaned in to kiss him and he hoped it was out of genuine affection and not just for the cameras.

'Hi Robbie,' Liz said. She kept her tone and expression neutral, as he tried to read her mood.

'All right, princess?' Robert said softly. 'You look stunning, as always.'

'Thank you.'

Robert took her hand and led her up the stairs, pulling out her chair for her to sit down – all in clear view of the photographers.

'It's beautiful,' Elizabeth said, nodding appreciatively at the stylish table décor, adding archly, 'Did you do it all yourself?'

'Napkin folding is my forte. I planned on making a career out of it, if the acting thing hadn't worked out,' Robert grinned.

The internal doors slid open and a waiter approached, offering them both a glass of pink champagne.

'Am I allowed?' Robert asked, hesitantly.

'For heaven's sake, you're a grown man, you make your own decisions.'

Robert frowned, playing with the stem of the glass uncertainly.

'Oh, go ahead,' Liz said, rolling her eyes. 'Champagne barely counts. It's the whisky that sends you wild.'

'In that case – cheers! To us.'

Elizabeth didn't respond to his toast, merely raising her eyebrows at him as the waiter returned with an amuse-bouche of blinis loaded with crème fraiche and caviar.

'I'm glad you came tonight,' Robert told her.

'Balls made it seem like it was non-negotiable.'

'Everything's non-negotiable with her,' Robert grinned. 'But I'm glad. It's better when it's just the two of us, and we can cut through all the bullshit.'

'Darling, I don't want you to get the wrong idea. I'm here because I'm contractually obliged to be. I haven't changed my mind about us.'

Robert felt a stab of frustration shoot through him and thumped his fist on the table, instantly regretting it, and hoped the paps hadn't caught the angry gesture. 'Christ, Liz, help me out here. What do you want me to do?'

'I *wanted* you to come home at night and not leave me on my own,' Elizabeth hissed, hurt and anger spilling out. 'I wanted you not to need half a bottle of Scotch in the morning before you could even function. I wanted you to not make me a laughing stock because some Vegas cocktail waitress sold her story of your one-night stand to the *National Enquirer*.'

'*Alleged* one-night stand.'

'Only because you were too drunk to remember what happened. You can't turn back the clock. You can't put those things right.'

'But I'll never do those things again. I've changed, I promise you. I'll do anything to prove it to you.'

'It's too late. I'm tired of having the same conversation over and over. You've well and truly burned your bridges.'

'I don't believe it, is there someone else?'

The waiter emerged through the sliding doors. He saw the looks on their faces and quickly retreated.

'Don't be an idiot. Of course not.'

'Can you honestly tell me you don't love me?' He was scrabbling for a toehold now, and he knew it; they'd never come this close to separation before and he could feel the ground shifting beneath him.

Elizabeth's eyes softened. 'Of course I still love you. That's the saddest part. I love you desperately, and yet I truly believe I'll be happier alone. I might never meet anyone again, but for my own sanity we can't be together.'

Robert stared sadly at her with dark, soulful eyes, his expression wounded as he absorbed her words. He stood up and walked over to her, offering his hand. Elizabeth frowned in confusion.

'Come with me,' he said tenderly.

'What . . .?'

'Come on, love,' Robert's expression was earnest, his blue eyes flashing with that irresistible twinkle.

Elizabeth let him guide her across the polished wooden deck, leaning against the railing and looking out at the view. To the north of them lay the magnificent sweep of the French coastline, with its clusters of honey-hued buildings and crescents of sandy beach; to the west, a vibrant sunset in vivid shades of crimson and gold. Robert stood behind her, wrapping his arms around her waist, his hands splaying over her hips. Elizabeth began to protest, but he whispered in her ear, 'Do you remember the first time we came here, after we'd wrapped the shoot for that bloody awful French and Italian co-production?'

She laughed easily at the memory. 'How could I forget,' she said. 'The Italian director didn't speak English, the production manager only spoke French and all the extras had been bused in from over the Spanish border.'

'I also hope you remember looking out over this view, and me telling you I'd never love anyone else again.'

Elizabeth felt her breath catch, 'Robbie . . .'

He could tell she was battling with herself. They'd always had incredible chemistry, the two of them sizzling between the sheets, unable to get enough of one another. The touch of her against him was driving him crazy, their bodies pressed tightly together, luxuriating in her sensuous curves. Robert began to kiss her neck in the way he knew she adored and heard her sigh with longing.

'Marry me,' he murmured.

She smiled, despite herself. 'We're already married . . . for a bit longer anyway.'

He held her beautiful face in his hand and met her gaze with his own. 'I mean every word. Let's renew our vows.'

Elizabeth turned to him so that they were facing each other, wrapped in one another's arms, lips inches apart. Neither were conscious of the photographers gathered on the jetty, waiting for the perfect shot. She stroked his forehead lovingly. 'I'm not getting through to that brain of yours, am I?'

'Think about it,' Robert whispered. 'Promise me.'

His lips brushed her ear, his breath hot on her neck. Fingertips danced across bare flesh, familiar yet forbidden. The electricity crackled between them.

'Maybe we should—' Elizabeth breathed.

Before she could finish there was a discreet cough from over by the door. Robert turned sharply, wanting to hurl himself across the deck and throttle the waiter with his bare hands.

'Give us a minute, mate.' He couldn't keep the anger from his voice.

'I'm so sorry to interrupt . . .' The poor waiter was almost shaking. 'We've had a call from Francesca Ballard. She said she's been trying your mobile, sir, but no one's responding. She said it's urgent.'

'What the . . .?' Robert reached into his back pocket and pulled out his phone. Eighteen missed calls from Fran. He was about to ring her back, but the waiter interrupted.

'She advised that you go inside first,' he said, wincing apologetically, before adding, 'there was also an urgent letter arrived from your agent, Mrs Chappell.' He handed her an envelope.

Robert realized that Fran didn't want the photographers to get pictures and wondered what the hell was going on.

He strode inside, oblivious to the opulent interior with its plush cream sofas and burnished gold fittings. Elizabeth followed him, concern etched on her face as she opened the letter, while Robert listened to what Fran had to say.

'Are you out of your mind? What the hell have you done?'

She was screaming so loudly it felt as though she was in the room with him, and he held the phone away from his ear.

'I don't know,' he shrugged, genuinely puzzled. Perhaps the paps had got pictures of him slamming his fist on the table and word had already got back to Balls.

'Who is she? Tell me her name, Robert, and by God I hope she was worth it.'

'I don't know what you're talking about,' he protested, glancing nervously at Elizabeth, who could hear every word, a sick feeling growing in his stomach.

'Don't try and deny it – there are photos. They're running them tomorrow – every single newspaper, TV channel, news outlet . . . The studio is going ballistic.'

'Photos of what?' Robert almost yelled, frustration and tension overcoming him. This was clearly serious, but he wished Balls would stop talking in riddles.

'You and some young, scantily dressed woman on a park bench. Your arms around her, in what is euphemistically described as "an intimate position".'

A cold sweat broke out on Robert's skin, scrabbling around in his mind for what it could be. 'What on earth. . .' he demanded, a nauseous sensation stealing over him.

At that moment, Elizabeth thrust a picture under his nose, in the grainy picture he could see himself and Estée on the bench in the park. Their faces seemed almost pressed together, he appeared to be whispering in her ear and his arm was around her shoulders.

'Holy crap,' he burst out. 'It's not what it looks like, I swear to God.'

He looked at Liz, who backed away from him, shaking her head, her expression one of disbelief and betrayal.

'Well, you'd better have a pretty good explanation,' Francesca said, sounding livid. 'Because I don't think even *I* can save you this time.'

Chapter 23

Oh hell, thought Ariana, as she opened her eyes and looked around sleepily. She'd done it again. She was at the Hotel Splendid, down by the old port, and this was Jonny's room.

When Jonny called suggesting she come over for a nightcap, she had almost said no, then she remembered Gabriel and his betrayal. To her surprise, her hurt and anger ran deep. By the end of the day, she didn't want to think about it anymore, so it seemed like the perfect opportunity to let off some steam. They'd flirted outrageously, drunk far too much, and the night had inevitably ended with her falling into Jonny's bed.

She rolled over to find she was alone and realized she could hear the shower running in the bathroom. Quickly, Ariana got up and dressed; she had far too much to do today, plus she didn't want to be naked when Jonny emerged. Last night had been a mistake, and one she didn't intend to repeat.

As she pulled on the minidress she'd worn last night, Ariana glanced around the room, comparing it to the Hotel du Soleil. It was similarly traditional in style, although she was gratified to see her hotel had the better view, being situated up on the hill. She peered around the curtains, noticing paint chips flaking on the windowsill, and was surprised to be greeted by grey skies, the yachts in the harbour bobbing on the choppy water.

With a pang, she remembered meeting Gabriel there only a few days ago, the romantic trip they'd taken to the Îlot Saint-Ferréol, and how ridiculous she felt to have believed there could be something between them. She felt humiliated when she recalled how good it had felt to kiss him, the way her body had stirred when he'd caressed her skin . . . Angrily, Ariana turned away from the window, letting the curtains fall and plunging the room back into gloomy darkness as she pushed the memories aside.

On the bed, Jonny's phone lit up as it began to vibrate. Ariana glanced at it, but didn't recognize the name on the screen. Perhaps it was a director, or a producer; she knew Jonny had been hustling hard this week for meetings that he hoped would further his acting career, but didn't seem to be having much success. Perhaps he was already becoming box office poison. Ariana considered taking his phone into the bathroom for him – the shower was still running – but she wasn't ready to face him quite yet.

As she turned, she noticed that the wardrobe had been partially left open and was amused to see ten identical black T-shirts hanging from the rail, with almost as many pairs of black jeans folded on the shelf below. She was about to close the door when something caught her eye and nagged at the back of her brain, her instincts urging her to look again. There was a shoebox at the bottom of the closet, the lid dislodged. She nudged it with her toe so that it fell off completely, revealing the contents.

Ariana gasped.

Inside were two enormous bags of white powder, beside a smaller bag of brightly coloured pills and a wad of cash bound by an elastic band. Her heart sank. Gabriel had been right all along, Jonny was bad news in every sense.

The phone on the bed began to vibrate again and Ariana jumped guiltily. She heard the shower turn off, and a moment later Jonny wandered through, stark naked, drying his hair with a towel.

'Hey babe,' he winked. 'Aw, why did you spend time getting dressed? Now I'm gonna have to undress you all over again . . .'

'Jonny—' Ariana began.

He noticed his phone flashing on the bed and strolled across to pick it up. He swore, throwing it back down as though it were on fire. His mood seemed to shift instantly, and he began to pace back and forth, clearly agitated, but not just in his usual moody way, she'd seen what was in the box, and knew that this was serious.

'Jonny,' Ariana pressed, her tone sharper.

'What?' he snapped.

'What the hell is this?'

He followed Ariana's gaze to the stash in the bottom of the wardrobe. A peculiar look came over his face, his brain working overtime as he weighed up the options – lie, deny, make a joke. He settled for a belligerent shrug.

'Do I really have to explain it? You used to be pretty familiar with that stuff yourself,' he said, making the choice to brazen it out.

'Are you *insane*? There must be at least two kilos there, not to mention all the rest of it. When did you start dealing like this?' Ariana asked furiously. She knew he used to do a little small-time dealing back in LA – it was the reason he always got invited to parties, why he could be sure to get his name on any guest list. After his last stay in rehab, he'd told Ariana he only used occasionally and had the situation under control.

'When did you get so judgemental, Little Miss Righteous?' he mimicked her accent, clearly furious. 'It's none of your goddamn business, OK? And why the hell were you snooping around, going through my things?'

'I wasn't,' Ariana retorted hotly, knowing that was exactly what she'd been doing.

His phone began to ring again and he snatched it up, swearing, not answering it but holding it in his hand like a grenade that was about to explode. Then it suddenly became clear to her, she realized he wasn't angry. He was scared.

Ariana watched him through her feline eyes. She'd never seen him like this before. Jonny was a charmer, a chancer, a smooth talker. Sure, he had a dark side, but she'd never seen him shaken like this, stripped of all his confidence and swagger.

'What's going on?' she frowned. 'Don't lie to me.'

Jonny finished drying himself and reached for a pair of Calvin Klein boxers. For a moment, he didn't speak. He seemed to be trying to decide how much to reveal. His long dark hair was hanging wetly in his eyes and he peeked out from underneath his fringe, giving her a hint of his boyish grin. 'Yeah, so I've got myself in a bit of trouble.'

Ariana sighed and flopped down onto the bed. There was a sinking feeling in the pit of her stomach. *'Quelle surprise,'* she commented darkly.

Jonny looked genuinely vulnerable. 'This is different. This is some serious stuff. This is . . .' Jonny sat down beside her, running his hands over his face. 'I think they might actually kill me.'

Ariana stared at him, trying to work out if he was being serious, or exaggerating for dramatic effect. 'You'd better tell me everything.'

'So I kinda fell back into it – don't be like that!' he exclaimed, as Ariana rolled her eyes. 'You know how expensive it is living in LA, you gotta have the best of everything or else you're no one. We don't all have billionaire fathers to bankroll us.'

Ariana bristled at the dig. 'Your dad's hardly short of cash, Jonny. He's a Hollywood A-lister.'

'Yeah, but he doesn't give a damn about me,' Jonny said bitterly. His phone rang again and he leapt up, clearly panicking as he fumbled with the buttons and eventually switched it off. His breathing was coming fast, his eyes wild. 'It was just a way to earn some extra bucks. I was partying hard anyway and it got me invited to all the VIP spots, met some cool people, made some good connections. You know how it is.'

Ariana understood that everyone made mistakes, but it sounded as though Jonny had been pretty stupid.

'I got behind on the payments. They'd give me the goods on credit, I'm supposed to sell it for a profit and give them their cut. Easy, right? Except I started to get confused. The next day I'd have all this money in my wallet and go out and buy, like, whatever, and then I never seemed to have enough to pay them back.'

Ariana winced, knowing how easily Jonny could have suckered himself into all of this. 'They were pretty understanding though. I thought they were nice guys. They'd just be like, OK, here's some more, sell it and then you can pay back what you owe out of your share. But I never seemed to make it all back.' Jonny looked haunted. 'I was using myself, giving it away to people for free, having a ball . . . I wanted everyone to like me, and they did . . .'

'Enough with the self-pity. How much do you owe them, Jonny?' Ariana said quietly.

Jonny no longer looked like the cocky guy she knew. He looked miserable. Terrified. When he spoke, his voice was a whisper. 'Half a million.'

'Jesus!' Ariana looked stunned. 'Half a million dollars?'

'Yeah, although I've been dealing in euros here, so . . . exchange rates and stuff. I dunno. They offered me a chance to redeem myself when I told them I was coming here. These are serious guys, Ariana. They're like, Russian mafia or something. They're not messing around.'

'Can you go to the police?'

'Are you crazy? They'll be fishing my body out of the ocean before I finish dialling nine-one-one.'

There was a loaded pause as Jonny turned to look at her, and suddenly Ariana knew what he was going to ask.

'No, Jonny.'

'Please, Ariana. I'm desperate. You don't know what it's like.'

'I can't.'

'These guys are gonna kill me, they're gonna string me up. I have to get them the money by the end of the week. *This*' – he jabbed his hand, indicating the shoebox in the wardrobe – 'isn't gonna put a dent in it.'

'I can't. Surely you can see that. It's madness. I can't give you half a million dollars to pay off some Russian gangsters – can't you hear how that sounds? No.' Ariana stood up to leave.

'Don't you dare walk out that door,' Jonny threatened, leaping in front of her to block the exit. 'Do you think it's that easy for me? That I can just walk away? Well, you wanted to know what was going on, and now you're part of it.'

'I don't want any part of this, or of you. I can see exactly what you are now, Jonny, just a selfish, shallow, nasty little cockroach. Get out of my way,' Ariana hissed. She knew Jonny was desperate and wondered how far he might go.

'Life's always been so easy for you,' Jonny ranted. 'You had everything handed to you, didn't you? It'd be a shame if someone burst that bubble. If someone decided to tell the cops about you and Liberty. What really happened that night.'

Ariana stepped back as though she'd been slapped. 'What?'

'You heard.' Jonny didn't even blink.

'Are you threatening me?'

'C'mon, babe, don't look at it like that. Think of it as helping out an old friend. I get half a million dollars, and you don't get locked up in jail with your mugshot splashed all over the tabloids. Orange never was your colour.'

'You bastard,' Ariana spat. She tried to push past him, but he grabbed her arm, holding it tightly. 'Get off me,' she growled.

Jonny dropped her arm, but his dark eyes were glittering dangerously. Ariana stared at him, struck by a sudden realization.

'Oh my God,' she whispered. 'It's you.'

'What's me?' Jonny frowned, wrong-footed by the sudden change in Ariana.

'The text messages. How could I have been so stupid? Was that your plan? Try to scare me and then demand money? I couldn't work out what the point of them was, but it seems so obvious now. You were going to blackmail me.'

'What are you talking about?'

'Oh, don't act the innocent, we both know lying is one thing you are really good at, Jonny!' Ariana grabbed her phone from her bag and thrust it in his face. *'I know what you did that night. How dare you.* Remember now?'

Jonny laughed cruelly. 'Aw poor little princess, so someone's threatening you about Liberty's death? *Quelle surprise,'* he mocked her again. 'Looks like you've made an enemy. But it's not me. Whatever else I might have done, that playground stuff just isn't me, babe, I swear to you.'

Ariana narrowed her eyes. Jonny was so convincing, she could almost believe he was telling the truth. She felt her phone vibrate in her hand and almost dropped it in shock, reading the message on the screen before turning it round to show Jonny:

**I HAVE THE TAPES. THE WHOLE WORLD WILL
KNOW WHAT YOU DID.**

Jonny held up his hands, protesting his innocence. 'Now do you believe me?'

'But if it's not you . . .?' Ariana trailed off. Her mind was racing in confusion and fear. Who was sending the messages? Were they bluffing about the tapes? What did they want? And if tapes did exist, what did they show?

Whoever it was had Ariana right where they wanted her. And they were still out there.

Chapter 24

Estée had never seen the hotel so busy. Every room was full due to the fire at Le Martinez and, although she was exhausted already, she was grateful for the extra hours. After her confrontation with Victor, she had decided against returning to La Châtelaine. That meant she needed every extra cent while she decided what to do next.

Robert Chappell had been a sympathetic ear when she'd needed one. After she had told him everything, he had tried to reassure her.

'Look, love, this business about the money you owe him is just a threat, to get you to do what he wants.'

'You think?'

'Definitely, that contract isn't worth the paper it's written on, and would never stand up in a court of law.'

'He still has my passport, though.'

Robert had scratched his stubble. 'You're a French citizen, aren't you? Report it lost and get another one. The guy's a chancer . . . he's just trying to scare you. Why don't you let me give you the money.'

'I couldn't let you do that,' she'd told him firmly, 'It wouldn't be right.'

'Just see it as a loan, you can pay me back, over time.' He winked. 'I charge a very low rate of interest, i.e.: none.'

'I'm not sure . . . what would your wife say?

'She's the most generous person I know and would do exactly the same thing,' Robert had replied.

Estée worked quickly and efficiently, humming to herself as she changed sheets and emptied bins, picked up towels and cleaned bathrooms. Fortunately, so far this morning, there'd been nothing too unpleasant. When people were on holiday, or away for business on the company tab, they behaved how they never would at home, with no consideration for the anonymous, unseen chambermaid who had to clear up after them.

Yet the job could be fascinating too, giving Estée a tantalizing glimpse into other people's lives. Yesterday, for example, she'd been rostered to clean Elizabeth Chappell's suite, and it was impossible not to notice the designer clothes hanging up in the bedroom, the luxurious products lined up on the vanity unit beside the expensive bottles of perfume. Even the handbag strewn on the coffee table was worth more than Estée earned in a month. *How the other half live*, she'd thought enviously. If only she could catch a lucky break, that might be her one day.

In the room she was currently cleaning, the guest had checked out early, leaving the remains of his breakfast tray and a newspaper beside it. Estée picked it up to throw it away, and it took a moment to realize what she was seeing: Robert Chappell's name was splashed across the front of *Le Monde*, above a grainy photo.

'*La Hausse et La Baisse*' – the Rise and Fall – read the headline, with photos of Robert on the red carpet at the premiere of *All Our Yesterdays* next to a picture of him with—

Estée's stomach churned. She instantly felt sick. No, it wasn't possible.

Her mind was racing so fast she could barely take in the words as she riffled through the pages, finding the series of photos showing Robert Chappell sitting beside her on a park bench in Juan-les-Pins, his arms around her, in an intimate, compromising position.

La Belle et Le Clochard read a smaller headline inside – The Lady and the Tramp – juxtaposing the poor-quality images of Estée beside Elizabeth Chappell in all her glory. Estée's gaze skimmed over the words, the writer lamenting what a fool Robert was to cheat on gorgeous, classy Elizabeth 'every man's fantasy' Chappell for a sordid hook-up with a 'cheap, ten-euro-per-ticket, dancer'.

Estée's world was spinning. She realized this story had been out there for hours now, the whole time she'd been going about her day, blissfully ignorant. She was headline news. Had everyone she knew seen it? Would Constance sack her, and throw her out? Christ, Elizabeth Chappell was staying at the hotel, and now the chambermaid who cleaned her room had been accused of behaving inappropriately with her husband. It was all such a mess, Estée thought with a groan, sinking down onto the bed and holding her head in her hands.

And what about Stefan? She'd tried to deny her feelings for him, but there was no doubt that she had stupidly allowed herself to hope they might become more than just friends. Would he think she was some low-rent floozy, out for whatever she could get?

Oh God, what if – a wave of fear washed over Estée's entire body – what if her mother saw the newspaper? She'd see that Estée had lied, that she didn't have the successful career she'd claimed. She would keep it from Emilie, of course, but what if her schoolfriends saw the article? She'd be teased mercilessly, shamed and upset by what her mother had done. It was just too terrible to contemplate.

Estée closed her eyes, exhaling shakily, feeling herself start to panic . . .

Constance had been run off her feet all morning. The influx of guests from Le Martinez had caused a lot of extra work, and she'd not even had time for her morning coffee. Now, the stream of queries and complaints had finally slowed down, and Constance sneaked into the back to make herself an espresso and pick up the newspaper she'd been meaning to read all morning. She skimmed through the headlines and almost knocked over her cup. *Mon Dieu!* Estée and Robert Chappell! She should have known something was going on between them that night he was drunk and Estée offered to take care of him, Constance thought darkly. She'd probably seduced the poor man and taken advantage of him.

Constance remembered that Marie had told her how Robert Chappell had turned up at the hotel with an enormous bunch of flowers and demanded to speak to Estée. Who would have thought it? He had such a beautiful wife too. Elegant and sophisticated, the polar opposite of Estée. You just never knew what went on behind closed doors.

No, she'd never liked the girl, Constance reflected, and now she'd been proved right. She'd always disapproved

of the way Estée earned a living: dancing for money –
and what else? Everyone knew what type of club La
Châtelaine was, Constance thought tartly. She'd tolerated
Estée because she felt sorry for her – and she was a good
little worker, if truth be told – but she would have to be
sacked immediately. What would the guests think if they
recognized her? And heaven only knew what poor
Elizabeth Chappell would make of Estée's presence just
a couple of floors below her suite. No, she would have
to go as soon as possible.

Constance had a copy of the paper open beneath the
desk and was drinking in the salacious details of the story
when the courier arrived.

'*Merci*,' she murmured, eager to get back to the article.
She was about to place the envelope on the side, but
something caught her attention: the sender's details were
Aristodemou & Partners Law Firm, and the return address
was in Athens.

Constance frowned, wondering what it might mean.
Her instincts were telling her that this could be an even
bigger problem than the Estée situation. Hurriedly,
Constance scribbled a note – *Back in five minutes* – and
popped it on the counter. Then, with a sinking feeling in
the pit of her stomach, she hurried up to see her mother.

The moment Ariana had had the idea, she'd sprung into
action. She'd have to do it without Gabriel's input, and
without her father's advice. Let them underestimate her,
she thought furiously. More fool them – she'd prove them
both wrong.

For the second night in a row, Ariana had barely slept.
She'd stayed awake planning, making notes, researching

and running on adrenaline. Her brain was working so fast, throwing out ideas and making calls, calling in favours. This morning had found her pacing the hotel, measuring up and making sketches, before heading to the kitchen to brainstorm with Stefan. And now it was time to make the phone call that would determine whether all her hard work had been worth it.

She drifted over to the window of her suite, looking out at the view – it wasn't quite as spectacular as the vista from Madame du Lac's terrace, but the Mediterranean shimmered beautifully all the same. A handful of wispy clouds drifted lazily across the sky, which was a perfect shade of cyan. Luxurious superyachts sliced effortlessly through the crystalline water, against a filmic backdrop of lush green mountains dotted with palatial villas. She'd adored the energy of this city when she'd first come here over a decade ago, and it had captured her heart once again. Ariana had the strangest sensation that this was right where she was meant to be, and she'd do anything to safeguard the inheritance her grandmother had left her.

As her gaze drifted along the Croisette, taking in the familiar shops and bars and restaurants, her eyes landed on Le Martinez. Work had already begun on the repairs, but the smoke damage was clearly visible, the distinctive white facade now blackened and charred.

One man's loss is another man's gain; another pearl of wisdom that Demetrios had passed on to her. Or, in this case, another *woman's* gain. Ariana certainly hoped so.

She took a deep breath and dialled the number. As the phone rang, she caught a glimpse of herself in the mirror. She was dressed immaculately in a smart shift dress, her blow-dried hair tied back in a low ponytail, and she looked fresh and polished despite her lack of sleep. Looking good gave her the confidence for what she was about to do.

'Good morning, Monsieur Dupont, my name is Ariana Theodosis,' she announced as Grégoire Dupont, President of the Palme Gala, picked up his phone.

'Ah, good morning, Mademoiselle Theodosis.'

'Please, call me Ariana.'

'Very well, Ariana. Shauna Jackson told me to expect your call. She was quite the cheerleader – you have a lot to live up to.'

'I'm sure it was all true,' Ariana laughed. She'd got in touch with her stepmother to ask for a favour; as an Oscar-winning actress with a long and successful career in Hollywood behind her, Shauna had connections throughout the movie world, and she'd been to the Cannes Film Festival countless times over the years. When Ariana had divulged her plan, begging her not to tell Demetrios, Shauna had agreed to speak to Grégoire Dupont and put in a good word for her. 'I think you can pull this off, Ari, and you'll make your father proud if you do,' she'd said on the phone, the lilt of her Irish accent still detectable.

'I don't want to take up too much of your valuable time, so I'll get to the crux of the matter,' Ariana continued smoothly. 'I was devastated to hear about the fire at Le Martinez – thank God no one was hurt – and terribly upset that you've been left without a venue for the annual gala. As I'm sure Shauna mentioned to you, I recently took over the running of the Hotel du Soleil and—'

'I'm very sorry to interrupt, Mademoiselle Theodo— I mean, Ariana. I think I can guess what you're about to suggest, but the Palme Gala demands a certain prestige, a certain cachet. While I don't mean to be rude, and while I'm sure the situation will change with you at the helm, the Hotel du Soleil is not synonymous with those characteristics. Admittedly, it's some time since I was last there, but I do know it by reputation. And that reputation isn't the best, I'm afraid.'

Ariana heard her grandmother's voice in her ear again: *One day you'll need more than your beauty to get you through life, you need to be charming too.*

I can do this, she told herself.

'Monsieur Dupont,' Ariana purred. 'I quite understand your concerns, but I can guarantee that the Hotel du Soleil would more than rise to the challenge were we to have the honour of hosting the Palme Gala. Due to our location, we have the best view of any hotel in the city from our beautiful terrace; if you're free this afternoon, I'd be delighted to personally give you a guided tour. Furthermore, I can assure you that I'm entirely au fait with A-list events and glamorous occasions – that's something of a specialism for me,' Ariana smiled. 'If you'd allow me, I'd like to send over some mock-ups of how the event space could look, as well as some menu suggestions. Our head chef here, Stefan Lavaux, is world class.'

'Yes, I have heard that his food is excellent,' Grégoire admitted.

'On that note, I wondered whether you'd had your lunch yet?'

'I'm sorry?'

'I have a courier arriving at your office, right about now, with a selection of dishes for you to sample. We have seared scallops with Gruyère and cream. Goat's cheese tartine laced with peach and thyme. Grilled balsamic chicken on a bed of crostini and black olive tapenade. Beef tataki rolls wrapped with spring onion and blanched baby carrots. And, for dessert, tonka bean panna cotta with roasted strawberries, and a chocolate orange and brandy mousse. All accompanied by a bottle of Dom Pérignon Brut 1973 – your favourite, I believe.'

'Well, your research skills are certainly impressive,' Grégoire conceded, sounding taken aback by the effort she'd gone to.

'Thank you. One more thing, before I leave you to enjoy your lunch. I understand that Shauna has spoken to her good friend, Michael Bublé, this morning. He's indicated that, were the gala to be held at the Hotel du Soleil, he would be delighted to perform.'

For a moment, Grégoire Dupont was speechless. 'I have to say, I'm most impressed by your ideas and your tenacity. My secretary has informed me that your courier has, indeed, just arrived. Let me enjoy my lunch, and I'll get back to you.'

'Of course. Take your time. I look forward to speaking with you later.'

Ariana hung up, a Cheshire-cat smile spreading across her face.

'So. It's the end,' Madame du Lac stated, her tone resigned.

'Little bitch,' Constance spat, surprised by her mother's matter-of-fact reaction. 'I knew the second I saw her that she was up to no good.'

Madeleine du Lac read over the letter once again, as Constance paced up and down on the worn carpet. It stated that Aristodemou & Partners were writing on behalf of the legal owner of the Hotel du Soleil, and serving Madeleine du Lac with three months' notice to vacate the hotel, as per the stipulations in the Last Will and Testament of Elana Theodosis. If she did not leave the premises within that time, legal action would be taken against her.

'Do you know who's behind this?' Constance demanded, her eyes blazing, her thin lips puckered in fury. 'Gabriel! He's been trying to get the hotel from you for years. That's why he's been hanging round that Ariana girl like a puppy dog. This is his chance. He's persuaded her to throw you out, and then he'll take over.'

Madame du Lac regarded her daughter levelly. Constance was consumed by rage and frustration and Madeleine wondered what, if anything, brought her happiness. She had no hobbies, no friends, no lover, and seemed to spend her life in a permanent state of bitterness and resentment. For a moment, Madeleine wondered how on earth Constance had ended up that way, and then she realized – that was the example she'd set her daughter for the past twenty years.

But Madeleine du Lac hadn't always been that way. The world might view her now as a dried-up old husk of a woman, but once she'd been the life and soul of the party. She'd adored her husband, Alain; they'd been deeply in love when they'd wed, and marriage had seemed like a big adventure they'd embarked on together. She'd thought Alain was mad when he bought the ramshackle property in Le Suquet, but they were young and beautiful, part of the beau monde, and they had friends and acquaintances in many different countries. For a time in the seventies and eighties, the Hotel du Soleil had felt like the centre of the world, where everyone who was anyone came to play.

Then things had soured. Alain had grown distant, started drinking too much, gambling every night. They'd almost lost the hotel – that's why Madeleine had to do what she did. She'd kept her actions from Alain as long as she could, but he'd been incandescent when he finally discovered what she'd done. And then there'd been the argument . . .

Madeleine closed her eyes, not wanting to relive that night. When she opened them again, Constance was staring at her, her face contorted in anger. She couldn't be more different from her brother, Madeleine reflected. Gabriel had gone out into the world and made something of himself. Madeleine would never admit it, but she was incredibly proud of him.

'I don't think it *was* Gabriel,' Madeleine said. 'We spoke, just the other day. He would not have me thrown out, I'm sure of it.'

'He's lying,' Constance retorted. 'When has he ever looked out for your best interests? I'm the one who did that. I'm the one who *stayed*,' she finished desperately.

Madeleine du Lac stared sadly at her daughter. She was grateful, of course, for everything Constance had done, but it was hard not to think that Constance had wasted what should have been the best years of her life. She was just as guilty of that herself, she realized. She'd spent twenty years chasing shadows, keeping all of them mired in the past.

'I know, *ma chérie*, but you mustn't worry. Everything will be all right. Ariana would never throw us out. She is a Theodosis, and they are our friends.'

'You foolish woman,' Constance spat. 'Ariana Theodosis is no friend of ours.'

Madeleine stared at her in shock; Constance had never spoken to her like that before, with such aggression in her tone.

'I'll prove it to you. Here, look at this—' Constance rummaged in her pocket and triumphantly pulled out the ring that Ariana had given to her.

Madeleine stared at it, at the delicate gold band mounted with a shimmering diamond in a rare pink hue. Suddenly, the room seemed to swim in front of her, everything growing hazy before her eyes. The jewellery was familiar to her – she knew it was significant – but the memories sparked then faded, leaving her faint and dizzy and confused.

Madame du Lac staggered across the room, reaching for her armchair. She sat down in relief and closed her eyes, breathing slowly, waiting for the mists to clear.

'Ariana had it. She asked me to put it in the safe,' Constance was saying.

'Then why didn't you?'

'I . . .' Constance was taken aback.

'Put it back,' Madeleine instructed. Her voice was low and commanding, taut with anger. 'You must leave well alone, Constance. Put it back in the safe and forget you ever saw it.'

Chapter 25

Victor Kolosov sat behind his desk in the windowless backroom of La Châtelaine, scrolling through gossip websites on his laptop. It wasn't something he usually did, but today wasn't a usual day.

The latest update in the Robert Chappell scandal, in which Victor was taking a particular interest, was that the movie star had personally requested this 'attractive young cabaret dancer' be added to the guest list for the *All Our Yesterdays* premiere. Some intern had leaked the information.

Victor read through the stories, becoming increasingly angry with each revelation. Well, this explained why Estée had been so reluctant to stay on after the show, so eager to dash off every night – she clearly had bigger fish to fry, setting her sights on a film star, no less. And she'd had the gall to lie to him, Victor thought furiously, as he realized that the night of the premiere was the night Estée had claimed to be sick and not turned up for work.

Now she'd given him the brush-off altogether –

evidently she thought that Robert Chappell was going to be her meal ticket out of La Châtelaine. Well, she would learn, Victor thought grimly. If she thought she could reject him like that, she was wrong.

He reached into his desk drawer. Beside a large bag of white powder lay a passport. Victor picked it out and opened it, staring at the photograph. Right now, he had more pressing matters to deal with. Victor liked to think of himself as a businessman, with a number of different interests. Whether all of those interests were strictly legitimate, or even legal, was a question he wasn't overly concerned with. But one part of his empire was causing him problems. His boss was demanding answers – and money. However high Victor rose, there was always someone higher up the chain, and right now he was having issues with—

The phone on his desk rang. Victor answered nervously, but was pleasantly surprised to hear a well-spoken female voice ask if he was the manager of La Châtelaine.

'I'm calling from *France Soir*,' she explained. 'We're running a story on a woman I believe works for you, known as Estée.'

Victor sat up a little straighter. 'Continue.'

'I'm wondering whether you'd like to tell me a little bit about her.'

'I might. It depends what I'd get in return.'

The journalist named a fee and Victor smiled. His day was starting to look brighter after all.

'Excellent, that looks superb,' Ariana beamed, as she sashayed through the ballroom, adrenaline firing in her veins.

Grégoire had called her back that same afternoon to

tell her that she'd made quite an impression, and to confirm that the 2009 Palme Gala would be held at the Hotel du Soleil. Ariana had thanked him profusely and, after she'd hung up the phone and finished screaming with excitement, she'd immediately got started, ignoring the niggling doubts at the back of her mind.

There was so much to do in so little time and, while she was no stranger to hosting a party, the gala was on a totally different scale. The eyes of the world would be on her hotel, and she knew that pulling off this event was going to be one of the hardest challenges she'd ever faced. If she succeeded, it would be a major coup, both personally and professionally.

She'd felt shaken after her run-in with Jonny, and the organizing of the gala had given her a welcome distraction. She couldn't stop berating herself for not choosing her friendship with Liberty over her affair. There were few quiet moments since then, but she'd tried again to reach her memories of that night in LA. She just couldn't believe she would ever have hurt Liberty.

Keeping busy was a blessing and Ariana had decided to start with the basics while she figured out the rest. The most pressing concern was the ballroom, and she'd set a team to work cleaning and painting, making repairs to the elaborate ceiling mouldings and polishing the floor-to-ceiling windows that opened directly out onto the terrace.

'Keep up the good work,' she called brightly, as she turned to go and quite literally collided with Gabriel. 'Oh!' Ariana exclaimed, as she looked up and realized who it was. Her cheeks flushed as she was assailed by memories of how it had felt to be wrapped in his arms, pressed tightly against him, to kiss his lips and run her hands over his bare skin . . . Then she remembered it had all been part of a plan and scowled.

Ariana met Gabriel's eyes, seeing hurt and confusion in there.

'I'm glad to see you. I was hoping we might be able to talk.' His voice was soft. 'Somewhere private.'

'I'm sorry, I don't have time. Perhaps we can schedule an appointment for another day.'

Gabriel frowned. 'Schedule an appointment?'

'Yes, that's right. Now if you'll excuse me—'

'Ariana, what's going on?' Gabriel's voice was firmer now, that familiar note of arrogance creeping into his tone. Ariana was pleased; it gave her a reason to dislike him.

'As I said, I'm very busy right now. I—'

'You've given my mother her notice to leave.'

Ariana paused. The room was teeming with workers who could easily overhear them, and this was not a conversation she wanted to have in public. 'All right, let's go somewhere quieter.'

'My office?'

'The one I told you to vacate a week ago?' Ariana's eyes were steely, but Gabriel held her gaze. 'Fine.' She marched off ahead, leaving him following in her wake.

They entered the room and he closed the door behind them so they wouldn't be disturbed. Now it was just the two of them, alone. The air was thick with tension of all kinds, and Ariana wondered if it had been a good idea to be so private after all.

'What's all this about, Ariana?'

'Your mother is occupying the best room in the hotel,

rent free. The situation can't continue. I have renovation work planned, so she needs to vacate the suite. I consider that I've been very generous letting her stay until now.'

Gabriel looked at her, and she knew he was wondering why she was acting so differently towards him. Where was the Ariana from their date; the sweet, vulnerable, vibrant girl he'd got to know?

'Of course, your decision is understandable,' he said carefully. 'It makes complete business sense. Although I thought you might have spoken to me first, or—'

'Why? The hotel belongs to me, remember? Why are you still here, anyway? Surely you have other business to take care of, other properties throughout the world to check on?'

Gabriel kept his expression neutral. 'Yes, but this is my childhood home. The place I grew up. Besides, I thought that you and I—'

'What about us?' Ariana shot back, her breath coming fast as she silently dared him to say it. She looked beautiful in her anger, her eyes blazing, her dark hair spilling out over her shoulders.

Gabriel walked towards her, stopping only inches away. Having him so close was intoxicating. She could smell his musky cologne, her gaze tracing the outline of his mouth.

'Why are you behaving like this?' he demanded. 'What's changed between us?'

Ariana wondered whether to tell him the truth. They stared at one another, engaged in a silent battle, until she finally blurted out the words: 'I overheard you, Gabriel. I know what you said about me – that it was all part of your plan.'

'I don't know what you're talking about.'

'The day after we went to the island. I went upstairs to speak to your mother, but you were already there and I heard what you said.'

'Eavesdropping again?' Gabriel raised his eyebrows, and Ariana felt her cheeks flame.

'*Ariana Theodosis has no idea what she's doing,*' she quoted, throwing the words down like a gauntlet. 'That's what you said. You can't deny it.'

Gabriel gave a Gallic shrug, seemingly unperturbed. 'I have no intention of denying it. What I said is true – you don't have any idea what you're doing. You've never run a hotel before. You've barely even had a proper job and, until very recently, your life seems to have revolved around parties. My comment was a statement of fact, not some kind of libellous smear.'

Ariana felt wrong-footed by his response. What Gabriel was saying might not be pleasant to hear, but she had to admit that it was accurate.

'You said the hotel belonged to you,' she stammered, feeling less sure of herself now. 'You said you had a plan.'

'Yes,' Gabriel acknowledged. 'I wanted to speak to you about that. Perhaps now is not the best time, but you've forced my hand. I have a business proposal for you.'

He sat down on the edge of the desk, right in front of where she was standing. 'You own the hotel, but you don't know what to do with it.'

'How dare you—' Ariana opened her mouth to protest.

'Calm down, it's true,' he added. 'I've lived here all my life and running luxury hotels is my business. I'm highly successful. That isn't arrogance, it's fact. So why not go into partnership? You and me, fifty-fifty.'

'Why should I?'

'It's the best solution, I get to keep an interest in the hotel, and you get the best hotelier in the business thrown in.' He folded his arms, holding her gaze confidently.

She felt momentarily blindsided; this wasn't what she had expected at all. Damn Gabriel, why did he always seem to have the upper hand?

'Look, we can sort out the finer details later,' Gabriel continued. 'Haggling is so undignified, *n'est-ce pas*? Anyway, I'm explaining to you what my "plan" was. Why, what did you think I meant?'

'I . . .' Ariana trailed off, embarrassed by what she had assumed. How could she tell him that she thought he planned to seduce her in order to steal back the hotel? 'It doesn't matter,' she said, her cheeks colouring.

'I think I can probably guess.' Gabriel stood up, so they were only inches apart and Ariana had to tilt her head to look up at him. He leaned in close and murmured, 'What happened between us wasn't part of any plan. I have a head, Ariana, but I also have a heart.'

Ariana stared up at him, longing for his words to be true. It was disconcerting, having him so close to her; her brain was telling her he was a smooth-talking businessman and she shouldn't believe a word, but her body was telling her something else entirely.

She took a step backwards, trying to gather her thoughts. 'I need to think. This isn't the right time.'

'Ah yes, the Palme Gala. I heard.'

'Good news travels fast.'

'Of course, it's impossible,' Gabriel shrugged. 'An event of this kind takes weeks of preparation, and you have only days. A seasoned professional would struggle –

and, as we've just established, you have zero experience in this industry.'

A bolt of anger shot through Ariana – mostly because she knew he was right. 'We'll see, shall we?' she shot back. 'I think you'd be surprised by what I can do.'

A smile played around Gabriel's lips. 'I can't wait to find out. But, like I said, I grew up in Cannes. Hotels are my business, and I know everyone worth knowing in this town. If you asked me nicely, I could help you.'

She narrowed her cat-like eyes. 'You're enjoying this, aren't you?' she said, as Gabriel burst into a wide grin.

Ariana felt torn. It was true that his contacts would be invaluable, but she hated the idea of being indebted to him. She still didn't know if she believed Gabriel's explanation that his 'plan' had been for them to go into partnership. His offer of help could merely be a ruse, to be involved in the Palme Gala and claim the credit. Or worse – to deliberately sabotage the event, ensuring the hotel would be ruined under her leadership and she would look like a laughing stock.

'Look, Ariana,' Gabriel began, 'you might not trust me, but you need me. You can't do this without me – and you know it.'

She was enraged by his arrogance but didn't think she'd ever found him more attractive than she did right now. He stood before her, completely confident, a smile on his lips and his eyes smouldering. Her anger had riled her up, her body humming with frustration that needed to find an outlet. She wanted him to sweep her over the desk and make love to her right there. From the look on Gabriel's face, he knew exactly what she was thinking.

'Let me show you what I can do,' he said.

She tapped her foot like a cat deciding its next move. Ariana knew she'd been outplayed, but she wasn't to be outdone yet. 'Fine, I'll let you help me,' she conceded.

'*Je te remercie infiniment.* That's very generous of you,' he said, his blue eyes sparkling, and she knew he was teasing her. 'I promise you won't regret it.'

'Just remember, though . . .' her dancing eyes returned his challenge. 'I'm the boss.'

'How could you be so goddamn stupid, Robert?'

'Do you know how humiliated I am? The whole world is wondering what's so wrong with Elizabeth Chappell that her husband had to snog some common little tart in a public park.'

Robert sat slumped on the luxurious sofa in his suite, his head in his hands. 'I've told you both, time and time again, it wasn't like that.'

'Newsflash,' snapped Francesca. 'It doesn't matter what the real story was. We've lost control of the narrative. In the minds of the public, Robert Chappell is a cheat who can't keep his hands to himself. You see the problem?'

'Christ, I need a drink,' Robert muttered, jumping up and pouring himself a large whisky. Elizabeth shook her head in disbelief, and Balls made a noise of frustration, but Robert figured he couldn't be in more trouble than he already was.

He, Elizabeth and Fran had assembled at the Hotel du Cap for crisis talks, and to 'figure out a strategy', as Francesca put it. The romantic dinner on the yacht had been abruptly called off; they'd been put on a boat to the harbour and bundled into a car amid tight security, the two of them hiding beneath blankets so no one could get a photo of 'Robert's guilty expression' or 'Elizabeth's tear-stained face'.

'We could lose the Palme d'Or because of this,' Francesca snapped.

'Well you've definitely lost your marriage. There's no chance of a reconciliation now,' Elizabeth told him tearily.

'The French don't care about infidelity,' Robert said grimly, downing a large slug of whisky.

'But *I* do,' Elizabeth wailed.

'I didn't mean . . . I was talking to Fran,' Robert explained. 'Look, princess—'

'Don't you *"princess"* me,' Elizabeth bawled. 'Don't speak to me. Don't even *look* at me.'

'Liz, I know you're angry – and you have every right to be – but we need to decide what our angle is going to be on this,' Fran interjected.

'Our "angle"? Why not just tell the truth for once?' Robert suggested.

'Oh, come on, you're not that naive, surely,' Francesca scoffed.

'For the thousandth time, I didn't *do* anything!' Robert roared in frustration. 'Why is no one listening to me?'

'Yes, you're right,' Elizabeth chimed in sarcastically. 'Let's put out a statement saying you met her last week when you were roaring drunk, then coincidentally saw her *again* this week, but all you were doing was trying to cheer her up because she felt sad. Oh, and I forgot to mention, she's a bloody *burlesque dancer*. Is that about the size of it?'

Robert was furious, struggling to contain his temper, as he and his wife glared at one another.

'Liz, I know you're angry, and I know I screwed up. Again. But nothing happened. It's been blown out of all proportion.' He knew the two women were struggling to believe his story. He had to admit, it looked bad. 'How many times do I have to tell you, I didn't—'

Robert broke off as a thought occurred to him. He'd been so busy trying to save his own skin, fending off the accusations and placating his wife and his agent, that he hadn't considered the impact on Estée. At least he had a whole team behind him, and a hotel suite to hide in while it all blew over. She was just a naive young girl, having to deal with the world's press by herself.

'I wonder how she's doing,' he said out loud.

'I'm sorry?' blazed Elizabeth, at the same time as Balls yelled, 'Are you out of your goddamn mind?'

'I just meant – she's not a bad person, and her family will see this. She's about to lose her job, and she has a young kid and—'

'All the more reason for you to stay out of this!' cautioned Fran. 'Seriously, Robert, are you having a breakdown or something? I'm *trying* to rescue your career and you don't even seem to care. Should I just leave? 'Cos I've got better things to do with my day than try and cover your sorry ass.'

Robert finished his whisky, swirling it round in his mouth and feeling the satisfying burn in his throat and all the way down into his stomach. Then he slammed the glass down on the counter. 'Tell the press whatever you want. I don't care.'

'Fine. Whatever. I'm done here. Oh, and as if I didn't have enough to cope with, I found out today that your beloved son's in town.'

'What?' Robert looked alarmed. 'That's all I need. What the bloody hell is he doing here?'

'How should I know?' Francesca snapped back, clearly at the end of her tether. 'I'm just warning you, in case he tries to make contact. The last thing we need is photos of the two of you brawling splashed all over the papers. On second thoughts . . .' she cocked her head to the side in thought. 'Maybe it'd be a good thing – it'd take the heat out of this story, for a start.'

Robert looked as though he might explode. 'I'm going for a cigarette,' he growled, as he stalked off towards the balcony.

Outside, the day was surprisingly overcast. The sea was dark and choppy, a strong breeze buffeting the palm trees and the manicured gardens below. Out over the bay, the skies were leaden, the dark clouds were gathering. Robert eyed them ominously as he pulled his lighter from his pocket. It seemed as though a storm was coming.

Chapter 26

The ballroom looked spectacular. The gold and crystal chandeliers had been polished until they gleamed, the traditional parquet flooring waxed and buffed, and everywhere Ariana looked there were enormous floral arrangements overflowing with dusky peonies and ivory-coloured roses. Clever lighting and carefully placed draping disguised the areas they hadn't had time to fix; smoke and mirrors transformed any lingering shabbiness into vintage glamour. If Ariana tried hard, she could detect the smell of fresh paint beneath the scent of lavender and lilies, but she was confident no one would notice. It was an incredible turnaround in forty-eight hours.

Ariana was uncomfortably aware that she couldn't have done it without Gabriel. He'd given her free rein with his little black book of contacts, crammed with designers, event organizers, PR companies and journalists. He knew the most exclusive florist on the Riviera and negotiated discounts with the top wholesalers. He'd been on hand to help her with everything she needed, no matter how insignificant, and whenever it all started to become too overwhelming, he was there to reassure her.

Ariana couldn't help but wonder what Gabriel's motives were; if he meant what he'd said about wanting to work together, or if it was all a lie. Perhaps the reason he was so involved in planning the Palme Gala was because he wanted to claim the credit if it was a success. If it was a catastrophe, he could slip away quietly into the background and let Ariana take the fall. *That's not who he is* . . . Could she really listen to that voice inside her, the one who wanted so desperately to trust him?

She daren't think about what would happen if the gala *was* a failure. She must have been insane to have taken on a project of this size with so little time. For all her bravado, her lack of experience showed, and she was incredibly grateful to Gabriel for rallying round. Ariana felt sick to her stomach when she thought of all the things that could go wrong, imagining Demetrios shaking his head and saying 'I told you so' as she was forced to admit that she was out of her depth. More than anything, she wanted to make her father proud of her.

She stared round at the small army of people working frantically to beat the clock: electricians and carpenters and landscapers and cleaners. Michael Bublé was finishing his soundcheck, and in less than two hours the crème de la crème of the movie world would be arriving at the Hotel du Soleil expecting a world-class event, yet there was still so much to do. She felt sick.

She walked out of the ballroom and onto the terrace. The event would be free flow, with guests served champagne as they arrived in the grand reception area, making their way through to the ballroom and out onto the terrace where a cocktail bar had been set up. The designers had brought in an abundance of greenery, with tiny fairy lights woven through the foliage to magical effect. It would look incredible when the sun went down.

The jewel in the crown was the incomparable view, the sweep of the Mediterranean as it traced the shoreline, the glamorous yachts in the old harbour. Although Ariana had only been at the Hotel du Soleil for a short time, she couldn't imagine leaving. She adored this place already and just hoped she could do it justice.

Yesterday, there'd been a huge storm, with thick black clouds and torrential rain, putting the event in jeopardy and forcing her to draw up contingency plans in case the terrace was out of action. But the storm had passed and was followed by a blazing sun that made the air feel almost tropical as the pools of rainwater evaporated from the ground. It was so hot that Ariana was running round in just denim cut-offs and a loose vest, her long hair pulled up into a topknot. She still needed to grab a shower and change into her gown, but first she wanted to check how everything was going in the kitchen.

On the way there, her phone buzzed and she felt a stab of panic. Opening the message with trepidation, she saw it was from Shauna and Ariana smiled as she read it:

So sorry I can't be there. You've got this xxx

Her stepmother was performing in her theatre show in London this evening, but she'd been supporting Ariana from afar, and it was sweet of her to text. It was nice to know that someone had faith in her, Ariana thought wryly, even if she didn't always have faith in herself.

She took the back staircase down to the kitchen. Inside it was a hive of activity, with people shouting and pans clattering and steam billowing in the air. On the counter were row upon row of tiny, perfect fruit tartlets, decorated with white chocolate curls and edible flowers. They looked like miniature works of art, and Ariana couldn't resist taking one. She bit into it with a satisfied groan.

'Everything OK?' she asked, as she located Stefan.

'It will be if you don't eat everything I've made.'

Ariana knew he was joking, but he looked under pressure. It was rare to see him stressed, but today she couldn't blame him. 'They're divine.'

'Thank you,' he said, with a small bow. 'We aim to please. On a serious note, we're running behind schedule. Mathieu and Sylvie both rang in sick, so we're two chefs down and could do with any extra help. I'm holding the fort for now, but if we fall behind, the whole thing could come toppling down if anything else goes wrong.' He drew his hand across his neck in a slicing movement. 'I can't be in six places at once.'

'OK, I'll sort it,' she reassured him with more confidence than she felt. Ariana had no idea where Stefan expected her to find two extra kitchen staff at this late stage, but she added it to her mental list of problems to solve quickly. Speaking of which, her next task was to speak with Estée. She was left with no choice but to fire the girl. Ariana sympathized with her predicament, but the whole situation was embarrassing for the hotel, not to mention humiliating for Elizabeth Chappell, currently their most high-profile guest.

'I've got everything under control,' Ariana gave Stefan

one of her million-dollar smiles, then headed out of the kitchen to do what needed to be done.

Victor Kolosov was having a bad day.

'I know. Yes, I understand. Don't worry, I have it under control,' he wheedled, trying to placate the man on the other end of the phone. 'There's no way he's going back to the States without paying what he owes. You'll get your money – I guarantee it. You can rely on me, I'm your man . . .' Victor trailed off as the man hung up.

He slammed his phone down on the desk and stood up, pacing the room. He'd had the misfortune of being lumbered with that arrogant American, Jonny Farrell. Jonny owed Victor's boss a considerable amount of money, and if it wasn't repaid by midnight tonight, they were both for the chop.

He'd been putting the pressure on Jonny, but the idiot kept protesting that he didn't have the cash. Victor knew he was lying. He was a Hollywood actor, for Christ's sake, with a movie-star father – of course he had a few million stashed somewhere. *No one* got away with cheating Victor Kolosov out of what they owed him.

Victor opened his desk drawer, reaching into the back for the gun that was lying there. He paused for a moment, then slipped it into his jacket pocket. Maybe Jonny Farrell needed some persuasion to produce the goods, Victor thought, his anger growing.

He could really do without this crap right now. Estée had failed to turn up for work again; it seemed she was serious about handing in her notice. How dare she disrespect him like that? After all the favours he'd done for her – giving her a job when she was desperate, and letting her get away with doing half the work that the other girls did. Did she think she was special or something? That she was too good for La Châtelaine? He thought back to the journalist who wanted some dirt on her. Any other girl would have been happy to use her notoriety to their advantage, and his. He could have been swamped with clients wanting a movie star's mistress, but now she'd killed that opportunity for him. He felt his anger stir again. She needed a lesson in respect.

But now that he'd told her about the money she owed him, she'd disappeared, just like Jonny. Victor had enjoyed thinking about what Estée could do to pay off her debt to him. She was an attractive girl, and he'd taken a shine to her. Her reluctance made her all the more alluring, it brought out his competitive streak. The thought of what he would do to her, of bringing her into line, flitted across his mind . . .

Yes, maybe he should pay her a visit before he went to find Jonny. He knew Estée lived at the Hotel du Soleil, and he'd heard there was a big party tonight. All work and no play would make Victor a dull boy. The doorman there owed him a few favours; he'd been to the club a few times after work, and Victor had hooked him up with some of his friendliest girls. He was sure the guy wouldn't want his wife finding out about that.

Yeah, maybe tonight was the night for a party, Victor thought. La Châtelaine would be fine without him for a few hours, and he deserved a little treat.

Victor made sure the gun was tucked firmly inside his jacket and set off.

* * *

'I'm so sorry,' Ariana said, 'but I'm sure you can understand my dilemma.'

The young woman in front of her was struggling to hold it together, and Ariana was keenly aware of the difference in their status. They were both around the same age, but Ariana was staying upstairs in a suite and had money, status and prestige. This girl was a chambermaid, living in the worst room in the hotel, and right now she was on the verge of tears.

'Please don't fire me,' Estée begged. 'Those stories aren't true – I didn't do anything wrong.'

Ariana looked at the girl's earnest face; she had felt the same way when Jonny implied she was involved in Liberty's death.

'The problem is, Elizabeth Chappell is a guest here, and she's paying a lot of money.' Ariana wasn't enjoying chastising the girl; maybe she wasn't cut out for management after all. 'The press are starting to pick up on the fact that you're employed here and, whether you did anything or not, the situation is embarrassing for her. I'm trying to improve the image of the hotel, and this is really not helpful.'

'I have a daughter,' Estée pleaded. 'I need the money. This is all I have.'

Ariana hesitated, feeling increasingly uncomfortable. It was clear the situation wasn't Estée's fault, so why should she suffer? Ariana had thought the easiest solution would be to fire Estée, but now she was here, sitting down with her face to face, she realized she just couldn't do it.

Ariana glanced round the tiny, impersonal room, taking in the cheap clothes slung over the chair in the corner, the tattered make-up bag spilling its contents onto the desk. This could have been her life, Ariana realized, if she hadn't been born into privilege. It was sheer luck of the draw that her father was a multimillionaire shipping magnate, and she was the heiress to his fortune. Without that, she'd simply be scraping a living however she could, trying to get through each day, just like Estée, who was still young and very pretty. Surely, she could afford to cut her a bit of slack?

'Look,' she relented. 'I need to think about this; in the meantime just try and lie low. The festival will be over tomorrow, Elizabeth will be leaving and then . . . We'll speak again, OK?'

'Oh, thank you. Yes, of course. Thank you so much.' Estée clung onto Ariana's words like a drowning woman to a life raft. 'I can't tell you how much I appreciate this. I know tonight is a huge deal for you and the hotel, and if there's anything you need me to do, just let me know. Seriously, anything.'

'It's fine, thank you.' Ariana turned to go, and her gaze fell on the framed photograph of what she presumed must be Estée's daughter. She was a carbon copy of her mother; the same curly, dark hair and identical deep, brown eyes, but her face still showed an optimism and naivety that Estée was beginning to lose.

'Actually,' Ariana said, an idea starting to form in her mind. 'There might be one thing. Do you know your way around a kitchen?'

Jonny had found himself in a garish Irish theme pub in the back streets of Cannes, just off the rue d'Antibes. It was a far cry from his usual sort of haunt, and he wasn't quite sure how he'd ended up there.

Dressed in a sleek Armani tuxedo, he cut a distinctive figure amongst the badly dressed tourists and backpackers, and he was attracting some curious glances. He'd convinced Ariana to put him on the guest list for the Palme Gala before their bust-up, and had been on his way there when he'd started to feel panic overwhelm him. He'd decided that the only thing that would keep him anywhere near calm was to stop off for a couple of quick drinks, and so he had somehow ended up here. Now he was holed up in a corner, mainlining Irish whiskey.

His phone had been ringing incessantly all afternoon. Then Victor had given him a deadline of midnight to get the money, and after that it had all gone quiet: no more messages, no more calls, no more threats. That was almost more menacing. Victor hadn't said what he'd do if Jonny didn't get the cash. He didn't need to. Jonny knew how guys like Victor operated. The Russian would hunt him down, and he might end up sleeping with the fishes before he got a chance to try and explain himself, Jonny thought dramatically.

The Palme Gala would be a great opportunity to sell his stash – all those movie moguls looking to blow off some steam – but even if he got rid of everything, he wouldn't raise that money by tonight. Jonny needed a friend, someone who'd be willing to lend him a large amount of money without asking too many questions. Right now, there were only two possibilities – his father or Ariana.

Jonny took a slug of his Jameson's and Coke, which was finally started to work on his nerves, and mulled over the options. His father would ask too many questions and probably refuse, like the selfish creep he was.

Anyway, he had enough going on at the moment judging by the front cover of the *National Enquirer* displayed on the hotel newsstand.

Which left Ariana. She owned a hotel, and her father was practically a billionaire. There'd be cash in the safe, surely. That might be enough to keep them off his back. All right, so she'd already said no and dumped him, but he knew she still wanted him really. No, she definitely wouldn't refuse him a second time, not once she realized how much trouble he was in. She could never say no to him. He was irresistible, he thought drunkenly. Yes, despite what she might have said earlier. A little bit of sweet-talking, nuzzling on her ear, and she'd be putty in his hands, just like every other time.

Jonny downed his drink and staggered to his feet, heading out into the street. He stuck out his hand for a taxi and tumbled onto the back seat, a cigarette in his hands and his fringe flopping over his slightly crazed eyes. The taxi driver eyed him warily in his rear-view mirror.

'Where to, monsieur?'

Filled with a new energy, he pointed vaguely towards the harbour, demanding, 'Hotel du Soleil. And make it *vite!*'

Chapter 27

Gabriel was making final checks to the champagne reception. He had to admit that Ariana had done an impressive job. Yes, he'd helped, but she'd been the one with the original idea, and the vision and determination to see it through. This was the biggest event at the hotel for more than twenty years, possibly the most prestigious in its history, and it unsettled Gabriel that Ariana had managed to achieve more in a week than he'd managed in a decade. She didn't have his mother and sister on her back, he reminded himself. Perhaps that was what the situation needed. Fresh eyes and fresh energy, no baggage.

It was wonderful seeing the place so full of life, a sense of anticipation in the air as the first VIPs began to arrive. He was reminded of how the hotel had been when he was a boy, always bustling, always exciting. The extraordinary had become commonplace to him back then. Gabriel shook his head, realizing that he was in a reflective mood tonight. He wasn't sure what had come over him recently.

The entrance was starting to get busier as a fleet of limousines pulled up outside and some of the most famous faces in the world entered the hotel to an explosion of flashbulbs. Hugh Jackman was amongst the early arrivals, closely followed by Juliette Binoche in a dazzling midnight-blue outré gown by Jean Paul Gaultier.

Gabriel turned to go and caught sight of Ariana. The last time he'd seen her, a couple of hours ago, she'd been dressed in casual wear, running around trying to do a million different tasks. Now she took his breath away.

She was dressed in black, and Gabriel immediately understood why; tonight, it wasn't Ariana's place to outshine the celebrities. She was the host, not the guest. But the gown's sheer simplicity highlighted how stunning she was, showing that she didn't need bright colours or a revealing cut to look incredible. The dress was strapless, emphasizing her slim collarbone and tanned skin, the fitted waist showing off her hourglass figure, before falling to the floor in a cloud of tulle. Her hair was swept up in an elegant pleat, and she wore no jewellery except for an enormous pink diamond ring.

She hadn't seen him yet, and Gabriel watched from a distance, feeling an inexplicable pang of jealousy at what-ever lucky person had her attention right now. Ariana was in her element, greeting the stars, charming the press and photographers. She was completely in control and had them all eating out of her hand. Gabriel was in awe of her.

He approached her, touching her lightly on the arm. She spun round, her face lighting up when she saw him. He inhaled the scent of her Chanel perfume, saw the flecks of gold in her amber eyes. He felt dazzled.

'You did it,' Gabriel congratulated her, looking around

him at the magic she had seemingly created effortlessly. The words seemed so inadequate; he wanted to tell her what an amazing job she'd done, how much he admired her . . . and how utterly radiant she looked.

'Thank you,' she smiled. 'I couldn't have done any of it without you . . . Gabriel, I—'

But whatever Ariana was about to say was lost as Princess Stéphanie of Monaco approached and Ariana turned to welcome her.

Gabriel melted away into the background and realized as he watched her that in fact there was only one thing he wanted to say to her at this moment.

He wanted to say *I love you, Ariana.*

Suddenly Gabriel knew it with absolute clarity. He loved Ariana with all his heart. He wanted to wake up with her every morning and make love to her each night, to travel the world together and build a future and spend every second by her side.

The excitement of the realization was followed by a crushing certainty: he could never tell her how he felt. It would never work between them. She didn't trust him, she'd made that very clear. There was too much distance between them, despite hardly knowing each other at all, so much had come between them already, with the unresolved tension over the hotel, and repeated misunderstandings. And, of course, there was Jonny Farrell, who always seemed to turn up like a bad penny. He treated Ariana appallingly, yet she seemed to find it irresistible, and Gabriel didn't think he'd ever despised another human being more.

Perhaps, if they were different people, without the shadows of the past hanging over them, it could have worked. But not now. There would always be something unknown between them, each of them wondering what lay undiscovered, what secrets were hidden that threatened to destroy them.

The knowledge felt like a physical blow to Gabriel; the first woman he'd fallen in love with, and the understanding that they couldn't be together, that he'd have to close himself off and shut down a part of him for protection. He couldn't get too close to her, it would hurt too deeply. Ariana had asked her lawyers to evict his mother from the hotel and, after tonight, Gabriel would leave too. It was the only way. It would be more than he could bear to be around Ariana all the time but not be able to be with her, to not kiss her or hold her or tell her how much he loved her. It would be better to forget about her altogether. In a few months his world would return to normal, and Ariana would be a memory. *The one you let go.*

A waiter approached, offering him champagne and canapés. Gabriel shook his head, but the interaction was enough to break his thoughts.

With an agonizing feeling in his chest, almost as though his heart was breaking, he tore his eyes from Ariana then turned and walked away, swallowed up by the crowd.

Elizabeth descended the sweeping staircase like a queen. She'd decided against taking the rickety old elevator – she didn't want to get stuck in there and miss the gala. Besides, why not put on a show, generate some positive publicity for the film, and make Robert see exactly what he was about to lose. Elizabeth had nothing to hide – why not take control of the narrative, as Francesca would say.

Besides, once the press got photos of her tonight, it would knock the other story – the one about her husband and a cabaret dancer – off the front pages.

She walked slowly down the Italian marble stairs, holding the curved mahogany banister – she didn't want to lose her footing in the vertiginous Manolos – looking sensational in a custom-made gown by ROX. It was a white silk sheath dress that poured over her body like water and wouldn't have looked out of place on a bride. Elizabeth's glossy blonde hair was straightened and parted in a simple, sleek, low ponytail, secured with a white band.

Liz wasn't stupid; she knew that turning up to the Palme Gala in something that resembled a wedding dress would send the tabloids into meltdown. There'd be a frenzy of speculation: Had she forgiven Robert? Were they renewing their vows? Was it all a publicity stunt?

Her confident gaze swept over the grand reception. It was busy now, the glamorous guests mingling, but she was pleased to note that her arrival generated a buzz in the exclusive crowd. She recognized almost everyone from the industry, colleagues and contemporaries and competitors, as she waved hello to Meryl Streep before blowing a kiss at Leonardo DiCaprio. Then her gaze fell on Robert.

He was wearing a tuxedo, and for once didn't have a hair out of place. His shirt was buttoned all the way to the neck, his bow tie correctly tied, the black-tie dress code emphasizing his dark good looks. Elizabeth knew he was under orders from Fran to play the game and not step out of line. Even though Liz was still furious, they'd agreed to present a united front – to look a million dollars and fake a smile. The show must go on, as the saying went.

Some news outlets had picked up on the fact that she and Robert were staying in separate hotels, and it was starting to filter through that Elizabeth was staying in the establishment where 'Robert's ill-judged dalliance' worked as a chambermaid. She didn't know if he'd already blown their chances of winning, but Francesca had told them candidly that, even if they'd lost the Palme d'Or, all this publicity would do wonders for the film when it was released.

Robert was waiting for his wife at the bottom of the stairs, looking up in wonder, with such adoration in those soulful, dark brown eyes. Elizabeth experienced a torrid mixture of anger and confusion. Why did he have to be such an idiot and make such bad decisions? He'd put her in an impossible position, leaving her with no choice but to go ahead with the divorce even though it was breaking her heart.

'You can still blow me away, Liz,' Robert murmured under his breath as she reached him. He went to kiss her, and she moved gently but firmly away.

'Please,' she murmured. 'Don't.'

She saw the hurt in his eyes and felt her stomach contract, but she knew he understood her reasons. Robert held out his arm and Elizabeth took it, the two of them drawing on their finest acting skills as they drifted over to the bank of photographers by the step, smiling and posing as the flashbulbs popped, convincing the world that they were a blissfully happy couple.

'I'll be glad when this is all over,' Robert murmured, slipping an arm around her waist. 'We can go home, just be the two of us again. We need to get back to normal, love.'

Elizabeth turned to him and stroked his cheek, feeling the smoothness of his skin where he was – unusually – freshly shaved. She leaned in, whispering in his ear so the cameras couldn't catch her words. 'My bags are packed and ready to go. I'm heading straight to the airport after tonight, and I'm going alone. This is it, Robbie. Our last goodbye.' Then she kissed him gently on the mouth, her eyes shut to ward off tears, but not before she caught the shock and pain in his eyes.

The photographers went wild. Robert held her tightly as he returned her kiss and she could feel the desperation in his touch; he knew that when they finally let go of each other, it was all over. When the kiss ended, they stared at one another for what seemed like an endless moment, both too full of regret and unspoken words. As Elizabeth turned away, the moment was broken.

Then a figure caught her eye and she couldn't help but exclaim, 'Oh, God, what's *he* doing here?'

Robert turned to see Jonny Farrell come sloping along the red carpet. There were dark circles under his eyes, as though he hadn't slept, and he looked as if he'd been drinking.

'Oh Christ,' muttered Robert. 'That's all I need.'

Jonny noticed them immediately – it was difficult not to – and headed unsteadily towards them. He turned to Robert, and Elizabeth sensed the tension as the two men eyed one another.

'Hello, Dad,' Jonny drawled, raising an eyebrow. 'Don't tell me you're not pleased to see your number one son?'

* * *

The kitchen was chaotic. Estée had thought that being a chambermaid was hard work, but it was nothing like the intense pressure down here. And the heat! Rivulets of sweat were trickling down her back beneath the white overalls that were too big for her, and she knew her hair must be a mass of frizz beneath the unflattering hat.

Estée had lost count of how many artichokes she'd peeled. As she was the most inexperienced, she'd understandably been given the most menial tasks, but reminded herself that she was grateful to have a job and knew she shouldn't complain. Stefan had demonstrated the correct technique, and it had taken him a matter of seconds. In contrast, Estée was painfully slow. It didn't help that she kept glancing at him out of the corner of her eye.

It was incredible to watch how he controlled the entire kitchen and everyone in it, she thought, trying and failing to concentrate on the pile of vegetables in front of her. The dishes that were coming out of the oven looked spectacular, and Stefan clearly commanded the respect of the entire staff. It was pretty sexy, if the truth be told.

'Keep those artichokes coming,' someone yelled.

'Yes, Chef,' Estée called back. She wanted to giggle at how ridiculous that sounded, but didn't think that would go down too well right now. She'd almost finished the enormous pile and wondered what the next task would be.

'Service! Come on, we need someone now, these plates are going cold.'

'We're short of waiters,' came the reply. 'Half a dozen agency staff let us down.'

A volley of swearing greeted the announcement. 'If these scallops don't get out there in the next three minutes, I'll need to throw the lot.'

Estée jumped as Stefan appeared at her side. He was clearly under pressure, but there was something attractive about his intensity – not to mention his smart chef's uniform. 'Don't worry about the artichokes, Estée.'

'Are you sure? I've almost fin—'

'Can you waitress?'

Estée paled. 'I used to, though not for a while.' As a jobbing dancer, she'd done all the classic freelance jobs over the years. 'But I can't tonight, Ms Theodosis said so. Elizabeth Chappell is out there.'

'We have no choice,' Stefan said urgently. 'Just keep your head down. We have spare clothes in the back – grab a white shirt and black skirt.'

Estée was torn. She desperately wanted to help but was terrified she'd be recognized. Then she caught sight of her reflection in the side of one of the enormous metal stockpots; with no make-up on and her hair tied back under her hat, she barely recognized herself.

'OK,' she agreed, gratified to see the look of relief on Stefan's face. 'I'll do it.'

'Thanks, Estée, I owe you one.'

With that, Stefan was gone, back to his alchemy, leaving Estée wondering if she would get away with it, and desperately hoping that she would.

Jonny and Robert eyed each other suspiciously. Robert spoke first.

'Jonathan, what brings you here?' Robert asked stiffly.

Jonny laughed mirthlessly. He was drunk and didn't care that there were cameras trained on them, capturing every excruciating moment of this unhappy reunion. His father had never been there for him. In fact, it was Robert's fault that he was in this mess, Jonny told himself. 'You're not the only face in town, and like you give a damn, Daddy,' he shot back, his voice drawling the last word as a taunt.

Robert balled his fists. 'Face?' he said incredulously. 'You look like something the cat dragged in!' Liz placed a restraining hand on his arm.

'Elizabeth,' Jonny nodded at her. 'Looking good as always. You're still standing by this one then, despite him cheating on you *again*. How many times is that now?'

'I'm warning you, son, I'm not taking any of your spoilt-brat bollocks today.'

'What's the matter, Dad, feeling cranky? Not had enough booze yet?'

Robert lunged for him. The cameras went wild, a burst of flashes lighting up the room, capturing the brawl on film to be beamed around the globe. It was over as quickly as it had begun. Even before security could intervene, Elizabeth had grabbed Robert and Ariana appeared at Jonny's side, hastily pulling him away.

'What the hell was all that about?' she snapped.

'Hey, I'm sorry,' Jonny apologized, remembering that he needed to keep on her good side.

'You know how important tonight is. Any more trouble and I'll ask security to kick you out.'

'Don't worry, babe,' Jonny replied, his eyes scouring the room anxiously. 'I'm sure everything is going to be just fine.'

Chapter 28

In the largest suite, on the top floor of the hotel, Madame du Lac stared out of the window at a world she'd almost forgotten. The hotel was bustling, with the great and the good out on the terrace drinking cocktails and dancing. Music was playing, and the sound of sparkling conversation and laughter drifted up to her window. It felt as though she'd been transported back thirty years. It was disconcerting, but it was also rather wonderful.

'Tell me again what's happening?' Madame du Lac said to Constance, who was sitting sulkily in the room with her mother. As the hotel was officially closed for the evening for the private function, Constance wasn't needed on reception.

'Take the night off,' Ariana had told her sweetly. 'You must rarely get the chance.'

Constance suspected that Ariana just wanted her out of the way, to ensure she didn't spoil the event.

'It's the Palme Gala, *Maman*.'

'The Palme Gala? Here? *Mais c'est impossible!*'

'Apparently not,' Constance replied through pursed lips. 'It's that Theodosis girl. Rumour has it she has Grégoire Dupont wrapped around her little finger, and he agreed to hold it here, after the fire at the Martinez. You remember the fire, *Maman*?'

'Of course . . .' Madeleine said distantly, turning to look in the other direction, out towards the Croisette where the Martinez was undergoing repairs. 'But I thought that was only a few days ago?'

'It was.'

'So how did she . . .? It's not possible to host this event in such a short time.'

'I believe Gabriel was very helpful.' Constance couldn't hide the disdain in her voice.

The ghost of a smile flickered across Madame du Lac's face. 'Ah, I understand. She is very impressive, *non*?'

Constance looked as though she'd sucked on a lemon. 'If you like that sort of thing, I suppose.'

There was a long pause. Madame du Lac turned her head once again, looking back at the party. She opened the French doors an inch or two so that the noise outside was amplified. The warm night air flooded in, carrying with it the salty tang of the sea, the scent of pine from the mountains and lavender from the fields, mingled with expensive perfume from the guests below.

'Do you know, it's over twenty years since I last went to a party.' Madame du Lac looked at Constance. A girlish excitement suffused her face, and her blue eyes sparkled with life. Constance stared back in alarm. 'I think I might like to go downstairs,' Madeleine mused. 'Take a look at what's going on.'

'Have you gone completely mad?' Constance asked in horror, wondering what on earth had come over her mother, the woman who'd hidden from the world for the past two decades.

'Perhaps. A little.' Madeleine wanted to laugh at the horrified expression on her daughter's face. 'Indulge me.'

She walked over to the mirror and gazed at her reflection. The woman who looked back was older than she remembered, her hair silvery-grey, her skin lined and wrinkled. She'd been forty-three years old when Alain had died, a youthful widow, and over twenty birthdays had passed, uncelebrated, in this room. A third of her life, wasted. She would waste no more.

Madeleine du Lac turned to Constance, an irrepressible smile stealing across her face. 'Are you coming, *ma chérie*? We aren't getting any younger and it's high time we started to enjoy ourselves, no?'

Gabriel made polite conversation with people he knew, and promptly forgot everything they'd said the moment they walked away. He was preoccupied with keeping a close eye on everything; when the rich and famous were crowded together like this, the risk was high, and anything could happen. He could still have Ariana's back, he vowed to himself, even if she never knew.

One man had caught his attention, arousing his suspicions. He was short and scruffy, dressed in an ill-fitting and dated suit that stood out amongst the dinner jackets and ballgowns. He wasn't speaking to anyone – no one seemed to know him – and he was helping himself to champagne and canapés as though they were going out of fashion. As Gabriel watched, the man accosted a waitress, who looked uncomfortable and quickly excused herself. There was something about him that made Gabriel feel uneasy.

He'd insisted they hire the best security team money could buy, and the crew were out there now amongst the guests, some dressed to the nines and blending into the crowd, others in head-to-toe black, standing unobtrusively around the edge of the room, kitted out with radios and earpieces and – in a few instances – weapons. It was crucial on a night like tonight, with so many high-profile guests. Some celebrities had even brought their own security with them; for those wearing priceless jewellery loaned by the top brands, it was an essential requirement.

Gabriel edged over to an enormous plain-clothes security man who was around six foot five and the width of a small car.

'You see the guy over there?' Gabriel said, nodding discreetly towards Victor. 'Keep an eye on him, will you?'

The man-mountain nodded.

Gabriel's gaze sought out Ariana, and he found her across the room, speaking with Jonny Farrell. Something in his stomach clenched. Perhaps it was jealousy, but Jonny made him uneasy, especially after the scene he'd just witnessed with Robert Chappell.

'And him too,' Gabriel added to the black-clad security guard, who acknowledged Gabriel's request and spoke discreetly into his radio. Gabriel hoped he wasn't overreacting, but tonight he felt on edge, like something was in the air, and he had learned to always trust his instincts.

Estée pushed through the double doors of the kitchen carrying a tray of black bread toasts topped with avocado and half a quail's egg. This was her third run out, and she was starting to feel more confident, holding her head a little higher and daring to make eye contact with some of the guests. She'd seen Robert and Elizabeth Chappell from a distance, and immediately swerved to the other side of the room. As long as she could stay out of their way, Stefan's crazy idea to have her waitress might just be possible – enjoyable, even.

It wasn't the way Estée would have chosen to attend the Palme Gala; she'd much rather be dressed in a designer gown with immaculate hair and make-up, and a glass of fizz in her hand, but it was better than sitting alone in her room, brooding on what she was going to do with the rest of her life. Everywhere she turned, she spotted another famous face: Pierce Brosnan had thanked her profusely for fetching him a Martini, while Liam Neeson had asked her to pass on his compliments to the chef. If it wasn't for the fact she would probably be sacked once the evening was over, Estée might almost have said she was having fun.

'Calm down, Jonny.' Ariana spoke to him in low, urgent tones. She could see he was hyped up, and had pulled him over to a secluded corner, far away from the cameras. Security had caught her eye questioningly, but she'd nodded to them that she was handling it. She didn't need their help – for now, at least.

In truth, she was furious with Jonny, and also annoyed with herself for forgetting to take him off the guest list. Before that she'd warned him that the Chappells were the guests of honour; they were the most high-profile couple at the event and were widely expected to win the Palme d'Or at tomorrow's awards ceremony. She'd instructed him to be on his best behaviour, and that for once he should keep his feelings about his father under control, but of course he'd turned up drunk and started a scene that could have ruined the gala. And now he was trying, unsuccessfully, to turn on the charm and defuse her anger.

'You're looking delicious tonight,' Jonny said, his eyes glazed as he grabbed Ariana by the waist and pulled her towards him. 'Totally edible.'

'Stop it,' she said sharply, extricating herself from his grasp. 'I told you it's over, and you should have stayed away, but now you are here then you'd better behave yourself or I'll throw you out.' He grabbed a glass of champagne from a passing waiter. Ariana snatched it out of his hand and placed it back on the tray. 'And you go and start a fight with your father.'

'I couldn't help it. He gets me so riled up, lording it over everyone like he's some bigshot, while I'm—'

Ariana remembered that Jonny was in trouble, that he owed some bad guys a lot of money. 'This is your own mess, and you need to clear it up.'

'Where the hell am I going to lay my hands on a pile of cash like that?' he said desperately. 'I'm screwed.'

'Look, I'm not going to talk about this. Right now I'm trying to—'

'Don't you get it?' Jonny's eyes were wild, sweat beading on his forehead. 'There is no later. I have until midnight tonight.'

Ariana saw the look in his eyes and knew what he was about to ask.

'Ariana, babe, I'm begging you. You're the only person—'

'No, I've told you already.' She cut him off, refusing

to listen to any more of his pathetic excuses. It was as though the scales had finally fallen from her eyes and she wondered what she'd ever seen in Jonny Farrell. He wasn't edgy or exciting or cool. He was a loser, a deadbeat, a hot mess. 'This is one of the most important nights of my life. If you cared about me at all, you'd support me, just like—'

'Like who?' Jonny scoffed.

Ariana's gaze drifted across the room, landing on Gabriel. He looked across at her and her stomach flipped, her pulse quickening. For a moment, it felt as though there was only the two of them in the crowded room. 'It doesn't matter,' she said quietly. 'I just— Oh no, what's she doing? She's not supposed to be out here,' Ariana groaned in frustration, as she saw Estée holding a tray of drinks, laughing at something George Clooney had just said.

All Ariana wanted to do was relax and enjoy the event, but it was just one headache after another. What if Robert or Elizabeth noticed Estée, or a photographer recognized her and snapped a picture?

Jonny followed Ariana's gaze. 'Hey, isn't that the chick my dad was—'

'Excuse me for a moment,' she said. 'And don't do anything stupid . . .'

Victor was strolling round the grand reception hardly able to believe his luck. All that security on the door, and he'd just waltzed right in like he owned the place. It came in useful having dirt on people. And now here he was, mingling with the A-list.

Victor knew he looked a little out of place – he wasn't wearing an expensive tux – but he told himself people would assume he was an eccentric director, or a famous actor trying to go under the radar. The idea amused him, as he downed a glass of champagne and grabbed another, helping himself to half a dozen canapés.

He'd had a couple of lines before he arrived, just to keep himself sharp. The drugs and the alcohol were mingling nicely in his bloodstream, and he was beginning to enjoy himself.

He hadn't been to the Hotel du Soleil in years, though he'd sent plenty of girls there in recent months to entertain the guests. He'd heard on the grapevine that someone new had taken over now, and they were clamping down on all of that.

Which reminded him – it was the delectable Estée that had brought him here tonight. He wondered where she might be. Clearly she wouldn't be part of this refined crowd, but one of the staff members might know where she was.

Victor looked around, searching for someone who could help him, then his sharp eyes fell on a person he hadn't expected to see.

He smiled.

It seemed like tonight was his lucky night.

Jonny swore under his breath as he watched Ariana stride off. Why had he been such an idiot? She was his only chance at getting that money, and now—

Great, that was all he needed. His father was making his way through the crowd, smiling and laughing like he didn't have a goddamn care in the world. Rather than risk Ariana having him ejected by security for creating another scene, Jonny took a step backwards to blend into the crowd – and collided with someone.

'*Bonsoir*, Jonny,' said a man's voice in his ear.

Jonny froze, then slowly turned to see Victor standing there.

'Why are you . . .? How did you . . .?' Jonny's eyes widened, panic twisting his features. 'No . . .' he muttered, shaking his head. 'I'll get your money, you'll have it, I promise. Just a few more hours, man, that's all I need . . .'

'Time's running out,' Victor hissed in heavily accented English. He let his jacket fall open, just enough so that Jonny saw the metallic glint of a gun.

Jonny backed away, a look of terror on his face. He almost jumped out of his skin as there was an enormous crash beside them.

Estée, standing just metres away, had dropped an entire tray of drinks on the floor. She was staring at Victor with a look of horror on her face.

Ariana had almost reached Estée's side when she saw her drop the tray of glasses. After that, everything seemed to happen in slow motion yet at the speed of light all at the same time.

As she turned in the direction where Estée was staring, Ariana saw Jonny with a look of absolute terror on his face, backing away from a sleazy little man who looked quite out of place. But before she could discern what Jonny was shouting about, the security team swooped in, heading for the little man.

Before they could get to him, he reached into his jacket and pulled out a gun, to the horror of the people around him, who backed away quickly.

Jonny shrieked, 'Don't kill me, man!' and tears rolled

down his cheeks as he grabbed Estée, pulling her in front of him as a human shield.

Ariana couldn't believe what she was seeing: how could Jonny be such a coward? Poor Estée was shaking and white-faced as Jonny tried to hide behind her.

'You think I won't shoot her, you snivelling little asshole?' the little man said, in what sounded to Ariana like a Russian accent. 'If I shoot her, you die too, right?' He laughed manically, and Ariana recognized the tell-tale sign of drug use in his dilated pupils. He was out of his head and might do anything. *God why didn't somebody stop him!*

Estée found her voice, which shook with terror. 'Please don't shoot, Victor, I have a daughter, she needs me—'

Then there was a cry of 'Get him!' and Robert pushed through the crowd, running towards Estée and Jonny, along with half a dozen security guards. The gunshot rang out so loudly that for a moment time stood still, before there was panic and chaos and shrieks of horror as guests scattered along the corridors, fleeing into the ballroom and out onto the terrace. Victor stood amid the chaos, still holding the gun, while Robert fell to the ground, looking down to see his white shirt was now crimson, blood gushing from his upper chest.

It was then that, seemingly out of nowhere, Gabriel appeared at the side of the man with the gun and, with a deft chopping action, knocked the gun out of his hand while he used the elbow of his other arm to knock him sideways, straight into the arms of one of the security guards. A second guard kicked the gun out of reach and tackled the man to the ground, pinning him down with his enormous bulk.

Ariana heard her own voice shout, 'Someone call an ambulance!'

Elizabeth ran to her husband's side as Robert sank to the floor, an expression of shock on his now-ashen face.

Gabriel ran over, ripping off his jacket and pressing it down on the wound.

'Don't move,' he instructed Robert, before telling Elizabeth, 'Keep the pressure on here. Hold it tight.'

'Is he going to die?' Elizabeth asked desperately. Her dress was covered in her husband's blood, dark red staining the pure white silk.

'Liz . . .' Robert croaked 'Don't leave me . . .'

'Oh Robbie,' Elizabeth's voice was ragged with sobs. 'Stay with me, darling. I promise I will never leave you, so don't you dare leave me, you hear?'

Robert said, 'That's all I wanted you to say, love.' Then his head fell back as he lost consciousness.

'Where the hell is the ambulance?' Gabriel called desperately, as Ariana and Estée looked on helplessly. Then, as the wail of sirens broke through the silence, they turned their eyes to where a long piercing wail came from above.

Everyone looked up at the balcony where Madame du Lac was standing with Constance.

'It's all happening again!' Madeleine cried, before crumpling to the floor in a dead faint.

Chapter 29

Blue lights were flashing outside the Hotel du Soleil, police cars and ambulances screeching to a halt as sirens blared. Robert had been rushed to hospital, Elizabeth by his side, but other than that no one had been allowed to leave. Victor had been arrested, bundled into a van and taken away. The police had assured Estée he was looking at a long spell in prison – not just for attempted murder, but it turned out he was involved in numerous other crimes, some more serious than others.

Everyone was being interviewed. The bar had been turned into a makeshift holding area, and glasses of brandy were being handed out to those most badly shaken.

Estée was sitting with Stefan, his strong arms wrapped tightly around her. She huddled against him, the solid bulk of him reassuring, comforted by his presence as she tried to take it all in. Robert had put his life on the line for her and she fervently hoped he would make it through. Such a kind and caring man deserved to. Now Stefan was here beside her, and for the first time in years, she actually felt safe. She leaned into him and kept praying.

A few tables away, Jonny and Montana were sitting together. Both of them looked white with fear, each wrapped up in their own thoughts. Jonny had spent a long time talking to one of the detectives and Ariana suspected that he wouldn't be able to wriggle out of this mess of his own devising quite so easily.

In a far corner of the bar, a small group had formed, consisting of the du Lac family – Gabriel, Madeleine and Constance – together with Ariana.

Madeleine had been brought round from her faint with the aid of one of the ambulance crew and a strong cognac. As soon as it was clear that she was fine, Gabriel had rushed over to Ariana and taken her in his arms. Ariana had clung to him, feeling as though she never wanted to let him go.

Right now, she was playing nervously with the ring on her finger, twisting it round and rubbing her thumb over its glittering surface. She glanced up to see Constance glaring at her, her lips tightly pursed. Ariana found herself wondering if Constance would ever like her. Even after everything that had happened this evening, she still couldn't let go of old grudges. Like mother, like daughter, Ariana supposed.

She looked across at Madeleine, feeling more curious than ever about the secrets she held. Tonight, it felt as though the sands were shifting, as though she might finally reveal what she'd been hiding. Gabriel clearly felt the same; he seemed on edge. Eventually, he couldn't restrain himself any longer and spoke:

'*Maman*, I know that now might not be the right time or place, but I have to ask. I need answers. You said, "It's all happening again." What did you mean?'

Madeleine closed her eyes. 'Patience, Gabriel. So impulsive. So eager.' She fell quiet for a moment, then seemed to come to a decision. She exhaled slowly, a long, shaky breath, and opened her eyes. 'Very well. Perhaps I should have told you this a long time ago. Forgive me. I did what I thought was right. It was such a very difficult time for me, and . . . forgive me.' She looked anguished suddenly, pain etched in the lines of her face.

'Of course, *Maman*,' Gabriel was saying. 'Take your time.'

Ariana looked across at him and felt her heart swell. Even in the midst of a crisis he kept a cool head, so calm and in control.

Madame du Lac reached out with shaking hands to pick up her tumbler of brandy. She took a fortifying sip and began to speak.

'It was 1971 when Alain and I purchased the Hotel du Soleil. Of course, it wasn't a hotel then – just a run-down old house – but the location was perfect. We discovered it one evening when we were out for a walk, climbing the hill above Cannes into the old town. Alain saw its potential immediately. In hindsight, it seems like madness. We bought the place on a whim, using all our savings, and Alain somehow convinced the bank to give him a loan to make the renovations.

'We poured everything into that place. It was hard work, but we loved it. We had friends from all over the world and invited them to come and stay. They brought their friends – wealthy, jet-set types, often celebrities. For a time, it really did feel like we were at the centre of the world. Every day was a party. We loved entertaining and having fun. It wasn't a hardship – it was a lifestyle, work was play and play was work.

'Our happiness only increased when we started a family. Constance, you arrived in 1972, and then Gabriel, you completed us three years later. For some people, having children would have been the death knell of the business, but you two seemed to fit right in. You were both sociable little things, happy to play with the guests, and everyone loved you both. Our life here, it was idyllic.' A shadow fell across her face. 'Then everything started to go wrong.'

Here Madame paused. Ariana was spellbound by the story. Despite all the commotion around them, she was eager to know what happened next but understood that Madeleine needed to take her time.

'Your father,' she continued, turning her gaze to Gabriel and Constance, 'had always enjoyed the good life, but it started to overwhelm him. He liked to gamble, but it got out of control. I didn't realize how bad the situation was until we'd lost almost everything. He hid it from me. All of our accounts were in the red, we owed money to everyone from the butcher to the boulangerie, and every centime we made was being used to prop up his habit. He was cutting corners at the hotel, firing staff until we were left with just a skeleton team because he hadn't enough money to pay all the wages. Of course, none of this is news to any of you.'

Madeleine looked pointedly at Ariana as she said this, leaving her ashamed at how she'd gone through their personal records, digging up family secrets.

'He sold our car, our antique furniture, our jewellery. At one point, all we had left was the hotel and each other. We had no money, no other assets. It was horrible – he became a changed man. Secretive, angry, aggressive. Of course, he was ashamed. He was in deep and couldn't see how to get out, but I was furious that he'd let us all down in this way. The arguments were terrible and, almost inevitably, he turned to drink. I was desperate. I couldn't let us lose the hotel, the only thing we had left. We would have been homeless, destitute.'

'So what happened?' Gabriel couldn't resist interrupting.

'I had to ask for help.' Madeleine closed her eyes, reliving the memory. 'But I couldn't let Alain know. He would have been so angry. He was a very proud man. At times, you remind me so much of him,' she smiled lovingly at Gabriel. 'Both ambitious, determined, fiercely protective of those you love.

'I turned to one of our best friends. Of course, we'd lost many acquaintances when it became clear we were having problems. It's true that you find out who your friends are in times of adversity. But a good man who remained loyal to us . . .' Here Madame looked Ariana straight in the eye. 'Aristotle Theodosis.'

Ariana gasped. 'My grandfather . . .'

Madame nodded slowly. 'Yes. He and your grandmother, Elana, were great friends of ours. And they were loyal. I confided in Elana one evening. She was horrified at what we were going through and offered to do anything she could to help. I asked her to take my engagement ring. I was terrified Alain would sell it. He wasn't himself, didn't know what he was doing. So she took it for safekeeping. It was—'

'—An enormous pink diamond.' Ariana finished the sentence for her. She'd guessed what Madeleine was about to say. All eyes fell on the ring on her right hand, as Ariana slowly removed it.

Madeleine nodded. No words were necessary.

'That's my mother's ring?' Gabriel looked startled. 'I admired it, I remember, over dinner, but I never realized . . . I never remembered . . .'

'I knew it was ours. When you asked me to put it in the safe, I knew. It seems the Theodosis family took everything that was ours,' Constance interjected bitterly. 'The hotel, the ring . . . Why didn't your grandmother give it back to *Maman*, that's what I want to know.'

'*Calme-toi, ma chère*,' Madeleine soothed her. 'I don't know the full story. I have not been quite myself for some time. I think that Elana did try. She wrote to me, many times. I have the letters – although perhaps I should pass them on to you, my dear,' she addressed Ariana. 'But I didn't want to see anyone after Alain died. I couldn't. The shame was too great. And now . . .'

'None of the family knew where the ring had come from,' Ariana explained, feeling inexplicably guilty. 'Yaya left all of her jewellery to me, and it was in the vault, along with everything else. I didn't know. I would never have . . .' She pushed the ring across the table towards Madeleine. 'It never belonged to me, and now I'm returning it.'

The ring sat between them. Madame du Lac made no move to pick it up.

'But you love it, yes? I can see it in your eyes.'

'It's a beautiful ring,' Ariana admitted. 'But it's not mine. It never was.'

Thoughtfully, Madeleine reached for it, holding it up to the light so it sparkled, momentarily lost in a haze of memories. Ariana expected that Madeleine would put it back on her finger, but instead she slipped it into her pocket with no further comment and continued her story.

'I didn't – couldn't – tell Alain, but I asked Aristotle for a loan. It was Elana's suggestion. I was desperate,' Madeleine said fiercely, still trying to justify her actions. 'The bank were about to foreclose on the hotel, and we had no way of meeting the payments. I would have done anything to keep a roof over our heads, to keep the business going. We needed something for our children's future . . .' She looked desperately at Gabriel and Constance. For the first time, Ariana saw the similarities between them – the determined set of the mouth, the arrogant tilt of the head.

'Aristotle bought the hotel outright,' Madeleine explained. 'He didn't want us scrabbling to pay back a loan, didn't want that insecurity hanging over our heads. He insisted he would be a silent partner – that he wouldn't interfere, and we would still take care of the day-to-day affairs – but he didn't want us to ever be in the position of potentially losing the hotel. To be running to him – or someone else – for yet another loan in a few years' time.'

'Now I remember,' Ariana almost knocked her brandy over, interrupting Madame du Lac but unable to help herself. 'The photograph! When Yaya died, my father and I were going through her old documents and photographs. We found a picture, and it must have been my grandmother and grandfather with you and Alain. That's why the hotel seemed so familiar.'

Madeleine smiled sadly. 'Yes, that sounds very likely. We were all great friends.'

'And when Pappous died, the property passed to Yaya. And then to me, in her will.'

Madeleine nodded slowly. 'Yes, that is my assumption. I have to confess, I was terrified when I heard that Elana had died. I didn't know what would happen to me.'

Gabriel frowned, and it was clear that something still wasn't adding up for him. 'I still don't understand. Why all the secrecy?'

Madeleine hesitated, steeling herself for the next part of her tale. 'Your father didn't know what I did – not for a long time. He never knew that I went to Aristotle for help, or that he was so indebted to our old friends. As I said, he was a very proud man.'

'But that's impossible,' Gabriel burst out. 'How could you have sold the hotel without him knowing – he would have needed to give his permission.'

Madeleine looked down at the table, shame stealing over her features. 'Your father . . . had a drinking problem. The more into debt he got, the more he drank to try and forget his problems. I couldn't confide in him. Gabriel, forgive me, I forged his signature.'

'Surely that's not legal?' said Gabriel, his mind working quickly. 'If Papa didn't legally sign away the hotel, then it still belongs to us, not to . . .' he trailed off as he looked across at Ariana.

Madeleine shook her head. 'Don't pursue this. What happened has happened. Aristotle was a good friend to us. He helped us when we needed him. Don't take away his legacy from his granddaughter.'

'No, of course not, I just . . .' Gabriel trailed off. 'I'm sorry,' he apologized to Ariana. 'I'm so used to thinking of the hotel as mine. Old habits die hard.'

Ariana smiled at him, forgiveness in her eyes.

'Did Papa ever find out the truth?' asked Gabriel.

Madeleine nodded, tears misting her eyes. 'He tried to sell the hotel – he didn't discuss it with me. The only thing we had left, and he tried to sell it.' She shook her head in disbelief at the memory of the betrayal. 'I know he wasn't himself by then. He was desperate. But he tried to sell this place behind my back, for a fraction of what it was worth. He was convinced the money would allow him to gamble back enough to pay off all our debts and start again some-where new. And, of course, when the lawyers became involved, they informed him that it had already been sold.'

'What happened?' Ariana whispered.

'He was furious. Beyond angry. I'd never seen him in such a rage. He accused me of . . .'

Madeleine closed her eyes as she remembered that night . . .

'Betrayer!' Alain roared. 'I know what you did. How dare you! You have humiliated me – with Aristotle Theodosis.'

It was past midnight. Madeleine was manning the reception when Alain came storming out of their room. He stood at the top of the grand staircase, screaming and hurling abuse.

Tonight, Gabriel was away, staying with a school friend, but fifteen-year-old Constance was seated beside her mother, reading a novel. She couldn't sleep, so Madeleine had let her come downstairs; in truth, she enjoyed the company. Madeleine was often terribly lonely these days, now that their friends had deserted them, and Alain had changed beyond recognition.

'Please, Alain, be quiet. You'll wake up the guests.' Madeleine hastily tried to quieten him.

'I don't care!' Alain roared. 'Why should I care about the guests when it's not even my hotel and hasn't been for months. Not since you betrayed me.'

Madeleine jumped to her feet. Alain was very drunk. He swayed unsteadily on the balcony, walking towards the stairs. She moved towards him, and Constance ran out to follow her mother.

'Stay there, ma chérie,*' Madeleine told her, not wanting her to see her father like this. Constance ignored her, sticking close to her mother, and Madeleine was too distracted to notice her daughter as she ran up the stairs towards her husband.*

'You had everything you could have wanted, and this is how you repay me?' he snarled. 'Sleeping around behind my back – and I'll bet he wasn't the only one. You've probably screwed half the hotel guests too.'

'How dare you!' Madeleine yelled, rage pulsing through her. She'd had enough of Alain's behaviour, his drunken rages. Couldn't he see that she'd done this for all of them? That he'd put her in an impossible position and she'd saved the hotel for the family. 'Don't you speak to me like that,' she yelled as she reached him.

'I'll speak to you however I want,' Alain yelled back. 'You're my wife – even if you don't act like it.' He grabbed her arm and Madeleine yelped in pain and fear.

'Let go of me,' she hissed, her eyes like daggers.

'You need to be taught a lesson,' he roared, lunging forward, striking out with his hand.

'No!' screamed Constance, as Alain overbalanced, falling over the banister at the top of the staircase . . .

There was a deathly cry from him, and a sickening thud as his body hit the black and white tiles below.

And then silence.

Tears were streaming down Madeleine's cheeks at the memory. She looked down at the table, too ashamed to make eye contact with anyone. The mood had shifted now, a mixture of grief and pity and sadness.

'So that's what happened,' Gabriel said matter-of-factly. 'That's how Papa died?'

Madeleine sobbed. 'It was all my fault.'

'It wasn't,' Gabriel insisted, reaching for his mother's hand and holding it tightly with his own. 'It was just a terrible accident.'

'But if it hadn't been for me, he wouldn't have died. That's why I couldn't leave my room – I couldn't bear seeing that staircase again, the scene where it all happened. I could hardly live with the guilt of knowing I killed him. That I was responsible for his death.'

Constance had been sitting silently throughout Madeleine's revelations. Ariana assumed she knew most of the story already and was surprised when Constance spoke.

'No, you weren't,' she said quietly.

'What do you mean?' Madeleine asked, dabbing her eyes with a napkin as she turned to look at her daughter.

'It was me. *I* killed Papa,' Constance confessed. Her face was contorted into a tortured expression, and she stared straight ahead. Ariana could see she was doing her best not to cry.

'*Chérie*, what do you mean? How could it have been you?'

Constance watched, horrified, as the argument unfolded between her mother and father. They'd argued before, many times, but not this viciously. She'd never seen her father this drunk, with such hate in his eyes, her mother no longer appeasing but prepared to stand her ground. She had never seen them be violent with one another. And when her father called her mother those names, and raised his hand to strike her, Constance acted instinctively, diving between the two of them, trying to push her father away.

'No!' she screamed.

And as she lunged for him, he lost his balance, falling over the banister . . .

'So you see, it wasn't you,' Constance sobbed. 'And I've let you live with thinking it was all these years. But I couldn't face the guilt. I couldn't believe what I'd done . . .'

'It wasn't either of you, don't you see?' Gabriel told them. Ariana could see that he was horrified by how upset his mother and sister were, how Alain's death had affected them so deeply for so many years, both of them thinking they were at fault. 'It was an accident, a terrible, terrible accident.'

'Perhaps I should go,' Ariana murmured, feeling like she was intruding on a private family moment.

Gabriel shook his head. 'Please stay,' he said, and reached for her hand. Ariana silently nodded, knowing he needed her support and determined to stand by him.

'How can you ever forgive me?' Constance wept, looking at her brother.

'There's nothing to forgive,' Gabriel assured her. 'Both of you are innocent of any guilt. We've suffered so much hurt as a family. Everything took place so long ago, and we've wasted so many years – fighting and grieving and hurting one another. It's time for us all to move on with our lives. To be a proper family again.'

As Ariana watched, Gabriel stood up from his chair and walked around the table, taking his mother and his sister in his arms, the three of them embracing, their tears cathartic, finally erasing the hurt of the past. The secrets had been revealed; they could only hurt them in the shadows. Now they were out in the light, it was time to move forward, and Ariana felt grateful to Madeleine for letting her be part of this moment.

'I need some fresh air.' Gabriel stood up, rubbing his forehead wearily. He looked as though he'd been through the wringer.

Ariana watched him uncertainly, unsure what to do.

He reached out his hand to her. 'Come with me?'

Ariana stood up, took hold of his outstretched hand, and let him lead her outside. At that moment, she knew she'd follow him to the ends of the earth.

Chapter 30

Ariana and Gabriel walked hand-in-hand beneath the moonlight, along the cobbled streets of Le Suquet and down the hill to the harbour. They looked as though they'd stepped straight off a film set: him, devastatingly handsome in his white shirt and tuxedo trousers; her, sultry and beautiful in the classic black gown that rippled out behind her as she walked.

They barely said a word to one another. Ariana knew that Gabriel needed time to take in everything he'd just heard. His world had been shattered, and he had to come to terms with what he'd learned about the death of his father, the guilt his mother and sister had carried, the circumstances around losing the hotel. Ariana kept quiet, squeezing his hand to let him know that she was there for him whenever he was ready to talk.

She was absorbing the night's events herself: the gunshot, Robert Chappell being ferried to hospital – the latest news was that he was critical and in intensive care, Elizabeth hadn't left his side – and the revelations from

Madame du Lac. The hotel was still swarming with law enforcement officers, and the only reason they'd been allowed to leave was because Gabriel knew the chief of police. Perhaps she should have stayed at the hotel, but right now it felt like the most important place for her to be was with Gabriel.

They reached the harbour and stopped walking. Gabriel sat down on the low stone wall beside the water, the sound of the sea lapping against the dock. Ariana recalled meeting Gabriel here for their romantic trip to the island. It was mere days ago, but so much had happened since then.

'How are you doing?' she asked carefully, sitting down beside him.

He turned to her, those blue eyes so intense it made her heart leap, sending tingles through her body. Harbour lights framed his features perfectly, and Ariana remembered how it had felt to kiss him.

'I'm OK. It's a relief, in a way, to finally know the truth. I think I'd come to terms with everything years ago, but it's good to know the details, to understand what actually happened. Of course, I feel terrible for *Maman* and Constance. I wish I'd been there for them, that I could have done more. At least now we can move forward and make a fresh start.'

'They're so lucky to have you,' Ariana said, reaching over to take his hand. 'By the way, where did you learn the ninja moves, taking that Victor guy out?'

Gabriel gave a wry smile. 'I went to an English public school. You need to be able to look after yourself, so I did martial arts for five years.'

For a moment, they sat in silence. Gabriel stroked her palm tenderly, their fingers lacing together.

'And you?' he asked softly. 'It's been quite a night for you too.'

'I still don't know exactly what happened. It was all going so well, and then . . . What an absolute disaster.'

'You certainly put the hotel on the map,' Gabriel couldn't resist saying, as Ariana shook her head helplessly in disbelief.

'I hope Robert Chappell's going to be all right. When that gun went off, I—' A look of panic crossed her face and Gabriel rushed to reassure her.

'He's in the best possible hands.'

Ariana nodded. 'And Elizabeth's with him, although Jonny stayed behind. The two of them have such a difficult relationship.'

At the mention of Jonny's name, Gabriel's face darkened.

'Yes, the infamous Jonny Farrell,' he laughed mirthlessly. 'I don't like the man and I suspect I never will. He's not honest. Not trustworthy.'

'No,' Ariana agreed. 'He's not.'

'And are you and he . . .?' Gabriel trailed off, letting the question hang. Ariana could hear the tension in his voice and rushed to reassure him.

'No, absolutely not. We're not together anymore. That's completely over.'

She saw Gabriel's shoulders relax in relief. Then another look stole over his face, his eyes full of questions, his jaw set tightly. 'Ariana, I can't bear this any longer. I need to know. I've fallen in love with you. I've never felt like this about any woman before. You're intelligent and wild and . . . unbelievably beautiful.' His eyes roamed her face, drinking her in, searching for clues about her feelings. 'If you don't feel the same way, I'll be out of your life. I promise you, you'll never see me again. But if you do . . .'

Ariana's heart was racing. She felt almost dizzy with joy, hardly able to believe the words he was saying. Did she love him? She'd tried to deny it – to Gabriel, to herself. But she felt light every time he was around, and as though a part of her was missing when she wasn't with him. She wanted him, desperately. Memories of his passionate kisses were etched on her brain. The thought of him leaving, of never seeing him again, made her heart ache. The mere suggestion left her in agony; she didn't know how she would survive. But it was impossible to articulate all of that, and all she could say was: 'Yes.'

'Yes?' Gabriel repeated, his forehead creasing uncertainly, wanting to be sure.

'Yes, yes, yes, I love you, Gabriel.'

He smiled at her, a wonderful expression of joy that lit up his whole face and seemed to transform him, all the stress and worry he'd been carrying melting away as he swept her into his arms and kissed her. In that one, blissful moment, everything else was forgotten – the hotel and the shooting and Madeleine's story. Ariana could think of nothing else apart from how wonderful it felt to feel his body pressed against hers, how right they felt together, and the intense longing stirring deep within her. All this time she'd been searching for a purpose. Now, she knew, she'd been searching for Gabriel.

Ariana could have stayed wrapped in Gabriel's strong arms forever. As he pulled back, she saw the desire in his eyes and knew it was reflected in her own.

'Come on,' Gabriel murmured, his voice low and gravelly, that melodious French accent sending tingles throughout her body. 'We need to go back.'

He held out his hand to help her up and they began the walk back up the hill. It felt as though everything had changed between them since they'd walked the same streets earlier that evening. Ariana could hear the music and laughter from the yacht parties and the beach clubs, but that felt like a world away from where they were wrapped up in their own little bubble.

They walked in silence once again, lost in their thoughts. Gabriel's arm was around Ariana's shoulder, holding her close. He cleared his throat and said, 'There's something I need to tell you.'

He sounded serious and Ariana looked at him in surprise. 'More secrets?' she said lightly, raising an eyebrow.

'Perhaps I shouldn't have done this, but I was worried about you – and with good reason, as it turned out.'

'Done what?' Her heart was thumping, wondering what Gabriel was about to reveal. She'd been feeling so happy and content, and selfishly didn't want anything to spoil it.

'I had my suspicions about Jonny, so I did some investigating. Perhaps I was a little jealous too,' Gabriel admitted, looking sheepish.

'And . . . what did you find?'

'Much of what you already know – that he has a problem with drugs, that his reputation with women is . . . less than stellar. Which brought me to Liberty Granger.'

Ariana's head seemed to fill with a roaring sound, her heartbeat racing, her hands shaking. She couldn't help but feel that way whenever she heard Liberty's name, as though she were about to have a panic attack. Ariana fought to stay calm as Gabriel continued to speak.

'I knew how worried you were about everything that had happened at that party. I was flattered that you had confided in me. I wanted to help. I felt sure you couldn't have been involved in any way. I know you, Ariana. You have such a good heart, you're not capable of anything like that.'

'What did you find?' she whispered.

'That night – what do you remember about it?'

'Please don't make me do this,' Ariana begged, suddenly close to tears. 'I've been over and over it in my mind. I don't remember. There are black spots, chunks missing. I'm so scared.'

'You took a cab home, do you remember?'

'I did?' Ariana blinked, desperately clutching for the memory.

'Yes, by yourself. There are witnesses who saw you. CCTV footage of you entering your building alone, not long after midnight. Jonny and Montana remained at the party.'

'Montana was still there?' Something didn't seem right to Ariana, an inconsistency niggling at the back of her brain. 'She told me she left early, that she had to be up the next morning for an audition.'

'Then she lied,' Gabriel said starkly. 'And if she told you that – if she was willing to make you believe you might be responsible for something so terrible – then I think you have to ask yourself what else she might have lied about.'

It took a moment for the wheels to turn as Ariana digested the revelation that if she'd left early, and if the party had continued long after she left, then she *couldn't* have been responsible for Liberty's death.

So why had someone been sending those texts, trying to make her think it was her fault and—

'The messages?' Ariana said. 'I thought they were from Jonny, but do you think . . .?'

'I don't have any proof, but that is my suspicion, that Montana Morgan has been sending them,' Gabriel said gravely.

'But she was supposed to be my friend. I trusted her, I told her how scared I was. She—'

They were almost back at the hotel. Ariana's expression changed, her eyes narrowing. 'She even asked me to put her on the guest list tonight. Christ, I was such a fool. Well, not any longer.' Squaring her shoulders, as though preparing for battle, she stalked off towards the entrance.

Ariana marched into reception. The hotel was emptying out now, the guests and waiting staff gradually making their way home as the police allowed them to leave. Ariana couldn't think about all of that right now. She had a single focus, just one target in mind.

She stared round the reception, her eyes steely, then headed for the bar. Madame du Lac and Constance were no longer there. After everything Madeleine had been through, Ariana expected she'd have returned to her room to recover. Jonny and Montana were still together. He was slumped on the table, staring into the distance, while she stroked his arm with her long fake nails, whispering into his ear.

Ariana stormed over and Montana looked up in surprise.

'Hey, Ariana—' she began.

'Don't you "Hey, Ariana" me. We need to talk.'

'What about?'

'Don't play innocent with me.' Ariana stared at her in disgust, her eyes blazing. Montana had gone pale beneath her fake tan. Her bleached blonde hair was dishevelled, her surgically enhanced breasts spilling out of her bandage dress. Everything about her was fake. Ariana found herself wondering what they'd ever had in common. She'd been a different person back in LA, she realized. She didn't want to be that person ever again.

'You told me you went home early from the party. You lied.'

A range of emotions flitted across Montana's face: surprise and fear, which she replaced with a shrug, deciding to brazen it out. 'I got confused.'

'Cut the bull, Montana. You tried to make me believe I had something to do with Liberty's death. That I was the one who killed her.'

Jonny was paying attention now, looking nervously between the two women as Ariana's voice grew louder. Gabriel watched anxiously. He knew this was Ariana's fight and didn't want to interfere, but if she needed him, he'd be there in a heartbeat.

Montana's face changed, becoming cruel and unpleasant. 'Aw, did poor little rich girl think she'd done something wrong? What did it feel like, huh? To have your perfect world messed up? To not get everything you ever wanted the second you snap your fingers?'

'What are you talking about?' Ariana stared at her in confusion.

'You had everything,' Montana spat bitterly. 'The looks, the money . . . Jonny.'

'What?' said Ariana and Jonny simultaneously.

'He would have wanted me if it wasn't for you, with your money and your designer clothes. You had the perfect life. God, I hate you.'

'B-But we were friends,' Ariana shook her head in disbelief.

'Oh, please. Spare me, we're talking about shallow LA, honey, not your crappy Greek loyalty schtick.' Montana rolled her eyes dramatically.

The pieces finally slid into place, and suddenly Ariana realized that her suspicions were correct. 'It was you. You sent the messages.'

Montana threw her head back and laughed. 'Oh, you should have seen your face: "I'm so scared, Montana. I can't remember what happened,"' Montana mocked her.

'But why?'

'Because you had Jonny. And Liberty had Jonny. How was I supposed to get a look in? I didn't stand a chance. He should have been *mine*. No one understands him like me. The two of you were always whining about him. Didn't you understand how lucky you were, that you got to be with him? I hated you, and Liberty too. She deserved everything she got.'

'Montana, what are you saying?' Jonny asked.

Montana looked at him, as though she'd forgotten he was there. 'Jonny, baby, you know it's true. No one knows you like I do. You know I'm more fun than those stuck-up bitches. I'll do anything you want me to. Whatever it takes to make you happy. All I want is to be with you.'

Ariana looked at Montana, draping herself over Jonny, who looked utterly bemused, and felt nothing but contempt. 'You're welcome to him. The two of you make the perfect couple.'

She turned on her heels and joined Gabriel standing a discreet distance away.

'Are you OK?' Gabriel asked.

Ariana realized she was shaking. 'What the hell just happened?' she said, looking shell-shocked.

'I don't know. But it sounds as though you don't have anything to worry about anymore. I'll hand over everything I have to the LAPD. They can decide what to do.'

Ariana nodded. Suddenly feeling exhausted, she headed for the stairs. All she wanted was to get back to her room. She began walking up the curved staircase, the wooden banister smooth beneath her palm and beautifully carved, but she would never see it in the same way now that she knew the truth about what had happened to Gabriel's father. The hotel was full of bad memories for the du Lacs; she hoped they could start making some good ones.

They were almost at her suite when something occurred to Ariana. 'You really did all that for me?' she asked. 'Looking into Montana and Jonny, and making sure I was OK?'

'Of course,' Gabriel shrugged, looking impossibly French.

A smile spread across Ariana's face, as she realized how lucky she was. Perhaps Montana was right – perhaps she did lead a charmed life. She'd been so suspicious of Gabriel's intentions, certain that he intended to betray her. Perhaps that had been his aim at first, but now she trusted him with her whole heart. 'But why?'

'I told you.' He looked at her intensely. 'I love you.'

Ariana let herself be enveloped into his arms, feeling so treasured, so safe. The last few days had been crazy, but now she knew she could face anything with Gabriel at her side. She tilted her head to kiss him and he responded, their embrace growing more passionate. She slid backwards against the wall, their bodies sliding together, heat flooding her belly.

'I don't think we should do this here,' Gabriel murmured, his lips brushing her ear thrillingly. They were still in the corridor, just outside her room.

Ariana smiled. 'Fortunately, I know a good hotel in the area.'

'I happen to know the owner,' Gabriel teased.

'I hear she's not a patch on the last one,' Ariana grinned.

As they fell through the door, the events of the last few days went rushing through her mind. The Hotel du Soleil might not be comparable with her father's empire, but Ariana was creating her own life, and doing what made her happy. Perhaps Elana had known her better than she knew herself; giving Ariana the hotel had given her a focus. And it had given her Gabriel.

Then Gabriel was kissing her neck, unzipping her dress, his body pressed against hers, and all she could concentrate on was how good it felt. Thoughts drifted away, and she surrendered to sensations.

Chapter 31

Arizona, November 2009

'God, grant me the serenity to accept the things I cannot change, the courage to change the things I can, and the wisdom to know the difference.'

Jonny murmured the serenity prayer, glancing around at the dozen other people earnestly reciting the words. They were an assorted bunch, a varied mix of ages and backgrounds, but they'd all found themselves here, at the New Beginnings treatment facility in the Mojave Desert. The room was plain, with everything designed to be soothing in natural wood and neutral tones, the integrated air-con keeping the fierce heat at bay.

His father was paying for it – *This is your final chance*, Robert had insisted – and it was costing an absolute fortune. But this time, Jonny was serious. He really wanted to change, to turn his life around, to settle down with a good woman and get a real job. Well, nothing too arduous. In fact, he could probably do the chat show circuit for a while, talking about how he was a changed man, hopefully get a new agent off the back of it and some lucrative new contracts . . .

'Good session, everyone. See you again the same time tomorrow.'

The session leader, a stern but caring woman who reminded Jonny of one of his childhood nannies, placed her hands together and bowed to everyone in a namaste. Across the room, Jonny caught the eye of the cute brunette who had arrived yesterday. He'd seen her in the gossip pages recently, a former Disney child star who'd grown up and gone bad – but oh, she looked good, Jonny thought to himself, with her creamy skin and shapely body shown to perfection in the tightly fitted gym gear she was wearing. Jonny lengthened his stride to catch up with her as she passed through the door into a glass-sided atrium, where a large Joshua tree was growing through the centre.

'Hey.' Jonny touched her lightly on the arm and she turned to look at him, an unnaturally white smile lighting up her face. 'Are you new here? I haven't seen you around before.'

'I just got here yesterday,' the girl explained, looking a little shell-shocked and embarrassed.

'Welcome,' Jonny beamed, running his hands through his dark hair. He'd had it cut short but was thinking about growing it again; he felt like Samson, losing his powers. 'I'm Jonny.' He held his hand out and the girl shook it.

'Bella. It's nice to meet you. Are we allowed to fraternize like this?'

Jonny shrugged. 'Everyone needs a friend, right? Especially in here.'

'Sure,' Bella nodded. 'That makes sense.' She stared at

him, her lips slightly parted, her pupils wide, and Jonny knew she was interested. Inwardly, he congratulated himself on not having lost his touch.

'I'm here if you need someone to talk to. I won't tell, what are you in for?' He gave her a concerned smile.

She hesitated. 'Um . . . well I'm here for sex addiction.'

Jonny said a silent prayer of thanks. 'That's tough, babe.'

'Thanks, Jonny,' she beamed, looking up at him with enormous Bambi eyes. 'I'll catch up with you later – I have to go now, I have a yoga class.'

'What a coincidence. Me too,' Jonny lied smoothly, unable to stop himself imagining Bella contorting her sexy, supple body into all kinds of different shapes right in front of him.

'Great,' she grinned. 'Let's go.'

Jonny followed behind, watching the way she walked, her hips sashaying, pert bottom swaying. He'd been nervous about coming back to rehab but now wondered why he'd been so worried. He had a feeling it wasn't going to be too bad after all.

'Beautiful,' Elizabeth declared, as she walked up behind Robert with a mug of tea. He took it from her gratefully, placing it down on the table beside him.

'Not as beautiful as you, my darling,' he grinned, pulling her in for a passionate embrace.

'Careful, you'll get my clothes dirty,' Liz half-heartedly protested.

'Better take them off then.' Robert wiggled his eyebrows as Liz laughed and shook her head.

'Honestly, you're incorrigible.'

She took a seat in a vintage armchair as Robert blew

across the steaming tea. They were on the top floor of the east wing of their new property, in a room that served as Robert's studio. It was a stunning Cotswold manor house, built in honey-coloured stone and wreathed in ivy, with stables and a lake in the extensive grounds. They'd sold up in California – both the Malibu beach house and the Beverly Hills mansion – and had no plans to return.

Elizabeth had been by Robert's side day and night after he was rushed to hospital in Cannes. They'd talked endlessly during his convalescence, and she'd realized how terrified she'd been that she might lose him; it was impossible to forget the sound of the gunshot or the sight of his blood seeping through his shirt. Elizabeth made the decision that, despite Robert's many flaws, she loved him desperately and wanted to be with him. She told her lawyers to destroy the papers, and the word 'divorce' had never been mentioned again.

They'd bought the Gloucestershire house sight unseen, and Liz had had a team of decorators and interior designers working on it for when Robert was ready to return. They'd moved in two months ago and it was perfect. Today had been one of those rare, idyllic, English winter days, the weather crisp and bright but freezing cold. Outside the mullioned windows the light was beginning to fade as the sun set and slid into dusk. A low mist rolled in across the fields, and a shimmering frost gave the scene a magical sparkle.

Both Elizabeth and Robert had been content to take a step back from their acting careers, to dial down the high-octane world in which they'd been operating. They revelled in wearing casual clothes and eschewing the gym, in not having to abide by a strict schedule or ensure they were always camera-ready. In a few months' time, they might get itchy feet, but for now, they luxuriated in their new-found freedom.

If they needed a reminder of their achievements all they had to do was look in their awards cabinet – the most recent addition was a Palme d'Or for *All Our Yesterdays*. Of course, neither of them had been at the ceremony, but Ross Anderson, the director, had attended and dedicated the trophy to 'absent friends', thinking of Robert and, of course, Liberty Granger. The movie had gone on to be a box office smash. Whenever the Chappells were ready, Hollywood would welcome them back with open arms.

Liz had devoted herself to Robert and his recovery. She liked to cook his favourite meals, run him a bath each evening, and pander to his every whim. She was incredibly proud of him for stopping drinking, and astonished that he'd developed a taste for green tea, of all things. Their lovemaking was slow and gentle, a rediscovering of one another, and Elizabeth blushed as she thought of their nights – and mornings, and afternoons – together.

She glanced across to where Robert had recommenced painting; he winced almost imperceptibly, and she was reminded that his shoulder hadn't fully healed. He'd been incredibly lucky; the bullet had missed his heart by inches, and the doctors had warned him the scar might never be pain free. Robert had had to reconcile himself to the fact that his days of playing action heroes were over.

The slower pace of life had brought out her husband's creative side with a vengeance. Robert had been trying his hand at writing, tinkering with scripts and short stories, but his true passion was painting, working in oil on canvas, mostly landscapes with the occasional portrait.

'Darling, it's simply incredible,' Liz continued, nodding at his current work-in-progress.

'Thanks. I called Fran the other day and suggested she might speak to a couple of galleries in London – maybe the Serpentine, or the Saatchi – about a potential exhibition next year. I thought she was gonna lose her mind,' Robert chuckled.

'Yeah, fifteen per cent of that isn't going to be comparable with the commission from a multimillion-dollar movie contract.'

'I know. She couldn't get off the phone fast enough.'

'It's a good idea though, an exhibition,' Liz mused. 'It would give you a goal. Something to work towards.'

'What about you? Anything interesting come through?'

Liz had let it be known that she was looking for a West End project, and theatre directors had been falling over themselves to send scripts to her. 'Nothing yet. I might have to delay that a little while anyway . . .'

'Oh really?' Robert was distracted, mixing just the right shade of magenta on his palette.

'Yes. I might need to take it easy for a few months. And you'll have to plan the timing of your exhibition carefully. We don't want it to clash . . .'

Robert was only half-listening. 'Clash with what?'

She hesitated, wanting to savour the moment. 'When the baby's due, Robbie . . .'

Liz couldn't keep the grin from her face as she watched the realization slowly dawn on Robert. He dropped his paintbrush and rushed over to her with a whoop, smothering her with kisses, not caring if he covered her in paint.

'Are you serious? I mean, when? How?'

'Surely I don't need to explain that last one to you,' Liz laughed. 'It's only early days,' she explained, as Robert began stroking her stomach, marvelling at the miracle cocooned inside. 'So let's not get carried away yet.'

'Are you kidding? I'm going to shout it from the rooftops. It's all going to be grand, I can just feel it. Me, you and our little girl.'

'Girl?'

'Yes, I'm sure of it. I love you, Liz. Seriously, I've never loved anyone more. And I'll be ten times the father I was to Jonathan – no, a hundred, in fact make it a thousand! We've weathered the storm and come out the other side. Nothing can break us now.'

Elizabeth snuggled up to him, feeling safe and protected as he enveloped her in his arms, knowing he meant every word he said. Robert was her husband, her lover, her best friend and the father of her unborn child. He had his faults, but she loved him deeply. And she knew she always would.

Intoxicating smells drifted from the bubbling pot on the stove where Stefan was trying out a new recipe. Estée lifted the lid and inhaled, dipping a teaspoon into the sauce and tasting it.

'Mmm, delicious. But it's missing something,' she teased, before turning round and kissing him.

The windows in their tiny kitchen were steamed up, the room warm and cosy. Their apartment in Montmartre, the charming hilltop neighbourhood in the north of Paris, felt comfortable and homely, and signified a new start for them. Estée was determined to start making changes to her life.

She'd cooperated fully with the police, giving evidence and an extensive witness statement. It had come to light that Victor's shady business dealings at La Châtelaine were merely a small part of a much larger operation, and the police had assured her that he was looking at spending a considerable time behind bars.

Estée had returned to Paris and her family. Her mother knew everything; she'd seen the stories on the news and, while Estée was embarrassed, Mariam was simply glad to have her daughter home safely, while Emilie was overjoyed to have her mother back. To Estée, it felt as though something was missing: Stefan.

If anything good had come out of the terrible incident at the Palme Gala, it had made Estée and Stefan admit how they felt about one another. Estée had discovered that life was too short not to be happy, and could no longer deny her feelings towards him. Stefan said that when he saw her with Victor, he realized he would have done anything to protect her. He handed in his resignation at the Hotel du Soleil – Ariana had offered him a generous salary raise to try and get him to stay – but Stefan knew it was time to move on.

He'd long dreamt of opening his own restaurant and, on a visit to see Estée in Paris, Stefan had found the perfect place in Montmartre. It was just off the tourist trail, high on the hill with stunning views over the city, and was situated in a delightfully quaint old building that housed the restaurant downstairs with two floors of living quarters above. Though Stefan didn't have the funds to buy the place outright, he'd managed to persuade an investor to come on board: Gabriel du Lac.

Despite being from very different backgrounds, the two men had always got on well, with a mutual respect for one another. Stefan knew that the decision hadn't been made out of charity; Gabriel was a successful entrepreneur, who wouldn't have done the deal if it didn't make business sense. Despite everything, Estée realized she had more than one reason to be grateful to the du Lac family.

'*Maman, Maman*!' The front door banged and a whirlwind blew in. Emilie was home from school. Estée heard her footsteps as she ran up the stairs, then burst into the kitchen to give her mother a hug.

'Her teacher said she got full marks in her test,' Estée's mother, Mariam, smiled as she followed Emilie inside. 'She's settling in well.'

Her mother had kept her old apartment in Saint-Denis, but spent lots of time at Estée and Stefan's new place, and was an invaluable help with her granddaughter. Estée had worried about uprooting Emilie from her school and her social life, but she was keen to move out of the suburbs, and regularly went back to stay with her grandmother and see her old friends. It was the best of both worlds.

Estée had thought long and hard about her future, and realized that the thought of traipsing round the audition circuit no longer filled her with excitement. She'd discovered a small dance studio near their new apartment and had been thrilled to land a job there, teaching small children the basics of ballet. It wasn't well paid, or prestigious, but the joy on the little ones' faces as they tried to master a grand plié or the perfect pirouette more than made up for that. The new arrangement seemed to be working well, and Stefan had been wonderfully embracing of her daughter and her mother.

Even now, Mariam wandered over to the hob and tasted the food. 'It needs more turmeric,' she pronounced, as Stefan shook his head in despair and Estée burst out laughing.

'By the way, there was a parcel downstairs for you,' Mariam said. 'I left it in the hallway.'

Estée went to get it, carrying it back through to the kitchen. It was large and securely packaged, and the sender's label said that it had come from England.

'It's from Robert,' Estée said in surprise, reading the return address.

The two of them had kept in touch via email, with Robert updating her on his convalescence, and Estée sending photos of her family. He'd refused to take back any of the money he'd lent her, and Estée had put it in an account for Emilie; her daughter, too, would benefit from Robert's generosity in the future.

Estée pulled off the packaging as everyone watched curiously, layer after layer of brown paper and bubble wrap falling onto the tiled floor.

'Oh,' Estée breathed. 'Look at that.'

It was an oil painting, the image recreated from the photographs she'd sent. It showed Estée with her arms around Emilie, an expression of joy on both their faces. Robert had called it *Mother and Child: Reunited*.

'He's very talented,' Mariam marvelled.

'Do I need to be jealous?' Stefan joked. Estée knew that he wasn't being serious; she'd told him everything that had happened – or rather, *hadn't* happened – with Robert.

Estée propped the painting on the kitchen worktop and they all stood back to admire it. Stefan wrapped his arms around Estée, planting a kiss on her shoulder, as Emilie came and slipped her hand into her mother's and Mariam bustled round preparing tea.

In that moment, Estée felt a surge of warmth and gratitude. After a tough few years, she'd finally found happiness and been brave enough to make a new start. She had a family, a man who loved her and treated her with respect, and she was thriving. She'd learned that life was a gift, and vowed to make the most of every day.

Epilogue

Ithos, December 2009

Ariana stretched luxuriously as her eyelids fluttered open. The Egyptian cotton sheets were crisp and cool, the dazzling white material highlighting her tanned, olive skin.

It felt strange to be back here, in her childhood room – well, it was more like an apartment, in the new wing of the villa that had been built when her parents got married.

It felt even stranger to be here with Gabriel lying in the bed beside her.

'Good morning,' she smiled, as he began to stir. Even first thing in the morning he looked impossibly handsome, with his wavy hair messed up, his face adorably crumpled, and a smattering of blond stubble on his chin. His piercing blue eyes sparkled as they looked at her and, as he propped himself up on one elbow, she found herself admiring his strong arms and the ripple of his biceps.

Ariana leaned in to kiss him, butterflies dancing in her stomach, wondering if she'd ever grow tired of waking up with him. Gabriel responded, their kisses growing more intense, until Ariana giggled and pulled away.

'Not this morning. I have plans for us.'

'I have plans for us too,' Gabriel growled.

'I'm taking you on a tour of the island, remember?' Ariana grinned, sliding out of bed and wrapping a silk robe over her naked body. Padding barefoot across the carpet, she pressed a button on the wall and the window blinds rolled away, revealing Ithos Bay and the picturesque harbour, the view she knew so well and that was imprinted on her soul.

Ariana had been so excited to bring Gabriel to the island that meant so much to her and her family. It was his first time meeting Demetrios, and the encounter appeared to have been a success. Last night, everyone had gone for a meal at Níko's taverna, feasting on spanakopita and kleftiko and all the traditional foods that Ariana remembered from her childhood. Her father and Gabriel had developed a mutual respect for one another, although Gabriel was clearly in awe of Demetrios, and the two men happily talked boats and business while Ariana caught up with Shauna and Alex, as well as Níko and his wife Teresa, and Christian and Grace with their baby girl, Thea.

Afterwards, as they walked up the hill back to the villa, she had left Gabriel chatting to Shauna and had run ahead to link arms with her father, who always strode up the hill much more quickly than everyone else.

'You do like him don't you, Papa?' she had asked her father shyly.

Demetrios pursed his lips as if in thought, and paused before he answered. 'Well . . .'

'Papa!'

'. . . No one is good enough for my little girl, Ari, you must know that.'

Ariana felt a moment of uncertainty, 'You are teasing me, right?'

'Oh no, not at all,' he said mock-seriously. 'No good father thinks that anyone is the right man for their daughter!'

'Papa, be serious!'

Demetrios laughed then. 'Oh all right, he's a businessman, he's an entrepreneur, he's hardworking and good-looking just like your old man, and he can handle himself. I think he'll fit right into the family, don't you?'

Ariana laughed. 'Papa, do you think Yaya would have liked him?'

Demetrios looked down at her tenderly. 'Your grandmother would have loved him, Ari.'

As Ariana stared out of her bedroom window, remembering the previous night with a soft smile, Gabriel came up behind her, wrapping his arms around her.

'I was going to take a shower,' he murmured, his voice low and husky, his delicious French accent sending shivers of delight right through her. 'Care to join me?'

It didn't take Ariana long to make up her mind. She supposed it didn't matter if they set off a little late; Ithos would still be there. Her eyes full of promise, she let her robe drop to the floor and took hold of Gabriel's hand, leading the way.

That afternoon, they were driving along Ithos's rugged roads in Demetrios's old jeep, as Ariana proudly pointed out her favourite spots on the enchanting island. They passed pretty little fishing villages where the old traditions were kept alive; fig trees and olive groves that stretched as far as the eye could see; a picture-perfect white stone monastery that sat on a craggy promontory lapped by the sapphire sea. The soaring mountains, sun-bleached and golden in the long, dry summer months, were now lush and green in winter. To Ariana, everything was both familiar and magical at the same time.

'Beautiful,' Gabriel murmured, although he was staring at Ariana. 'Shall we stop somewhere soon? It'd be good to stretch our legs and breathe in the sea air.'

'Yes, let's,' Ariana agreed easily. 'There's the most beautiful bay on the other side of this headland. I swear, it has the softest sand in the whole world.'

'Sounds perfect.'

They continued driving. It was mild for the time of year, and the winter sun sparkled off the Aegean Sea, the foamy, white-tipped waves crashing onto the rocks along the shoreline. The jeep easily handled the descent as they made their way down from the cliffs to sea level, parking up on a deserted stretch of land beside a pristine beach. There was no one around, not even boats on the horizon, and it felt as though they were the only two people in existence.

Demetrios's chef had packed them a mouth-watering picnic, and Gabriel carried the basket across the beach where they set up on a blanket. Ariana was wearing a long-sleeved floral dress with ankle boots, but she kicked them off, wiggling her toes in the fine white sand. Gabriel, dressed in a smart blue shirt and chinos, wrapped his arms around her and kissed her tenderly, as though she were the most precious thing in the world.

'So, how do you like Ithos?' Ariana asked expectantly.

'It's beautiful. I can see why it's so special to you. Thank you.'

'What for?'

'Bringing me here and sharing your home with me. Letting me be part of your life and showing me everything that's important to you.'

'The most important things to me are you and my family. I'm glad I could finally bring the two of you together.'

So much had changed over the last few months. Ariana and Gabriel had grown closer than ever. Although theirs was a tempestuous relationship, they hated being apart, and had fallen deeply in love.

The Hotel du Soleil was undergoing a revival. It turned out to be true that there was no such thing as bad publicity, and the drama of the Palme Gala had put the hotel firmly back on the radar of the jet-set, who'd flocked there over the summer months. Ariana had swallowed her pride and allowed Gabriel to lay to rest the demons of his past, letting him buy into the hotel on a fifty-fifty basis. Together, they'd set about transforming it.

'Let's celebrate,' Gabriel said, reaching for the cool box.

'Celebrate what?' asked Ariana. She was staring out at the view, letting the sound of the sea and the warmth of the sun revitalize her.

'You, me, being here together. And one other thing.'

Ariana turned and her hand flew to her mouth in surprise. Gabriel was down on one knee, holding out a ring. She felt tears spring to her eyes even before he uttered the words she knew he was going to say.

'Ariana Elana Aphrodite Theodosis, I love you more than anything and I want to spend the rest of my life with you. Will you do me the honour of being my wife?'

Ariana was too stunned to speak. At first, she could only nod her head, but then she found her voice. 'Yes, yes, yes!' she cried, overwhelmed with happiness.

It was only when Gabriel went to slip the ring on her finger that she realized.

'This is your mother's ring,' she murmured. 'I couldn't . . .'

'She wanted you to have it. She gave it to me and asked me to pass it on. She knew how much you loved it. Given that your grandmother had it for so long and kept it safe, she felt it was only right to keep it in your family. *Our* family.'

Gabriel popped the champagne cork and poured his fiancée a glass.

'To the future,' he said softly, as they toasted.

'To the future,' she murmured back, snuggling into his embrace as he wrapped his arms around her and kissed her deeply.

Ariana felt like the luckiest girl in the world as she held out her left hand to admire the brilliant pink diamond on her third finger, its myriad facets sparkling in the Greek sunlight. The ring had been cherished by both of their families, and it was as though their pasts and their futures were intertwined, held together by an invisible bond that could never be broken.

It was as though the two of them were always meant to be.

Acknowledgements

To everyone who bought my first book *Under a Greek Moon* and took the time and trouble to review it. I am overwhelmed by your positive comments, and beyond delighted that you enjoyed it.

My grateful thanks to all my family, friends and colleagues who have bolstered my confidence in my ability to do this, especially when I doubted myself. Your encouragement and support is so appreciated. Thank you.

To Steve. Your patience knows no bounds! You are such an inspiration to me. Thank you from the bottom of my heart.

To my wonderful family for believing in me, and for being there through thick and thin, not only now, but all through my life.

Philippa and Chris Howell, you are like family to me. Your support is never-ending. Your pride in me is humbling.

Kerr MacRae, my publishing agent. None of this would have been possible without you. Your sage advice and guidance is phenomenal!

Kate Bradley, my editor at HarperCollins … I think we were separated at birth! You have such a sound understanding of my vision. I love working with you. You make the whole process easier and enjoyable.

Finally, my grateful thanks to HarperCollins for publishing this book and to the wider team who made it all possible, including CEO Charlie Redmayne for his encouragement, Elizabeth Dawson and Emma Pickard for their publicity and marketing expertise, publisher Kimberley Young for her support, and Claire Ward who designed the fabulous cover.

Read on for an extract from Carol's new novel

The Secrets of the Villa Amore

Coming summer 2023

Campania, Italy

Carina Russo was standing on the Juliet balcony of her bedroom, in her family's palatial countryside villa. The land as far as she could see belonged to the Russos; the undulating hills in shades of sage and sun-scorched ochre stretching away to the distant horizon. Beyond the manicured gardens that bordered the house, lush with greenery and leading to a secluded Romanesque swimming pool, lay row after row of sprawling vines, the dark grapes hanging like priceless jewels in the vineyard that had made the Russos' fortune.

The Russos' land bordered that of the Bianchis, the two estates separated by a wide, shallow stream that began in the Avella mountains. It was this natural spring, with its mineral-rich water, that gave the grapes such a unique flavour, and made the Casa di Russo wine so special.

The fierce heat of the day had reached its zenith, the late afternoon sun bathing the landscape in a magical golden light. The whispering breeze lifted tendrils of Carina's thick, honey-blonde hair, which had escaped the long plait in which they were tethered. The trace of a frown crossed her youthful face; her skin was lightly tanned, her almond eyes a rare shade of violet, her lips full and pillowy.

Carina had lived here all her life – except for her university days studying business in London – and her existence had been a charmed one. Adored by her parents, she and her twin brother, Lorenzo, had had an idyllic childhood, spending their days roaming the estate, climbing trees and searching for buried treasure; shrieking with delight as they raced through the vineyard sprinklers on the hottest summer days. Now Carina was entering her final days as a single woman. In less than a fortnight, she would wed her true love, her childhood sweetheart – Giorgio Bianchi.

'Carina? Carina, are you listening?'

'*Sì, mamma.*' Carina turned back into the room to find her mother looking at her questioningly.

'We still need to make a decision about the stemware for the champagne reception. Which do you prefer, flutes or coupes?'

'Whatever you think is best, Mamma. Your taste is always impeccable.'

'But it's *your* wedding.'

'I don't care about glasses,' Carina insisted happily. 'All I want is to be married to Giorgio.' She beamed at her mother, who returned the smile indulgently.

Carina's mother, Emma, was Scottish. At first glance, people often thought Carina was too, with her light skin and fair colouring, but those close to her knew that she was Italian through and through – fiercely loyal, quietly determined, with a stubborn streak that meant she wasn't afraid to fight her corner and stand her ground.

Her mother was the epitome of British elegance combined with Italian style. She was in her early fifties, her long, blonde bob expertly cut and styled, the perfectly blended highlights given that little something extra from exposure to the Italian sun. She wore an Armani shift dress in cream linen with a tan-coloured belt that emphasised her slim waist and slender figure, whilst a simple gold wedding band encircled her ring finger, classic pearls at her ears and throat.

'All I want is for you to be happy, darling, but there's so much to do. We have Costa Bianchi coming for dinner tomorrow evening – your brother is coming home especially.'

Carina grinned at the mention of her twin. 'How is my little brother?'

'There's barely moments between you being born,' Emma smiled fondly. 'The same as usual, still not interested in settling down, and having the time of his life in the city from what I hear.'

Lorenzo was the younger of the two of them – by eleven minutes – and was great friends with Carina's fiancé, Giorgio. The three of them had grown up together, thick as thieves. Lorenzo had always been creative, passionate about art and fashion, and now lived in Milan where he was studying architecture. To their father's disappointment, Lorenzo had shown little interest in the family business. Carina, however, was an expert in wine, instinctively understanding how the frost or storms, or a fierce sun would affect this year's grape harvest. She could tell with the merest glance which ones were ready to be picked, and which should be left on the vine to ripen.

Her nose was refined and her palate sophisticated, able to detect the full depth and range of flavours from sweet vanilla to fruity berries to aromatic spices. In short, wine-making was in her blood, in the way it had never been in Lorenzo's.

'. . .And then we must leave the following morning for the coast, to finish the final preparations,' Emma was saying.

The wedding of Carina and Giorgio was to take place in the celebrated town of Amalfi, where the Russos owned a palatial hillside property overlooking the sea – the Villa Amore. The nuptials would unite the two families, both great wine dynasties, neighbours and friends.

Carina turned as she heard footsteps outside in the tiled hallway, and her father, Salvatore, knocked once then walked in without waiting for an answer. He strode over to Emma and kissed her distractedly before turning to Carina, taking hold of her hands.

'*Cara mia*, you grow more beautiful every day.'

'I think you are biased, Papà,' she laughed.

'No, it's true – your mother will agree with me,' Salvatore said, grinning broadly. He was in his fifties now, but it seemed to Carina that he was in his prime, undoubtedly still a handsome man. His thick black hair was flecked with grey, giving him a distinguished air, and his rich brown eyes sparkled with life. He was more physically active now than he had been as a young man – playing tennis or heading out on the boat they kept in Amalfi, when his hectic work schedule allowed – and his solid, muscular body was testament to that.

'I came to tell you both the wonderful news,' Salvatore announced. 'I've signed a deal with Heritage Estates. They've agreed to be the exclusive distributor for Casa di Russo across the whole of North America, with an agreement to increase the supply year on year over the next decade. We'll have to expand the vineyard and increase production, but this is what we have been working for, yes? It secures our future – for the whole family, but especially for you, my number one daughter,' he told Carina.

'Oh, Papà, that's incredible,' she exclaimed, as she threw her arms around him.

'Darling, I'm so happy for you,' Emma congratulated her husband, kissing him on the cheek.

'Come, Carina, and I'll tell you all of my plans.' Salvatore strode towards the door.

'Can't it wait until later?' Emma interjected, her lilting Scottish accent taking on a firmer edge. 'We were discussing the wedding.'

Carina looked from one parent to the other. She could sense her mother's frustration and felt torn between the two of them.

'Nonsense, that can wait.' Salvatore waved away his wife's words. 'The wedding will take care of itself. Everything is in hand.'

'We have less than two weeks—' Emma began, but Salvatore cut her off.

'Walk with me, Carina. There's so much to discuss, and you know how I value your opinion.'

Swept away by his enthusiasm, the wedding preparation temporarily forgotten, Carina hurriedly followed her father out of the room.

Emma stood alone, feeling forgotten, as her husband and daughter walked out of the door. She glanced around Carina's room, taking in the make-up and perfume bottles neatly lined up on the vintage dressing table, the antique wardrobe overflowing with clothes, in poignant contrast to the soft toys propped up against the pillows, the child-hood trinkets tucked on the bookshelves. Emma felt a whirl of emotions. Her daughter's whole existence was here, and soon she would be leaving to start her married life. Emma knew her own life would change enormously.

Carina had moved away before, for university, but this felt more final. The last of her children would be gone, and an empty nest loomed. As the mother of the bride, Emma had thrown herself into organising her daughter's big day and wondered how she was going to fill her time when it was all over. Even though Salvatore had insisted they hire a wedding planner – Bianca – the poor woman had been left with very little to do, Emma reflected with a wry smile. Which reminded her, she really needed to speak to Bianca about the timings for the reception . . .

Emma left the room, walking through the grand house as she headed for her private study. She knew Carina was thrilled about her upcoming nuptials, but even that once-in-a-lifetime event was trumped by the needs of the family business. All her husband and daughter seemed to care about was wine.

In the long, stately corridor that ran the full length of the house, with its panelled walls and elaborate stucco ceiling, Emma stopped and looked out of the window. She watched as Salvatore and Carina emerged onto the terrace, passing the fountain with its statue of Bacchus, the Roman god of wine and festivity, on their way to the vineyards beyond. Sometimes, Emma felt that she loved and hated those grapes in equal measure. Yes, they had given her a wonderful life, with two beautiful houses, holidays to the South of France and the Seychelles, as well as the opportunity to mingle with the rich and famous, but it felt as though she was forever coming second to a pile of fruit – at least in her husband's eyes. It seemed to be a theme with the men in her life, she thought wryly.

Lately, that sensation was stronger than ever. Salvatore seemed distant, his kisses perfunctory, and Emma didn't know how to reconnect with him. She told herself that after the wedding it would be different – she would be less busy, able to devote herself to him once again – but deep down she knew it was more than that. They'd been married for twenty-five years, having celebrated their silver wedding anniversary in the spring, but their relationship had never felt the way it did right now. Salvatore had always treated her like a queen; now she felt like a ghost, her presence barely acknowledged.

Hopefully this wedding would sprinkle its romance on Emma and Salvatore too, she thought with a sigh. They certainly needed it.

Carina linked her arm through her father's as they left the garden behind and stepped into the gently sloping vineyards, the familiar feel of the soil beneath her leather sandals, the sweet, fruity scent of the grapes perfuming the air. She was wearing a long, floral dress that fluttered around her calves as she walked, bracelets jangling on her bare arms. Her diamond engagement ring sparkled in the sunshine.

'. . .And I've been speaking to some investors,' Salvatore was explaining. 'I don't want to give away more than ten per cent, but we'll need to upgrade the fermentation tanks and buy additional barrels, not to mention expanding the winery itself, hiring extra staff . . .'

'That's wonderful, Papà. You've worked so hard all these years, you truly deserve it.'

'Thank you, Carina. I know you love this business as I do.'

They made their way between the rows of vines and Carina plucked a grape from the bunches nestled amongst the sun-dappled leaves, popping it in her mouth. It was delicious – crisp and juicy, with a hint of tartness. In a couple of weeks they would be ready for the harvest – a process which was still done by hand at the Russos' winery – but Carina wouldn't be here to see it. She'd be a married woman, off on her honeymoon, beginning her new life with Giorgio.

'*Deliziosa*,' she proclaimed. 'In a fortnight, they'll be perfect.'

'You're right of course,' Salvatore said, admiringly. Then, almost as though he'd read her mind, he added, 'But you won't be here. I don't know how we'll cope without you.'

'Papà, I'm hardly moving to the other side of the world,' she hastened to reassure him. 'After the honeymoon, we'll be living on the Bianchi estate for a while. I'll basically be next door.'

She waved her hand across the fields, indicating the Bianchis' land on the other side of the stream. There was a small villa on the estate that was to be given to Carina and Giorgio as a wedding present; they would base themselves there until they decided where to settle permanently – an issue that was still a cause of disagreement between the two of them. And it wasn't the only subject they'd quarrelled about recently. In the lead up to the wedding, with all its stresses and pressures, she and Giorgio been arguing more than ever before.

'Ah, but once you're married you'll forget about your old papa,' Salvatore said knowingly, interrupting her thoughts. 'Your life will be all about Giorgio, and having babies.'

He tried to keep his tone light, but Carina knew her father too well. She recognised that he was genuinely fearful of what the future might hold for their relationship. The two of them shared a special bond; he'd been reluctant to let her go to London to study, and he hated the thought of losing her now.

'Of course I won't forget about you and Mamma,' she insisted. 'Besides, I'm only twenty-five. You and Giorgio are both so old-fashioned, assuming I'll want children straight away. There's plenty of time for that.'

They fell silent as they walked, lost in their own thoughts. Around them, the labourers were hard at work, removing the weeds that threatened to choke the precious crop, alert for any signs of mildew, which could kill a plant and infect the whole vineyard.

Carina's mind turned to her handsome fiancé. She loved Giorgio deeply. The two of them had grown up side by side, and she believed it was their destiny to be together. They'd been inseparable as children then, during their teenage years, as they matured into adolescence with the accompanying rush of hormones, Carina began to see Giorgio in a new light, as more than simply her childhood friend and playmate. They'd had their first kiss by the stream and gone on to spend countless hours together, sharing dreams and secrets.

Surprisingly, the physical side of their relationship had never progressed much beyond those first innocent fumblings. Giorgio had been raised Roman Catholic, as had Carina, and he'd impressed upon her the importance of saving herself until she was married. He was unashamedly traditional, explaining how much it meant to him that she should remain a virgin, pure and deserving of a white dress on her wedding day.

Their marriage would unite the two families, the two business empires, and Carina would have been happy to stay in Campania forever. She adored the region, the way the landscape changed with the seasons, often joking that she'd been grown from the earth in the same way as the grapes. If it were up to her, she'd raise her family here, like the generations before her. Until recently, she'd thought that Giorgio felt the same way, but lately she'd sensed some reluctance from him, a feeling of restlessness with his life. He was the adored only child of Costa and Vittoria Bianchi, and he was expected to take over the family business, a role which had taken on greater significance following the sad death of Vittoria a few years earlier. Costa Bianchi was adamant that his only son should continue the work of previous generations, and Carina knew her fiancé would never turn down his duty.

'There's something I need to talk to you about.' Her father's deep, melodious tones cut into her musings.

'Yes?'

'We're going to have an unexpected guest staying with us in the run up to the wedding.'

'Oh, who?' Carina was intrigued, but she could tell her father was holding something back.

'I'm hiring someone to look after you. I'm finalising the details, but they'll act as your driver and bodyguard.'

'Papà, I— '

'I'm not taking any chances.'

'You're being ridiculous,' Carina burst out angrily. She

hated the thought of this special time being overshadowed by anyone or anything. She certainly didn't want to be followed round by some oaf when she was having her final dress fittings or visiting the beautician. Was he going to come with her when she went to the spa, or the masseuse? 'You're being paranoid. It was an accident.'

Carina thought back to that terrifying incident, almost a month ago now. She'd tried to banish it from her mind, but sometimes when she closed her eyes at night, it all came flooding back. . .

'I can't believe how pretty it is here,' sighed Edie Stone, as she stared round at the picture-perfect streets of Positano from behind her enormous sunglasses. The enchanting, pastel-coloured buildings were nestled at the foot of the verdant mountains, the idyllic terraced gardens sweeping down to a turquoise sea that was almost too beautiful to be real.

'I know,' Carina sighed happily. 'I feel like the luckiest girl in the world right now.'

It was just six weeks until Carina's wedding and her best friend, Edie, had taken advantage of a break in her filming schedule and flown over from Los Angeles for a girly weekend. They'd been browsing in the stylish boutiques, picking out dresses for Carina's honeymoon and lingerie for her wedding night, and their arms were laden with stiff paper shopping bags tied up with ribbons. Now they were heading to a café for a refreshing drink and a proper catch-up.

The two women made a striking pair. Carina was undoubtedly beautiful, in a pale blue chiffon maxi dress by ROX that draped perfectly around her slender body; her long, blonde hair swept up in a top knot with tendrils falling loose to frame her face. Edie's style was more edgy, her hair cropped short in a pixie cut and dyed platinum-blonde, her long legs encased in denim shorts teamed with a cropped shirt that showed off her tanned midriff. They turned heads even in a town known for attracting the cream of the glitterati.

'You don't get views like this in London,' Edie laughed, waving her arm to indicate the cobbled piazza leading to Spiaggia Grande beach, sleek white yachts bobbing on the Tyrrhenian Sea beyond.

'Oh, we had so much fun back then, didn't we?' Carina reminisced, as she linked her arm through Edie's and they turned into a quiet backstreet where the stone walls were draped with bright pink bursts of bougainvillea, the subtle scent suffusing the air as the sun blazed overhead.

Carina and Edie had met during Carina's time in England, when she was studying at the London Business School. Against her father's wishes, she'd taken a part time job working in the box office of the Wardour Theatre, which was where she'd met aspiring actress, Edie Stone. Where Carina was cool and composed, Edie was loud and gregarious, and the two complemented one another perfectly, quickly becoming fast friends and renting a flat together in fashionable Notting Hill. Now Edie was on the verge of superstardom, her career going stratospheric, and they rarely found the time to see one another.

'I'm so glad you're here,' Carina told her. She had to raise her voice as she spoke, the noise of a car engine getting louder behind them. 'We hardly ever get chance to talk—'

'Look out!' Edie screamed.

Everything happened so quickly. Edie grabbed hold of Carina, so hard it hurt, yanking her out of the path of the oncoming vehicle. Carina turned, her eyes widening in fear, as the black Maserati swerved across the narrow street, appearing to drive straight at her. The windows were blacked out, and she couldn't see the driver.

Carina screamed, and it took a moment for her to realise she was safe as the car sped off, tyres screeching. Edie had pulled

*her into the recessed doorway of a chapel; if she'd remained in
the narrow street, the car would have hit her.*

*The two women stood for a moment, hearts pounding, adren-
aline rushing through their bodies. In all the commotion, Carina
had dropped her shopping bags. The contents had spilled out,
strewn across the road, the delicate white lace underwear now
spoiled and dirty. She stared at it, dumbly, as Edie went across
to pick it up, her hands shaking. Carina knew that she would
never wear it now – it felt tainted and unlucky.*

'What the hell just happened?' Edie said, her voice shaking.

*'I. . . I don't know,' Carina stammered, shocked to find that
her voice was trembling too.*

*'Probably just a paparazzo,' Edie said, attempting to shrug
it off. 'I've had a few following me in LA recently.'*

*'Yes,' Carina paused before nodding numbly. 'You're probably
right, why would anyone do that on purpose, who else could it
be?'*

*But she couldn't shake the chill that had crept over her and
that stayed with her for days afterwards . . .*

'Please, Carina.' Salvatore turned to her, and Carina saw the
concern etched on his face. 'Let me do this. Giorgio would
never forgive me if anything happened to you. I would never
forgive myself.'

Carina sighed. Did it really matter if her father wanted
to hire a bodyguard for a few days? She could ignore
them completely. In fact, she could probably give them
the slip and sneak off. If it would make her parents feel
better, who was she to argue?

'Of course, Papà,' she said meekly. 'As you wish.'

He put his arms around her and kissed her on the forehead. She felt like a child again, safe and protected in his
arms. Her father was being ridiculous, clearly overreacting,

but it was easiest to appease him. After all, Carina felt sure that she had no enemies. Who could possibly want to hurt her?

And if you can't wait, try Carol's *Sunday Times*
bestselling debut novel . . .

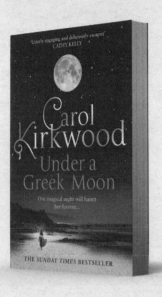

A-list actress Shauna Jackson has the perfect life.
Fame, fortune, marriage. Or so it seems.

Running from a scandal, Shauna flees to the place
that changed her life twenty years ago, the idyllic
Greek island of Ithos.

Captivated once more by the azure seas and
scented olive groves, bittersweet memories resurface
of one summer, one unforgettable man, and a
long-hidden secret.

Shauna can escape Hollywood,
but can she escape her past?